WE ARE MAYHEM

ALSO BY MICHAEL MORECI

Black Star Renegades
The Throwaway

MICHAEL MORECI

WE ARE MAYHEM

WITHDRAWN

ST. MARTIN'S PRESS ☙ NEW YORK

WE ARE MAYHEM. Copyright © 2019 by Michael Moreci. All rights reserved. Printed in the United States of America. For information, address St. Martin's Press, 175 Fifth Avenue, New York, N.Y. 10010.

www.stmartins.com

The Library of Congress Cataloging-in-Publication Data is available upon request.

ISBN 978-1-250-11785-4 (hardcover)
ISBN 978-1-250-11786-1 (ebook)

Our books may be purchased in bulk for promotional, educational, or business use. Please contact your local bookseller or the Macmillan Corporate and Premium Sales Department at 1-800-221-7945, extension 5442, or by email at MacmillanSpecialMarkets@macmillan.com.

First Edition: April 2019

10 9 8 7 6 5 4 3 2 1

For my family. Every single day, it's all for my family.

WE ARE MAYHEM

The Black Star Renegades may have won the battle, but the war is far from over.

Although Praxis's *War Hammer* has been destroyed, the kingdom still maintains a tyrannical grip on the galaxy. In the wake of Praxis's devastating defeat, fear and terror reign as Renegade forces struggle to match overwhelming odds.

But there is hope.

Kira Sen has a bold plan that will win more star systems to the Renegades' side—enough to defeat Praxis once and for all.

And Cade Sura is still in possession of the Rokura, the most powerful weapon in the galaxy. He just needs to learn how to use it before the evil Ga Halle tracks him down and takes the weapon for herself. . . .

PROLOGUE

Cade cried.

He tried to stifle the tears he'd been holding in all day, but the fact that he couldn't stop himself from crying like he was a silly little baby made him so frustrated that he cried even more. His house was quiet, and though everyone in it was asleep, the thought of someone catching him like this made him sick to his stomach. So, of course, that's exactly what happened. The floorboards creaked and sighed behind him, the sound magnified by the house's silence, and Cade knew he wasn't alone anymore. Filled with shame and anger, he considered running out of the house; he considered hiding and hoping that whoever had been awakened by his sobbing figured it best to just leave him alone. But, as he sat in the dark on the stairs that led to the cold, damp cellar, he knew that all he could do was wipe away his tears with the back of his hand and act like everything was okay even though it wasn't. And a lot of good even that did; his efforts to brush his tears away only smeared them across his face.

"Cade?" a voice called from the darkness. "Is that you?"

Cade turned and saw a silhouetted figure, large and imposing, standing in the doorway at the top of the stairs. His father, Benji.

"Is everything all right?" Benji asked when Cade didn't respond. And then, when Cade still couldn't bring himself to say anything, Benji continued. "I'm going to come down there. Okay?"

Benji walked down the stairs, the old boards moaning under the pressure of his heft. Cade's father was a large man, and at a passing glance, he'd seem intimidating. But, other than his mother, Cade couldn't imagine a kinder and gentler person. Sure, Benji looked like someone who could clobber anyone who ticked him off, but that required him to get ticked off. And that never happened. Benji preached tolerance and patience, peace and understanding. Which was all the more reason Cade didn't want to discuss why he was so upset.

"So," Benji said as he sat next to Cade, "this is unusual."

Cade turned away, realizing it was a futile gesture only after he'd done it. His father clearly knew he'd been crying.

"Are you going to talk to me, or should we sit quietly? Whatever you want to do, Cade. I'm happy to just sit here with you if that's what you need."

Cade sniffled and used his sleeve to dry the tears that he'd pressed against his cheeks. He wasn't crying anymore, so he could at least clean himself up a little.

"I'm okay, I just had a—" Cade paused as the words began to come out in a stutter. The tears threatened to come again. They were totally out of his control. "I had a bad dream is all."

Benji nodded. "I know you're twelve now and practically a grown man, but I'm still your dad, and I can still help you. You have to tell me how, though."

Cade buried his face in his knees and covered his head with

his arms. He just wanted to shrink away; he wanted to fold up into his own body, fall through a crack in the stairs, and be gone. It was the only way he could avoid this conversation, which he knew his father was going to coax him into having even though he didn't want to. And realizing that only made him frustrated at himself, and embarrassed, all over again.

"Is this about what happened today?" Benji gently prodded. "I heard there was an . . . incident with you and your brother. Were some kids picking on you?"

Cade's head shot up, and he threw his father a righteously indignant look.

"Picking on *me*? No. I'm way too cool for that."

"Cade," Benji gently reproached, "do we need to have the ego talk again?"

Cade sighed. "No," he said. "But I wasn't getting picked on. It was this other kid, Lakum. He's . . . such a lost cause. He's scrawny and nerdy, and he just practically begs the other kids to mess with him. And they do. All the time."

A low, nasally rumbling came from Benji; it was the sound he made when he was contemplating something. "Does it bother you, these kids picking on this boy?" he asked.

Cade's face turned red, flushed with anger, and he turned away. "I hate it."

"So what happened—with Lakum?"

"His mom is always there to walk him home after school, but she didn't show up today. Lakum was alone, and the kid didn't even know what to do with himself. He should have just walked home and not waited around—everyone knows only the older kids hang out after school. And they're the ones who give it to him the worst.

"I had to go back to my locker because I forgot one of my books. That's the only reason I was even there. And when I came out . . ."

"The older kids were giving Lakum a hard time," Benji said, trying to say what Cade could not.

"A hard time? Dad, they were beating the crap out of him. These kids took turns punching and kicking him, and Lakum just lay there, curled in a ball on the ground. He didn't even fight back; it was like . . . like he was okay with what was happening. Like this was just the way things were supposed to be."

"And how did that make you feel?"

"Mad!" Cade snapped, almost yelling. "I wanted him to fight back, to do something to stick up for himself. But . . . I was even madder at those stupid bullies. They think they can do whatever they want and push around whoever they want, but they're really cowards. They only act that way because they're bigger than everyone else and because they're always together."

Benji sighed. "That's usually how bullies work. Most of them act that way because they're insecure and afraid. If you stand up to them, they're usually quick to retreat."

Cade rolled his eyes. He couldn't imagine a more quintessential thing for his father to say. "Yeah, well, not these ones."

"What happened?"

"I wanted to go back inside to get help—find a teacher or something," Cade said defensively. "I know that's what you're going to say I should have done. But, Dad, the way those kids were pounding on Lakum, I thought he might be dead by then.

"So . . . remember how I said I had to go back inside and get that book? Well, I made good use of it," Cade said uneasily. He could see his father already starting to wince as he anticipated where this story was heading.

"Good use of it *how*?" Benji asked.

"I charged those bullies and cracked the nearest one over the head with it."

"Cade," Benji said, but it was less like he'd said it and more like he'd groaned it. He was the only person who could express Cade's name in such a way, and he was made to do it often. "That was probably not the best way to intervene in that situation."

"I know," Cade said sheepishly. "But, you know, I sometimes have trouble thinking things through."

Benji shook his head, and his scowl turned into a smile. He even laughed. "You're right about that, my son. You certainly have your mother's tendency to act on your impulses."

Cade hung his head. "I'm sorry."

"Don't be," his father said. He clasped the back of Cade's neck and gently lifted his head. With his gaze directed upward, Cade saw the worry in his father's eyes. Benji cupped Cade's chin and studied his son's face, searching for any kind of scratch or bruise that he might have missed before. "Are you okay?" he asked. "Did they hurt you?"

Cade tore his face out of his father's grasp and looked away. Without wanting to—he'd thought he'd gotten all the mucus and tears and pathetic whimpering out of his system before his father joined him on the stairs—he started to cry again. And once it started, it only got worse. He tried to hold back his outburst, and the fact that he couldn't made him feel weaker than he did in the first place.

"Cade?" Benji asked, angling his body so he could see Cade's face. Cade withdrew further into himself and the darkness of the stairway. "Cade, what happened? What did those boys do to you?"

"*Nothing*," Cade said. "They didn't do anything to me."

"Then, what?" Benji asked, confused. "If they didn't hurt you, then what has you so ups—"

"They didn't do anything to me because of Tristan. Okay? Tristan stopped them."

Benji drew back. "I'm having a hard time following. Why's that a problem?"

"Because, it . . . I . . ." Cade stumbled over his words until they mashed into a prolonged growl. "Just . . . never mind." Cade sharply rose, knocking the back of his hand against his face as he did, furiously wiping away his tears.

Benji followed him.

"Cade, wait," he said, calling out in a hushed tone as he followed his son through the living room. "Please, tell me what's wrong. It's just you and me here, no one else."

Cade turned and faced his father, but he couldn't bring himself to say what he wanted to say.

"I promise," Benji continued. "I won't say anything to your mother or Tristan. I just . . . I want to know."

"It's just . . . ," Cade began, but he had to pause. He suddenly knew he was being ridiculous and petty over what had gotten him so upset, what he'd let gnaw at him for far too long.

"I don't want to be saved by Tristan," Cade admitted. "I don't want to be shown up by him in everything I do. I know he's older than me and bigger and stronger, but it's like . . . it's like he's *perfect*, and everything I do he beats me at. He's better than me *all the time*, and I feel like nothing because of him."

Benji sighed pityingly. It was like he'd been expecting this moment to happen. "I will never lie to you, son. And it's from that place of honesty that I admit to you that your brother is a remarkable person. We all know it. But—and I need you to listen to me—so are you."

"I'm your kid." Cade sniffled. "You have to say that."

"No," Benji said sternly. "You impress me so much—you have no idea. You fill me with more joy than I ever thought possible, and you have the biggest heart of anyone I know. And that includes your brother.

"I mean, look at what you did today, sticking up for Lakum. Cade, most people would not get involved. Most people would see the odds stacked against them, and they wouldn't dare stick their neck out. They'd turn and walk the other way. But not you.

You threw yourself in front of this boy because you care and because you're brave. I'm not sure I approve of your methods, but that's a different conversation. The point is that you put the well-being of someone else over your own, and it takes a certain kind of person, a *rare* person, to do that."

"A lot of good it did," Cade said, his voice small. "I would have gotten my face stomped in if Tristan hadn't shown up. Nothing I do is good enough."

Benji looked at Cade with a skeptical expression. "Let me ask you one question. Once you intervened, did those boys leave Lakum alone? You stepping in, did it help?"

"Lakum took off. I've never seen a kid run faster in my entire life."

"Sounds like you did exactly what you set out to do. You saved Lakum."

"All I did was give those bullies a new target," Cade said, slumping even farther. "If Tristan had been the one to step in, it would have been a totally different story."

Benji stepped toward Cade and grasped him by his shoulders. He again angled his face to meet Cade's downcast eyes.

"Cade, you did what was right, and you did it *your* way. You are you, and that's all you can ever be. It's all I want you to be."

Cade let his father's words and his prideful gaze soak in. He thought he'd be at best dismissed for harboring such feelings against his brother, at worst admonished. But his father had listened and treated Cade with the exact care that he'd needed. Cade felt silly for having expected anything less.

"Thanks, Dad," Cade said, and Benji wrapped him up in a hug. When Cade pulled away, he looked up at his father uneasily. "So . . . you're not mad about me hitting that jerk in his head? I mean, he had it coming."

Benji smiled. "No, I'm not mad. I'm not sure I'd agree that he had it coming, but . . . look. I know I preach high standards for you boys. But I also realize that the galaxy can be a complicated place, and you have to figure out all the challenges and problems that it's going to throw at you in your own way. Not my way, not your mother's, not Tristan's. Now, it's very late. We should both try to get some sleep."

Cade agreed, and he was heading to his bedroom when Benji called him back.

"Is everything okay?" Cade asked when he spotted his father standing exactly where he'd left him.

"Everything's fine, I just—I wanted you to know that I understand that it's not easy for you. Your brother casts a long shadow, there's no doubt about it. But, Cade, if there's one thing I know, without question, it's that you'll figure things out.

"I promise you, Cade. You *will* find your way."

CHAPTER ONE

More enemy fire deflected off the *Rubicon*'s shields, causing both the ship to bounce in space and Cade's stomach to bounce into his chest. He wrapped his hand around a strap that hung from the cargo hold wall, steadying himself as he swallowed his insides down. After taking a deep breath, he looked over and saw Kira smirking at him.

"*What?*" Cade asked, agitated.

"Nothing, nothing at all," Kira said. "I just didn't know you were so delicate. But it's fine. Totally cool."

Cade groaned. "You know, even by our standards, this is excessively stupid."

Kira put up her hands. "Hey, don't look at me. This is your friend's idea."

"Huh?" came Mig's voice from the back of the cargo hold, where he was tinkering with something or other. "Is Cade complaining again?"

"I'm not complaining," Cade said. "I'm just . . . processing. Verbally. I'm verbally processing."

"Verbally processing your complaint," Kira said. "We got it."

"You know what? I'm ready. I am ready to jump out of this ship now."

"Such a sensitive Chosen One." Mig snickered as he stepped in front of Cade and started fiddling with his grav suit. "I'm just going to shut this clasp. If you're going to leap into the cold, deadly abyss of space, it's best if your enclosure is airtight."

Cade rolled his shoulders, unable to find any comfort inside the cumbersome exoskeleton. Grav suits were nothing new; crew members used them all the time, especially on larger starships, to make exterior repairs. But in those instances, the grav suits were tethered to the ship. They moved slowly and safely.

Mig's version was neither slow nor safe. He'd reinforced Kira's grav suits so the exterior was harder to penetrate, but Cade was less concerned with the ramifications of taking enemy fire and more concerned with the suit's propulsion capabilities, which, thanks to Mig's upgrades, could now power a small starhopper. Having that kind of power right beneath his feet and hands didn't sit well with Cade. Especially since he was supposed to use that power to propel himself through space and hope nothing went wrong—and in this case, wrong could send Cade careening off into space, where he'd die a long, excruciating death. Cade had one fear in life, and that was it. He could take on a squad of Praxian drones with hands so steady you could rest your drink on them; he could fly any ship through a furious dogfight with a smile on his face. While he didn't relish the idea of meeting the sharp end of a quanta staff or being incinerated by an enemy starfighter, at least those ends would be quick. But confronting the vast, emptiness of space? Where he'd float for days and do nothing but *think*? That scared the crap out of him.

The ship was rocked by enemy fire again, and Cade nearly lost his lunch.

"You know," Kira said, "if I could hand over the control of my ship to your cranky drone, you should be able to handle this."

"I never thought I'd say this, but for the first time, Duke is actually the least of my problems," Cade said.

From over his shoulder, Cade heard 4-Qel's heavy gait as he lumbered down the cargo hold's ramp. He "whistled" a monotone tune as he joined Cade, Kira, and Mig.

"Personally, I'm excited," the drone said. He'd been equipped with the propulsion units, but he didn't need the grav suit. Because, apparently, nothing could kill him.

"So you like the idea of hurtling through space with a questionable amount of control over your body?" Cade said. "Why doesn't that surprise me?"

"I'll be like a graceful speck among the cosmos, as close as I will ever get to being united with the fabric that binds all sentient life."

Cade and Kira shared a curious look.

"Or," 4-Qel continued, "a weapon of massive power, out to exact my destructive purpose."

"That's more like it," Kira said.

Mig punched in the code on the cargo hold's control panel. The hold's door lowered slowly, revealing a deep blackness punctuated by pinpricks of stars.

"From here, the drop to the Kundarian trade ship should take no more than two minutes," Mig informed the team. "Use the suit exactly like I showed you; let it do most of the work, and you're good."

Mig joined Cade, Kira, and 4-Qel, and together they walked toward the lip of the cargo door. In just seconds, they'd be jumping off it; Cade tried to convince himself that he was relieved to finally have it done with. He'd been sweating this solution to liberating the Praxis-occupied Kundarian vessel ever since it was conceived, and no matter how hard he tried, he couldn't bring himself to liking it. In fact, he hated it.

"Oh, one other thing!" Mig yelled over the din of the cargo door's hydraulic system. "Do *not* forget that last thing I told you!"

Cade shot a panic-stricken look at Mig. "Wait, what?" he asked. "What last thing?"

"Huh?" Mig said, holding his armored hand up to where his ear was, beneath his helmet. "Sorry, I can't hear you."

"What last thing? You didn't—" Cade looked over and saw Kira practically bursting as she tried to hold in her laughter.

"Oh, hilarious," Cade said. "Real mature."

"Still can't hear you," Mig toyed.

"Then read my lips!" Cade yelled, and then he mouthed, very clearly, a pointed obscenity.

But then the noise stopped as the door was completely lowered.

"All right, boys," Kira said. "Time to fly."

The space above the planet Kundar was punctuated by streaks of light screaming across the sky. Kundarian freedom fighters engaged Praxian Intruders with the goal of drawing them away from the trade ship that'd been hijacked by the evil Praxis kingdom weeks earlier. It'd been sitting inert since, a bargaining chip against the Kundarian freedom fighters who were waging a bloody ground assault against Praxis's occupation of their planet. Praxis's deal with Kundar was simple: Surrender, join the kingdom, and the trade ship carrying essential supplies would be released from orbit. Kundar's answer, as evidenced by the dogfight taking place over their planet, was clear.

Resistance to its imperial ambitions—ambitions that wouldn't settle for anything less than complete control of the entire galaxy—was new to Praxis. The kingdom used to be able to rely on its *War Hammer*—a massive starship that had the power to drain the energy from a planet's nearest star, leaving it dark, cold, and dead—to be the ultimate deterrent, but Cade and his friends changed all that. Defying the odds, defying orders to relent, Cade, Kira, Mig, and 4-Qel pulled off what had previously been an unthinkable task: They blew the *War Hammer* into a million little pieces, and that strike wound up being the opening salvo in a war across the galaxy.

But Praxis wasn't about to relinquish its control so easily.

In the wake of having the crown jewel of its fleet blown out of the sky, the evil kingdom doubled down on its assault of neutral planets like Kundar, forcing more and more worlds to fly Praxis's bloodred flag. Praxis smothered planets with numbers; no system could match its air and ground forces. The planet's enlistment rate was ten times higher than the next highest planet, and if that wasn't enough, Praxis also conscripted ancillary forces from the planets they annexed. Still, the destruction of the *War Hammer* proved that sometimes might doesn't matter; sometimes sheer numbers aren't enough. Not when you have willingness. Not when you're fighting for what you believe is right. And that's why Cade was hurtling through space at a clip he didn't even want to think about, soaring toward the Kundarian trade ship so he and his friends could free it from Praxis's control and, from there, aid the planet's freedom fighters in their efforts to evict Praxis from their home once and for all. Cade and his friends—referred to as the Black Star Renegades, a moniker Mig anonymously spread through the galaxy because he said it made them sound "more legit"—had become Praxis's fulcrum, balancing its agenda of conquest and control with the hope for freedom. The hope to resist and *win*.

Below Cade, Kundarian starfighters, with their sleek dual engines and chromium shells, executed evasive maneuvers as they deftly flew circles around Praxis's Intruders; the Kundarians unleashed proton blast after blast, but only as a defensive measure and to keep the Intruders off-balance. The barrage filled the space with innumerable points of light; to Cade, it was like looking through a kaleidoscope while high on kerbis. Still, it kept Praxian fighters away from the trade ship for the time being. This little plan of Mig's was plenty suicidal already; the last thing Cade needed was to navigate his way through airspace that was littered with both enemy and friendly fire and the flaming wreckage of countless starships. That'd be the only thing that could make this worse, Cade thought.

Until things got worse in a way Cade didn't anticipate.

The Kundarian trade ship was in Cade's sights and coming on fast. But as he got closer to the vessel—shaped like a crescent moon with a bulbous command console in its center—Cade noticed small disks launch from the ship's starboard side. Dozens of them spun in Cade's direction. Hundreds of them.

His heart sank into his guts.

"Guys!" he yelled into his comms. "We've got incoming!"

"*Damn it,*" Kira snarled. "Razor drones."

Destruction didn't even begin to describe a razor drone's purpose. Cade had to make up a word because no existing word appropriately captured the razors' single-minded penchant for carnage. Annihilatory. That would do. The drones were designed for one purpose and one purpose only: to magnetically attach to the hull of a ship and tear it to shreds. Which was bad. Because ships without exteriors to keep them, among other things, pressurized and stabilized? They tend to fall from the sky. Uncontrollably. And the people inside fare even worse than the ship after it crash-lands.

Cade was currently covered in a material identical to the hulls of most ships. He had seen the razors' work with his own eyes. It didn't take much for him to conjure an image of what the drones would do to his grav suit and then his skin, intestines, and so on.

But Cade wasn't a ship. He wasn't just some sack of meat in a grav suit. He was the *Paragon* . . . kind of. Of sorts. A Paragon in training. Despite his leveling up, or maybe because of it, Cade still relished any opportunity to be reckless. Possessing the Rokura was just an excuse for him to double down on his wanton disregard for his own well-being.

"So, Mig, weren't you the one saying how we'd be too small to be picked up by the trade ship's sensors?" Cade ribbed, exacting a small amount of payback on his friend. "That *was* you, right?"

"Well," Mig casually responded, "looks like I was wrong."

"All right, here's what we're going to do," Kira said, taking the lead. "Mig, Qel, push yourselves toward the center, to Cade and me. We'll tighten formation and blast our way—"

"Nah," Cade interrupted. "I've got this."

Cade fired his thrusters to maximum burn and was just getting out of suit-to-suit comms range when he heard Kira yell, "I hate it when you do that!" Cade smiled; Kira really did hate it. The thing was, Kira would have flung herself headfirst into a hive of razor drones if it meant fulfilling the mission, even though the odds of her not making it out were slightly worse than taking a sidewinder blast point-blank to the face. Cade recognized how similar they were in their appetite for danger, although their motives were different. Kira chased it because she was a dedicated soldier, and no risk was too great when doing the right thing was at stake; Cade because he had a massive chip on his shoulder— circumstance had yoked him to the belief that he had something to prove, that he'd *always* have something to prove. What separated Cade and Kira now was simple: Cade had the most powerful weapon in the galaxy at his side, and the upside of that was that he could take stupid risks; the downside was that he often had to strand his friends on the sidelines. The Rokura was too dangerous, and Cade wasn't certain he could tame the weapon if its powers exceeded his control. Still, even if it was for their own good, Cade couldn't help but feel like he was drifting away from the people closest to him.

As Cade drew within spitting distance of the razor drones, their finer details came into focus. Two amber-hued ocular lenses were set into the core of their bulbous bodies and, protruding from their sides, four pincers snapped greedily, anticipating their prey. Cade knew he was an easy target; the Rokura, though, was no one's lunch, and these drones were about to learn what it was like to have the power of destiny shoved up their tailpipes.

Cade aimed the Rokura forward. White-hot energy began to spark off its three blades. Cade thought he should say something witty and clever, but so far, his attempts to craft a catchphrase had only yielded "Taste the heat," and he wasn't sure what that even meant. Besides, his friends already had a lifetime's worth of fodder to bust his chops about in his sometimes-clumsy attempts to play the role of Paragon. So instead, he'd just kick back and let the mystical weapon perform its magic. That's how this whole thing worked; though Cade would never admit it to anyone, he knew the truth: The Rokura was in charge, not him.

Sure, they'd settled into a tense truce since the weapon chose him over Ga Halle. Cade used it as seldom as possible, and in those instances, the Rokura obliged his commands. It helped free him and Kira from a nakal beast's den on Ryson, and it destroyed Praxis's prototype mobile drone garrison on Bondra before it could escape the planet's orbit. The Rokura had no choice. Until Ga Halle could prove her worthiness over Cade or another true Paragon—like Cade's brother, Tristan—came along, it would just have to make the best of whatever the galaxy threw its way, even if it was a second-best destiny. Still, even though the Rokura was as stuck with Cade as he was with it, he felt its darkness swirling on the periphery of their alliance. Deep down, the weapon was still intent on shaping Cade into the Paragon it deemed worthy of the mantle. And that worthiness, it seemed to Cade all too often, required pursuing a path that was darker than he'd ever be comfortable with. The weapon still spoke to him, still urged him to quench a thirst for power that he didn't possess. Light existed in it as well, and Cade felt it struggle for domination against the darkness. What kept Cade awake at night was his fear that he'd never find a way to harmonize both sides. As he struggled, the Rokura's more aggressive half taunted Cade with the promise of unlocking its full, true power. In his meditations, Cade caught glimpses of what that power had to offer, and it terrified him. Images of a city engulfed in flames, of a Praxian warship being torn apart, of innocent, frightened people begging for mercy clouded his mind, and Cade knew that he'd never acquiesce to such terrifying expectations. But he also knew that, until he did, he'd never be the Paragon's true master, let alone partner. And that meant he was vulnerable. That meant, one day, the Rokura would stop working on his behalf.

What happened after that was anyone's guess. Cade could only hope, as the razor drones buzzed around his head, that that day wasn't today.

Energy of incalculable might poured off the Rokura, and the first razor drone that tested that crackling white light received the teeniest taste of its power. It was enough to obliterate the drone from existence. One jolt from the Rokura and the drone convulsed, briefly, and then it was gone.

Cade wished that small sample of the Rokura's might would be enough to deter the hundreds of other drones from attacking. But no one ever learns.

"Stupid machines," Cade grumbled as the drones descended on him en masse. He shut off his propulsors, and the abrupt end of his momentum was enough to drop Cade out of the capsule the razors were attempting to cover him in. As he drifted back, Cade aimed the Rokura at the pursuing drones and let it rip. A single blast shot out from its head and shredded the drones in his vicinity. His path clear, Cade activated his propulsors and carved an upward arc with the firing Rokura leading the way. With the razors in pursuit, Cade angled the Rokura down and widened its blast radius; he eliminated swaths at a time, but the relentless drones still continued their pursuit.

Nonetheless, Cade assumed victory was just a matter of letting the weapon wrap up its large-scale destruction and then mopping up whatever stragglers remained. What he didn't know was that there was a second wave of drones at his back, purged from the trade ship while he wasn't looking. But Cade got a good feel for their presence when he detected one chewing through the back of his grav suit. Before he could swat it away, Cade felt something crash against his suit, strong enough to jolt his body upright; he looked over his shoulder and saw Kira, a sidewinder in each hand, picking off the drones that were zeroing in on him.

"You really have to stop shooting at me," Cade said.

"Oh, come on," Kira said. "I've only done it twice, and I saved your butt in both instances. Literally this time."

Cade and Kira closed the distance to each other; Kira continued to pierce drone after drone between their orange lenses, and Cade took out a batch with the Rokura. But the things kept coming.

"I'm running out of charges!" Kira said, and though Cade was focused on obliterating the drones in front of him, he could feel more and more coming at his back. A lot more.

They were about to be overwhelmed.

"Cade, we've got to get out of here. There are way too many of them."

Cade broke off the Rokura's killing spree and turned to see what Kira was looking at.

"Come on! What is that, *all* the drones?"

If Cade's knowledge of Kundar's star chart was correct, he should have been able to look out to this swath of space and see the Erso Nebula. But no. Instead, all Cade saw was a wall of razor drones so immense that it blotted out the world beyond. And these drones were coming on *fast*. Even with their propulsors pressed to maximum burn, Cade figured they had a fifty-fifty chance of outrunning the drones, though Duke wouldn't be able to get the ship to their location in time to save their asses. Which meant Cade had to do something that probably wasn't safe. In fact, he knew it was definitely unsafe, but it was all they had.

With a firm grip, Cade grabbed hold of Kira's waist and pulled her close. He held her in an embrace, their bodies pressed together, and brought the Rokura close to his chest.

"Hey!" Kira snapped. "What do you think you're doing?"

"Saving us, I think?" Cade said. "Now hold still."

This was the moment Cade dreaded. Sure, the Rokura provided him with enough juice to look cool and win some battles, but there was a danger in allowing himself to slip too close to the weapon. He felt that danger down to his core, and it made him think that should his connection to the Rokura get too deep, and vice versa, he might not be able to pull back out. But he had no choice, so he pushed his fear of potential consequences aside and concentrated. Cade channeled himself into the Rokura and felt it flowing into him in return. The effort made him grimace; Cade squeezed his eyes shut as he pushed his will outward, straining with every fiber of his being. Kira called for him, but her voice was lost as his mind went deeper into his focus. Cade began to feel his efforts taking shape; the Rokura's energy was expanding outward, forming a shell around himself and Kira. He opened his eyes and realized they were safely cocooned in crackling white energy.

"Whoa," Kira said.

Cade looked at her and smiled. "Yeah? Well, check this out."

Suddenly, an immense surge of energy erupted from the cocoon, a 360-degree blast that vaporized every single razor drone in sight. Nothing was left of them but barely visible particles shimmering in the eruption's afterglow. They rained down over Cade and Kira, brilliant specks glowing and fading all around. Kira reached out a hand and let them fall into her palm, where they evaporated like snowflakes. It made her smile.

They were safe, but when Cade looked down, he realized he was still holding Kira close to his side. He loosened the grip his fingers had on her grav suit, but his arm wouldn't let go. His eyes drifted to her suit's helmet; there, the remaining luminous bits of the razor drones reflected in the glass casing, obscuring half her face in wonderment.

"Hey," he said.

"Hey yourself."

"I feel like . . . like we never see each other anymore," Cade said, and it was true. With Cade training with Percival to become a more suitable Paragon and Kira strategizing the rebellion against Praxis, there had been hardly any time for much else.

"Well," Kira said, "here I am."

Cade stammered. He wanted to tell Kira that he missed her, but to what end? The separate paths that created a wedge between them—not to mention the burgeoning war—weren't going to converge anytime soon. If anything, the demands placed on Cade by Percival were only driving him further from Kira. Further from all his friends. And taxing Kira with his feelings for her—however genuine, however true—was unfair to her. The squadrons under her command were counting on her to deliver on the promise she and Cade forged together: that they could defeat Praxis. That their risk and sacrifice was worth it. To fulfill that promise, Kira needed to remain focused on the task at hand; she needed to rally enough systems to contest the Praxis kingdom at their almost immeasurable scale. Kira needed to be more than diligent, more than dedicated; she had to be an unstoppable force, and Cade had no doubt that it was the role she was destined to play.

Still, Cade had to spit out *something*. He opened his mouth to speak, not knowing what would come out, but he was mercifully cut off by the sound of Mig's panicked voice breaking through the comms.

"Sorry to break up your moment, but we have to get out of here!"

Cade looked over his shoulder and spotted Mig and 4-Qel racing toward him. And behind them, an Intruder chasing after a Kundarian starfighter. The starfighter was supposed to stay out of their way and avoid situations exactly like this one. But as it drew nearer, rapidly, Cade noticed that the ship was bucking uncontrollably as sparks popped from its rear. The pilot, Cade assumed, must have taken his vessel off course in an effort to preserve the ship's integrity, or what was left of it. But it didn't work. Now, the starfighter was zeroing in on Cade and his friends. And it was likely going to be blown to pieces very, very soon.

Before Cade and Kira could even recalibrate and propel themselves away from the incoming starfighter, Mig and 4-Qel were on them. Mig grabbed hold of Cade, 4-Qel grabbed Kira, and together they blasted off toward their destination, the Kundarian trade ship—with the failing starfighter, as well as the Intruder that pursued it, on their heels.

"This is going to be close!" Kira yelled, and as she did, Cade dared to look back over his shoulder one more time. The starfighter was making quick work of the distance between them; Cade could almost feel the engine's heat warming his grav suit.

"I'd say it already is close," Cade replied. "Where are we supposed to land in the trade ship?"

"There," Kira said, leading them all forward. "My contact on the inside left that docking bay's shield down for us."

Cade looked at the trade ship and noticed a small docking bay that, unlike the others, wasn't protected by faint red shielding. It wasn't a surprise; Kira's missions were always as tight as a drum. Things in her control never went wrong. The problem was the unexpected things. Like, for instance, a starfighter pilot who, in the process of trying to save his own hide, veered dangerously off course and was threatening to crash into the very people he was supposed to be safeguarding. And while Cade didn't know any instances of starships crashing directly into people, it didn't take much of an imagination to figure out how those stories would end: with the guts of those not protected by a starship (i.e., him and his friends) splattered all over the place. So they were going to have to hurry.

"I knew I should have given the propulsors more power!" Mig yelled.

"Any more juice on these things and they'd tear our limbs from our bodies," Cade reasoned.

"A price I wouldn't mind paying at this point!"

They were all pushing their propulsor units to their limits, but it was no use; the starfighter was outpacing them with more speed than they could account for.

"We could always move out of the starfighter's path," 4-Qel evenly suggested.

"And have it crash into and destroy our only entry into the ship? I don't think so," Kira said. "We're making this."

No sooner had Kira's rejoinder been made than Cade looked back just as the Intruder erupted two shots out of its cannon—two shots that landed directly into the Kundarian starfighter's rear. The shots proved to be all the ship could handle, and Cade could only watch as their problem went from critical to catastrophic: The starship erupted into a ball of fire that burned across the sky before quickly extinguishing. What was left was a junk heap's worth of debris blazing toward them, countless pieces of fiery scrap metal that were just as problematic as the ship, if not worse. Instead of one thing roaring toward them, it now was thousands.

Not to mention the Intruder that, having cleared the pesky starfighter out of its way, was now laser-focused on Cade and his friends.

"We're dead," Mig said.

"I don't think so," Kira said as she turned around and started firing her sidewinder at the incoming debris. "Everyone, shoot the scrap closest to us! The more junk we create between us and that Intruder, the harder it'll be for its weapons to lock on to us!"

Cade, Mig, and 4-Qel did as instructed, firing round after round at the debris, sending pieces careening between themselves and the Intruder. The Intruder retaliated with blasts of its own, but none came close to their intended targets. Not until Mig teased the limits of their luck.

"Can't hit what you can't see, jerkfac—"

And that's when one of the Intruder's proton blasts sailed directly over his head, close enough to nearly singe the helmet of his grav suit. Cade turned to Mig; he looked like the shock alone was about to kill him.

"Whoa," Mig breathlessly said.

"Enough messing around!" Kira yelled. "Everyone in!"

Cade spun back around to see the cargo bay within reach, but the Intruder was bearing down on them, hard. Shot after shot sailed overhead—thankfully, people were a lot harder to hit than starships—but it would only take one hit to reduce any of them to a smear in space. Cade pushed his propulsors even though they were already burning at capacity. Still, any little boost could spell the difference between life and death.

At last, he rocketed into the docking bay, Kira, Mig, and 4-Qel at his side. They smashed onto the metal floor and rolled, carried by their momentum, deeper into the bay. None of them had any time to even think about slowing down; landing in one piece with broken bones far outweighed not landing at all. But the grav suits, Cade learned, offered enough protection to prevent serious damage to their bodies. Cade continued to bounce across the floor, and he didn't stop until he crashed into the rear wall. It was a painful way to land, but at least their time in the grav suits was over.

Cade felt his muscles and joints already aching as he stumbled to his feet. "This one's going to linger for a while."

The pain he felt in his back, legs, and ribs was forgotten when he looked ahead and saw the Intruder still racing at him. It was thundering toward the cargo bay, and it wasn't slowing down.

"It's going to crash into us!" Cade yelled.

"Everybody move!" Kira ordered. "Move!"

But Cade knew there wasn't time for them to get clear of the Intruder's path. There was only one way to save their sorry butts. Cade grabbed the Rokura and held it like a spear. Trying to forget all the coin he'd lost to Kira in darts, Cade ran ahead and launched the weapon directly at the opposite wall. There, it landed squarely into the docking bay's control panel, smashing it.

In the blink of an eye, the dim red shield spread across the bay's opening, and just as it did, the Intruder flew right into it. A pulse of dark red screamed across the shield, and the Intruder burst into pieces.

Cade turned to look at his friends, who were still holding their breaths, expecting to die. Except 4-Qel, who didn't breathe, which was why he was the first to talk.

"See?" he said, clasping Cade's shoulder as he walked by. "And you were worried about our adventure in the grav suits."

Cade wanted to fire a barb back at the drone, but all he could muster was a pitiful wave of his hand, shoving the drone away.

4-Qel was unphased. "No time to lose," he chirped. "We have a ship to liberate."

"The bridge is this way," Kira said, leading Cade, Mig, and 4-Qel down the dark, narrow hallway that snaked away from the cargo bay. They went up to the ship's main level and to a forking path. "My contact told me sentry drones are standing guard between here and the bridge, but nothing we can't han—"

From the darkness of the path on the left came a reptilian voice that cut off Kira's words. "Mr. Sura," the voice said. "I've been waiting for you."

Before he even twisted his head to see the figure emerging from the leftmost path, Cade already knew who the voice belonged to: Ortzo, the Fatebreaker who'd been relentlessly pursuing Cade since before he blew up the *War Hammer.*

"I've *missed* you," Ortzo said with an exaggerated sibilance.

Cade armed himself with the Rokura and took a step in Ortzo's direction. "I bet you have; Ga Halle must be a real pill these days."

Ortzo smirked. He was dressed in the traditional Fatebreaker armor—a black tunic with protective gold scales shielding his arms, legs, and torso—though without the mask that covered his face. Not that it mattered; unlike Cade's shido, the Rokura had no problem slicing through anything that was in its way.

"My master is doing just fine," Ortzo replied. "Praxis still controls the galaxy, and the small matter of her claiming what rightfully belongs to her—the very weapon you hold in your unworthy hands—is soon to be resolved."

Cade snorted. "You are a confident one, I'll give you that. Delusional, but confident."

"Why are we even wasting time entertaining this fool?" Mig said, his finger twitching over his sidewinder's trigger. "Let's dust him and move on."

Cade held down Mig's arm just as he was about to raise his weapon. He could see Ortzo flashing a devilish smile across his face.

"No," Cade said. "He wouldn't make it that easy."

"Heat-sensitive explosives," Ortzo said, answering the question he hadn't been asked. "One shot from that uncivilized hand cannon of yours, and this entire hallway goes up in flames. That means the so-called *Paragon* will have to deal with me the old-fashioned way: with a duel."

"He's insane," Mig whispered at Cade's side, but Cade kept his focus on Ortzo. The Fatebreaker burned so hot Cade could practically see the flames roaring in his eyes. There was no telling how much misery and suffering the Fatebreakers had caused across the galaxy, and Ortzo was their commander. The most fanatical of them all. If he wanted a fight this badly, then Cade was happy to oblige him. And make the galaxy a little brighter in the end.

"Get to the bridge, take the ship," Cade told Kira. "I can handle this."

Kira eyed Ortzo, then rested an uncertain gaze on Cade. "Are you sure about that?"

"I'm sure," Cade said, forcing a confident smile. "You have your path, I have mine. Now go, do what we came here to do."

Kira nodded, and Mig and 4-Qel followed her down the fork that led them away from Cade and Ortzo. With his friends gone, Cade turned his attention to the maniacal Fatebreaker, who was waiting. Armed with his battle-scarred shido, he began to walk toward Cade, and Cade toward him.

"You may have fooled part of the galaxy. You may have even fooled your friends," Ortzo said as he swung his shido down on Cade. Cade blocked his parry easily, but Ortzo pressed his weapon down on Cade as the fire burned even hotter in his eyes. "I know what you're hiding, Sura; I know what no one else does."

Cade was about to shove Ortzo off him with ease, reinforced by the Rokura's power, when Ortzo flung his armored elbow across Cade's face and then kicked him in his chest, sending him backward. It'd been some time since anyone had touched Cade in a fight, and not since his battle with Ga Halle had he confronted someone who *knew*. The nakal beasts, the razors, the gunners and sentries from Praxis's unending arsenal, they didn't know the truth. They didn't know that Cade was a fraud, a liar, a pale substitute for the real thing. But Ortzo did, and his knowledge filled Cade with dread. He didn't feel invisible with the Rokura in his grasp—he felt exposed.

"You're not in control, you can't be," Ortzo taunted. "You're a *faker*, and I'm going to *prove* it."

Ortzo charged at Cade, and suddenly, Cade was on the defensive.

He was vulnerable.

CHAPTER TWO

Kira expected more from the *War Hammer*'s destruction. For so many years, it'd been the symbol of terror and oppression throughout the entire galaxy, and she'd hoped that the image of it falling in pieces from the sky would galvanize people from one end of the galaxy to the other. That it would remind them what life was like before Praxis's reign. What it was like to have hope. To be free.

There was a ripple effect following the news of Praxis's stunning defeat at Ticus. Rebellions sparked in a number of systems, wreaking havoc on Praxis's long-standing methods of control. The kingdom's patrols were attacked, supply lines sabotaged, even fortified outposts were overrun. Some systems declared freedom from Praxis's cruel reign, and there were even a few planets and rebellious cells that found Kira and Percival and either pledged their loyalty in the coming war or joined their ranks.

But then, Praxis fired back.

The kingdom enforced strict curfews on systems with the most dissension; it dropped brutal military forces to occupy planets that even murmured their support for the renegades who'd struck the *War Hammer*; or, like Kundar, it found creative ways to cripple a planet by kneecapping its access to food, medical supplies, and other essential goods. Praxis tightened its grasp across the galaxy, and while its stranglehold wasn't enough to completely stem the tide of defiance, it was enough to maintain control. Granted, the number of people on Kira's side—known as the Renegades, a moniker that made her roll her eyes—had grown, and more individuals volunteered every day.

Kira didn't need individuals, though. She needed planets. She needed entire systems to stand up and wave a middle finger at Praxis. Because at just a few volunteers a day—some of whom were trained, useful fighters, but too many of whom were not— it would take a thousand years to match Praxis's might, and no rebellion had that kind of time. Kira, Cade, and Percival were the little guys, and the little guys ran on heart, hope, and a whole lot of optimism. But those things aren't in limitless supply, and once they run out, all that's left is a grueling conflict against impossible odds. And that's when rebellions die.

It was also why this mission to deliver the Kundarian trade ship was so vital. If just a few dedicated people—the Renegades and Kundar's freedom fighters—could claim a victory against Praxis, Kira's hope was that it would spur the Kundarian royalty, already sympathetic to the cause, to actively join the fight. To stand up as an independent system, shake off Praxis's yoke, and inspire others to do the same.

But first things first: Before systems started lining up to resist Praxis, Kira had to clear the sentry drones that bottlenecked the path between where she, Mig, and 4-Qel were pinned and the ship's bridge.

Kira twisted her head around the curved edge of the ship's narrow hallway, only to meet blaster fire bursting out of the sentry drones' standard B-18s. The errant shots raced above Kira, popping sparks from the ceiling that rained down on her head. She fired off a return shot that struck one of the sentries directly in its shoulder; the shot must have hit the drone in just the right spot, because when it attempted to raise its arm to return fire, nothing happened. The arm hung loosely at its side, blaster pointed at the ground. The sentry made a whirring, revving sound, almost like it was determined to raise its arm, but the sound was cut short when the sentry on its left shot it point-blank in the head. The injured sentry dropped to the ground, and its squad mates—if they could even be called that—kicked it out of the way to make room for the unit one row back to step forward and take its place.

"They really have to program those things to shoot with either hand," Kira said to herself as the blaster fire from the sentries continued unabated.

"So," Mig yelled from the other side of the hall, "this is taking forever!"

"I wish they'd advance, or do *something*," Kira yelled back. It was a strange wish, but all those sentries parked in front of the door that opened to the bridge were more an inconvenience than a danger. Sure, she could bide her time and, with Mig and 4-Qel, pick the drones off one by one. But they didn't have all day. Praxis knew they had boarded the ship, and it was only a matter of time before they deployed reinforcements. This wasn't a mission where you dig in for the long haul; Kira needed to strike hard, strike fast, get the ship back to the Kundarians, and get herself and her team out.

"Mig!" Kira yelled over the screeching blaster fire. "You have any of your magnetizers on you?"

Mig cocked an eyebrow. "My magnetizers? The things you said were a complete waste of time? That we'd never have a use for? *Those* magnetizers?"

"Those'd be the ones," Kira replied.

"Yeah, I've got one. How come?"

"Because we need to clear a path to the bridge. And those drones are made of metal."

Mig squinted at Kira, studying her as if she knew something he didn't. "But the entire ship is made of metal. If we start drawing metal to a single point and, like, the walls start getting torn off, we'll get sucked out of the holes and die. Which goes back to your whole reasoning on the magnetizers being a bad idea."

"As a being made partially of metal, I agree that this is a bad idea and object to us doing it," 4-Qel added.

"Not if we destroy the magnetizer before things get out of control," Kira said. "We let the magnetizer do its thing on the drones, then *boom*—one blaster shot solves our problem."

"And if you can't get a clear shot?" Mig questioned. "If you miss? My aim sucks, Kira. If we end up having to rely on me, we're gonna die."

"And I'll be too busy being sucked into the magnetic vortex to help," 4-Qel sardonically added.

"Just toss the magnetizer toward the drones," Kira ordered. "I'll handle the rest."

Mig looked over his shoulder at 4-Qel, who shrugged. Mig did the same, then pulled off his backpack and began rummaging through it. He pulled out the orb he was looking for and began twisting it into position, all while Kira ran the briefest cost analysis in her mind. The risk? She couldn't destroy the magnetizer and they'd all die. The reward? If she pulled this off, they'd free the ship and Kundar would align with the Renegade movement, a victory that could very well prove to be the turning point in the war. Or there was the path where they did nothing at all: They wouldn't win over Kundar, Praxis would squash their rebellion, and they'd all die anyway.

Two out of three paths ended in death—which, as far as Kira was concerned, meant business as usual.

Mig nodded at Kira, giving her the "all ready" sign.

"All right, hand it to Four-Qel and let him throw it in the middle of the sentries," Kira instructed. "I'll cover you, Four-Qel."

"What, *I* can't be trusted to throw my own creation?" Mig huffed.

"You throw like my dead grandmother," Kira said. "Hand it to Qel."

"It's true, you have very weak throwing capabiliti—"

"Well, excuse me for not being able to do everything!" Mig sulked.

4-Qel took the magnetizer out of Mig's hands and gave Kira an enthusiastic thumbs-up. Despite the grim possibilities, the highly advanced drone loved these kinds of situations.

Kira popped out from behind the security of her cover and opened fire on the drones. She managed to blast small craters into a few before those in the unit collectively turned their attention to her. Right as that happened, 4-Qel stepped away from the wall he'd been hugging, giving himself enough clearance to toss the magnetizer at the drones. It was a perfectly arced throw that glided right over the unsuspecting drones' heads and dropped to the ground with a *clink*. The sentries stopped when they heard the noise, craning their heads like a dog that'd heard a whistle, curious of its source. When nothing happened, they turned their attention back to laying suppressive fire in Kira, Mig, and 4-Qel's direction, but they never got a single shot off.

The drones began to bend. Backward, forward, left, right—whatever their position to the magnetizer was, their bulky bodies began to be pulled in that direction. At first, the pull was moderate, buckling the sentries at their waists. They rattled and buzzed, communicating something with one another. And just when it seemed like their bodies couldn't take any more strain, the magnetizer shot up from the ground and hovered just over the sentries' heads. There was a brief pause when the magnetizer relinquished its hold on the sentries, and they were as sedentary as the worshipping monks on Tatone. But it was only the slightest respite, because right when the magnetizer emitted a soft beeping noise, things got a little out of hand.

The sentries were the first to go. They were yanked off their feet, and then their feet were yanked from their bodies. Then their arms, their legs, their heads, and so on. The shredded appendages swirled around the magnetizer with tremendous efficiency, every single scrap of metal compressed with the force of an armored transport rolling over a tin can. The sound of metal crunching and squealing made Kira wince, but the goal had been accomplished. Not a single sentry remained, which meant it was time to take out the magnetizer.

The magnetizer, though, seemed to have ideas of its own.

In an instant, all the compressed drone parts unified into a collective heap that orbited, like a shield, around the magnetizer. And the device was just getting warmed up. More metal began to groan as the magnetizer's pull increased dramatically; Kira could see paneling and other hardware, all metal, start to pull from the walls and toward the magnetizer. The device was getting stronger, a lot stronger, and there was still the issue of the shield it'd constructed to contend with.

"I thought you said the build to critical mass was gradual!" Kira yelled at Mig.

"Pfft. You think this is critical mass? Just you wait."

Kira shot him a poisonous look.

Mig shrugged. "I'm just saying."

The magnetizer had to die. Knowing that, Kira stepped out from behind cover and took aim. When she did, she immediately felt the device pulling at her weapon, which was crafted almost entirely from metal. The blaster jumped in her hand just as she fired, sending her shot wide. Kira tried to steady her hand, resisting the device's pull; first her hand started to shake under the strain of trying to keep her sidewinder steady, and before long, her entire arm was convulsing uncontrollably. Kira held strong against inevitability, but it was too much. She was over-powered, and her blaster was sucked out of her grip.

Kira turned to Mig and 4-Qel, who'd both directed their sidewinders at the magnetizer, but it was too late. Before either could even got a shot off, their weapons were pulled out of their hands and joined the other swirling bits of scrap metal. Mig spat a panicked curse as 4-Qel grabbed hold of a vertical banister bolted to the wall. Kira could see him resisting the magnetizer's pull, shifting his weight and strength backward so he didn't end up crushed and cubed by his best friend's invention. 4-Qel was freakishly strong, but Kira had a feeling that the magnetizer wouldn't rest until the entire ship was turned inside out.

Metal continued to screech as it tore from whatever it'd been attached to. The reinforced material, made to withstand enemy attack, curled and buckled like it was being heated at an unimaginably hot temperature. Kira was exceptionally grateful that there was more than one layer before the outer hull, but it was only a matter of time before the magnetizer got to it, and a short time at that. Kira's window to save their butts was closing fast.

"Now it's reaching critical mass!" Mig yelled as he held on to 4-Qel's waist, helping to keep him in place.

"Great!" Kira vented. "Any ideas?"

Mig pursed his lips to the side and searched the ground, as if the answer were somewhere on the flooring that was about to get torn out from beneath their feet. "No. Not really."

Kira groaned through a tightly clenched jaw, then muttered a curse to the sky. That's when an idea presented itself. "Hello, beautiful," Kira said as her grimace turned into a smile.

Above their heads, a sliver of a support beam was tearing away from the ceiling, creating a nice point on its end. Pointy things can be used for stabbing, Kira mused, and stabbing something sounded ideal at that moment. She needed to reach the make-shift spear, though, before it got caught in the magnetizer's orbit, and she couldn't do that without some help.

"Listen, I have a plan," Kira said, projecting her voice over the chaotic din. "But I need Four-Qel to give me a boost when I say so."

"A boost?!" Mig howled. "If Four-Qel lets go, he's dead."

"If I don't nail this, we're dead anyway," Kira shot back, see-ing the spear about to loose itself. "Four-Qel, I need you to get me to that spear. You see it?" Kira nodded to the ceiling.

"I've got it," 4-Qel replied.

Kira stood at the ready, anticipating her moment to run and jump. The spear was barely holding on, and when it twisted just a little bit more, the metal shard would break free.

"Now!" Kira yelled and ran toward 4-Qel. Just as she reached him, he released his grip on the wall and tossed Kira into the air just before his body was sucked into the magnetizer's orbit.

Kira soared upward, her trajectory perfect to reach the spear just as it broke free from the ceiling. It raced toward the magne-tizer, drawn fiercely by its pull. Riding it to the device's orbit, she gave the spear the strongest shove she could muster, throwing her body into its momentum.

And she was rewarded by the spear breaking through the mag-netizer's orbit, its point driving right through the magnetizer's core.

Blinding light poured from the magnetizer as it violently spasmed before bursting into pieces. In its wake, the hallway boomed with the thunder of all that metal dropping to the ground.

"Hot damn, Mig. What was in that thing?" Kira questioned as she got up from the floor, dusting herself off.

"Ohhh . . . ," Mig said as he helped 4-Qel get to his feet. "You don't want to know."

"Well, at least your device did us the favor of opening the bridge's door," 4-Qel said. "And by 'opening,' I mean tearing off its hinges and crushing it into a jewelry box."

Kira stepped through the gaping hole and onto the bridge. Mig and 4-Qel followed. A single floating disk emanated light and did its best to illuminate the room, but its projection wasn't nearly strong enough. The soft light cast a beam across the ceiling, exposing bits of dust that fluttered aimlessly. The rest of the area was almost imperceptible, lit only by the control panels that curved a horseshoe shape surrounding the command deck at the ship's nose.

"Wasn't your contact supposed to be meeting us here?" Mig questioned.

Kira cast a suspicious glance around the room. This was all wrong. The crew should have been on the bridge, maintaining the ship's functions. Slipping into auxiliary control was safe only for short-term use; flipping the ship into automatic was a good way for it to get bombed out of the sky.

Unless that's what someone wanted.

Kira was about to order Mig and 4-Qel off the bridge, off the entire ship, when 4-Qel called her to the command deck.

"Is that your contact?" 4-Qel asked, pointing to the dead Kundarian slumped over in a chair. A single blaster wound drilled a hole through the side of his furry head; blood and brain matter had dried around the gaping point of entry.

"Shaddac," Kira said, looking down at the lupine face she'd never seen in person until now. Sorrow struck her heart; she'd never met the man who'd risked so much to help his people and the Renegade movement—and paid the ultimate price for it. "His name was Shaddac."

The Kundarian's eyes were open, freezing his face in a look

of perpetual shock that bordered on horror. Kira gently rubbed her hand over his forehead, closing Shaddac's eyes for the final time. She then relieved her ally of his blaster rifle, a Kundarian blaze rifle, and handed it to 4-Qel.

"Stay sharp," she instructed. "We're caught in a—"

Before the word "trap" could escape Kira's lips, the bridge's comms crackled to life, showering the room in a fluorescent-blue glow. 4-Qel spun on his heels, brandishing the blaze rifle with one arm and guarding Mig with his other. But there was nothing for the drone to blast into oblivion—just the outline of a face taking shape as the line of communication became clearer and clearer.

Kira took a step forward, squinting as she studied the face coming through the comms. Slowly, as if it happened one muscle at a time, her expression shifted from suspicious curiosity to simmering rage. If the rifle were in her hands instead of 4-Qel's, she would have shot the face forming before her eyes, if only just because.

The image came into focus, and though the person hovering just above Kira's line of sight was bathed in blue, she knew his true face. It was seared in her mind forever: those cold, gray eyes, flat nose, and sharp jawline, the dramatic red uniform, crisp and spotless. She tried to view the enemy before her as just that, an enemy. But that wasn't possible.

"Baron Ebik," Kira said, trying to keep her tone steady. "I almost didn't recognize you with that collar around your throat. How's it feel to be Ga Halle's pet?"

Ebik offered Kira half of a smug smile. "I feel alive, which is more than my fellow Barons can say. Or your friend—Shaddac, was it?"

Kira chewed on the inside of her cheek at the grating sound of Ebik's voice; the mention of Shaddac's name and the reminder of what Ebik had done to him made Kira draw blood. She tasted warm iron as the blood slid over her tongue and down her throat. She couldn't bring herself to speak, so full of rage as she was.

"I see," Ebik continued, "you don't want to talk about your coconspirator. The traitor to the Praxis kingdom. Perhaps a different topic, then? After all, it's been so long since we last spoke. So, tell me . . ." Ebik paused and cleared his throat. He leaned in closer to the comms and shot a satisfied grin at Kira. "Have you missed your father?"

"Um . . . what?" Mig said, taking a step toward Kira.

But Kira couldn't answer. She swallowed hard, knowing that the man who was her father—in biology only—was baiting her into a psychological ploy. That's what he did best, and Kira was no stranger to his games. For most of her life, she'd suffered under his mental warfare: the way he lured her into trust and betrayed it; the way he made her question her instincts; the way he planted seeds of doubt that, in time, grew into a plant that strangled her own self-worth. But she'd learned, after enough tortured years, who her father really was and what he was capable of, and she would be damned if she was going to let him run his game on her again.

"No, seriously," Mig said after a quiet moment. "What is this whole father busine—"

4-Qel put his hand on Mig's shoulder and drew him back. "I don't believe now is the appropriate time."

"What have you done here, Baron Ebik?" Kira questioned, her voice icy and distant.

"Well, if we're going to stick to formalities, *Kira*, you can call me Admiral Ebik Gendry. The Baron caste has been . . . retired."

"I believe 'slaughtered' is the word you're looking for," 4-Qel interjected.

Kira wasn't surprised 4-Qel took issue with Ebik's flippancy at the Baron massacre; it was the same kind of rhetoric the royal family of Eris used when they "retired" a line of Qels every time an upgraded model became available.

Ebik shrugged at 4-Qel, then turned his attention back to Kira.

"I know why you're here," he said, his voice as cool and his words as precise as Kira remembered. "You have an excellent military mind, Kira, but let's not forget where you get it from. It's no accident that I've been made admiral of the Praxian fleet; I still hold the highest score for the war game trials at the Praxis Military Academy, and no one has graduated with more honors than I have."

"Congratulations," Kira snarked. "No one simulates warfare better than you."

"Discount my abilities all you want, but you only work to discredit yourself. Everything you know is because of *me*. And what is the one thing I told you, time and time again?"

"Always use the bathroom *before* a dogfight?"

"Know your enemy," Ebik spat. "And *I* know *you*."

Kira laughed in the face of Ebik's arrogance and began walking around the comms projection, scanning the image of her father as if she were sizing it up for a brawl.

"Rescuing this ship was so important to you because you thought bringing these supplies to the Kundarians would galvanize them to fight at your side," Ebik continued. "It's a good plan, but transparent to anyone who's looking. And I've been looking, watching your every move to learn how you think."

"And what's your strategy, Ebik? To bore us to death? Because if so, bravo. It's working."

Ebik stroked his cheeks down to his chin as he studied his daughter with an indifferent gaze. Hardly anything affected Ebik; he was a tactician in his heart and mind, always calculating every move he made. His high cheekbones, his perfectly parted black hair—turning gray, perhaps, Kira ventured to imagine—and the savagery in his eyes marked him as an aristo-crat, and a proud one at that. Yet it also kept him in control. Kira knew he was too skilled to give anything away by flashing his emotions, assuming he even had any. She liked to goad him anyway.

"Symbols work both ways, my daughter," Ebik said, return-ing Kira's jab with one of his own.

Kira felt a shiver run up her spine, but she maintained her poise. She refused to let Ebik feel like he was getting to her; he could blow up this ship with her on it, but he wouldn't do so without the pleasure of knowing he'd gotten past her defenses. Ebik liked warfare; he found it amusing. What he enjoyed more, though, was warfare of the intimate variety. He took pleasure in getting inside people's heads and breaking them from the inside out. Kira had seen him relish this twisted delight on too many occasions.

"You intended this victory to be a symbol of hope, to inspire people to rebel against the galaxy's ruling power. Now, it's about to become the opposite. Your failure will be a lesson to those who dare defy Praxis. They'll see what happens to those who oppose our order."

"And your failure is in thinking that just because you own today that you own tomorrow as well," Kira said. "You think you know us, but you don't. You're dealing with people who've ex-perienced lifetimes of being beaten and broken. We're resilient, and no single defeat is going to make any of us quit."

"Defiant as ever. You may have my tactician's mind, but you have your mother's fiery spirit."

Kira's hands balled into fists so tight she could feel the blood pumping in her fingers as it pushed to circulate. The mention of her mother was deliberately designed to elicit a rise out of Kira. That's how Ebik operated, that's how he won. By working people's emotions, by preying on their weak spots and traumas, he kept his opponents rattled just enough to distract them from his true purpose.

Kira refused to fall into Ebik's hands.

"We will not fail," she snarled.

"Who will stop us?" Ebik's voice raised a pitch, expressing his incredulity of the very idea of being defeated. "Your mother tried to stymie my plans, and look where it got her. The Barons attempted to undermine Ga Halle, and now they're all dead. And through it all, little girl, I remain. I'll *always* remain."

Now it was Kira's turn to scoff. "Remind me, Ebik, what happened to the girl who refused to follow your rules and plans? The girl—the *little girl*—who persistently stood up to you, even when you tried to *kill* her?"

Ebik's lip twitched as his perfectly composed countenance showed signs of cracking. Kira smiled and took a step toward the projection of her father, pressing her fiery gaze deep into his eyes.

"You're not the only one who remains, you son of a—"

Ebik snorted a short puff of air, then forced a smile.

"The ship is lined with explosives, which I've just activated," Ebik said. "The Kundarians can watch their supplies—the ones you promised to return to them—burn. You and your friends have precious little time to escape or you, too, will go up in flames."

Kira wanted to blast Ebik with overtures on how getting off the ship in a hurry—all of them, Cade included—was something they could do in their sleep, but before she could wrap up a barb of words and spit them at her father, Mig took hold of her elbow and dragged her away from the comms.

"Time to move," he whispered, and Kira went along with his momentum.

For a moment.

Because Kira wasn't done. She might not have time to boast and brag about her team's abilities, but she wasn't going to leave her father—the man she hadn't seen since he'd dug a triblade into her shoulder and sliced her across her chest—without saying one final thing.

Kira turned back to the comms, just as the transmission was starting to fade.

"Hey, *Dad*," Kira said, and Ebik's flickering blue projection turned to face her.

"Forgot to say good-bye?"

"Not quite," Kira said. "I want you to know something, and I want you to understand it as clearly as possible:

"The next time I see you, I'm going to kill you."

Ebik rolled his tongue along the inside of his mouth before curling his upper lip, unable to conceal his disdain. "We'll just see about that," he said as the transmission evaporated.

Kira turned to Mig and 4-Qel, who were waiting at the blown-out doorway.

"Well, what are we waiting for?" she asked. "Looks like we have to go rescue Cade. Again."

CHAPTER THREE

"Your brother murdered before your eyes, the Well and all your fellow Rai scattered across the galaxy. Your own Master, a man who was like your father, betrayed and tried to kill you. Face it, Cade Sura: You're *alone*."

Cade wiped away the blood that streamed from the wound Ortzo had sliced across his cheek. He left behind a smear of crimson that ran from the side of his face to his tightly pursed lips. The fight with Ortzo had spilled into the trade ship's belly, the level that most crew saw only if they needed an escape pod. The rest belonged to mechanics. In the space softly lit by deep-blue and orange lights that spread beneath the floor and cast their illumination up, Ortzo had managed to contest Cade's strikes at every turn. Ortzo was a tenacious, skilled, and deter-mined fighter; Cade understood that within seconds of their duel's start. But with the Rokura guiding his way, Cade should have been able to dispose of Ortzo, regardless of how fierce Ortzo was, without breaking a sweat. But Cade was sweating. And bleeding.

And the more Ortzo taunted him, the more Ortzo got under his skin, the further he was from connecting to the Rokura and being able to draw on its power. Without it, Cade wasn't certain he could get out of this fight alive.

"You have no idea what you're talking about," Cade said, trying to push Ortzo's words out of his mind. The darkness they cast over him was proving to be deadlier than anything Ortzo could do with his shido.

Ortzo, standing opposite Cade, kept his shido at the ready as he began stalking a circle around the room. "Oh, that's right," Ortzo sneered. "You have your friends. Is that what you're clinging to?"

"I'm warning you, Ortzo," Cade said as he wrapped his hands tighter around the Rokura's hilt. Visions of the Fatebreaker he'd disintegrated on Quarry—that the Rokura had disintegrated—flashed in his head. "I'm *warning* you."

Ortzo huffed. "You think they, what, *care* about you? Percival is a coward and a liar, a terrorist. He sees you as a means to an end and nothing more. What do you think will happen when he finally accepts what I already know, that you will never, ever become a true Paragon? Do you think he'll continue to waste his time with you? The same goes for your friends and this threadbare thing you're calling an uprising. They'll either abandon you or die; they'll die because of *you*. Because you led them into a war under the lie that you could be something you're not."

Cade's chest welled and caved as he panted with rage. He was smoldering, his fear and doubt having transformed into fury over the course of this fight. He wanted to throw Ortzo's words in his face, but he couldn't. His focus was dedicated to pushing back the Rokura's influence, which was bleeding into his mind. It was as if the weapon had been waiting for this moment, for Cade to be unsettled enough to welcome its twisted purpose. It wanted him to seize power through mayhem and murder; it wanted him to find the control that eluded him by traversing its dark path. Somewhere in the back of Cade's mind, he knew that the relationship he'd forged with the Rokura had been a ruse; it lent him enough of its power to keep him alive and enticed, but in the end, it wanted Cade for its puppet. And its pull was *strong*. Cade thought he could work with Percival and learn how to master the weapon through rigorous training and focus, but he was wrong. This side of the Rokura would always come bubbling to the surface, the side that covetously lusted for power, and Cade knew he couldn't hold it back forever. He wasn't strong enough, and he never would be.

Cade would never be the Paragon.

"It's the nature of the world," Ortzo continued. "We forge relationships that benefit our ends so we can fulfill our most basic impulse: to survive.

"Just give me the Rokura. Accept the truth, and you'll be the one who survives. You have my word that the entire Praxis kingdom will leave you in peace. You can unburden yourself and disappear, Cade. Because they will turn on you— Percival, the Renegades, even that girlfriend of yours, I believe her name is—"

"GRAH!" Cade screamed as he charged Ortzo and slammed the Rokura down on him. Ortzo blocked the strike with his shido, but the defensive measure knocked him back on his heels. The Rokura was coursing through Cade, its influence taking over, and there was nothing Ortzo could do to combat its power. There was nothing anyone could do.

Cade swung the Rokura away from Ortzo's shido and, with unmatchable speed, brought its blunt end around into Ortzo's chest. The blow shattered the Fatebreaker's armor, and Cade heard Ortzo's ribs crack just before he started choking on his own breath. Futilely, Ortzo swung his shido at Cade, yelping in pain as he did. The Rokura in his off hand, Cade swatted the shido away and, with Ortzo defenseless, he sliced his weapon across his enemy's thigh. The wound hobbled Ortzo, who staggered back until he was caught by the outer wall. He remained there, clutching his wound—which was gushing blood—as Cade crept slowly toward him.

Just as Cade reached striking distance, Ortzo looked up. He looked Cade dead in his eyes, and he started to laugh.

"Go ahead, kill me," Ortzo taunted, looking up at the Rokura that Cade held just above his head. "It won't change the fact that you're a fraud. And when everyone around you figures that out, you'll be all alone. You don't even have parents to run to, *boy*."

Energy began to pour off the Rokura's tip, and Cade could see its brilliant sheen reflected in Ortzo's eyes. Cade swallowed three deep breaths as he forced the Rokura's sway out of his mind.

Kill him now, it said. Destroy him. Destroy them all.

The influence was so hard for Cade to resist, but he knew he couldn't relinquish control. If he let the Rokura in, he feared he'd become nothing more than a vessel for its dominant will. That he'd be forever lost under the Rokura's power.

Cade wanted to resist. He had to. But the question lingered in his mind, one he couldn't let go unasked.

"What do you know about my parents?" Cade growled.

Ortzo propped himself up against the wall, angling away from the Rokura's crackling power.

"Killed by a tragic ship malfunction, that's the version you were told. But no, no, no. And you know it isn't true. They were conspiring with Kaldorian scum—troublemaking idealists, like you and your Renegades."

The Rokura surged. Cade felt the weapon's white-hot power pulsing through it and his own body. Cade tried to control the rage that wanted nothing more than to blow Ortzo to bits right then and there. Leave him nothing more than a stain on the ship's wall before he could say another word. But he was compelled to listen, as sick as it made him to hear Ortzo recall his parents' death.

"My parents," Cade snarled, "were aid workers."

"Your parents were conspirators and enemies of the Praxis kingdom, and that is why their ship was blown out of the sky by cloaked dreadnought bombers," Ortzo said as he pushed himself off the wall and neared Cade.

"It's why I killed them," Ortzo spat.

Cade was blinded. Light burst in cycling waves off the Rokura, and all he could see was its burning power. And in that power was the capacity to satisfy his deepest desires and heal the wound that'd been festering in Cade's heart since the day his parents left and never came back. He could have his *revenge*. All he had to do was release the Rokura's might on Ortzo, and Ortzo would die an excruciating death. His skin and muscle and everything else, down to his atoms, would be eradicated from existence. Ortzo would be gone, obliterated, and Cade would claim the justice his parents deserved. All he had to do, he knew, was let the Rokura take charge. It taunted him with the promise of giving him everything he needed and wanted. Revenge, power, justice. He could have it all if he just surrendered, and he was ready to do it. Consequences be damned, because there was no way he could let the man who'd murdered his parents suffer anything other than the worst death possible.

But then, through the din of the Rokura's power and the voice that crowded his head, he heard his friends call his name.

"CADE!" they screamed, and in his mind flashed an image, one of himself the way Kira, 4-Qel, and Mig would see him in that moment—maniacal with unimaginable power. Cade shuddered and tried to shake the image off, but the moment took hold of him. And then, the image began to change. Cade's form was morphing before his eyes; soon, he was shrouded in all black, his face pale and ghastly. But then the blackness took hold, spindles of vicious vines wrapping around his body, until standing before him was nothing more than a featureless shape. Cade could see the shape's shoulders rise and fall as it breathed. He cautiously reached out his hand and placed it on the thing's shoulder; he wanted to turn it around so he could see what'd come of it, but the shape pulled away. It retched violently, and a shrieking unlike any Cade had ever heard before stabbed at his ears. Suddenly, daggers tore from the shape's head; they twisted and turned, forming hideous, deadly shapes. Cade felt revulsion; he felt terror. Before he could pull himself away from the shape, its head began to turn. And there, staring into Cade through bloodred eyes, was Ga Halle. Ga Halle donning an obsidian helmet of gnarled horns, smiling with delightful malice.

"The Rokura is mine," she hissed, and before Cade could shake off the horror he felt, he was jolted back to his waking life.

And in this waking life, the Rokura was exploding in his hands.

The revulsion Cade felt as he pictured his friends responding to the Rokura unleashing its furious power came rushing back. While Cade knew his friends would never abandon him, he questioned whether they would abandon the Rokura. Of all the grim possibilities the Rokura presented, that was the one Cade could least abide.

Just as the Rokura was about to erupt in Ortzo's face, Cade flinched. He pointed the weapon over his head, and instead of atomizing Ortzo, the blast tore through the ceiling. And the ceiling above that, and the ceiling above that. Cade was thankful to be in the bottom of the ship; otherwise, his decision to defy the Rokura might have sent him propelling into space through the hole he'd made.

Ortzo, meanwhile, capitalized on the window Cade created sparing his life by trying to kill him. He swung his shido around like a club, its blades on a path to smash into Cade's skull. But just before that could happen, a single blast flew over Cade's shoulder and drilled Ortzo backward. He was knocked off his feet, and Cade turned to see 4-Qel with a smoking rifle in his grip. Cade saw the drone shoot him a thumbs-up just before he collapsed.

Every part of Cade—emotional, physical, and spiritual—was completely and utterly spent. He felt as if the vital thing that made him who he was—his soul, his essence, whatever name the galaxy wanted to ascribe to it—had been scooped out of him, leaving a husk behind. And that husk was now prone on the ground, the world spinning around him. Cade tried to push himself up, but he slipped under his own weight and dropped face-first back onto the floor. Through his bleary vision, Cade saw Ortzo dive into an escape pod. 4-Qel fired shot after shot at the pod, but the door closed before Ortzo could be touched. The Fatebreaker jettisoned into space, and all Cade could do was lie there, wondering what was happening to him.

Cade fought to keep his eyes open, but he couldn't ward off the darkness overwhelming him. Just before he succumbed to unconsciousness, Cade felt Kira rush to his side. She propped his head up and called for 4-Qel to help lift him off the ground.

"It's going to be okay," Kira said. "Duke's on his way. We're getting out of here."

Cade caught a glimpse of Kira just before his head lolled back and his eyes rolled behind his eyelids. She looked distraught. Haunted, almost.

Something was wrong with her. Something was wrong with both of them.

In the cockpit of the *Rubicon*, Kira took a deep breath and focused on the tasks in front of her: regrouping with the other

Renegades, getting Cade the aid he needed, and salvaging what she could of the Kundarian failure. It was all she could do to prevent herself from bursting into tears. She'd kept herself together and led her squad off the Kundarian trade ship before it exploded, but it hadn't been easy. Aided by the power of Mig's propulsors, 4-Qel used his sheer strength to tear a hole through one of the thin doors that covered the escape pod hatches. They'd discovered that all but one pod—the one Ortzo had escaped in—had been decommissioned.

Together, Kira and Mig angled Cade through the do-it-yourself exit 4-Qel had made and, using his grav suit, sent him rocketing to 4-Qel, who was waiting to receive him. She let Mig propel himself out of the ship next, and Kira followed. She caught up to 4-Qel and grabbed hold of Cade, who was still unconscious. Together, they flew away from the ship and were intercepted by the *Rubicon*, piloted by Duke. Kira made it aboard just in time to watch the trade ship, not that far in the distance, erupt from one end to the other.

The ship she'd come to rescue was completely destroyed, and it was all her father's doing.

Now, she was alone in the cockpit of her custom-made assault cruiser, unable to decide if she should cry, scream, or break her hand punching whatever was closest. She went with a little bit of all three as she howled madly before slugging the storage locker adjacent to the cockpit door over and over while hot tears formed in her eyes. Exhaustion combined with the recognition that hurting herself wouldn't help her in the least finally brought her outburst to an end, and just as she was about to collapse against the locker she'd just beaten the snot out of, she stopped herself.

Kira refused to let this happen. She would *not* let Ebik do this to her.

She also realized Duke was in the room with her, operating the ship from her command chair.

"Oh, don't mind me," the cagey old drone said as he swiveled the chair to face Kira. "I fly with Cade; I'm accustomed to watching humans throw temper tantrums."

"Well, I'm not used to throwing them," Kira said as she pulled herself away from the dented locker. She straightened her clothes—a tight-fitting jacket and black pants combination, designed to fit well under the grav suit she'd been wearing—and when she raised her hands to push away the dreads that were hanging in her face, she noticed blood was dripping from her hands. She'd split her knuckles and shredded the surrounding skin to ribbons. She grinned defiantly at the sight of the crimson trickling down the back of her hand and beneath the sleeve of her jacket. Ebik had his little bit of her blood; he wouldn't get a single drop more.

"How's my ship?" Kira asked as she stood beside Duke at the command chair.

"Would you like to get cleaned up first?" Duke asked.

"Why? The sight of blood makes you uneasy?"

"Nothing makes me uneasy. I'm a robot. Where's Cade? How is he?"

Kira exhaled sharply and turned away from Duke. She didn't know what was happening with Cade, not exactly, and she didn't feel like talking about it. Especially to Duke. Talking about whatever was happening to Cade would be an admittance that something was wrong, and she wasn't prepared to cede that point. Not even to herself. Because then she'd have to come to terms with her lingering suspicion that, in the end, the Rokura would prove to be anything but the weapon of salvation it'd been hyped up to be. She was afraid. Afraid that neither Cade nor Percival really knew what they were dealing with as they tried to tame the weapon; afraid that it had the potential to destroy everything she'd fought so hard to build.

And, more importantly, she was afraid that it would be the

death of Cade. Yet that concern felt distant and abstract, obscured by her failure at Kundar. And Ebik. His voice echoed in her head, and she couldn't exorcise the words that'd haunted her ever since the day she'd fled Praxis.

Personal ties only make you weak, Ebik had told her just weeks before he'd tried to kill her. They give you a reason to compromise the one thing you should never negotiate—your own destiny. And that works both ways. You'll have to betray the ones you love, or they'll betray you. It's how these things always end.

Kira winced. Not because Ebik had been remarkably true to his word but because his words exposed the deep concern she had over Cade and the Rokura. Would the weapon be their downfall? Would she have to step in and destroy it, despite Cade's and Percival's protestations? They didn't see the weapon the same way she did; they thought they could bring it under control despite its instability, despite its darkness. Their progress, so far, hadn't been encouraging; it seemed that, at times—like just now in the belly of the trade ship—the Rokura was the one controlling Cade. Kira knew a time might come when the Rokura would have to be stopped, but would Cade stand by her side or in her way?

"Kira?" Duke prodded, snapping Kira out of her reverie. "I asked about Cade."

"He's resting in the medical bay," Kira tersely said. "He's stable."

"Did you know that I retrieved Cade from the spire on Quarry after he first acquired the Rokura? He was as near death as anyone I'd ever se—"

"The ship, Duke," Kira interrupted. "Let's focus on the ship."

Duke threw up his hands, surrendering. "You humans are so confounding," he said. "It's why I'm grateful to not have emotions obscuring my programming."

"Duke."

"You're the boss," Duke said, turning back to the control panel. "While you were gone, I took the liberty of performing a complete diagnostic, and I discovered a number of items . . ."

Of all the things Kira needed right now, listening to Duke prattle on about the ship's functionality couldn't be further from the top of the list. A warm bed would be nice; a drink even better. But she knew it would be more of a hassle to try to stop Duke than it was to just let him get it over with. So instead, Kira clasped her bloody hands behind her back and strolled to the *Rubicon's* viewport. Normally, gazing into the endless wonder and beauty helped Kira feel at least somewhat at peace. She didn't have the patience for spirituality, but she could look out to the stars for hours. But there was no peace for her today. Not with the numerous, unending scraps of metal obscuring her view. Shards of a mass-jump system. Slabs of what looked to be a sensor array and a thrusting panel. Together, all these parts and the technology that made them function constructed the Kundarian trade ship. But now the wreckage was nothing more than junk floating in space, waiting for an opportunistic scrapper to come along and haul it away.

Kira knew better, though. She knew this ship was the hope so many people on the Kundarian surface were waiting for; they needed supplies, food, and medicine, and Kira was supposed to deliver it all to them. But she didn't. She'd stepped right into a trap laid by her father, and nothing was going to be the same with him in the picture. Because now, Kundar would slide into acquiescence rather than join her in the fight for freedom. Her failure to do as she promised would ripple throughout the galaxy, and other systems that flirted with the idea of revolt, like Kundar had, would cower back into silent obedience. Better to be whipped and alive than bold and beaten into misery. Though, to Kira, Praxis's cruel punishment of Kundar—sabotaging their acquisition of essential goods—was all the more reason for planets to fight back. Sure, Praxis boasted order and peace, but anyone thoughtful enough to care about the fate of the galaxy knew that was a lie. The attack on the Kundarian trade ship was a manifestation of that lie, a revelation of Praxis's true edict: control on its terms, enforced by any means necessary.

"—and the *kkzzzztt* hydraulic sensor is reading *kkzzzztt* below acceptable levels of *kkzzzztt*—"

Kira swiveled back to Duke, whose body was twitching and whose eyes were flickering like he was having a power malfunction or the drone equivalent of a stroke. "You okay, Duke?"

Seeing Kira, Duke's head snapped back into focus. "Why, yes. Yes, I am fine. Thank you for asking."

"Oooookay," Kira said, slowly pacing toward Duke. "Why don't you let me take over? I can get us home from here."

"Not to worry, I can handle it while you rest. If you could just punch in the coordinates for our return trip, I'll guide us there without delay."

Kira shot a sideways glance at Duke. The drone was a lot of things—insubordinate, rude, and helpful only when forced to be. Polite and caring? Those traits had been weeded out of his programming over the years, if they'd ever been there at all. Which meant something was wrong.

"Why don't you go ahead and put in the coordinates, Duke. You've got the control panel right next to you."

"Oh, yes. Yes, of course."

As Duke went for the control panel, Kira slowly reached across her body with her left hand, hoping not to draw Duke's attention, and went for her sidewinder. But she was a second too slow on the draw.

Instead of going for the control panel, Duke thrust his hand toward the ground and came up firing with a snub-nosed charger pistol.

Kira dove to the ground at the sight of Duke's sudden movement, just in time to avoid getting a hole blown through her face. She yanked out her sidewinder as she fell to the floor and fired off three wild, defensive shots; they came nowhere close to hitting Duke, but they gave her enough time to scramble for cover.

"Did you really think I'd let you leave?" Duke said as Kira pressed her back against the steel pillar that kept the cockpit together when it flipped on its axis. "I knew at least a few of you, if not all of you, would survive the ship's explosion. I took the liberty of having your drone's mainframe rewired so he could be my remote puppet."

Though the voice belonged to Duke, Kira knew that the words belonged to Ebik. It was the second time he'd pulled the rug out from under her today, and she really did not appreciate her father's underhanded diligence in trying to kill her. Though at the same time, she shouldn't have expected anything less.

Kira whipped her head around the pillar; she was going to drill a dozen blaster rounds into Duke's face and then dump him out the airlock and shoot him some more from the ship. She'd just have to apologize to Cade for killing his stupid drone later. Just as Kira turned, the *Rubicon* bucked like it'd taken a direct hit to its rear from a warship's cannon. But Kira didn't hear any impact, and she knew there were no other ships nearby. They hadn't been hit with a ton of force, which meant Ebik had done something *worse*.

The ship was now screaming toward the Kundarian atmosphere, accelerating at a forty-five-degree downward angle and at maximum thrust, straight for Kundar's surface. Or, if Kira knew her geography, they were more accurately heading for Rendariac, Kundar's ice-capped mountain range.

"Ebik!" Kira screamed. "I swear, when I get my hands on you—"

Kira poked out her head, only to be greeted with a litany of blasts from Duke's charger pistol. She ducked behind the pillar, and as she did, she heard the cockpit door whoosh open.

"What in the—ahhhh!" Mig screamed as he stepped into the cockpit and immediately took fire from Duke. He dove and avoided getting shot, but 4-Qel wasn't as lucky. A blaster bolt bounced off his chest plating and ricocheted across the room. Getting shot didn't hurt or damage 4-Qel. But it did make him mad. Very, very mad.

With Duke focused on 4-Qel and Mig, Kira rolled out from behind the pillar and drilled the drone with blast after blast from her sidewinder. Because he was an older-model drone, Duke had a reinforced exterior that protected it, to a certain degree, from blaster fire. As Kira's blaster fire rattled Duke, even penetrated him at some points, 4-Qel rushed him. With one quick movement, just as Duke was about to turn his pistol on the drone that was bigger, faster, and stronger than he was, 4-Qel grabbed Duke's head and ripped it off his neck. Sparks snapped from the shredded wires, yet the drone still had enough juice stored in his dome to keep going.

"Futile," Duke said. "Everything you've done, everything you plan to do—"

"I never liked you," 4-Qel interrupted, then he smashed Duke's head between his powerful hands like it was a munta bug. He then tossed Duke's crushed, severed skull over his shoulder.

"What the—why?!" Mig yelled as he slid forward with the ship's downward trajectory toward the control panel. "Everything we do ends up crazy!"

Kira, like Mig, had to glide to the control panel. Only 4-Qel, with his gravity-lock legs, was able to move without taking into account the ship's trajectory. She considered taking the stick and trying to pull the *Rubicon* up, but she knew that whatever was causing the ship to dive required a much more profound fix than a pilot could provide.

"All right, listen: My father hot-wired Duke to control him remotely, and he somehow sabotaged my ship. You're up to speed, so no follow-up questions until we're horizontal again. The question is, how do we do that?"

"Uh . . . ," Mig said as he tried to flip through the control panel's functions, only to discover none of them were functioning.

Kira, meanwhile, turned her gaze toward the viewport just as the ship was breaking through Kundar's atmosphere. Mountains, hazy and fog-covered, were starting to come into view. "Time's a factor here, Mig."

"Okayokayokay," Mig said. "So, he couldn't have cut any actual mechanical functionality, which is good. But he must have, I don't know, rerouted . . . argh, just let me get under there!"

Mig dove beneath the control panel and, as far as Kira could tell, started to pull out wires at random. Meanwhile, the mountaintops weren't getting any farther away.

"Are you sure you know—"

"Zzt!" Mig barked at Kira. "Genius working!"

Kira looked at 4-Qel, who shrugged. "He *is* a genius," he said.

As much as Kira appreciated Mig's brilliance, she appreciated her own life just a little bit more. Coming on faster than she was comfortable with was a wall of solid rock that, without question, would rob both Kira and Mig of those things they loved the most. And, using her judgment as a guide, both were about to be taken away unless she pulled the ship up—

"Now!" Mig yelled. "Get us out of here!"

Kira hopped into her command chair, wrapped her steady hand around the stick, and, with all the force she could muster, pulled the *Rubicon* up and out of its descent. The ship had a tremendous amount of momentum dragging it down, but Mig's fiddling had wiped out its autopilot commands and equalized the power back to the ship's engines, giving it enough juice to overcome gravity. Eventually.

"We're not going to make it!" Mig yelled, clutching the control panel.

"Yes. We. *Are*," Kira replied through gritted teeth. The stick rattled wildly in her grip, overpowered by the gravity that was hot to keep the ship pulled toward the ground. But Kira kept it firmly in place despite its protestations. And just as the top of a mountain's alabaster-capped peak came into view, she was rewarded with the feeling of her ship leveling out. It climbed and climbed, angling away from the jagged outcropping, and right when a blanket of snow was about to smother the viewport, the *Rubicon* thrust upward. The bottom of the ship skidded against the rock face, jostling everything and everyone aboard, but it was just a scratch. Kira had regained control of the ship, and no one had died in the process.

Well, except for Duke.

"Just for the record," Kira said as she huffed to catch her breath, "if that were Cade flying, we would have crashed."

"Oh, no doubt," Mig agreed.

"Without question," 4-Qel added. "Paragon or not, he would have ended us all."

With the *Rubicon* heading in the right direction, Kira set the controls to cruise and flopped back in her seat.

"I'm guessing Duke is beyond repair?" she asked.

"Good only for scrap," 4-Qel said. "I'll dump him in the engine room."

"No, wait," Kira interrupted just as 4-Qel was grabbing the decapitated drone. "Scan him for a transponder. A tracking device."

4-Qel did as requested and, sure enough, he located a tracking device in Duke's back. He went to yank it out, but Kira stopped him.

"Keep it on him. Keep it right where it is, and dump him out of the airlock."

Again, 4-Qel did as instructed and returned to the cockpit just in time to see Duke fall out of sight.

"Good," Kira said. "Now Ebik thinks we're dead. At least he will for a little while."

"Yeah, about this whole Ebik thing," Mig began. "What's, um . . . what's the deal with that? He's your dad—like, your for-real dad?"

Kira bit her lip. This was a past she worked very hard to keep hidden, and she couldn't do a thing but watch as the gravediggers dug it up, spadeful by painful spadeful. "I'll explain another time," Kira said, gaining a temporary respite from the question she knew, eventually, she'd have to answer. "Right now, we have to get back to base and figure out what to do before Ebik finds out that we're still alive. Because I promise you, he won't relent until he's won."

As much as it frustrated her to admit this, she knew it was true. Ebik was out there, prowling the stars with the single-minded purpose of destroying everything she stood for and fought for, and when he discovered she was still alive, he'd turn to destroying her as well. History was repeating itself, but this time, Kira vowed, things would be different. She wasn't a helpless kid anymore, unable to stop her own father from running a triblade across her chest with the clear intent of murdering her. Kira drew a furious breath at the memory, picturing the remorseless look in Ebik's eyes as he'd dug the blade into her flesh. And all because she refused to sit idly by as Ebik imprisoned Kira's mother and usurped her seat on the Baron's quorum. Kira's escaping Praxis before Ebik could toss her in prison too threatened to make him look weak at a time he needed to look strong. Because only through his untarnished strength could he seize the power he lusted after and join the chorus of Praxian leaders who supported Ga Halle and her imperial ambitions. Despite her penchant for genocide. Despite the fact that she was completely out of her mind.

For her disobedience, Ebik tried to discard Kira like she was someone he didn't even know. Worse, someone he utterly despised. There was no telling his recourse for the trouble she was causing now. And as much as Kira relished the opportunity to give her father exactly what was coming to him, the remembrance of everything he'd done to her and her mother filled her with a particular kind of fear and dread that was unlike any other she'd known. She'd faced down squadrons of Intruders in skies punctuated by the battered remains of her own squadron's starships; she'd protected families against attack ships that were setting their crops ablaze for a perceived act of sedition; she'd raced toward a burning star and delivered a massive payload onto its surface, defying all odds, and struck a blow against Praxis the likes of which no one had ever seen. Still, she couldn't help but feel a profound discomfort at her father's reentry into her life.

The feeling must have projected onto her face, try as she might to suppress what was inside, because when she glanced at Mig, Kira could see the genuine look of concern on his face. It was almost like he was saddened by what he saw in Kira, and maybe he was; Kira knew that, like her own father, neither Mig's mother nor father would ever win an award for how they nurtured their children.

"I know you don't want to talk about everything with your dad, not in specifics, but do you want to talk about how you're doing? I mean, are you okay?" Mig asked.

Kira shook off all the thoughts and feelings Ebik brought back to her and forced a smile. She'd made a vow to herself, long before she'd found a home at the Well, to always look ahead, to never dwell on what was behind her. And there was no way she'd allow Ebik to compromise her focus and make her break that vow. Not now, with all that was at stake.

"I'm good," Kira told Mig. "Ebik stopped being my father a long time ago; at this point, he's just another Praxian jerk who wants all of us dead. He can get in line with the rest of them as far as I'm concerned."

"Yeah," Mig said, nodding. "Yeah."

"Besides, you know what? I should thank dear old Dad, because he was right; we're never going to win over the galaxy one planet, one system, at a time. It'll never happen."

"I'm failing to see how this is a good thing to realize," 4-Qel said.

"Look, we've gained a lot of allies since blowing up the *War Hammer*, and that's great. But we're still nowhere close to having the numbers needed to topple Praxis. And we don't have the resources to win that kind of long game, not to mention we can't possibly expect to stay hidden while we're playing it."

"So . . . what does that mean?" Mig asked. "Don't tell me this is it."

"No, this most definitely is not it," Kira said as she punched in the coordinates for their base into the mass-jump drive. "This war isn't over, not even close. We just need to change things up.

"And I know exactly how."

CHAPTER FOUR

C ade woke with a start and gasped.

A gentle breeze brushed over the contours of his body, and with it came an earthy aroma, rich with a hint of derig spice. He breathed it in deeply as his eyes adjusted to the starlight that filled the narrow slits he'd exposed to the world. As his eyes focused, so did his sense of smell; he caught a whiff of recuperative balms mixed in with the earth and spice and knew they were coming from his own body. The acrid scent was just potent enough to make Cade relish the idea of a hot shower. He pushed his body up from whatever it was he'd been sleeping on and groaned. Everywhere ached. His arms, his back, his head—Cade felt dehydrated, beaten up, and on the brink of catching a cold all at once. Metal sighed beneath him as he swung his feet around and forced himself upright. He rubbed his hands on the metal frame beneath his legs and the textured canvas mat that was tautly wrapped around it. He'd been curled up on a cot, but both where the cot was located and how long he'd been there were total mysteries.

Incrementally, Cade's eyes adjusted. In the foreground, he was able to discern long, narrow stalks of derig grass swaying all around him. He stood on uneasy legs and walked into the field, running his fingertips along the spice grass's coarse umber tips. With the force of his thumb and forefinger, Cade squeezed a derig bulb until its tangerine powder dusted his fingertips; he brought those tips to his nose and inhaled the aroma. He felt his senses sharpen. Derig was a potent stimulant, and Cade needed all the help he could get shaking off his slumber.

Though Cade's vision had yet to fully return, the derig placed him back on Raja Prime. Back at the Renegade base.

He'd taken the smell of derig for granted in the four months he and all the other Renegades had occupied the small moon in the Vossalos system. The native spice had been lost in the stench produced by the makeshift encampment Percival and his Rising Suns had established. The grease of blaster fire, the heat of too many bodies too close together, the roasting of botho meat—all of it overwhelmed the small but abundant plant, and Cade didn't again have an opportunity to appreciate it until now.

Until he was alone.

Cade rubbed the bleariness from his eyes and forced his sight to sharpen. He tried not to panic. The derig field began to take shape, and as it did, Cade began to recognize the outlines that marked where his camp used to stand. The oval shape of the mess hall on his right, the derig flattened where the building's frame pressed into the ground. Cade swiveled to his left and spotted the outline where the armory once stood. He spun around. Surrounding the cot he'd just been lying on was the form of the medical tent. Peppered in between were the smaller marks left behind from where the sleeping quarters had been. All of it, gone. The cot was the only trace of the base that'd been there.

Deep in the distance, Cade spotted a dozen Dundals—one of the three tribes native to Raja Prime—working the fields. Draped in a golden mesh that fell from their wide-brimmed hats all the way to the ground, they plucked derig bulbs as they hummed a spiritual chant that, according to what Cade had been told, warded off malevolent spirits. Cade often found himself wondering how much stock the Dundals could have realistically placed in this chant of theirs, especially when considering it'd been malevolent spirits that had forced them into a devilish pact with Percival. For years, Raja Prime's ruling tribe, the Faros, had been squeezing the Dundals for increased derig production while claiming higher and higher takes of their harvests. As a result, the Dundals were a starving people. Less derig meant less trading power on Klyzon, a nearby commerce moon. That meant less food, medicine, and other essentials. The Dundals had been beaten down, demoralized, and famished, yet they were still forced to deliver however much the Faros demanded, even if it was killing them.

Percival knew of the Dundal plight, and he also knew of Raja Prime's value as a strategic location. Not only was it a remote planet in a backwater system, but it possessed the unique characteristic of being surrounded by narrow mass-jump lanes. That put Praxis, not known for its humility in the ships it built, at a profound disadvantage. Sure, one of their warships might be able to position itself just right to make the jump, but it was more likely it'd be torn apart, its pieces belched out upon reaching Vossalos. So, Raja Prime became the coveted location for the Renegades' base, but it wouldn't be as easy as making planetfall and setting up shop. All three Raja Prime tribes were known for their fierce hostility to outsiders, and history had proved that whatever their differences, they'd put them all aside and repel whoever tried to infringe on their land.

But if someone could make an ally of one of the tribes, which was no small feat, then an understanding could be reached.

The Renegades hadn't introduced themselves to the Vossalos

system with drop ships, numbers, and weapons hot. That was how you started a war, Percival cautioned, and the last thing they needed was a six-month campaign fighting natives while trying to establish a base of operations. Instead, they entered quietly. Percival, Cade, Kira, 4-Qel, Kobe, and Mig approached the Dundal leaders with a simple offer: They'd "negotiate" fairer terms of harvesting and sharing derig and, in essence, halt the genocide the Dundals were gradually enduring. In return, they'd be given space to set up their base. Though anxious to protect their generations-old isolationism, the Dundals had grown desperate enough to accept Percival's offer.

Cade looked the other way, stuffing down his own inner conflict as Percival and his followers worked out a deal with the Faros tribe. All Cade knew was that Percival returned three days later, and when he did, the Faros were ready to grant the Dundals the relief they'd been promised. Like that, the Renegades had their new home.

And now, in the blink of an eye, it was gone. At least Cade thought it was, though one vestige of the camp still remained.

"You are not in control of the Rokura," a voice called from over Cade's shoulder.

Cade turned, and he spotted the back of Percival's head popping above the tips of the derig that gently swayed in the breeze. The former Paragon was just ten yards away from Cade, sitting cross-legged in a meditative pose. He didn't turn as he spoke to Cade; instead, he remained fixed on the rambling fields that broke at the horizon, giving way to a line of jagged crystalline mountains. Settling over the mountains was Raja Prime's deep-blue sky, streaked with plumes of orange and pink as the planet's triple dwarf stars set on another day.

"All of your training, all of your work fashioning your mind and body to forge equilibrium with the Rokura—if not dominance over it—has been for nothing," Percival continued. "You are *failing*, and your lack of discipline is dragging everyone else down with you."

"What do you want from me?" Cade asked. "To be perfect? To be my brother? Because if that's what you're expecting, you're going to die a disappointed man."

"I expect you to focus," Percival said as he got up from the ground. He turned to face Cade, the Rokura in one hand and his own shido in the other. "I expect you to discipline yourself enough to rule the Rokura, not the other way around. I expect you to be *better*."

Percival flung the Rokura in Cade's direction; Cade flinched as the weapon landed right at his feet, its blades digging into the ground and kicking dirt over his pants.

"No," Cade said, pulling the weapon out of the ground and gripping it tightly at his side. "You expect me to do what you want. To be what you want. You're no better than this damn weapon."

Percival sneered. "And you're as stupid as you are stubborn."

"What about what I want, Percival? Ortzo killed my parents. That son of a—" Cade stopped and sucked in a deep breath, trying to cool the smoldering within himself. "If I had let the Rokura unleash on him, it would have been no more than he deserved. But I didn't. I stopped it from happening, which—you have no idea what that's like. Though maybe you would have at least a vague notion if you hadn't been such a coward when you were chosen to wield the Rokura."

"You selfish brat. Do you really think you're the only one who's been made an orphan by Praxis? Parents, spouses, children—no one is spared Ga Halle's rage and cruelty. No one. And you hold in your hands the means to stop her, and you're going to squander it. You can justify your failure to yourself any way you want. You're not the Paragon. You're not made for this."

"And what about you? Praxis would have never even happened if you had taken the Rokura when you had the chance."

"And I've been paying for my mistake ever since that day. How about you? You won the Rokura from Ga Halle; you have your chance. But when I look at you, I don't see someone willing to fight. All I can think about are the people suffering and dying because you can't get over your own self-pity."

"I never asked for this!" Cade yelled, pointing the Rokura at Percival. Though he hadn't moved any closer, Cade noticed Percival had raised his shido in a defensive position.

"Your parents never asked to die. Neither did your brother, neither did all the other people—real people, Cade—who lost their lives because of Ga Halle's madness. The galaxy is a cruel place, and I will not stand idly by and let you waste the chance to make it less so."

The anger drummed so hard in Cade's chest he could hardly breathe. He was tired of being the one burdened with cleaning up everyone else's messes. Percival's failure with the Rokura; the Well's failure to stop Praxis when it had the chance; even the entire galaxy's failure to recognize how evil Praxis was, unify, and fight back without having to be coaxed into doing so by a messiah. Because Cade was no messiah. He was afraid. He was uncertain. He was flawed, deeply and thoroughly. That wasn't the stuff of saviors, and it was only a matter of time before everyone else—Percival, the Rokura, maybe even Kira—came to recognize what Cade already knew. And when that happened, when it became abundantly clear Cade wasn't the one who could meet their expectations, he'd be all alone. Just like Ortzo had said.

"What are you going to do, Percival? Are you going to make me be the Paragon?"

"If I have to? Yes."

Cade gripped the Rokura in its center and crouched into a fighting position. "I'd like to see you try," he said.

Percival took a deep, hesitant breath. "So be it," he said, then charged at Cade.

Cade met Percival halfway, and against the three suns disappearing behind the horizon in the distance, their weapons clanged together as they exchanged their opening strikes. Cade and Percival pushed against each other and locked into a standstill; with no aid from the Rokura, Cade was equally matched with the former Paragon in strength and, in this moment, determination. Driven by pride and a shared, deep-seated need to be right, neither Cade nor Percival allowed themselves to surrender an inch for fear of what it might mean to lose.

"And what if you had let the Rokura kill Ortzo?" Percival asked as he continued to shove his shido against Cade's Rokura. "You'd really surrender everything to see one man dead?"

"Maybe," Cade huffed. "Maybe I would."

"Then your parents died for *nothing*," Percival said and kicked out Cade's knee, sending him stumbling forward. Percival spun out of Cade's way and came around, ready to defend himself.

"What are you talking about?" Cade asked, quickly getting back into fighting position. "My parents *did* die for nothing. They were casualties of a war they had nothing to do with."

"Mig told me what Ortzo told you. All this time, have you really believed that your parents were just aid workers? Cade, they were helping the Kaldorians fight for freedom; they were helping them defeat Praxis."

"You're LYING!" Cade yelled.

"Your parents believed in something. Your brother believed in something. What about you, Cade? Do you believe in anything?!"

Cade rushed at Percival, fast and nimble. He swung the Rokura high, thrust it forward, then swiped it at Percival's legs. Each strike was defended, but each strike also sparked the Rokura's intensity. Energy was once again crackling off its blades, building to an uncontrollable summit.

When Cade tried to drill the bottom of his weapon into Percival's stomach, Percival quickly sidestepped the attack; with Cade unbalanced just enough, Percival was able to use his shido to catch Cade in a choke hold.

"Good," Percival whispered into Cade's ear. "Now is the time to control yourself. To focus. Use the weapon to defeat me. Don't let *it* use *you.*"

"I am in control," Cade snarled back as he drove an elbow into Percival's side, breaking his hold.

Cade held the Rokura up to his face, ready for more. He felt the weapon's heat warm his skin, and through its cycling energy he saw an obscured image of a self-righteous Percival square up for continued battle. Cade couldn't tell how he felt about Percival's temerity: glad his so-called mentor was still willing to fight, or concerned over what would happen to himself and Percival if their duel went on much longer. The former was winning out, and Cade had a flash in his mind that it was the Rokura, not him, that was enthused to keep an unnecessary fight going. But it was just a flash.

This time, Percival was the one to take the offensive. He swiped his shido in a downward arc at Cade, and its blades crashed against the Rokura. Cade was ready to turn Percival's momentum against him, but he was too slow. Nothing about his fighting felt right; he couldn't concentrate, couldn't get a feel for himself or the Rokura. He was lost, too concerned over what kind of influence the Rokura might levy on him and what the unintentional results might be. Percival used his distraction to get a step ahead. When Cade went to make his attack, Percival beat him to it; he drove the blunt end of his shido across Cade's face, knocking him off-balance. Just as Cade staggered a half-step, Percival swung his shido hard against the Rokura, driving its crackling head into the ground. The weapon drove into the dirt, and the entire ground lit up as bolts of searing white light shot out in every direction. Cade tried to wrench the Rokura from the ground, but Percival drove a knee into his abdomen, and then he grabbed Cade by his shirt and used his weight to shove him to the ground. Cade lost his grip on the Rokura, and it remained stuck where it was as he fell onto his back.

By the time Cade looked up, Percival was standing above him, his shido pointed in his face.

"Control, you say?" Percival panted. "If you were in control, you would have beaten me before I could even lay a finger on you."

"Just tell me the truth about my parents," Cade breathlessly said, slumped on the ground, defeated. He had to know if his parents were victims or martyrs; it was a distinction that, to Cade, was everything. Victims were something to mourn; martyrs were something to fight for. "I need the truth."

"I didn't know either one of them, but I knew of them; they were the couple on Kyysring who could get you supplies and help move them. They were resisters, Cade. Like all of us."

Cade let his head drop against the ground as he felt an enormous weight press against his chest. Tristan, Kira, Percival, the entire galaxy, and now his parents. All pressing their hands on Cade, directing him to become something he was convinced he could never, ever be.

"This isn't over, Cade," Percival said as Cade remained on his back. "You might think it is, but it's not. I won't give up on this. I won't give up on you. You can do this. You and I, together, can do this."

Cade groaned like he'd aggravated a deep wound. But with the Rokura out of his grasp, at least his head was regaining a semblance of clarity. No longer were shards of glass corkscrewing in his mind, twisting every thought he called his own while, simultaneously, a foreign presence buried its impulses into his psyche. "We've trained. We've meditated and focused and pushed, and here we are, at the point where we're fighting each other. The Rokura is meant to be with the Chosen One, Percival. And I think we're both understanding why."

"Let me ask you a question. Do you think Wu-Xia was the Chosen One when he made the Rokura? When he used it to bring peace to the galaxy?"

"That's different," Cade said as he pulled himself into a sitting position. "In case you hadn't noticed, I'm not Wu-Xia."

"It's only different if you choose it to be. Strip the legend down, and all you have is someone willing himself to become something better, something more. It's what I see in that story, and I know for certain it's what Ga Halle sees."

"So what? You think I haven't tried convincing myself and the Rokura that I deserve to be the one who controls it?"

"Your belief in yourself is questionable, Cade, but that's not the point. The point is that neither one of us knows how to do this," Percival said as he pulled the Rokura out of the ground and handed it to Cade. "I was born being able to claim this weapon, which means I know nothing of having to will myself into using it. As much as I hate to admit it, I'm not capable of showing you how to become a self-made Paragon. That leaves us one option: We have to bring you to someone who can."

Cade grabbed the weapon hovering in front of his face. He wasn't through with this weapon, and vice versa. Not yet.

"I told you I knew things about the Rokura and its legend, things they didn't tell you at the Well," Percival continued. "Well, it's time to put that knowledge to the test."

"Meaning what?" Cade asked. "I'm sorry to sound skeptical, but who out there is going to help make this Paragon thing happen for me?"

"Who? Who do you think?" Percival said as he turned and walked away from Cade. "There's only one person who can help you now . . . Wu-Xia himself."

In the shelter of a narrow pass, protected by a natural canopy created where the impenetrable sides of two mountains abutted, the Renegades made their new, temporary camp. Cade decided to make the journey on his own, using coordinates given to him by Percival. By the time he arrived, night had taken Raja Prime and darkness reigned. Using the soft light he'd coaxed from the Rokura, Cade moved across the landscape a single glowing fok to anyone watching from a distance. After two hours of walking, the derig fields began to thin, giving way to the unwelcoming mountainous terrain that supported no crops and, thus, were home to none of the Raja Prime tribes. Cade negotiated this land with care; he was certain there was a trail that provided a more direct route, but he didn't know where it was, nor did he have any interest in sending a comms to anyone for help. Cade needed solitude; he needed time to clear his mind in preparation for the journey ahead. Time to consider just how desperate he and his allies had become.

His field scanner rendered useless by the unbroken night that surrounded him, Cade's visibility was limited to the little bit of space illuminated by the Rokura's glow. That's why Cade failed to spot the camp until he was nearly on it. First, he caught the faint glow of a fire's spark; its embers cast just enough light to shimmer off the crystalline mountain walls that crowded the space overhead. Soft hues of indigo and emerald played a visual harmonic off the rough exterior as the small bits of glowing crystals caught the light and then bounced it from one side to the other. For a brief moment, Cade stopped to watch the show. His reverie, though, was short-lived. He didn't have time to waste.

The temporary base was more of an encampment when compared to what'd been dismantled while Cade was recuperating. The Renegades had recruited a lot of new faces in the months since the *War Hammer* had been destroyed, allies that came from all over the galaxy. Some were motivated to join the fight because they were born soldiers and war was all they'd known since as long as they could remember; others had never held a weapon in their lives but joined simply because it was the right thing to do. Cade hardly recognized any of the men and women he passed as he walked through the canyon. But he recognized the looks on their faces: demoralized, tired, and full of doubt. Percival had told Cade the reason they'd dismantled their hard-won base; he told him about the hotshot admiral who boasted a brutal and efficient record and now had the Renegades on his radar. Percival had no choice but to take extra precautions to hide their presence while he still could. He ordered some to orbit a nearby asteroid field, sent others on missions, and, knowing Percival as Cade did, he surely had plans for those who remained on Raja Prime. All this maneuvering to avoid the cunning wrath of one Admiral Ebik.

Percival also explained who Ebik was to Kira.

Cade found Kira at the opposite end of the canyon, alone, working on her ship by floodlight. The harsh light cast the *Rubicon*'s oval shadow against the far wall of the pass, dulling the subdued light of the crystals embedded there. Cade went to the side of the ship, where Kira's legs stuck out from beneath. He was about to duck his head under and say, "Knock, knock," when a sidewinder poked out from the *Rubicon*'s underbelly.

"Stay right there," Kira ordered.

"Whoa, easy," Cade said. "It's just Cade. The one who doesn't like being shot at, if you need me to be more specific."

Kira wheeled herself out from beneath the *Rubicon* and looked

Cade over before getting to her feet. "You look terrible," she said.

"Yeah, I think this is one of those situations where I actually am worse for wear."

"Assuming you were all that sharp to begin with."

Cade forced a smile at Kira's barb, knowing this banter for what it was: a way to avoid talking about the road ahead. For both of them. He followed Kira to the *Rubicon*'s ramp, where she took a rag out of her back pocket and used it to scrub the grease off her hands.

"So," Kira said, "I hear you're going on a mystical journey to find some dead guy."

"I'd like to say it's not like that, but . . . it's exactly like that." He laughed, trying to bring some levity to the moment. Kira wasn't having it, though.

"Well," Kira said as she brushed past Cade, "good luck with that."

"Kira, wait," Cade said, calling after her. She turned, her face hard, her eyes refusing to meet his. "Just . . . don't. Please."

"What do you want me to say, Cade? We make a good team, all of us, and it sucks that you're leaving."

"A *team*?" Cade said as he stepped toward Kira. "Is this about all of us, or about me and you?"

Kira looked up at Cade and exhaled sharply out of her nostrils. She didn't say a word, though.

"Look," Cade continued, "Percival told me about Ebik, about . . . you know. I'm sorry—really sorry—that this is happening to you. To have him back in your life . . . I don't even know how hard that must be."

"It's nothing," Kira mumbled. "*He's* nothing."

"Kira, this man tried to kill you when you were just a kid. And now he tried to kill you again. He's not nothing, and we both know it."

"I'm dealing with it," Kira said, reclaiming her resolve. "Ebik is my problem, and I'm handling it."

Cade arched an eyebrow at Kira. He'd been concerned about how Kira was handling the sudden insertion of her crappy father back into her life. Now, he was concerned in an entirely different way.

"What are you planning?" Cade asked. "What's this secret mission that Percival won't tell me about?"

"Well, it wouldn't be much of a secret if everyone went blabbing about it, would it? Besides, you're not part of it, so you don't need to care."

"Is that what you think?" Cade said, his voice conveying his growing frustration. "That I don't care?"

Kira shrugged and forced a flippant tone into her words. "Want to tell me again what you're about to go do?"

"I know what you're doing," Cade spat. "I get that you're mad, but you don't have to throw up your walls with me."

"What's the problem?" Kira asked, casually defensive. "Just tell me what your next step is."

Cade's lips tightened, then he drew and exhaled an angry breath. "You know what I'm doing. And I thought you understood why I'm doing it. Why I *have* to do it."

"Have to? Says who?"

"Says . . . I don't know," Cade responded, flustered. "This is what I have to do for the Rokura. It's what has to happen."

"And *that* is your problem, Cade," Kira said, drawing close to him and staring him in the eyes. "Where do you draw the line with the decisions that the Rokura makes for you?"

Cade broke Kira's gaze and looked around, searching. But the answers he was looking for—so many answers to so many complicated questions—were nowhere to be found. "I don't know," he whispered. "I just . . . I don't know."

Kira backed off, shaking her head as she put distance between them. "That stupid weapon is creating a wedge between us, between all of us. You have a choice, and you're choosing to follow the Rokura."

"Yes, so we can win this fight," Cade implored. "That's why I'm doing this, that's why I'm following Percival on some ridiculous mission. We're fighting for the exact same thing."

"No, it's not the same!" Kira yelled. "Everything we've made, everything we are, is built on people. On our hope and our courage and our will to *fight*. That weapon is not what makes us what we are; it's not what makes *you* who *you* are."

Cade took a step toward Kira, reducing the space between the two of them to no more than a few inches. "You're right about what you said. Deep down, I don't care about your mission. I don't care about the Rokura, either," Cade said, drawing even closer. "I care about you, Kira. I care about *you*."

Cade expected Kira to yell in return. Maybe hit him, but probably just shove him away. Instead, she looked right at him, and with tears forming in her eyes, she said softly, "Then don't go."

For a moment, Cade couldn't think of a word to say. Because it wasn't like he hadn't explored the possibility of abandoning the Rokura. Just like he'd planned on doing when he'd first held it. But as he walked for hours from the fields of derig to the crystal mountains, one thought, and one thought alone, plagued his mind: What would happen if he failed? If this gambit to find the ghost of Wu-Xia turned out to be a fool's errand—which could very well be the case—there was no plan B. There was nothing other than him, Percival, and the wild hope that they could find Wu-Xia, and the Paragon Prime would impart wisdom salient to controlling the Rokura. And if that didn't happen, it could very well be the end of everything. Because when Tristan pulled the Rokura from its stasis, he unleashed a powerful thing onto the galaxy that no one understood and only he could control. But

Tristan was gone, and the Rokura wasn't going anywhere. Worse, Cade had experienced its terrible power and purpose; in moments like the one he'd had with Ortzo, Cade was granted a vision that played out in flashes on the periphery of his mind. And in those flashes, darkness. Darkness spreading across the galaxy, extinguishing the light from one end to the other. It brought pain. It brought suffering. It brought the end of all things. It was that vision that Cade fought most ardently against, and if he failed to find a way to rule this thing that was beyond his or anyone else's understanding—save the dead guy he was hopefully soon to meet—it would find its way into someone else's hands.

It would find its way to Ga Halle.

Should that happen, Cade knew the vision that'd brought him to his knees on the Kaldorian trade ship—of Ga Halle twisted and more dangerous than he could have ever imagined—would no longer be a vision. It would bleed into reality like the blackest ink dropped into a shallow pool of water. Destruction first. Then death. Then absolute darkness.

"I have to," Cade murmured. "I don't want to go. I don't want . . . any of this. But I *have* to. Percival knows what he's doing. He has the best idea of what—"

"Then leave," Kira interrupted. Her eyes grew dim and hard, and Cade could see the hurt and the anger burning inside of them. "Go."

His heart heavy with sorrow, Cade tried to think of the words that would make everything better. But there weren't any. Going with Percival was both the right and wrong thing to do. He had to take this one last chance to figure out the Rokura—either how to use it or how to destroy it. The cost, though, was being separated from the people he cared about when they needed him most.

There was no time left for Cade to consider options and outcomes. As he watched Kira squat beside her ship, he heard a dasher bike rumbling behind him. Cade knew who was there, and why, without having to turn around.

"It's time to go," Percival said solemnly.

Cade looked back at Kira.

"Be careful," he told her, then he walked away. He thought he heard her say something, but he was too afraid to turn back and find her gone.

Cade boarded the dasher bike and took a deep breath. He had to do this; he had to focus on what was in front of him. What he was about to do could win the war or at least prevent it from being lost. Still, he couldn't stop himself from looking back. And he saw Kira, still waiting at the edge of her ship, watching him go.

Cade kept her in his sight even as Percival pulled away. She became more and more distant until, finally, Cade couldn't see her anymore.

He was afraid it was the last time he ever would.

CHAPTER FIVE

Kira had never seen such a sorry collection of soldiers in all her career.

Though, to be fair, she was hesitant to call them soldiers. Most of them were not. They'd been steadily taking on recruits from across the galaxy since the *War Hammer* had been blown into a billion pieces in the space over Ticus. But of those recruits, many of them—too many, in Kira's opinion—were sorely lacking the stuff soldiers were made of. Some were too old; some were too young. Some joined because they had nothing else to do and leaving where they were, even if it meant the possibility of engaging in armed combat, was better than staying. Some were the troublemakers looking to skip out on whatever bounties, warrants, or payback homed in on them like a heat-seeking torpedo. Most of the lot had little to no training or the discipline to be trained; a good number of them were unpleasantly surprised when they realized what the day-to-day life of a grunt was like. Still, Kira had to believe that each and every one of them joined, despite whatever dubious reasoning motivated them, because they wanted to see the Praxis kingdom crumble. Or that they at least harbored a personal grudge that burned so hot within that it compelled them to put their lives on the line in exchange for the chance to exact some revenge. Even that would do. Because there's no bounty in the galaxy that's worth the exhausting grind of warfare; there's no dead-end planet so bad you'd put your life on the line—with a group of underdogs, no less—to get away from it. No, Kira was convinced that despite whatever circumstances brought them into the Renegade fold, deep down, each and every one of these recruits was here for a noble reason. They were here because it was the right thing to do.

The light of righteousness, Kira knew, only burned so brightly. And when it's already faint and sunk way down deep to begin with, it is that much easier to extinguish. Inertia and entropy were becoming as real an enemy to Kira as Praxis. As she looked out to the faces awaiting her command, she saw a lot of fires dwindling before her eyes. With Percival gone, it was her job to find a way to reignite those flames.

While Kira recognized her leadership style didn't always make for smooth sailing—she was abrasive and blunt, and held tough, but fair, standards—she won troops over by being honest with them and by never ordering her squads to do something she wouldn't. In that spirit of honesty, Kira had no choice but to recognize the difficult road they'd all faced since the *War Hammer*'s destruction. Even the recruits who shared Kira's gusto for kicking Praxis's collective teeth in showed signs of weariness. Until now, the Renegades had managed to balance their little defeats with little victories, and they could all cling to their marks of progress. But then Ebik came along and reminded them all of the power they were up against. Now, they were reeling from their first major defeat; now, they were forced to run from their homes and scramble into a cave for shelter like timid animals. Frightened, demoralized, exhausted. These weren't the conditions for victory; these were the conditions in which rebellions come undone. The onus was on Kira to reverse course. And fast.

"They look like men and women who've just witnessed their own executions," 4-Qel said as he joined Kira on the boarding ramp of their newly acquired starship. "Would you like me to defeat the strongest among them in combat and win their respect? That might inspire them to do as they're told, if only out of fear. I hear this tactic is very popular in prison."

"Let's keep that option in our back pocket for the time being," Kira said as she leaned over the ramp, down to the space below the rear of the ship. "Mig, how's this boat looking?"

Mig rolled himself out from under the ship, removed his soot-covered goggles, and tossed them to the ground. "On fifth inspection, it still looks *fine*. The problem isn't going to be getting there; the problem is going to be getting *in* once we're there."

Kira nodded. Mig was right, but she could only tackle one problem at a time. That was her mantra. One problem to the next, solving one after another after another on a chain that had an unknowable number of links. Kira, though, was less concerned with the number—two links or two hundred, it didn't matter—and more concerned with where they led: Praxis's doorstep. The final link that would lead to the kingdom's end. Kira would never stop breaking off links until she either reached its conclusion or was incapable of following the chain any further. Whichever came first was the only way she would stop.

"You're certain of this mission?" 4-Qel asked as Kira turned back around. "I don't mean to question your command. It just seems very . . . risky."

Kira cracked her neck and squared her shoulders. Maybe 4-Qel was right. Maybe her plan would prove to be a terrible mistake. But Kira didn't have the time or the luxury to allow doubt to stymie what little momentum they had left, not when the galaxy was racing toward totalitarian domination. Swift action was demanded of her, and she'd deal with whatever her decisions wrought, good or bad, when the time came. But right now, she had to save the Renegades. She had to strike a major blow against a relentless enemy that dwarfed everything her forces had to offer on their best day. To do so meant taking risks.

"Go get Kobe and tell him if he's coming, he's coming when we fire up our engines," Kira ordered 4-Qel. "I'm not waiting around for him to finish murmuring his spiritual grocery list to the wind."

"I believe he's practicing a form of meditation similar to—"

"*Qel.*"

"Right," the drone responded and headed down the ramp.

Kira watched as he left, then turned her attention back to the beaten and demoralized faces that awaited her, huddled in this damp, glittering canyon. They were searching for something, anything—even the outlaws, even the dead-enders—to light the way. It was all they had left: a path that led them forward.

"I want all of you to look at me," Kira said, raising her voice less to be heard and more to command attention. "Look me in the eyes, because I want there to be no uncertainty in the words I'm about to say:

"We. Will. *Not*. Lose."

Eyes widened. Heads rose a little higher. The crowd stood a little taller. They'd all been suffering from a feeling Kira hadn't felt since she was a child, a feeling that she had Ebik to thank for: that losing, that *submitting*, was their destiny. And if Kira's mother had not been there to tell her otherwise, Kira would have lived a life of submission. That's how kingdoms like Praxis and men like Ebik won. Wars weren't decided on the battlefields; they were decided in the hearts and minds of those who fought them. As long as you were still breathing, as long as you still had a shred of resistance left in you, you weren't defeated until *you* decided.

More than anything, they wanted to rob you of your audacity to resist and your will to fight. But Kira refused. She wouldn't allow it for herself, and she wouldn't allow it for those who followed her command.

"If you think this is defeat, then you don't know defeat. If you think this is the breaking point, then you don't know what it means to be broken. This is what Praxis wants, to deliver one big hit against us and destroy our collective will. Think about all the time Praxis devoted to that counteroperation against myself and my team. Think of the resources they expended. And for what? To kill me. To kill Cade and take the Rokura for themselves. Well, I'm still here. And Cade still has the Rokura. So, who was it that failed? We took this one on the chin, there's no doubt about that. But Praxis did *not* walk away with a victory. Far from it."

Kira let her words linger as she studied the ragtag collection of men and women of all different species who would topple a kingdom and free the galaxy. If there was one thing Kira had learned in her life, it was to never underestimate people from whom no one expected anything. When provided the right motivation and even the smallest opportunity, there was nothing they couldn't do. Kira was living proof of that. She led them because she was one of them. Misfits. Scoundrels. Renegades. But most of all, they were survivors, fighters. It was written all over their faces; these were people who'd *endured*.

"We all come from different places, and we're all here for different reasons, but one thing connects us all: the thorough, unwavering knowledge that Praxis is wrong and must be stopped. Let them think we're down. Let them think we're out. We know this place, all of us. And we know how to come back from it. So, when they least expect it, we'll get them. Then we'll do it again and again and again until they're the ones running from *us*. That day will come, and when it does, Praxis will stay down. They don't have your resilience, your ability to pick yourself up and keep moving. And that is how we'll win—we will not stay down."

Kira nodded to Captain Temple, a grumpy old war veteran who, if the legend was to be believed, was responsible for ending the plunder of Carthaton with his own two hands. He'd been picked by Percival to command the Renegades in their absence, and Kira couldn't think of a better choice to lead the mission to find a new home.

"Damn fine speech," Temple said as he moved to take command. "I'm ready to eat a warship for breakfast."

"I'll be back soon enough, Captain," Kira said, taking his hand. "Save some for the rest of us."

A rare smile spread across the Carthaton's smooth, olive-green face; Kira turned to board her ship and leave the captain to start his leadership. As she walked up the ship's boarding ramp, she heard a voice call her from behind. She turned to find a Sulac woman whose skin was as dry and tough as her home planet's arid topography. The woman called Kira again, and the crowd, who'd begun murmuring after Kira's speech ended, went quiet.

"Yes?" Kira asked, then the Sulac's name came to her. "Private Dekaa?"

"You're leaving us? On *that*?"

"I am," Kira responded, twisting her neck around to espy the ship she was entering while trying not to acknowledge the nervousness that carried on Dekaa's words. "A mission."

"A mission? A mission where?"

Kira gazed at the crowd, the expectant eyes that, like Dekaa's, were filled with fear and uncertainty. They were losing not only their leader but their inspiration; Kira was the heart and soul of their will to resist, and everyone—Kira included—knew it. To remove that now was potentially a loss too many. Which meant Kira had to tell them. She had to leave them with something big, bold, and inspiring. Something to see them through.

"Praxis," Kira said, and the entire canyon went silent. "I'm going to Praxis, and I'm going to take the entire planet out from right underneath the kingdom's nose."

4-Qel and Kobe joined Kira in the ship—a Praxian cargo vessel that Percival had somehow gotten his hands on—and just as the boarding ramp started to rise and close, the silence was broken.

The entire Renegade forces broke into a holler that shook the canyon walls. The sting of her very personal defeat at the hands of Ebik was starting to wear off, and Kira felt readier than ever for what was ahead.

In the belly of the cargo ship, the dual engines hummed rhythmically as they pushed the vessel closer and closer toward Praxian space. It was white noise to Kira, a cocoon of sound that helped ease her racing mind. She had to come down to the engine room to give herself a mental break. Up top, she was double- and triple-checking the ship's signature, making sure it remained authentic to Praxis's most current landing codes. She was running the weight scanner, ensuring that their forged mass—forged to maintain their guise of coming to the surface with cargo to deliver—stayed consistent. There were dozens of things to keep a watchful eye on, all of which had to be totally perfect for the ship to clear Praxis's rigid landing standards. They'd only get one shot at this, and if they failed, not only would it mean mission failure but also life failure. A Praxian patrol likely wouldn't think twice about shooting down a ship trying to deceive its way to the surface. And while Kira was a great pilot— the best, she contended—she wasn't a miracle worker. Should a squad of Intruders press an attack, there was little she'd be able to do; the ship had the maneuverability of a botho stuck in a swamp, and if that wasn't enough, its weapons array was *maybe* capable of shooting a model starcruiser out of a child's hand. Maybe.

It was best that they didn't fail their authentication.

If it were up to her, Kira would spend the entire trip monitoring the ship's carefully manipulated signature. But it wasn't. Not with Mig and 4-Qel in her ears, forcing her to do trivial things like eat, sleep, and take breaks. Visiting the engine room was more to appease them than satisfy anything she needed. Because Kira didn't need breaks. And she especially didn't need the quiet that allowed her mind to dwell on how she hadn't set foot on Praxis in years.

Luckily, the quiet was short-lived. Between the cycles of the engine's shifting rotations, she heard the soft, almost imperceptible sound of something pressing against the metal floor.

Kira wasn't alone.

Hand pressed against the butt of her sidewinder, Kira stalked the length of the starboard engine, expecting something, or someone, to jump out at her. She was ready to shoot first and ask questions later if whatever she shot was alive to talk.

Kira reached the back end of the engine, and she was about to unholster her weapon and let it lead her way around the turn when she heard a sigh coming from the other side. Then, a voice.

"You've scanned this ship to the ounce how many times? And you still think there's a stowaway on it?"

Kira rolled her eyes as Kobe walked out from behind the engine. He was down to his tank top and sweaty from head to toe.

"You're truly a glutton for punishment to make yourself exercise in the hottest spot in the ship," Kira said, feeling beads of sweat starting to form along her own hairline.

"I suppose I want to be extra cautious for this kind of mission."

Kira cocked an eyebrow, detecting just how loaded Kobe intended his response to be. "And what kind of mission would that

be?" she asked, stressing a tone of authority in her voice as a reminder to Kobe.

"A foolish one," Kobe said, then he took a long drink from his
water bottle.

Kira, fighting the urge to slap the bottle right out of Kobe's
hand, attempted a more diplomatic approach. After all, Kobe
technically wasn't under her command; he was Percival's right
hand, out on loan to Kira while Percival and Cade were off on
their mystical journey. Speaking of foolish missions, Kira mused,
but she quickly shoved that thought out of her mind. She couldn't
bring herself to think about Cade. The mission required nothing less than her total focus, which in turn allowed her to stifle
how she was really feeling—

Afraid.

Kira was afraid that the Rokura would force Cade to betray
her, just like her father had; either that or she'd lose Cade, just
like she lost her mother.

Kira cleared her throat and focused. "You want to tell me why
our mission is foolish, Kobe?" she asked.

Kobe smirked. "I don't know if your friends didn't read your
briefing. Or it could be that they're too close to you to confront
you on it, but have you considered that personal ties to this situation might be clouding your judgment?"

"No," Kira said without hesitation. "This is our only chance—
our *only* chance—to cripple Praxis in a way they can tangibly
feel. It's our only chance to keep our fight going."

"Maybe it's our only chance this week," Kobe replied. "Maybe
if we waited a little bit instead of rushing into enemy territory
to—"

"You expect our battered, demoralized forces to sit around and
wait while we hope for some kind of opportunity to present itself? Waiting for opportunities doesn't win wars, Kobe. *Making*
them does."

Kobe huffed a deep breath and looked away from Kira briefly, then turned his attention back to her. "You might be right. But that doesn't change the fact that you're taking us into the enemy's lair on a mission to rescue your mother."

Kira took a step forward, bringing herself right into Kobe's face. "We're rescuing the last living Baron, the one person who can legitimately take control of Praxis and destabilize its military forces from within. *That* is our objective, and don't you ever think twice about it."

"If you say so," Kobe said as he brushed past her.

"And what about you, Kobe?" Kira asked to his back. "From what I understand, you were so eager to volunteer for this mission. Why? You're going to tell me it has nothing to do with revenge for what Praxis did to you, to your entire planet?"

Kobe turned and shot Kira a look that could freeze the entire bottom half of the ship. "It doesn't," he said.

Kira shook her head. "You might have convinced yourself of that, but I don't buy it."

Kobe walked back toward Kira, his expression still cold as ice. But Kira couldn't detect any of the rage or pain she'd expected to find pushing just beneath the surface of his controlled veneer.

"When my planet was dying after Praxis robbed us of the light from our star, my family did everything it could to escape. But we were poor. Had no transport, nothing to trade or barter for a way out of our own graves.

"My father was the first one to go. My mother followed soon after. That left just me and my little sister, alone, terrified, freezing, and starving. I had to tell her that everything was going to be okay. That help was going to come for us. I knew it probably wasn't true, but I figured, if nothing else, hope would keep her going. And it did, for a while. But only for a while. She died with her hand in mine, believing a lie I'd told her."

Kira felt a pang of regret. She'd heard plenty of stories like

Kobe's before, but something about the rawness in Kobe's words—like this had just happened to him—unnerved her. Most of the stories she heard were about guerrilla squadrons shot down over a Praxian base, or people who'd lost their lives in one of Praxis's bombing strikes. She could digest those tragedies because they were so big and, sadly, so common. But Kobe's experience wasn't an abstraction, it was intimate. Kira tried to steel herself with the reminder that what happened to Kobe's sister was exactly why she was fighting, but it was cold comfort. Nothing she could do—no amount of victories, no amount of systems liberated—would give Kobe back what he lost.

"I don't know what to say," Kira whispered, choking down her feelings of shame and sadness. "I . . . I'm sorry. Sorry that happened to you."

"Don't be. My point isn't to share my grief. See, I nearly died, too. I was just about there, and I was ready. But then a ship came. Out of nowhere, here was this ship dropping from the sky. Percival had intercepted our distress message. He'd come when no one else had. He got me on board, and I was . . . out of my mind. Delirious, in shock, barely conscious. But I remember one thing about that moment, and it was the vow I made to myself, and it wasn't for revenge. Revenge is a selfish journey of darkness, and it was meaningless compared to the magnitude of what my people and I suffered. The vow I made was simple:

"Never let this happen again. To anyone, ever. And I've been living that vow since."

Kira gripped Kobe's story close. She held it inside of herself like so many other similar stories that cataloged the anguish and terror Praxis had inflicted on the galaxy.

She looked Kobe dead in his eyes, pressing forth the conviction of her words with every fiber of her being.

"I swear to you, I haven't put us on this mission for personal reasons. All the doubts you have about my motivations, I've had them as well, except multiplied by a million. I've thought about the strategy behind what we're doing so many times I can barely stand it. But every time, every single time, I come back to the same conclusion:

"This is the right move. Praxis will never see this coming, and if we pull this off, we can turn the tide of this whole damn war. This isn't about revenge; it isn't about all the misery Praxis has caused us. It's about ending their reign. Period."

Kobe turned up his chin at Kira and glared down at her. He studied her for a few tense seconds before extending his hand toward her.

"I've always liked you," he said. "Now I trust you."

Kira accepted Kobe's handshake and wanted to expel a giant sigh of relief. She always knew Kobe would fight for her as duty demanded. Now, he was going to fight *with* her. Kira strove to earn that distinction with each and every person in her command.

And now, with Kobe truly in her ranks, they were stronger than ever.

Kira was eager to bring this war to Praxis's doorstep.

Except war, it would seem, was already there.

Kira raced to the cockpit and found 4-Qel frantically working the control panel and Mig running diagnostics from beneath the dashboard. The alarm wailed a sharp pitch that only succeeded in pissing Kira off. She was about to order Mig to slice the cord that powered the warning system when the ship was hit hard on its port side; Kira was thrown off-balance and would have been knocked off her feet if Kobe wasn't behind her to break her fall. Something was wrong, Kira thought with a shudder. More than wrong, intuition screamed within her. In a mission simmering with the potential for catastrophe, calamity found them quicker than it should have.

"Somebody tell me what's happening *now*!" Kira yelled as she reestablished her footing. "Who's shooting at us?!"

"I have no idea," 4-Qel said. "We plotted our mass jump to come out just beyond Praxian airspace, and our coordinates say we're at the exact jump location."

Kira gritted her teeth. She didn't want explanations. She wanted answers to two points of concern: Who was shooting at them, and how could they kill it?

"That doesn't answer my question, Four-Qel," Kira barked. Just then, the ship was rocked again. Kira didn't break stride, though, as she hopped into the pilot's seat and brought the weapons online. "Who's out there? I want to know so I can personalize the protons I'm about to send up their as—"

"Diagnostics must be shot, because the radar isn't picking up any other ships," Mig said from underneath the dash. "I'm not seeing a single problem down here, though."

"So, let me get this straight," Kira said, trying to stifle her anger before she released it on the wrong people. "We jumped exactly where we were supposed to, and that dropped us right in the crosshairs of an enemy that doesn't exist on our scans?"

"Consider yourself fully briefed on our current situation," 4-Qel said, still trying to manipulate the ship's dusty and dated equipment into not sucking.

Kira exhaled sharply, waiting for another blast to pound their woefully unprotected cargo vessel. But the strike didn't happen. Nothing happened. Kira knew Praxis enough to know they didn't waste time shredding enemy fighters—or ships they assumed, guessed, or just had a feeling were enemy fighters—to pieces. Meaning: The ship should be destroyed, and they should all be dead. But they weren't.

"Open the cockpit shielding," Kira ordered.

Mig rolled out from beneath the dashboard and cocked an eyebrow at Kira. "You do realize any Praxian fighter will be able to establish visual recognition then, right? Like, they'll see us."

"Just open it," Kira affirmed.

"If you say so." 4-Qel shrugged as he activated the mechanism that rolled up the viewport's shielding. "At least we'll be able to flip off whoever's out there before this ship gets compacted into a cube. With us in it."

Everyone in the ship anxiously waited, in total silence, for the viewport to reveal an enemy fleet waiting to finish off their ship. They expected a squadron hovering on the edge of their view, biding its time before it fired enough torpedoes to torch the cargo ship into a pile of smoldering space dust. Kira wasn't buying that scenario, and her gut feeling was right. Because when the shielding pulled back, there were no enemy fighters anywhere.

"Did we know the coordinates we set the mass jump to were for an asteroid field?" Kobe asked.

Kira knew that the floating bits of debris swirling around them, seemingly for miles in either direction, weren't asteroids. She'd seen this before, and so had 4-Qel and Mig.

"That's no asteroid field," Kira said. "That's debris."

"Just like when the *War Hammer* blew up," Mig added, dumbstruck. "But—huh?"

"It's a Praxian vessel," 4-Qel said, having run a scan of the floating parts while everyone else gaped at the wreckage. A small chunk ricocheted off the port side, and Kira took the controls, navigating the ship slowly through the field. "But how," 4-Qel continued, "does a Praxian ship—presumably a warship, judging by the size of the wreckage—get destroyed over its own planet?"

Kira was delightfully puzzled. "That is a damn fine question," she said. "There's only one way to find out."

"And what way is that?" Mig asked, his voice conveying how unenthusiastic he was about the answer.

"The careful way," Kira replied.

Kira angled the ship down, putting it back on its designated landing vector. They were heading toward the central landing terminal, just outside the capital's metro center. The idea was to land the ship in the most populated area and assimilate into the bustling urban crowd as quickly as possible. Kira, Mig, and Kobe were provided with fashionable Praxian clothing, fake IDs, and enough coin to bribe their way to wherever they needed to be. 4-Qel would just have to do his best to blend in as a service companion. Kira didn't expect that cover to last long, but if they found themselves on the surface long enough for 4-Qel to be identified by the wrong people, they were probably burned anyway. This mission relied on their ability to move quickly and efficiently; they had to find Kira's mother, Akima, free her, and somehow get her in position to assume the power that was by law hers. It was a binary mission—succeed or fail. There was no middle ground and, therefore, no half measures to be taken. They all knew there was one rule and one rule only: Don't get caught. Everything else was fair game.

As she smoothly cruised the cargo ship toward the landing checkpoint, Kira hoped they'd gotten their one surprise out of the way. But she knew that was wishful thinking. She knew, down deep, that the pulverized warship wasn't a mission aberration; it was the first sign of what was to come.

The second sign was no one responding at the checkpoint station.

Intel was clear: Two alpha drones operated the station that floated just beyond Praxis's atmosphere. They scanned every ship that came in, verified their codes, and, at times, performed random searches just to keep the crews of all incoming vessels on their toes. Alphas were the most efficient, thorough, and lifeless creation the galaxy could ever conjure and a true mark of the Praxian spirit. For them to abandon their post or be in dereliction of duty was inconceivable.

Unless something had gone terribly wrong.

"Why aren't they answering?" Mig asked, his voice cracking with panic. "Alphas answer. It's what they do."

"Well, they certainly didn't go for a coffee break," Kira said. "So, my guess is—"

"They're dead," 4-Qel interrupted. "Unlike me, alphas aren't equipped with technology that shields their signatures from ship scans. I'm reading nothing on that ship, so either they left, which we all know is impossible, or they no longer have a signature to emit because they are no longer beings of energy, artificial or otherwise."

"This doesn't make any sense. A destroyed warship, dead alpha drones . . . what's happening here?" Kobe questioned.

"None of this is right," Mig said. "It was one thing to head into the dark, beating heart of the Praxis kingdom under carefully planned conditions, but this . . . I don't know what this is. None of us do. As important as this mission is, I don't think it warrants us going on a suicide run."

Everyone was silent, letting Mig's words float around the cockpit like a storm cloud. Kira eased the throttle, bringing the ship to coasting speed, but still angled toward Praxis's surface and whatever was down there. She tried to think of what to do, tried to weigh her options, but there was no complexity to consider. The choice was either to stay on mission and fly into the unknown or abort. That was it, and Kira wasn't fond of either selection.

"So . . . anyone want to chime in?" Mig asked. "Do we pull back?"

All eyes shifted to Kira. She was the commander, and this was her call to make. 4-Qel, she knew, was up for anything. She looked to Mig, who had fear and uncertainty in his eyes, but not defiance. And Kobe's eyes simmered with the fire of determination. He nodded at her, dead set in the choice he'd made. And Kira agreed. They were here, knocking on Praxis's door. It would take more than some unusual occurrences to send them running.

"We're going in," Kira said, and she grabbed the throttle and accelerated the ship through the planet's atmosphere. Kira could feel everyone gripping the arms of their seats tightly. There was no turning back now; the ship was too slow to even attempt an escape, and its shields didn't provide the protection they'd need to punch their way through any resistance they might encounter. They'd either land or die trying.

The ship cleared the layer of clouds, dropping directly over the densely clustered skyscrapers that shimmered gold, silver, and red as the planet's star set over the horizon. Light cascaded over the buildings, giving an almost viscous sheen to their exteriors. The skyline shone brilliantly, and for a moment, Kira had to break her gaze away, as if the reflecting light was too much for her eyes. It had been a long, long time since she'd seen her home planet, and the memory of leaving was burned in her mind forever. She was just a child, alone on a starcruiser, bleeding out from the wound her own father had inflicted. The planet was radiant then, too, the buildings of its urban center glowing brightly against the nighttime sky as if in defiance of darkness. So much of the planet was eerily the same, with its tightly packed buildings scraping against one another as they stretched to the sky. Kira strangled the throttle as she pushed the ship forward in its landing approach, arcing it so she got a clear, direct view of the Praxian skyline. There, centermost of it all, was the towering Megaron, a massive edifice that gleamed gray and white and reflected light like fire in the sky. Standing head and shoulders higher than the landscape and topped with what looked like an aggressive claw reaching down, the Megaron was built as a testament to the endurance and strength of the Praxian people after they had repelled attacks from barbaric invaders who had come to seize the planet generations earlier. Kira knew how that meaning had been perverted over the years, coming to represent blind, obedient jingoism, leaving the ideal of fighting for a noble, necessary cause when called upon buried in history's graveyard. Kira took it all in with a shudder, and the shudder carried all the way across time and space and hit her again, so many years later, as she drew closer and closer to the planet she'd vowed never to return to unless it was to burn it all down. Although she'd meant it quite literally then, her mission now was close enough. Everything Praxis had come to represent— repression, terror, hatred—would burn, and she'd make sure the entire galaxy witnessed the flames.

Unless someone else beat her to it.

Because suddenly, from the lower half of the Megaron, an explosion ripped through the exterior, sending roaring flames bursting from its side. The blast was followed by another in a nearby building, then another. Three buildings were burning, tarnishing what was once—and had been as long as Kira could remember—an unblemished skyline. The plumes of smoke rose skyward, dissipating in the atmosphere. What didn't get lost in the air, though, was the message the blast sent:

Praxis was under attack.

"What the—what is happening?!" Mig exclaimed as he sprang from his seat.

"Sit down and strap in," Kira commanded as she pushed the throttle down, narrowing the ship's trajectory to the surface. Landing became less important than getting a closer look that, Kira hoped, would provide an answer to Mig's question. Because right now, she had no clue what was happening. Ships were destroyed; stations were abandoned; buildings were burning. It was a battle, that much had become clear. But waged by whom? That was the question that occupied Kira's mind as she accelerated the ship toward the Megaron.

"That appears to be blaster fire on the ground," 4-Qel said, making the most of his advanced optics. "*A lot* of blaster fire."

"It might be time to reconsider our strategy," Kobe said, getting up from his seat. "Civil war, coup—whatever this is, we're not prepared to be in the middle of it."

Kira gritted her teeth and contemplated pulling rank. She knew Mig shared Kobe's urging for caution, and looking at 4-Qel, she sensed he did as well. While the throttle was hers to control and rank gave her authority to follow whatever course of action she damn well pleased, Kira knew Kobe was right. It stung her right in her heart to be this close and be forced to fall back, but anything less than at least rerouting their course was flirting too closely with death or at least capture. She was close enough to see the surface now, and there, she spotted the blaster fire bolts that were being exchanged over the entire area, blanketing it in warfare. Kira was made jealous by it, but not enough for her to compromise her first rule as a commanding officer: Never unnecessarily risk the lives of your squad. And she wouldn't. Kira pulled the stick back and turned the ship starboard, getting them away from the action below.

But it was too late.

An alarm rang out, a long, incessant wailing that was different from the normal alert. Kira knew this type of alarm because she had it on her own ship. It was reserved for special occasions.

It was reserved for when you were truly screwed.

"Qel!" Kira yelled. "Give me a status report!"

"Ground-to-air missile," 4-Qel responded. "Bearing on us at an increasing rate."

"An increasing—damn these sensors! How much time until impact?"

Kira looked up at 4-Qel, and while she knew it was impossible for him, as a drone, to have an expression, she swore she detected fear in his bulbous eyes. It was the last thing she saw before their ship was hammered.

"None," 4-Qel said.

For a moment, there was darkness. When Kira opened her eyes, she couldn't hear a thing, though she knew everything around her was screaming. All she could feel was the violent motion of their lousy Praxian ship spinning and bucking as it roared toward the ground. Kira blinked hard, then wiped her eyes. The backs of her hands came back bloody, and suddenly Kira became aware of the pain in her head—a gash on her forehead that was oozing blood. She felt light-headed from the wound, disoriented from the turbulence, but her wits were still with her. They were crashing, hard and fast. The missile that had struck the ship shredded its port wing, that much she knew. Escape was impossible, and stabilizing the ship enough to execute something that resembled a landing was equally out of the question. Her only chance was to do whatever she could to minimize casualties.

"Four-Qel!" Kira yelled. "Four-Qel, are you with me?"

Though Kira felt like she was catching 4-Qel with her head dunked underwater, she still could hear the drone's tinny voice as he called out his confirmation.

"All right, listen," Kira said, taking hold of the stick even though it was trying its hardest to dance out of her grip. More blood flowed into her eyes, but she didn't have time to wipe it away. "Shoot all the power to the ship's front engine. Any power we have, you plug it into that engine. I don't care if it comes from the toaster—send it.

"Mig, Kobe," Kira said as she shot her head around the cockpit, ensuring they were still alive and with her. "Hang on for dear life. We're going down, and it isn't going to be pretty."

Kira turned back, and she could feel the stick beginning to fight her less. That was the good news. The bad news? They were seconds—precious seconds—from their inevitable union with the surface. And while there was no chance of it being a happy one, at least they had the saving grace of being pointed away from the skyline and toward the adjoining docks. If there was one thing that could complicate the situation, it would be gigantic buildings standing in their way.

With all power diverted to the front engine, Kira was able to do the one and only thing she could: prevent them from crashing nose-first. That's how people got decapitated.

With the buildings shimmering and racing past Kira's port side and the docks coming on fast, Kira pulled back the throttle with all her might. They were spinning less and the bucking had been subdued, but the only thing that mattered was getting the ship angled so its rear took the brunt of the crash. Kira couldn't have cared less about what direction they were facing when that happened.

"I might not have always shown it," Kobe yelled over the ship's howling metal, "but I enjoyed being part of the same fight with you guys. You're all crazy. I mean, you're seriously out of your minds!"

"Save the eulogies," Kira said through her clenched jaw. "Something stupid will probably kill us all, but this won't be it."

Kira screamed, bringing the nose up as much as she could before the inevitable occurred: impact. The ship pounded into the concrete surface, but it did so leading with its tail. Metal screeched and shredded as the ship's exterior was ripped apart, and the angle of the crash propelled it into a mighty bounce. They landed flat on the ground, hard, but the worst of the crash had been absorbed by that first hit. Now, it was just a matter of physics taking over to slow the ship down and eventually bring it to a stop. And though they'd undoubtedly be battered and bruised, they'd survive. That's all Kira cared about.

As the ship dug in and scraped against the pavement, Kira allowed herself a moment to take her hands off the controls and wipe the blood from her eyes. She'd gone through the crash in near blindness—not that it mattered—and when she regained her vision, she wished she hadn't. Because the first thing she saw was where the ship was taking them, and it was nowhere good; their direction of spin had sent them on a course toward the buildings. In fact, they were skittering between them at the moment and heading right toward the mouth of a glass-and-steel building directly ahead. All Kira could think about were civilians, and she hoped, desperately, that whatever fighting was taking place all around had cleared out the premises.

"I'm detecting no life-forms ahead," 4-Qel said as if reading Kira's mind. She looked at him and smiled, and before she could turn back around, glass exploded all around the ship. The steel frame was pulverized, and for a moment, Kira was hit with the horrible fear that the building was crashing down on the ship and was burying it. Assuming the ship held and they survived, they'd be trapped in their own grave beneath however many metric tons of building materials.

But that didn't happen. Instead, at last, the ship lurched to a stop right before they smashed through the building's other side. Kira held tightly to her harness, afraid to exhale for fear that the entire ship would fall apart all around them. Mig and Kobe must have felt the same, because neither of them said a word. It was 4-Qel who broke the silence.

"Well," he said, unstrapping himself, "that wasn't so bad."

Before Kira could question which part of their near-death experience wasn't so bad, before she could even peel herself out of her seat, an explosion rang throughout the cockpit. Kira's heart leapt up into her throat, and she wasted no time throwing off her harness and pushing herself from her seat. In all the ship's tumult, a sidewinder had somehow found its way to the floor just a few feet in front of her, but by the time she noticed it, it was too late.

The door to the cockpit blew off its hinges, the solid hunk of metal spinning right past Kira's head. She whipped around to see it race by her, and when she turned back around, a trio of soldiers armed with A-10 automatic blasters were storming the cockpit. Kira eyed the sidewinder in front of her, considering her odds of diving for it and getting a shot or two off before her guests could return fire. Her odds weren't good. But still, it was the only play she had.

"Don't even think about it," the commander said as Kira angled her body maybe an inch forward. "Don't."

Kira pulled back and could only watch as the lead soldier stayed positioned in the center, his gun trained on her head, and the other two soldiers covered the flanks.

"Wait," Kira said. "Just wait."

But there was no waiting to be had.

"Good-bye, warlords of Praxis," the commander said, and then a shot echoed throughout the cockpit.

CHAPTER SIX

B attlefields drenched in blood. Wars for conquest and for sport waged across the galaxy. An entire world of barbarians born and raised for the sole purpose of battle. You want to know what the real legacy of Wu-Xia is? That's it."

Cade kept his gaze fixed on the *Rubicon*'s viewport. The opening displayed nothing but a distorted view of the stars streaking past as they made yet another mass jump, but Cade preferred looking at that rather than having to look at Percival. It'd been a tense trip to wherever they were going. Cade didn't know. Nor did he know why they were going there—not exactly—or what they were supposed to do once they arrived. This was the type of game Percival liked to play, hoarding and controlling knowledge like it was currency. To him, it was, Cade realized. It gave him leverage and power, two things Cade was certain Percival found essential in his war against Praxis. Though Cade was loath to admit it, information could be a powerful tool of control and survival. And like Percival had told him time and time again, if they were going to defeat Praxis, they would have to use every tool in their arsenal. Cade just had a strong distaste for those tools being used against him. He'd pressed Percival for insight into their journey, but the responses he'd received from the burned-out ex-Paragon were cryptic at best and usually colored with ominous foreboding.

"We're going to a place we're not supposed to be," Percival had said when Cade questioned him about their destination during one of their meditation sessions. "It isn't going to be easy, and I have a feeling we're both going to learn things we might not want to know."

The time to pull back the veil, apparently, began now. Percival had called Cade to the cockpit, and Cade was still amazed that Kira had put her prized ship out on loan. Percival vowed not to get a scratch on it, and he'd better not. Whatever damage the *Rubicon* suffered, Cade knew his punishment would be tenfold. Cade wondered if Percival was having trouble navigating the ship. After all, he'd grown accustomed to flying his Boxer, a forgotten relic of the Quarrian War. Twice their arrival coordinates didn't match their plotted coordinates, and Cade felt compelled to remind Percival that accuracy in space travel was pretty important. There was a lot of junk floating around out there, so it was best to stick to the points that were known to be clear. Otherwise, you might find yourself jumped into, say, the heart of a star. Or rammed into an asteroid. Or dropped into dark space, where no one really knew what happened. Percival waved off Cade's concerns, and all Cade could do was give him the finger when he wasn't looking. Cold comfort, but at least it was something.

With Cade situated at Percival's side in the cockpit, he finally began to open up. The jump they were in the middle of, Percival explained, would finally get them to their destination. But before they arrived, Cade needed to better understand what he was getting into. Specifically, he needed to know the truth about

Wu-Xia; he needed to know that the man who'd forged the Rokura wasn't the peaceful warrior that everyone in the galaxy knew him to be. Wu-Xia, if Percival was to be believed, was a dangerous, violent warlord.

And all Cade could say to that was, "Botho. *Dung.*"

"Oh, really, Cade? So you believe the fairy tale that Wu-Xia was this sweet little monk who looked around a war-torn galaxy and said, 'You know what? Praying is nice, but how I can really fix the galaxy is by forging an all-powerful, terrifying weapon that'll utterly decimate anything that stands in the way of my quest for peace.'"

Now, it was Cade's turn to scoff. "I'm not sure either one of us is in a position to question the degree of ridiculousness associated with the Rokura."

"I'll give you that," Percival said, "but the weapon had to come from somewhere, and the story we've been told doesn't make the slightest bit of sense."

"You're right, it doesn't," Cade said, folding his arms tightly against his chest. "Unfortunately, I have my hands full trying to figure out where you're taking me, so I really can't add another riddle to my plate."

Percival continued, undeterred. "And isn't it odd that Wu-Xia, according to legend, forged the Rokura on Quarry, when just one glance at any depiction of him tells you he's clearly not a Quarr—"

"Cut the mysteries, Percival. Okay? Just—enough. You know something about Wu-Xia that no one else does. Great. Either tell me what it is and why it's important without a dozen questions leading me to what you want me to know, or turn this piece of junk around and bring me back to my friends."

"Listen, you think—" Percival started in a scalding tone before catching himself. He slumped and ran his hand through his thinning gray hair before taking a deep breath and starting over.

"Being . . . candid isn't an easy thing for me. I've learned some hard lessons over the years. Very hard, and I guess I'm just used to having to play things close to the chest."

Cade studied Percival and couldn't help but feel a strange sort of pity for him. He had no idea what he'd endured in his years waging more or less a one-man war against the Praxis kingdom. Sure, Cade had brought the fight to Praxis, but he was one in a unit. Percival was one man on an island, exiled and presumed dead. In some ways, they weren't all that different. If nothing else, they had the Rokura and the misery it caused both of them in common. After all, one thing they understood about each other was the trauma the weapon inflicted on everything, not to mention the profound burden it levied on its wielder. Even though Cade didn't know who Percival was before he'd yanked the Rokura out of its stasis, he was certain he wasn't the man he was now. He couldn't be. And for all his grit, determination, and ferocity, deep down, Percival was lost. The Rokura had robbed him of who he once was, gutting everything he knew—namely, that he was born to do something noble with a noble tool—and insinuating a reality that was nowhere close to the fantasy he'd been sold. Cade didn't like how Percival treated him—keeping him at arm's distance, testing him at every turn—but he understood it was all for the purpose of protecting both Cade and himself. They might be the best people in the galaxy to act as the Rokura's proxy, but that didn't mean either one of them was properly equipped for the task.

"How do you know all this stuff about Wu-Xia?" Cade asked, careful that his tone conveyed curiosity and not doubt. "I mean . . . who even knows anything about him anymore?"

Percival smirked, gathering himself. "The galaxy's a lot smaller when everyone thinks you're dead. After everything that happened in the spire with Ga Halle, the Rokura, and me, I ran. I was terrified by the idea that someone was going to drag me back and force me to use that weapon. I didn't sleep for weeks; I feared what would happen if I let my guard down for even a second. But eventually, I realized no one was looking for me, that the Well was so concerned with hiding their shame that they were more than happy to let Ga Halle and me both fade into obscurity. Obviously, only one of us made good on their wish.

"Once I stopped looking behind me, I started looking ahead. And when all the pity washed away, I found myself angry. Very angry. The Rokura was supposed to be my birthright, an extension of everything I was down to my very core. What did it mean that I was repulsed by it? Was there something about me that made the Rokura act the way it did in my possession? Not knowing ate away at me. I had to understand what went wrong, and that meant that I had to find the truth. Remember, Wu-Xia was just a man. He lived, he breathed, he died. What I wanted to know is what he did in the spaces between—who he really was and how he became a myth. That is the journey I went on.

"For years, I traveled the galaxy, following any mentions of Wu-Xia wherever they took me. And my mission did indeed take me to some interesting places. Folklore, myth, legends—those I encountered in abundance. But eventually, I found what I was looking for. I found answers."

Cade studied Percival as he worked the ship's controls. "Found answers where?" he warily asked.

Percival looked back at Cade as he manually switched off the mass-jump drive. "Here," he said.

Suddenly, the *Rubicon* halted in its jump and snapped backward like a taut rubber band released. Once Cade straightened himself in his seat, he looked outside the cloudy viewport and couldn't believe his eyes. There, floating beneath a layer of fog that glowed purple and maroon, was a celestial body that had erupted from the inside out. At least, that was the legend as Cade knew it. And yet, despite the cataclysmic damage it'd endured, the planet hadn't been destroyed. Not entirely, at least. A gaping hole was punctured through the surface all the way to the planet's core, and everything that'd erupted out was now caught in its orbit; a veritable asteroid belt encircled the planet, cutting through the misty haze surrounding it. It was a sight that defied the laws of the galaxy, and it certainly defied everything Cade had been led to believe. He was beginning to think this wasn't the only legend soon to be shattered.

"Is that really—" Cade stammered, still unable to grasp what his own two eyes were seeing. "It can't be."

"The Ruined Empire of Monaskis," Percival said. "It is."

"But . . . it was ruined. It's in the title."

"Yet here we are."

"Here we are," Cade whispered. He'd always known about the legendary empire of Monaskis, especially the legend part. Growing up on Kyysring, every cheap hustler, every hapless smuggler, every wannabe pirate boasted about all the riches to be found there and how they had in their possession a map that would take them to this supposed paradise. And every year, those same lowlifes were kicking around the streets of Kyysring, as broke as they were the year before. But the official story behind Monaskis, the one they'd written in the history archives, was that Monaskis was defeated in the Great War by Wu-Xia himself. The Monaskin people celebrated a culture driven by war and conquest, and the mark they left on the galaxy, dating back centuries, was an unpleasant one. Pillaging, conquering, and slaughtering were just a few of the empire's favorite pastimes. Thinking of that, it all clicked into place in Cade's mind. The legend, their mission, what Percival had told him about Wu-Xia. It added up to one thing:

"This is where Wu-Xia is really from," Cade said.

"It is. He may have decimated the planet for its atrocities, but he couldn't destroy his past. Not completely."

"But if he was this brutal warlord, why the about-face? Why would he make the Rokura and dedicate himself to bringing peace to the galaxy? And did peace really mean," Cade said, gesturing to what was left of Monaskis, "*that*?"

"Those are good questions, and I've often pondered the answers myself. Unfortunately," Percival said, taking the ship's stick and bringing them toward the planet, "I've never been able to discover the finer details of Wu-Xia's life. But that's what we're about to discover."

"Whoa. Whoawhoawhoawhoawhoa," Cade said as he took Percival's hand off the stick. "Wait. If you don't have the answers, that means you've never been to Monaskis. Have you? And by the way, your answer had better be 'I have; they're expecting us.'"

"I've never been any closer to Monaskis than we are right now," Percival coolly said. "There's a reason our mass jumps and our coordinates have been off, same as there's a reason I manually pulled us out of our last mass jump. We're bordering dark space, Cade. Things don't follow the same principles here as they do where we're from. Monaskis stays hidden that way, and anyone who finds it or stumbles upon it doesn't live to tell people what they've discovered."

Cade squinted and shook his head; it hurt his brain to try to make sense of what Percival was telling him. "So . . . what are we doing then? We didn't come all this way for the novelty of having an ancient civilization kill us, did we?"

"Only one person, and one person alone, is permitted to land on Monaskis."

"Don't even tell me. Don't even say it."

"The Paragon."

Cade flung his hands in the air. "Great. *Terrific.* I hope you know where the Paragon is!"

Percival smiled at Cade and grasped his shoulder. "He's you. Or at least you're the closest thing there is."

"No," Cade said, firm in his rejection.

"Listen, I know this is risky, I know it's dangerous, but it's the only chance we've got. All we have to do is flash the Rokura as proof of who you are. Then we learn Wu-Xia's history, his *real* history. If we can find out how and why he forged the Rokura, we can better understand what this thing is and have a shot at using it to win this war."

Percival swiveled his chair away from Cade and retook the stick. This time, Cade didn't interfere. He slumped in his chair, knowing that even if he thought Percival was wrong, there was no turning back anyway. As Percival put them on a landing vector, Cade had only one thing to say:

"We're gonna die."

Static. Every channel, every frequency. Percival had parked their ship so they were looking directly into the cavernous maw of the planet. Through Monaskis's orbiting remains and the mist that was so thick it seemed viscous, Cade couldn't discern any finer details of the surface. Just darkness, and Cade found it hard to imagine who could possibly inhabit this planet. Judging by Percival's repeated failed attempts to elicit any kind of response through the comms, Cade started to think that the planet—despite what Percival had been led to believe—was desolate.

"*Rubicon-1* to Monaskis surface, do you read?" Percival said into the comms for what felt to Cade like the millionth time. "Do you copy?"

"There's no one here, Percival," Cade said. "We're wasting our time."

Percival shook his head, rejecting Cade's sound conclusion. "No, they're there. It's just a matter of reaching them. It's just a matter—" Percival perked up his head, and his face brightened.

"It's just a matter of what?" Cade asked as he watched Percival open the entire array of comms channels. Normally, that was a bad idea. A very bad idea, because you never knew who was listening. But considering that they were literally on the dark side of the galaxy, Cade figured there was no harm in blasting a message into the void.

"Of saying the right thing," Percival responded, a clever smile on his face. He turned to his comms and continued. "Monaskis surface, this is the vessel that you have no doubt detected on your radars. I am requesting permission to land and to land safely. I have the Paragon on board," Percival declared, and Cade leapt out of his seat.

"Why would you—don't say that!" he yelled.

Percival waved him off, then said it again.

"I repeat, I have the Paragon on board."

Cade couldn't decide if he should knock out the comms or knock out Percival. Both seemed like reasonable things to do.

"You said it again!" Cade said, already feeling the weight of the target Percival had just affixed to his back. Sure, he assumed no one was listening on Monaskis or from anywhere close enough to be in comms range, but on the off chance there was someone out there, Percival had just revealed the galaxy's most lucrative bounty and given up their location in one big, dumb swoop.

"Someone's there, and they need to be compelled to open the door for us," Percival said matter-of-factly, making Cade even madder.

"And did you ever think that this someone might now be compelled to open this door so they can murder us both and collect the cargo-load of coin Praxis has on our heads?"

"Yes," Percival said. "That did cross my mind. But the risk is worth it, and we can handle ourselves if need be."

Cade fumed, and he was about to explain to Percival what he could do to *himself* when a blinding white light scorched the entire cockpit. Cade closed his eyes and turned away, but the light receded from the ship as quickly as it had burst inside. Its effects, though, lingered. Cade turned to find the ship's systems going haywire, everything from its mass-jump drive to its shields flickering between being off- and online. The overhead lights surged so brightly Cade expected them to pop, but right when they hit their maximum threshold, they went soft, only to surge again. Cade's frustration from a moment earlier suddenly seemed trivial compared to the uneasiness he was experiencing now.

"Percival, what have you gotten us into?"

Like Cade, Percival was scanning the cockpit with his hands held close to his body, afraid to touch anything. "I have no idea," he said. "But look."

Percival pointed through the cockpit window. There, through the mist, Cade saw a double row of fiery yellow lights burning near the Monaskis surface. There were at least twenty beacons in total, ten on each side, and they blinked in unison, maintaining a steady, hypnotic rhythm. Cade followed the lights as best as he could to their ending point; as far as he could tell, they only led deeper into the planet's darkness.

"We should follow them," Percival said.

"Something tells me we really don't have a choice," Cade said.

Guiding the ship despite its diminished capacity, Percival navigated them around the asteroid field and then punched through the mist. Beyond those obstacles, the guiding lights that rose out of the ground on massive pedestals of rock shone with more clarity. Under Percival's eager hand, the *Rubicon* cut through the miles to the guiding lights, but Cade wasn't so sure about their journey. Especially when he saw where it led.

At the end of the line, Cade spotted a blue, shimmering wall. It stretched to cover the entirety of a gaping chasm that separated the planet's exposed crust they'd been flying over.

"That's a shield," Cade said, his tone wavering somewhere between wonder and terror.

"It is," Percival agreed. "They must be leading us inside."

"Inside . . . the planet?"

Percival looked at Cade and took a deep breath before accelerating toward the shield. "If there's one thing I've learned in my travels," Percival said, aligning the ship with the barrier ahead of them, "it's that the galaxy is filled with mysteries."

And with that, the shield disappeared, and the *Rubicon* flew inside the Ruined Empire of Monaskis.

The breadth of the world within the Monaskin core was unimaginable. The walls were a deep ruby red, veined by streaks of gray that looked like lightning breaking across a bloody sky. Lights like the ones Cade and Percival had encountered leading to this place jutted out from innumerable points, and Percival followed their path down and deeper into the planet. The lights revealed sentry post after sentry post dug into the rock wall, each manned by a team of guards armed with impossibly large blasters that had electrosaws affixed to them. The guards glowered at the ship as it passed, helping to balance Cade's feeling of awe with a dose of disquiet. He didn't know where he was headed, and it was very much looking like whoever was leading him there held an impossible advantage. The shield, the guards, and who knew what other surprises lying in wait all spelled one thing: Should things go bad, there'd be no escape. Cade knew he had to succeed in whatever he was supposed to do, or he'd die a long, long way from home.

Percival guided the ship slowly through the heavily fortified artery and into what seemed to be the heart of the Monaskin interior. As they proceeded, Cade began noticing flakes of gray and red wafting around the ship. It was ash, and Cade could only assume that the planet's topography was still suffering the consequences of Wu-Xia's destruction.

After passing through a brief, narrow canyon, the world opened up so big, so wide, that Cade nearly caught vertigo looking at it. Cade gasped. "How is this even possible?"

"I don't know," Percival murmured from over Cade's shoulder. "I really don't know."

There was no telling how massive the clandestine Monaskin civilization was. Cade's eyes followed the rock walls up and then down, trying to get a sense of how high and low they reached, but distance and fluttering ash obscured any telling detail before Cade could reach a conclusion. And like the sentry posts, countless structures were carved into the dark red walls, their purposes unclear. Cade thought he could discern what looked like storefronts and a few family homes, all tarnished by the falling ash—each unit was accessible to the others by small vessels, like open-air elevators, that ran horizontally and vertically across the rock face. It was a metropolis in miniature, and the sight of so many crafts traveling in every direction over such an immense space was dizzying. Still, Cade marveled at the system's chaotic efficiency. He was so caught up that he failed to see what was materializing in front of the ship.

"Cade," Percival said, tugging Cade's sleeve. "You might want to see this."

Peeling his gaze away from the strange world unfolding along the *Rubicon*'s starboard side, Cade was about to ask what he was supposed to be looking at, but there was no need; he knew the moment he turned around.

The ship was positioned on a slight downward trajectory, and coming into view straight ahead and below them was an opulent, iridescent golden palace.

"Oh, man," Cade said, astonished. "They have a castle?"

Percival was in awe. "It's magnificent."

A pair of deep-blue spires twisted their way skyward, framing a set of double doors that stood at least twenty feet high. An exterior wall made of alternating gold and blue columns was set in the rock, framing the door and ensuring its impenetrability. Golden, unblemished stairs led away from the doors to a long esplanade that stretched toward the center of the canyon and ended in a crescent shape that Cade took to be a landing pad. And all of it, every inch, was untouched by ash. Not a single speck tarnished the palace grounds.

Guards were stationed from the pad all the way to the palace, two single-file rows of armed sentries mirroring one another. Cade wondered if the Monaskins always maintained this kind of vigilance. If so, it was a tad much.

"I'm guessing this is where they want us to go," Percival said, bringing the ship down toward the landing pad.

"Why aren't they saying anything on the comms?" Cade asked. "You'd figure people this crazy about security would at least give clear directions."

"Because they want to hold all the cards," Percival said. "We have no idea what this place is or who's behind those palace walls. Keeping us in the dark prevents us from taking any kind of action."

"Or maybe they assume we're stupid enough to lead ourselves into their trap."

"The thought did cross my mind," Percival said as he brought the ship down on the landing pad.

"Terrific," Cade said as he strapped the Rokura to his back. "There's not a whole lot of scenarios that don't end in very bad things happening to us, are there?"

"Only one: You convince them you're the Paragon, and out of reverence for Wu-Xia, they help us get the answers we need."

Cade groaned. "Very bad things it is, then."

"And remember," Percival said as the boarding ramp hissed and lowered, "you're the Paragon. The Chosen One. Act like it. Do not piss these people off."

"Hey, give me some credit," Cade said as he strode alongside Percival across the esplanade. "I don't piss off *everyone* I meet."

Percival shot him a look that expressed his disagreement.

"Fine," he said. "I'll be good."

A row of guards assembled at the foot of the palace stairs, waiting to intercept Cade and Percival.

"I guess this is as far as we go," Percival whispered to Cade as they stopped about ten feet shy of the barrier. The guards, who were dressed in black leather tops that buckled tightly over their chests and dark pants to match, eyed Cade and Percival wordlessly, and Cade was impressed by how well they could maintain their brooding intensity. He was about to comment on it when he remembered what he'd promised Percival, so he bit his tongue. The pull to mock the excessive seriousness was strong, but Cade was saved by a rumbling noise that drew his attention to the palace doors. They were opening at last.

For all the theatrics that their arrival engendered, Cade expected a battalion of Monaskis's best to storm out of the palace, or at least a royal entourage that exuded intimidation. But that's not what came out of those doors. Instead, a band of four men in light tunics—blue like the palace itself—and armed with compression pikes holstered at their sides stepped forward. They walked in perfect unison with one another, forming a square around a young woman who stepped gracefully down the stairs under the protection of her guards.

What became most apparent as the woman and her retinue drew closer wasn't just that she was young. She was *really* young. Sixteen at best, Cade figured. Dressed in a white robe that tied with a golden belt at her waist, she had long, black hair that flowed freely over her shoulders and smooth, dark bronze skin that seemed to glow in the light. But beyond all these polished touches, Cade noticed more—namely, her toned arms, the quiet intensity behind her eyes, and the gold-painted gamma blaster that was meant to blend with bangles hanging from her belt. Whoever this woman was, she was likely royalty, but Cade got the impression that she could hold her own in a dangerous situation. Even though she was pretty much just a kid, Cade still hoped whatever relationship they were about to embark on didn't involve him finding out just how capable she was.

But then she spoke, and Cade felt a piece of that hope die.

"Kneel," she commanded once she reached the bottom of the stairs.

All the guards save one parted to make way for her, and she stepped just far enough past them so there was nothing between her and Cade and Percival. And standing directly behind her was what Cade took to be her personal bodyguard; he stood at least a foot over her head, and he didn't appear to have an ounce of fat on his muscular frame. His head was totally bald, and his eyes were wide and alert, though he stared into the distance, not settling on anything or anyone. Cade was caught up admiring his stature when the woman spoke.

"Kneel," she repeated. She looked both Cade and Percival in the eye, holding their attention.

Cade looked at Percival, who stood up straight, put his chin and chest out, took a deep breath, and then knelt.

"Seriously?" Cade asked.

"*Cade,*" Percival implored.

Knowing he wouldn't get anywhere with Percival, Cade turned his attention to the mysterious queen or princess or whatever she was standing in front of him. "I'm sorry, but who are you?"

"I'm the one who commands the many weapons that can kill you in the time it takes to draw a breath. Now, as I've said twice already—"

"Yeah, that tells me what you can do. It doesn't tell me who you are."

The woman clenched her teeth hard—Cade could see her jaw-bones protruding beneath her skin—and then tore her icy gaze from Cade and redirected it onto Percival. "Do you always allow your squire to speak with such insolence?" she asked. "And why in the world would you entrust him to carry your Rokura?"

Percival looked up at Cade and groaned, much to Cade's satisfaction. For a moment, he considered explaining to this woman that he, not Percival, was the Paragon, but he stopped himself. He'd let Percival do it while he stood idly by, smiling. It was the stupid grin, Cade was certain, that agitated Percival the most.

"Your Majesty—I assume it's proper for me to call you that?" Percival asked.

"It is," the woman replied, her tone gentler than it had been with Cade. "I'm Queen Lux Ersia, ruler of Monaskis. And you are the Paragon come to my planet. But why?"

"Actually, Your Majesty, I'm not the Paragon."

"I am," Cade blurted. He couldn't help himself.

An amused smile spread across Ersia's face as she turned her attention back to Cade. "Is that so?" she asked. "And why, Paragon, have you come here?"

Cade's eyes roamed, taking in everything around him—the palace, the guards, even Ersia—and he reminded himself what was at stake: the countless systems and the lives spread across them all. None of them were quite like Monaskis, but Praxis hardly discriminated when enforcing its tyranny. Whether other systems liked it or not, Praxis bound them all together. They would either be unified in fighting back or unified in living under a cruel oppressor. To help ensure the former, Cade knew he had to get serious.

"We need your help, Your Majesty," Cade said, trying to put his best foot forward. "To defeat Praxis, to free the galaxy, we need your help."

Ersia toyed with Cade, flashing an expression of mocking confusion for everyone to see. "But you're the Paragon. Why would you possibly need *my* help?"

"That is a great question, Your Majesty," Cade said, trying to buy himself some time as he decided whether he should tell Ersia the truth or lie. Since he couldn't think of a lie that made the least bit of sense, he had to go with option number one. Unfortunately. "I need to learn. About the Rokura, about being the Paragon—everything that Wu-Xia lived and understood when he created this thing. He was from Monaskis, right?"

"Indeed he was," Queen Ersia said as she slowly paced the area in front of Cade, studying him with passing curiosity. "Wu-Xia was a Monaskin through and through; he was bred for battle, trained to be a warrior since before he could walk. But then he betrayed everything Monaskis stood for and turned the weapon that he made on his own home. His own people."

Cade cast a sidelong glance at Percival, and he could tell they were thinking the same thing: This wasn't going anywhere good.

"I didn't know any of that," Cade said. "But I promise you, we're not here to cause anyone harm. I just . . . there are things I need to know in order to do this right."

"You're not the first to come to our gates posing as the Paragon," Ersia said as she stepped back toward her guards. "Some claim to be the descendant of Wu-Xia; others simply try to pass themselves off as the Chosen One, flashing a weapon of their own making as if we don't know any better. They demand our riches, they demand our weapons, they demand our ships. Do you know the one thing they share in common?"

Cade swallowed hard. "I don't."

"They never leave this planet."

Cade eyed Ersia skeptically, then moved to take a step forward. The guards flinched at his slightest movement, so Cade withdrew. "I'm guessing you're not implying that they fell for Monaskis's charm and decided to stay of their own volition, right?"

Half of Ersia's mouth rose in a smile. "Nope."

"Your Majesty," Percival said, still kneeling, "we demand no riches, no weapons, nothing. We seek only knowledge and guidance."

Ersia barely acknowledged Percival, choosing instead to keep her focus on Cade. He felt increasingly uneasy under her gaze, which was equally dignified and deadly.

"So . . . you're the Paragon?"

Cade groaned with uncertainty as Ersia's walls closed in on him. "I sure am," he said with as much conviction as he could muster.

"Good," Ersia responded. "Then you're prepared to prove it."

"Um . . . sure?" Cade said. "But prove it how?"

Ersia smiled in a way that Cade didn't like at all. "By surviving the Trial of the Paragon, of course."

"The wha—" Cade didn't have a chance to inquire any further.

Suddenly, Cade's world went black as one of the guards threw a mask over his head. At the same time, a set of strong, large hands gripped him hard at his shoulders and forced him forward.

"Hey!" Cade protested as he fought against the momentum and the guard that was carrying him forward. He pulled with all his strength, but his arms wouldn't budge an inch, and he continued to be pushed along. "What do you think you're doing? Answer me!"

"Throw him in a cell, Xeric," Cade heard Ersia say. "Then make preparations for the trial."

No one else said a word. Nothing from Xeric—who had to have been Ersia's top guard—nothing from Ersia, and nothing from Percival.

"Percival?" Cade yelled, but there was no response. He hadn't heard a blaster fire, so he could only assume Percival was in no worse condition than he was. And at the moment, his condition was bad. He was being led up on the stairs, which could only mean he was being brought to the palace. What awaited inside, Cade couldn't even venture to guess. This trial, whatever it was, couldn't be good.

He reached the top, and the hands held him solidly in place.

"There sure are no shortages of Paragons in the galaxy," Xeric said.

Cade could tell Xeric was standing just a few inches from his face; he could feel the heat of his breath through the mask that'd been pulled down over his head.

"You're making a mistake!" Cade snarled. "You don't know what you're doing!"

"We'll see about that," Xeric said. "For now, where you're going, you won't be needing *this*."

At that, the Rokura was torn from Cade's back—and it *hurt*. Cade's head filled with pain, like he'd had the blunt end of a sidewinder smashed into his skull. He howled, feeling his entire body burn, but no one cared. Xeric resumed the march, and as much as Cade violently wrenched his body, it was no use. He couldn't break free.

"Don't you dare try to use that weapon!" Cade screamed. "You have no idea what it can do. You hear me? Do you hear me?!"

No one responded. No one uttered a single word. The only sound Cade heard was the palace doors slamming shut behind him right before a jolt of electricity plunged into his spine. His body went limp, and before the device was torn from his back, Cade was out cold.

CHAPTER SEVEN

Kobe moved impossibly fast. Kira didn't know if the soldier nearest Kobe had taken his eyes off him or if he'd just blinked for too long. It probably didn't matter. Kobe leapt against the viewport and catapulted his body forward, right at the soldier. He kicked the blaster right out of the soldier's hand just as he pulled the trigger; the shot went errant and bounced around the cockpit before burying itself into the floor. The lead soldier turned at the sign of distress, but he had no chance. With his inhuman speed, Kobe had the disarmed soldier gripped by the collar of his jacket and the seat of his pants, and when the commander turned to address the trouble beside him, he was met by his companion being flung in his direction. The disarmed soldier, charging uncontrollably forward thanks to the momentum Kobe forced into him, slammed into his commander and knocked them both off their feet.

Whoever these people were, their siege of Kira's ship was over.

Using the distraction as an opportunity to make his move, 4-Qel charged at the remaining soldier and pinned him against the cockpit wall. He grabbed his blaster at the barrel and crushed it in his grip.

"I think I broke it," 4-Qel said, effortlessly lifting the soldier off his feet. The soldier looked ready to cry.

The commander—a Poqlin, from a race of refugees that came to Praxis just before Kira was born and had been serving as the underclass since arriving—wasn't as willing to surrender so easily, though. Using his uncanny Poqlin strength, he shoved his mate off him and, positioned on his knee, trained his blaster at 4-Qel.

"Let him go, or I will be forced to shoot you," the commander said, but Kira had serious doubts about his resolve.

Plus, she was standing behind the commander with her sidewinder pointed right at his head.

"Ahem," she said, and the leader's shoulders visibly sank.

"Awww, man," the commander said.

"That's my friend you're pointing your blaster at."

Still, the commander persisted, even though his body language screamed how much he wanted to surrender. Kira could tell that he knew he was screwed. "But he's about to kill my friend," the commander responded. "That will really pull down the squad's morale."

"No one," Kira forcefully said, "is killing anyone. Four-Qel?"

4-Qel nodded and gently set the soldier back on his feet. He then patted him on the head.

"Your turn," Kira said, addressing the commander. "Drop it and push it over to me."

The leader hesitated, and his body sank even farther. But he had no choice, so he dropped his blaster to the ground and raised his hands to the sky.

"Go ahead and kill me. I won't make you feel bad about it; you got me fair and square," the commander said. "Just, please, give my men fair treatment. Try not to be half as savage as Ga Halle."

Kira looked back at Mig, who shrugged his confusion. "They think *we're* Praxian? But they're also Praxian, so why they'd want to kill us . . . is kinda confusing," he said.

"Wait a minute, wait a minute," Kira said, turning back to the commander. "You attacked us because you think we're Praxian?"

"Ummm . . . what is the answer you'd like to hear?"

Kira sighed. "Take a look around. Do we look Praxian?"

"You're in a Praxian ship," the commander said, perplexed.

"Okay, that's a fair point," she said. "But even if we were Praxian, why would you attack us?"

"I knew we were doing a poor job of marketing this thing," the commander said ruefully. He stood up slowly and brushed off his pants while keeping his eyes on Kira.

Kira kept her sidewinder trained on him, but she had a pretty good feeling there'd be no sudden, rash movements from him.

"Trying to kill us is one thing," Kira said, making no effort to conceal her agitation. "But now you're testing my patience and—"

Kira was cut off when an explosion—a plasma detonator, she assumed, likely no more than a hundred yards away—invaded the relative quiet of the cockpit. Its blast reverberated off the walls and through Kira's teeth. Everyone but Kira flinched.

"Better make your story quick," Kira said when she was confident she'd be heard again.

"My name is Gunk," the commander said.

"Gunk?" Mig asked, stifling a laugh.

"Yes, well, our language is different from yours," Gunk asserted. "In Poqlin, 'Gunk' carries a different meaning."

"What does Gunk translate to?" 4-Qel asked.

"Aren't we getting personal awfully fast," Gunk said defensively. "I'll have you know it's a family name. My mom is a very sentimental lady."

"All right, let's cut the family history here," Kira said. "What we really want to know is what this thing is that you're leading. Who are you, all of you?"

"We're the people's movement, of course," Gunk said as he puffed out his barrel chest. Poqlins were known for their physical strength, but how their physiology actually worked escaped people. Poqlins were made of rock. They looked exactly like humans, if humans were covered head to toe in thin sheets of some kind of beige stone. There were a few details about their species most people didn't understand, particularly reproduction, but Kira spent as little time thinking about that as possible.

"You're looking at the tip of the spear," Gunk continued.

"If you're the tip of the spear, let there be mercy for its hilt," Kobe said.

"Quiet," Kira snapped at Kobe. Then to Gunk, she said, "People's movement—for what? Who are you fighting against?"

Gunk's mouth crunched in an O shape, and he looked at Kira in complete bafflement. "You really don't know anything about what's happening here? This is so disheartening."

"Remember what I said about testing my patience?"

"Right. The Praxian uprising," Gunk said. "The people's movement? The fight against the military regime? None of this rings a bell?"

Gunk's eyes jumped from Kira to 4-Qel to Mig to Kobe and back to Kira. He was obviously looking for some kind of recognition. He found none.

"We're in the middle of a civil war."

"How's it coming?" Mig asked.

Gunk tried to suppress a wince. "Peaks and valleys."

Kira holstered her sidewinder, picked up Gunk's weapon—a hefty tri-blaster—and shoved it in his chest. "Let's go," she said. "You're going to take us to your leader."

"He's kinda in the middle of something right now," Gunk replied. "Can it wait?"

"No. It looks like your people's movement needs all the help it can get. What's your mission anyway? I mean, you didn't think launching a campaign in the middle of the business district was a good idea, did you?"

Gunk put his hands to his temples as if fighting off a headache. "Wait, who are *you*?"

"We're the Black Star Renegades," Mig said proudly.

Gunk's eyes lit up. "*The* Black Star Renegades? The ones who blew up the *War Hammer*?" His awe, though, quickly turned into embarrassment. "Of all the ships to shoot down, we shoot down the Black Star—"

"That's not—we don't have an official name," Kira said, smothering a groan. "Let's stay focused. What is your objective? What's your mission?"

"We have a Shadow, one of the best," Gunk said. "The plan is to get him to the financial core and have him hack it to bits. That'll keep the treasury out of Ga Halle's hands for at least a little while."

"Huh," Kira said with a smile. "That's actually a good idea. But you need to pull it off. What progress had you made before you shot us down?"

"Us personally? None. But I understand that the general has gotten his team and the Shadow inside the core. They had breached the interior when we took down your ship."

On the side panel of the cockpit's port side was a storage panel, secured by a fingerprint recognition pad. Kira pressed her fingertips against the pad, and it hissed open. Inside was artillery enough to arm a small militia. Kira grabbed the compression whipblasters and tossed them to Kobe and Mig. The heavy-duty tri-blaster went to 4-Qel, who whirred with excitement. Kira grabbed a whipblaster for herself—and had to suppress a gleeful squee when she did—as well as a couple of plasma detonators.

"Okay," she said, slamming a charge into the whipblaster—an automatic blaster that sported a spinning barrel for the most effective suppressive fire imaginable. "Let's go find this general of yours."

Uninterrupted blaster fire smothered the confined area that contained the financial center's cluster of buildings. Cylindrical towers erupted as the hail of blaster bolts pulverized their exteriors; it wasn't that difficult of a demolition, Kira noted, seeing that the exteriors, from the bases all the way to the tops—each of the four towers capped with a gleaming steel spike—was made of glass. Only Praxian architects could be arrogant enough to slap glass over the entirety of a building's facade, assuming that the planet was untouchable. Yet here they were.

From Kira's perspective, the financial cluster couldn't have been located in a worse strategic position. The six financial buildings occupied the core of Aragorn Square, and the area itself was distinguished by the Aragorn Museum, a hundred-foot-tall fortress that surrounded the square on three sides. Praxian forces were currently perched on the top floors of the Aragorn, firing indiscriminately at the financial buildings in order to keep the opposition pinned down. If Kira had to guess, an ancillary team of Praxian ground forces was on its way through one of the city's lower levels and would soon come up right into the financial buildings and squeeze its enemies into a vise. That's what she would do.

Assuming whoever was in charge of Praxis's counteroperation was as smart as she was—Kira tried to at least be open to the possibility—the window to pull this thing off was very, very narrow and closing fast. She had to act quickly.

"The one thing we cannot do is hesitate," Kira said, instructing both Gunk and the soldier he'd kept with them, Stark. "You both know what to do, right?"

Gunk nodded enthusiastically, but Stark seemed far less certain. This was the problem with recruiting people off the street, shoving a blaster in their hands, and calling them soldiers. She'd seen it too many times in her own revolutionary movement, where the people in charge placed value on warm bodies, even if they had no chance of staying warm for long. Since they still had a little bit of time to kill before her plan kicked into action, Kira explained the strategy one last time.

"Listen," Kira said, making sure to catch Stark's attention, "what we're doing is called a timed advance. Okay? Now look—"

Kira drew Stark's attention ahead.

"You see that overturned aero barge straight ahead, right? That's our first stop. Four-Qel, Kobe, Mig, and . . ." Kira snapped her fingers, trying to remember the name of the soldier who accompanied her friends.

"Qin," Gunk said.

"Qin, right," Kira said. "They're setting explosions on two sides of the museum that will distract the fire directed at the buildings. Not for long, but enough time for us to get to the barge, and then—"

An explosion again drowned out Kira's words. She looked up to see that a chunk of the museum's northern wall had been blown out; replacing the seemingly impenetrable fortress's edifice was a wall of smoke and fire pouring out into the evening air. As anticipated, the sudden, unexpected blast brought Praxis's suppressive firing to a stop.

"Move! Move!" Kira commanded as she led Gunk and Stark forward, crouching as she ran to the aero barge.

She dove for cover behind the barge and pressed her back

against the commuter transport's metal underbelly, which was still warm. Gunk was beside her and Stark beside him. Kira had no doubt that Praxis would send some of its forces to investigate the blast, but its assault on the financial cluster, after the brief pause, was undeterred.

"They don't take much of a break, do they?" Gunk asked. "Very diligent, those Praxian soldiers."

Kira craned her head around the barge and spotted the concrete block that housed one of the spotlights that were placed in the square's four corners. It was a straight shot from their position but a lot longer of a haul than it had been to the barge. "We'll just have to be faster, then."

"If they spot us—"

"War's a whole lot of ifs, Gunk. Deal with it."

Another explosion pulverized a block of the museum's exterior, this time on its eastern face. Kira wasted no time sprinting to the spotlight. It was farther than she would have liked, but there was nothing she could do about that, so instead she dug every footfall deep into the ground and propelled herself forward as hard as she could. Small bits of metal and rock crunched beneath her feet, and she could smell smoke and blaster fire in the air. All she could do was push through it, hoping she would reach her destination before the never-ending blaster fire that was pulverizing Aragorn Square's buildings turned on her.

But that's exactly what happened.

She, Gunk, and Stark were just ten yards away—the longest ten yards of her life—when she felt the first blaster bolt crackle over her head. She gasped like she'd been punched in the chest, but she didn't stop. They were target practice, Kira knew it, but she also knew that the hardest target to hit is a moving one.

Stark, being young and untrained, tragically didn't possess the same knowledge.

Kira didn't know what caused her to turn around, but she

whipped her head over her shoulder just as Stark was drawing his tri-blaster. She had no idea what he intended to do. Praxis was shooting at them from at least fifty yards away, and even Kira only had a vague sense of the shooters' positions within the museum. But fear of death didn't listen to reason or logic. Fear of death only knew survival, or at least what it thought was survival. For Stark, survival meant fighting back.

Before Kira could scream at Stark and order him to keep moving—why hadn't she reminded him while they were at the barge?—a blaster bolt drove directly into his chest. Stark remained still for just a moment, though it felt like hours to Kira. She could see the confusion behind his eyes as his arms went limp. He shuffled two steps forward and dropped to his knees. Even though every part of her screamed for her not to, Kira wanted to race back and pull him forward, to get him out of harm's way even though she knew the damage had been done. Just as she was about to turn, Gunk's body slammed into hers; he drove them both to the ground as a stream of blaster bolts rushed overhead. Side by side, as bolts scorched the ground all around them, they crawled behind the spotlight's housing and were safe. For the moment.

Kira turned to Gunk. "Thanks. I owe you one."

"Total accident; I tripped and you broke my fall."

"Oh boy," Kira huffed.

War was all around. Kira felt it on her skin; she sucked it in with every breath she took. It made her feel dirty, and not just in a literal sense. Who knew how many lives, like Stark's, would be lost in this relatively small skirmish? Who knew how many irreplaceable Praxian artifacts and pieces of art would be destroyed? It was almost as if one of the tenets of war was to demolish both the future and the past by killing off so many youths and decimating remembrances of generations past. That way, there'd be too few people who remained to describe the terrible things they'd endured, and nothing would be left to learn of the past's mistakes.

"We're in trouble," Gunk said.

"We'll be fine," Kira said as blaster fire tore into the other side of the concrete block, bringing bits of rubble down on their heads. "Just wait for it."

Kira shut her eyes and took a deep breath, and as if she'd willed it, the shooting stopped.

"Okay, now!" Kira said, grabbing Gunk and darting around their shelter. She looked up at where she assumed the Praxian shooters had been positioned just as one of them was flying out of the window. 4-Qel poked his head out of the same open space and wiped his hands clean.

"But what about the other shooters?" Gunk yelled.

"Bad angles to hit our building's entrance. That's why I planned it this way!"

With Kira leading the way, she and Gunk made it into the square at last. The remaining shooters opened fire, but just as Kira had said, they weren't in position to hit them; shots ricocheted off buildings and landed errantly by a good measure. As they neared the building where Gunk's general was supposedly located, Kira tore her whipblaster from her back and opened fire. The force of the blaster's recoil almost knocked her off her feet, which Kira found exhilarating, but she was able to stay upright as she decimated the building's glass facade. The whipblaster's spinning dual barrels covered a much larger area than she needed, but Kira didn't mind the cushion. Nor did she mind indulging in the whipblaster's destructive capacity.

With the ground-level windows out of the way, Kira and Gunk could dash inside the building without pause. They'd finally made it.

"Where's the general?" Kira demanded.

Gunk wheezed. "Just give me a . . . let me take a—"

"Praxis is going to be swarming your general and his team at any moment. We'll breathe later."

Gunk nodded quickly and led her toward the elevator. "The core's three levels down," he said, calling the elevator. "With any luck, the Shadow's in the system and almost done."

Kira and Gunk stepped inside the elevator when it arrived. Gunk let out a deep breath, then turned to Kira as the doors closed. "Well, that was terrifying. And look at you, calm as the sunrise. Things aren't always this crazy with you, are they?"

"No," Kira replied. "Usually they're crazier."

Down in the frigid subterranean heart of Praxis's financial cluster, Kira dug her boots into the smooth metallic floor and kept her weapon tight in her grip. She felt the heat of a half dozen tri-blasters trained at her head. But it didn't bother her. As long as she kept her whipblaster targeted at the one person in the room who mattered, nobody was going to make a move.

"I think there might be some kind of confusion," Gunk said. He was standing next to Kira and had been frozen there since Kira had pressed her whipblaster against her shoulder, holding it steady. "That's . . . that's the general. He's the person you wanted to see."

"Oh, I know who this is," Kira responded. "But not as any general. No, this is the Warden. Warden Kay."

Kira's eyes remained fixed on her target. Still, she couldn't help but notice, blurry in the background, the Shadow Gunk had mentioned. Kira noted his presence, though it wasn't much of one. As the tension of an armed standoff mounted over his shoulder, he kept his focus on whatever he was doing. Sitting on his long, gaunt legs that crossed over one another in an unnatural position, the apricot-skinned alien had his hands pressed against the base of a massive tower before him. Kira flicked her eyes up, following the tower that spiked through the building's center, rising so high it was consumed by darkness before she could see its end. How Shadows corrupted technology was a mystery to the entire galaxy, and seeing one at work did nothing to demystify who they were and what they did. Not that Kira cared all that much; she corrupted tech with detonators and whatever gadgets Mig cooked up, and that was good enough for her.

"Kira Sen," Kay said. He was standing ten feet directly in front of Kira, his arms casually hoisted above his head. "The girl who escaped."

Kira considered killing Kay right then and there. It would be the quickest and easiest way to defuse whatever he was *really* up to. Were her death not guaranteed the second she pulled the trigger, she would have. With murdering the former Praxian Warden off the table, Kira knew she'd have to get him talking— Kay, she remembered, had a passionate love affair with the sound of his own voice—while she came up with a plan B.

"I can only imagine the disappointment you felt when I evaded your plans to kill me," Kira acerbically snarled.

Kira expected a barb in exchange. She expected Kay to respond with arrogance and disdain. But the Warden only shook his head.

"It's not at all what you think," he said. "It truly isn't."

There was a genuineness behind Kay's words that Kira hadn't expected. Conciliatory, even. It made her pause to study the man in front of her, a man she hadn't seen in over ten years. He'd at least matured since she'd last seen him. His hair seemed to have darkened to a deeper red, and he'd grown out a thin beard that was graying in patches. He was still broad-shouldered and lean around his waist, but the cocksure way he'd once carried himself had transformed into a more thoughtful posture. Kay was only a few years older than Kira, though the thing she remembered most clearly was him being the perfect portrait of young, brash, and stupid. Under Ebik's close guidance, Kay had risen through the military ranks at an unparalleled pace, especially for his age. He was leading battalions in his late teens and strategizing the entire ground infantry's training and tactical operations soon after. A lot of good he'd done with all that drive and talent, Kira lamented. Still, she couldn't help but detect a weariness behind his eyes, the same weariness she saw in herself whenever she looked in the mirror. On Kira, it revealed someone who'd had everything they'd known taken from them and had to build a new world over the ashes of what once was. She was curious what it meant on Kay.

Even so, Kira wasn't interested in the trials and tribulations of Warden Kaller J. Kay. What mattered were the facts, and she wasn't about to negotiate the fact that Kay was her father's personal lapdog.

"So you *didn't* aid my father as he imprisoned my mother and tried to murder me? You were the chief Warden, the person directly responsible for the protection of the Barons and their families. Oh, and you just happened to be appointed to that position by my father."

"I was young, and your father . . . no one is better at manipulating and using people. You might know that."

"I do," Kira sneered, "which is why I don't buy you as the noble leader of some people's movement for one second."

"You think this whole thing is an elaborate game orchestrated by your father?"

"Prove me wrong," Kira said, wrapping her finger around the whipblaster's trigger just a little tighter.

"I don't have to," Kay said as his face wrinkled into an indignant scowl. "I gave you your moment, and now your moment is done. Any minute now, this tunnel is going to be overrun by gunners, and I plan on having my squad out of here before that happens. We've got a job to do; we've fought and died to get it done, and if you think you're going to get in our way—"

Kira's eyes darted side to side. The six men and women flanking Kay tightened their grips on their blasters just enough for her to notice. Kay had the upper hand—he always had the upper hand, Kira knew—and he was ending this showdown in one of two ways: Kira's surrender or her death.

"—you're mistaken," Kay finished.

There wasn't much of a decision to be made. Killing Kay and then dying in a hail of blaster fire would accomplish nothing. Even if her instincts were true and Kay was acting as an agent of her father, cutting him down would effectively break the chain, and she'd never find out what Ebik was plotting. And her death would be a significant obstacle to her desire to see the Praxis kingdom burned to the ground. So Kira did the only sensible thing; she lowered her whipblaster.

And then a shot was fired.

Time slowed to a crawl. Kira could only watch as one of Kay's soldiers' heads snapped to its side and then recoiled. One moment he'd been standing next to Kay, tri-blaster trained on Kira, and the next moment he was facedown on the floor, bleeding from his head.

It didn't take Kira long to figure out they all had to run.

"Take cover!" she yelled, turning her whipblaster toward the long, dark tunnel from where the shot originated. She unloaded her weapon and moved toward the tower, a step behind Kay's squad who were just coming out of their stupor.

"You were saying something about me working with Ebik?" Kay yelled over the hail of blaster fire.

"Defend our position first! Worry about yourself later!" Kira snapped in reply.

Blaster bolts searing the air all around them, Kira and Kay joined what was left of the squad behind the mainframe tower. Another soldier had fallen, leaving just four remaining squad members, plus Gunk and the Shadow. Gunk was nursing a flesh wound on his right bicep, and the Shadow continued his work, oblivious, like nothing out of the ordinary was happening around him.

"Well, the gunners are here," Kay said as he slammed home a fresh charge into his blaster. "My guess is they're eight strong with more soon to follow from the other end of the tunnel."

"Darkness is their friend," Kira pointed out. "Hard to hit what you can't see."

Kira poked the Shadow on his shoulder and was startled to find how cool to the touch he was. He turned to face her, his oblong, ashen-gray eyes wide, like it was the most curious thing in the world to have another sentient creature nearby.

"Hey, can you access the building's mainframe from here?" she asked.

Kay intervened, carefully taking Kira's hand off the Shadow's shoulder.

"He doesn't like to be touched," Kay said. "And we need him to focus on his task."

"We need to thin their numbers. Whatever economic chaos the Shadow is able to cause won't mean squat if we're all dead."

Kay grimaced, almost baring his canines like a cornered animal. "Fine," he growled, and then he whispered something into the Shadow's ear. The Shadow nodded and turned to the terminal, and a second later, the lights in both tunnels were blazing.

"Let's give 'em hell!" Kira said, and the squad followed her command.

Using every inch of the tower's real estate, including a pair of support beams that jutted out from both sides, each member of the seven-person squad carved out enough cover to protect themselves and fire back at the approaching gunners. The roles had been reversed; not expecting to be exposed by the tunnel's light, the gunners were now the ones scrambling for their lives. The only way to permanently down a gunner was a shot to its AI module, located on its wrist. It was a one-in-a-million shot from this distance, but a solid hit to its chest, even protected by its armor, was sure to knock a gunner clean off its feet. Which was Kira's exact strategy. Switching her whipblaster to a single-barrel blast, she set her sights on the chest of her enemy. If she couldn't stop them, at least she'd slow them down.

"Better hurry up with that!" Kay yelled to the Shadow, who was busying his fingers over the keypad at a dizzying clip. He intoned something by way of reply, though Kira was clueless to its meaning.

"You fluent in weirdo?" she asked Kay. "Was that sound an affirmative or what?"

"No idea, and since the Shadow's handler is currently bleeding out of his skull, we're gonna just have to hope for the best," Kay said.

As Kira turned to continue her assault on the gunners, she saw another one of Kay's soldiers fall. She was propelled back off her feet by a blast to her upper body, and before she could recover, another blast struck her near where the first had landed. The soldier dropped to the cold metal ground with a lifeless thud. Anger tightened Kira's jaw, and when she twisted back around, she spotted a gunner with a plasma detonator in his hand.

"I don't think so." Without wasting a moment, Kira activated the second barrel of her whipblaster and directed all fire toward the gunner. Catching him in mid-throw, she riddled his armor with one blast after another. The sheer force of the assault sent the gunner spiraling back. As the detonator rolled away from him, Kira waited, anxiously, to see if it'd been activated.

It had.

A plume of orange death rocked half the tunnel, erupting flames up to the ceiling and, more importantly, engulfing three gunners in its fiery tomb. Their armor was made to withstand a great many things, Kira knew all too well, but she was certain incineration wasn't one of them.

"I'm impressed," Kay said, half a grin appearing on his face.

"I don't care," Kira snapped.

Kira peeked over the partition that acted as her cover but withdrew when she saw the Shadow stand up and start walking away from the station. His long legs brought his height to a good seven feet, and his double-jointed knees gave him the most awkward of gaits. He again intoned something indecipherable at Kay as he went on his way.

"Should I even ask?" Kira questioned Kay, who could only shrug. A blaster bolt raced between them; it led Kira's attention down the other tunnel, where she saw another squad of gunners coming on fast.

"Damn it, we've got more company!" Kay yelled.

Kira moved to repel the gunners remaining on the other side, and Kay called for Gunk to check the Shadow's work.

"I—yes?" Gunk said as he studied the terminal. "It looks properly broken to me."

"Good enough," Kay said. "Gunk, Sen and I will get you cover; lead everyone out on my command." He turned to Kira. "How are you doing on charges?"

"Last one," Kira said as she slammed a fresh reload into her whipblaster.

"Make it count. Spray the incoming gunners. I'll hold the ones on the other side. Good?"

Kira nodded. She didn't like taking orders from Kay, but it was the exact call she would have made, and there was no time for grandstanding.

"All right, everyone out!" Kay commanded, and Gunk led the four remaining soldiers back toward the exit. "And hold that elevator!"

The fresh batch of gunners was just getting in range as Gunk took off, but they were met by an erratic storm of blaster fire courtesy of Kira. It was enough to send them scrambling, but Kira, with the whipblaster going full tilt, knew her ammo wouldn't last much longer.

"If we plan on getting out of here, it's gotta be now!" she yelled to Kay.

Kay didn't say anything, and Kira could sense him focusing on his squad as he fired at any gunner who dared pop their head out while the escape was happening. "Okay, they're safe at the elevator. Let's go!"

Kira bounced up and continued to spray fire; she'd make every single bolt she had count, and when those ran out, she'd find another way to fight. Praxis wasn't going to kill her that easily.

Killing Kay, though, was apparently less of a challenge.

They'd barely made it ten steps when a bolt from somewhere lanced Kay's thigh. The blow dropped him down to one knee, but it did nothing to stymie his fight. Kira was impressed by his ability to take a shot and hardly skip a beat. He kept on firing, keeping the encroaching gunners back as best as he could.

"Go!" he snarled at Kira. "I'll hold them back!"

At Kay's command, Kira pulled the trigger on her whipblaster for the final time. She was fresh out of ammo, standing completely exposed as enemies pressed her on both sides. The sensible thing would have been to follow Kay's command and run. To save herself. But sensible actions, particularly the kind that came at the expense of others, weren't something Kira could abide.

"Give me this," Kira said, snatching Kay's tri-blaster from his hands. "And come on."

"Sen, get out of here!" Kay protested. "That's an order!"

"Oh, shut up. I'm not in your army," Kira said, firing at whichever gunner came closest as she helped support a hobbled Kay. As they inched their way toward the elevator, blaster fire suddenly shot out from behind them; Kira turned her head just enough to see Gunk and the others firing back at the gunners, enough to keep them at bay. They reached the elevator, and everyone kept shooting until the doors closed. The exterior was pounded by the gunners' assault until, at last, the elevator climbed out of range.

"Up top is likely to be even worse," Kay said as he accepted his blaster back from Kira. "We can find cover between the buildings, but it won't take long for the Praxian forces to swarm on our position."

"I'm not planning my funeral just yet," Kira said as she took the comms unit from her pocket.

"I hope you have an army up there," Kay said.

"No," Kira said, exhaling a deep breath. "But hopefully we won't need one."

She flipped open the line for the comms and raised 4-Qel. "How's it looking up there?" she asked.

"They're adequately reinforced—and by 'adequately,' I mean excessively. *Very* excessively. Who knew they had this many drones?"

It was the exact report Kira didn't want to hear. She sighed, trying to conjure a plan out of thin air.

"But don't worry," 4-Qel said. "We're incoming."

Kira and Kay exchanged curious looks; 4-Qel's statement was hard to fully comprehend.

"What do you mean 'incoming'?" Kira asked. "Are you in a ship?"

"Hey, we've been busy while you were storming the city," Mig chimed in, the happy satisfaction evident in his voice. "Prepare for evac. I'm pretty sure you won't be able to miss us."

No one said a word. There was nothing to say. Everyone, save the Shadow, refreshed their charges. Kira drew her sidewinder and sighed wistfully. She missed her whipblaster, especially since there was a drone army waiting for her on the surface. Ragtag bands of rebels didn't win battles against armies; they survived them, and that's all Kira hoped to do. It just would have been easier to do that with a weapon that was able to kill so many, so fast.

"Do you think they're going to start shooting right away?" Gunk asked. "Or maybe do that thing where they tell us to surrender first?"

No one answered.

"Right. Probably the former then."

The car was silent until the elevator dinged to mark their arrival. The doors slid open, and Kira's breath caught in her throat at the sight of how many drones were waiting for them. Sentries and alphas were to be expected, but Praxis had also spared no expense and called in their big guns as well—breaker drones, oversized units that hulked head and shoulders above the rest and packed the kind of heavy artillery that was made for those times you just had to kill en masse. They were going to be especially tricky to put down.

The drones' formation created an impenetrable shell around the building's exterior. Shoulder to shoulder they stood, countless rows deep, blasters at the ready. Given the conditions—Kira and her group pinned down with little ammunition and nowhere to go—these drones weren't an army; they were an execution squad.

"Holy sh—"

But Kira didn't even have time to get her stunned reaction out before cannon fire tore through the sky and rocked the ground directly in front of the building. Kira couldn't tell what exactly had been fired, but she felt its impact from her feet all the way to her hair. But the drones felt it even more. Sentries and alphas blew apart in every direction—arms, legs, heads, nuts and bolts, everything they were made of erupted in an ashen plume that sent those parts skyward. The irreparable drones then rained back down, landing with a thud against the smoldering surface.

Neither Kira nor Kay wasted a moment mobilizing their followers. They darted out of the elevator—with Gunk shouldering Kay's weight—and toward the shattered exterior, wagering high that their pickup would arrive any moment. The remaining drones had paused, reconciling whether their core directive of protecting themselves overrode whatever their primary objective had been. It didn't. The drones resumed their objective, which was unmistakably to not let the individuals who'd infiltrated the financial core live. Kira and the others were ready, though, firing whatever they had at the drones as they neared the exit.

Even with their numbers thinned, the remaining drones were way more than Kira, Kay, and the rest could handle. Fortunately, they didn't have to. Just as the drones were about to open fire and shred their targets, a ship swooped down from the sky, firing into the crowd of drones as it came. The ship—a black-and-maroon oblong vessel with a single massive thruster at its rear—vectored to the ground hard and fast, jolting to a stop just inches from the surface. Once steady, it spun 180 degrees and fired maximum burn to its thruster. Every drone within striking distance, even the breakers, was propelled clean off its feet and sent soaring backward.

"How in the world did your men secure an officer transport, Sen?" Kay yelled as they ran toward the ship's boarding ramp.

Kira shook her head, amused. "No idea. But I'm sure there's a colorful story that explains it."

Kobe greeted them inside the ship, eager to get the ramp back up so they could extricate themselves from this war zone.

"That everyone?" Kobe asked.

Kira nodded, and as the ship rose, Kobe pressed the button to bring in the ramp. It had barely closed halfway when blaster bolts began scoring its shielded exterior, causing the transport to buck, but only a little.

"I see you've made some friends," Kobe observed.

Kira looked at the group behind her, particularly Kay, and huffed. "We'll see," she said. "Come on, let's get out of here."

Kira was leading Kobe out of the hold when Kay called her name. She stopped but didn't look back.

"You won't get far," Kay said. "Praxis has this entire city under strict patrol with Intruders and transports like this one. If they raise you and you don't respond with the correct clearance, we all die."

Kira finally turned and shot Kay a deadly glare. "And I assume you have the correct clearance."

"No, I do not. But I know their patrols well enough to get around them and get us someplace safe."

"That'd be a great offer if we were working under the assumption that I trusted you," Kira said. "But I don't."

Kay pushed off Gunk with a wince and limped toward Kira. "I'm not going to die over something that took place over a decade ago," he snarled. "Now, you listen to me—I've shown perfectly well what I'm doing here. What about you, Sen? Why are *you* here? Let me guess. Exacting some payback against dear old Dad? If that's the case, then you're going to have to take a number and get in line. And that line starts with *me*."

"I'm not here for Ebik."

"This is the last time I extend my hand," Kay said, nearly choking on his agitation. "What's it going to be? We either work together or you let us out of this ship right now."

Kira broke her stare with Kay and looked to Kobe. He met her hard gaze with a shrug.

"We have no idea where to find shelter, and this ship isn't even equipped to break the planet's atmosphere."

Kira had to fight to prevent her posture from slumping. Nothing in her mission had gone according to plan, and now she was being forced to cooperate with her father's right-hand man—the man who'd been trained and groomed by Ebik himself. The man who'd helped strip her mother of her role as Baron, imprison her, and leave Kira open to be discarded by her father.

"We'll work together under the condition of getting us both to safety," Kira said. "But that's where this alliance ends."

Kay nodded, then sat down on one of the chairs that folded out from the hold's wall. His leg was evidently still troubling him, and begrudgingly, Kira decided she'd provide whatever medical aid the ship had to offer.

"Gunk will navigate your pilot to our base," Kay said. "But under one condition."

"The condition is we don't drop you back off where we found you," Kira snapped.

"No, you wouldn't do that—not when you think there's a chance we can be useful to you. And I can tell by the look in your eye that's exactly what you're trying to determine," Kay said. "So, while you figure that out, I want to know something. Why are you here? Why return to the planet you escaped so many years ago?"

Kira stood tall in the frame of the door's exit, the reminder of her mission rallying her strength.

"I'm here for my mother," Kira said. "I'm going to rescue her."

Kay looked at Kira, unblinking, then leaned his head against the hold's wall and started to laugh.

"Kay, you either explain to me what's so funny, or I *will* drop you where I found you—except now, I won't give you the courtesy of lowering to the ground first."

"I'm sorry, I'm sorry," Kay said, stifling his outburst. "But that's truly why you're here?"

Kira took an aggressive step toward Kay, hand on her sidewinder. She felt his squad mirror her movement. "Do you know where she is? Because if you get in my way—"

"Do I know where she is?" Kay said, incredulous. "Sen, who do you think is leading this uprising?"

CHAPTER EIGHT

D arkness.

   Then, like a flint striking steel, a spark of light.

   This world, wherever it was, whatever it was, existed in varying shades of gray and black. The sky resembled a sheen of soot, smeared across the atmosphere and choking the life out of any light that even attempted to break through. Cade's trembling eyes danced around, trying to discern any hint of shape or form that might define this place. But the ashen fog extended like a curtain to obscure any and all features down to the horizon line—assuming there was a horizon. Beneath his feet, the ground was obsidian stone, smooth and layered like it'd been polished by a long-forgotten tide. And Cade was compelled by a powerful external force unknown to him to follow a path on its upward rise. Step by step he climbed, somehow feeling like he was descending and not the opposite, unable to see more than a few inches ahead of himself. He reached out with an apprehensive hand, trying to push away the darkness that obscured his vision, but the gloom persisted.

Slowly, one cautious step in front of the other, Cade continued until wisps of murky smoke plumed just ahead. Effervescent colors burst and rained down deep hues of red, green, and indigo. And as the colors spread, they cast enough light for Cade to discern the outlines of three shadowy shapes—human, almost, but too ethereal to be understood as flesh and bone. Cade halted, unable to draw any closer.

With Cade frozen in place, the shapes began to chant in a language he had never encountered before. The pitch of their voices and the cadence of their words rang sharply in Cade's mind; he winced and covered his ears, but it did no good. The echoing melody still penetrated into his brain, piercing it like daggers.

Cade didn't know what he was being forced to watch, but he knew his purpose: to bear witness. But Cade knew whatever message was being conveyed was wrong; it felt like a virus burying itself deep within his very core. Twisting it, squeezing it, spreading its darkness within. Cade let out a soundless scream, and as he did, the three figures began to change right before his eyes.

Among the three spectral shapes stepped another figure—this one more human but also more menacing, and Cade shuddered as a jolt of cold spread throughout his body. The figure was wrapped in all black, and from Cade's vantage, it seemed formless until it started to change. It was his vision all over again, the one he'd slipped into in the Kundarian trade ship. Horns like horrible, knotted tree roots twisted out of the shape's head, curving and gnashing their way forth. As the demented crown took shape, the chanting intensified, growing faster and louder. Cade's knees would have buckled beneath him if they weren't so firmly paralyzed. The shapes' voices—if Cade could call them voices—and the subtle noise made by the spawning horns were so otherworldly that he could hardly take it. He could only stand where he was, gripping his ears, as the shapes began to sweep their arms across the mist. As they did, the ashen air cleared, and the formless figure came into view. Similarly, the specters' chanting took on a more recognizable pitch, though Cade didn't need to hear their words to know who he was looking at.

"Ga Halle," the shapes said, their gravelly voices stretching out each syllable.

Ga Halle—Ga Halle bearing her crown of twisted horns, Ga Halle with bloodred eyes—stepped forward. The shapes parted for her as she strolled, lithe as a feline, right up to Cade.

"Release your hold on the Rokura," Ga Halle whispered into Cade's ear. "You aren't strong enough to possess it for much longer. Surrender, and you can *live*."

"You're insane," Cade said, breathless.

"Your brother had what few people had. He was absolute. His goodness was complete; it was total. I, too, am absolute. Just in my own way."

Cade shied away from Ga Halle; he found it difficult, almost impossible, to look into her fiery eyes, and he couldn't determine what she could do to him in this place. He kept waiting for her to strike him, to tear one of the horns from her own head and drive it through his heart. He imagined his blood wafting into the air and turning into soot as he lay there dying. He hoped this wasn't real. The vision, the place, none of it. But he knew that hope was false. The place might not be real, not exactly, but the moment between him and Ga Halle was. It was happening to him; it was happening to her. Still, that didn't mean it made any sense. At least to Cade.

"What are you talking about?" Cade asked.

"Good. Evil. Two sides. Two paths to power. You don't have enough good in you, and you're certainly not evil—and that dooms you to *fail*."

Cade opened his mouth to speak, but he choked on his own growing feeling of dread. He knew she was right. He was going to fall, and something words couldn't express was going to rise in his wake. Ga Halle—whatever she had become.

"My transformation is complete," Ga Halle said as the three shapes gathered at her back. "I am the absolute I need to be, and now it is time that I came for you."

"Ga Halle," Cade said, his pleading tone surprising even him.

"There's no turning back," Ga Halle said as she and the shapes receded. "No undoing what's been done."

Cade still couldn't move. Even as he felt the ground begin to tremble and crack, he couldn't so much as take a step. Suddenly, it felt to Cade like the ground was getting soft, brittle. As he fought to tear his feet away—where he'd run to, he didn't know—Cade realized that the ground was dissolving. He barely had time to acknowledge that fact before everything that was beneath him broke apart and vanished, leaving him to fall and fall and fall through nothingness.

Until he jolted back, awake in another place he didn't know. He shot up from the metal slab he'd been lying on and gasped like he hadn't breathed in days. And when Cade felt a hand grasp his shoulder, he snapped his body around and grabbed the neck of whoever was behind him. Adrenaline raced through his body, compensating for the disorientation and fatigue that otherwise would have sent him falling to the floor. It was that overwhelming adrenaline that kept Cade's hand wrapped around Percival's throat for a moment past recognizing it was him.

"Cade," Percival gasped. "Let . . . go."

Cade took three calming breaths, each one deeper than the one that preceded it. He loosened his tightly constricted jaw muscles and then finally relinquished his hold on Percival's neck.

Percival took a step back and rubbed his throat while Cade studied his surroundings. They were in a cell, that much was obvious by the shielded door that shimmered across the room's only point of entrance or exit. A single metal slab hung from a flawlessly smooth indigo wall, and it was clear by the size of the space and the one sleeping accommodation that this room was made for a single occupant. Which, Cade assumed, could only mean that he and Percival weren't going to be staying there long. And not because they were going to be let free.

"You were having a nightmare," Percival said, stretching out his neck's discomfort. "I tried waking you, but you wouldn't respond."

Cade pressed his fingers over his eyes, trying to piece together everything he'd seen. He remembered every detail; he just couldn't figure out how any of it made sense.

"I don't think it was a dream," Cade said. "It was too clear, too real. It was more like a vision. I've been having them lately, but . . . I don't know what they are or why I'm having them."

Percival cast a gaze at Cade; his expression was inquisitive but laden with a shadow. "These visions . . . what are they showing you?"

Cade folded his arms across his chest. The remembrance of what he'd seen made him cold all over again. "Ga Halle," Cade replied. "It's always Ga Halle. I was in some . . . strange place. It was dark everywhere. The ground, the sky, everything was dusted in ash. Ga Halle was . . . I don't know, part of some kind of ceremony. She was being transformed into something. Something horrible."

"Who performed the ceremony?" Percival asked. "Anyone you recognize?"

Cade shook his head as he struggled to find words to describe the shapes—priests, witches, whatever they were—and the form they took. "There were no people there," Cade said. "Just these three . . . specters. These three black, kinda viscous shapes."

Percival narrowed his vision as if trying to bring his thoughts to bear out of the emptiness of their cell. "The dark seeds of Mankarta," he said.

Cade rolled his neck over his shoulders and groaned. He didn't want to inquire any further, because he knew what Percival's answer would reveal: This was all just more of Ga Halle's bothodung that Cade would have to deal with. Still, he asked, "What are the dark seeds of Mankarta?"

"Purveyors of the occult. It's said that they're immortal conduits to the galaxy's dark energy, whatever that is. Even if we assume they're more than just legends, the question is why Ga Halle would have anything to do with them. She does little without reason or at least without knowing what her gain ought to be. But the dark seeds are evil incarnate, thoroughly."

"Then I guess it makes sense for Ga Halle to hit it off with them so well," Cade said. He stretched his stiff, sore body, and he was taken back to the pain he'd felt when Ersia's guards had prodded him like cattle into the palace and then electroshocked him until he was unconscious. His body still tingled from however many volts had been pumped into his spine.

He shook off the pain and continued, "In this vision, Ga Halle was going on about how the Rokura was rightfully hers and how she was going to take it from me. Which is nothing new. But the thing is, this time it was different. It *felt* different. These dark seeds, they did something to her. And . . . I don't know. She kept talking about good and evil and being absolute in one or the other." Cade paused, and the cell was silent. He squeezed his eyes closed, and he knew he had to share the truth he'd been trying to deny since he'd encountered Ga Halle in his vision above Kundar. The truth of what the future held for himself and everyone around him. He spoke his words solemnly. "Percival, if I saw her right now, I don't think I'd be able to stop her. She's . . . whatever's happened to her, she's not the same."

Percival's eyes flickered from Cade to the floor. He smiled, then it died on his face. When he looked back up, he bore an expression of sympathy that bordered on pity.

"I haven't . . . ," Percival started, but his words trailed off into a gentle sigh. "I haven't taught you as much as I should have."

Cade sank back down onto the bunk and squeezed his shoulders, bringing his elbows together to form a steeple at his chest. He turned his attention to the shielded door, the only thing in the cell he could fix his eyes on other than Percival.

"It's not about the teaching, Percival," Cade said. "It's about things neither one of us can change. Whatever it is that guided you and Tristan and even Ga Halle, it doesn't guide me. I'm not that person. I'm sorry, I'm just . . . not."

Percival slid onto the bed next to Cade, though he kept his gaze ahead. "It's all a lie, Cade," he said. "The whole myth of the Paragon—it's not real. Not in the way you think it is."

Cade scoffed. "Said the person who pulled the mystical weapon from its stasis."

"I pulled it out because I was certain I could do so. My whole life, I'd been told that seizing the Rokura was my destiny, and I believed it. I believed the Master Rai when they told me becoming the Paragon was an inevitability. Tell me, did they do the same thing with your brother? Did they build him up like he was a god walking among us? Did they position him to be the supreme best in everything he did?"

Cade feigned like he was thinking about Percival's line of inquiry, but he knew the answer. They both did.

"I'm not special, and I never was," Percival continued. "Neither is Ga Halle. The only thing we shared was this absolute belief in ourselves. I got over my inflated view of myself; apparently, she did not."

"But . . . why? What's this all for?" Cade asked, feeling his heart sink.

"Belief can be a powerful weapon, Cade. If Ga Halle gets the Rokura, that dark influence you feel within it will take control. Why? It's not necessarily because Ga Halle is evil; it's because anything she does with that weapon justifies itself. How can she be wrong, after all? She's the Paragon. Once you convince yourself that you're the highest power—once you're absolute—then by your own virtue, you can never be wrong. That's ultimately what everyone wants, Cade. They want a god to come along and tell them what to do and what's right and what's wrong. The Masters saw what Praxis was turning into, they recognized the deep discord happening across the entire galaxy, and they knew there wasn't a thing they could do about it. But a Paragon? Now that's a different story. All they had to do was make one.

"But things went wrong, and the Masters blinked. Their absolutes turned out to be anything but, and without their godhead, they figured there was nothing they could do for the galaxy, and they didn't come around again until they got desperate enough to try with your brother. And just like last time, everything went terribly wrong."

Cade fell back on the metal slab of a bed. "Maybe that's what the Rokura's real secret is—it holds the power to create tragedy."

For the first time since Cade woke up, he heard a sound coming from outside his cell. A distant, echoing sound of a series of locks being opened. Someone was coming.

"Listen, we don't have much time," Percival said, getting down on his haunches so he was eye to eye with Cade. "Everything I taught you was wrong; I realize that now. I wanted you to believe the way I believed—that you had to be convinced of your power and your control. It's—" Percival started, then he gave way to shaking off his regret. "Don't believe in me, or Tristan, or even the Rokura. Believe in yourself. You've done it before, back on the *War Hammer.*"

"Which was a fluke."

"Which proved that you could beat Ga Halle."

"No," Cade snapped, fighting back tears. "All that showed was how, deep down, I want to die."

Percival frowned as he stood up, and Cade watched as his upper lip curled into a stubborn snarl. "I don't buy that for a second. I know you, Cade. Like it or not, I do. And I know you weren't willing to sacrifice yourself because you wanted to die. No. You were willing to die so everyone else would live. *That* is your power; *that* is what makes you worth following. It's why I follow you."

The door's shielding faded; as it did, two stocky guards armed with a kind of compression pike Cade didn't recognize came into view. Wordlessly, they entered the cell, and the larger of the two twisted Percival's arms behind his back and slapped on restraints that covered his hands, fingertips to wrists. Percival didn't resist, but Cade sprang to his feet and stood between the leading guard and the door.

"What's going on here? Where are you taking him?" Suddenly, Cade felt panicked. He felt afraid, but not about what was going to happen to him. He was worried about Percival, and in his concern for his mentor, a thought flashed across his mind. Maybe, just maybe, Percival was right.

The guard leading Percival out didn't say anything; he didn't have to. Before Cade could utter another word, the guard's partner drove his forearm into Cade's throat and pinned him against the wall.

"Let me go!" Cade rasped, resisting the hold the guard had on him. But it was no use; he was too weak and the guard was too strong. "You don't know who we are! You don't know what you're doing!"

"Save it, Cade. Save it for whatever's coming," Percival said as he was dragged past Cade and out of the cell. "And just know . . . know that I'm sorry. I failed you, Cade. But if I can't convince you to believe in yourself, then at least be convinced that *I* believe in you."

Cade felt a momentary easing of the pressure being applied to his throat, but it was immediately followed by the guard grabbing him by his shirt and tossing him onto the slab.

"We'll be back for you soon enough," the guard grumbled. "The trial awaits."

Though he knew it was futile, Cade rushed toward the cell's open doorway. Just as he reached it, the shield popped back into place, and he ran right into its solid mass. The impact knocked Cade onto his ass. He didn't stay down, though. In an instant, Cade was on his feet and at the cell door; he tried to look down the hallway, but the shield was too thick to see through. Cade had no idea where Percival was being taken or what would be done to him when he got there. He couldn't even see what direction he was heading.

"Percival!" Cade screamed, pounding his fists against the shield. "Percival!"

But it was no use. Percival couldn't hear him. No one could hear him.

Cade was all alone.

Until he was dumped into the arena.

A guard removed the mask from Cade's eyes, exposing a massive fighting pit—and he was in the middle of it. He could almost smell hot blood wafting in the air, rising from the faint crimson stains that streaked across the dirt ground. The crudity of the pit, though, was contrasted with the grandstand's glossy sheen. Like the castle's exterior, walls of deep gold streaked with a royal blue marked the arena's perimeter; impressive, winding pillars rose to the ceiling with banners depicting what Cade assumed to be Ersia's royal crest—a winged beast armed with a golden pike—draped down their sides. Cade glanced at the audience; the seats were filled with guards and the other denizens of Monaskis. They sat silently, leering at Cade with disdainful eyes.

"Hello," Cade called out. "I'm glad you could all make it to see me do . . . whatever I'm going to be doing."

There was no response.

Cade peered at the ground and sighed unpleasantly. "I do not have a good feeling about this," he said to himself.

His spirits were lifted, though, when he spotted the Rokura sticking out from the ground. It'd clearly been slammed, blades first, into the dirt just ten feet away from him. The solace he took seeing the Rokura, of all things, made the depths of this situation's awfulness abundantly clear: He was captive in the core of a dead planet, Ga Halle was breathing down his neck, and now he was trapped in a fighting ring where he'd be forced to prove he was something he was not. And if he didn't, he and Percival would be killed. And his friends would likely be next, followed by Praxis having an uncontested tyrannical rule throughout the galaxy.

So, things were not great.

Like usual, Cade figured he'd just have to react to however things unfolded. The first step was retrieving his Rokura. For better or worse, it was the only weapon available to him, and he had a feeling he was going to need one. The moment he stepped forward, he was blasted with a beam of light shining directly in his face. Cade shielded his eyes just as music started playing from somewhere, music that cued the audience to roar. And roar they did. Their feverish, frenetic cheers reminded Cade of the drone fighting pit back on Kyysring, and it made him realize just how far he'd come. At the onset of this journey, he'd finally gotten to see the infamous drone pit for himself; now he was going to die in one just like it.

A few moments of pompous music accompanied by obnoxious cheers passed, and the light was removed from Cade's face. When his sight finally returned, his gaze was directed to the center of the arena. There, perched on stilts just above the pit's scarred gray walls, was a glass-shielded luxury suite—home to Ersia and her inner circle of guards. And Percival, just to Ersia's left, bound to a chair. Xeric stood menacingly over him.

Ersia was finishing a ceremonial series of benevolent waves to the crowd when she swung her focus onto Cade, looking at him as if he were a Kyysring street rat. Which he kind of was, but still. She stepped toward the suite's edge, and Cade kept his eyes on her the entire time, knowing the menace that was shooting from his glare. He and Percival had come to Monaskis in peace, seeking guidance and wisdom, and this person—who kept herself and her people conveniently hidden from the galaxy and its many problems—was obstructing Cade's quest to free the galaxy from tyranny. Who knew what Ga Halle was becoming or what she was planning while Cade and Percival languished in Ersia's custody? Who knew what kind of danger Kira, Mig, 4-Qel, and Kobe were in, danger that Cade should be protecting them from? And it was all because this Monaskin queen—whatever that was even worth, considering the entire galaxy thought her race was extinct—refused to even hear him out. Cade didn't have time to suffer fools, and as far as he could tell, Ersia was a grade-A fool who knew nothing of him or what he had to do. Yet she'd made herself an impediment anyway.

"You come to us claiming to be the Paragon," Ersia said, her voice carrying sharply through the hushed arena. "As such, Monaskin culture demands you prove your claim."

"And who said I have to care about you or your demands?" Cade yelled back. "I know you think this little exhibition of yours matters, but it doesn't. My companion and I—that guy you have tied to a chair—are trying to save the galaxy. Maybe if you all weren't living with your heads up your butts hidden deep in this rock, you'd understand what is at stake and get out of our way!" Cade flashed a conciliatory smile that he hoped would assuage what he'd just said. He'd gotten carried away and forgot that he needed Ersia's help. "Though, you know, to each their own, and we could really use your help. Please and thank you."

Cade felt the crowd tense, and even from his considerable distance, he could see Ersia's face go dark.

"And do you know why we're, as you so eloquently say, hidden deep in this rock?"

Cade sighed. His stupid smile hadn't worked. "I have no idea," he replied. "But I'm guessing you're going to tell me."

Ersia responded, "Because you put us here."

Cade pursed his lips and rolled his eyes like he was giving the accusation a modicum of contemplation. He wasn't. "No," he said. "I didn't. I think I'd remember that."

"You're the Paragon, are you not? Then it is in your legacy. *You* are why we're here. *You* are why our planet was destroyed."

"I'm not following," Cade said impatiently.

"Wu-Xia was one of us, as you already know. He was our greatest, most skilled warrior. He protected our planet back when it was still whole; he conquered worlds and made it so the Monaskins were feared for our power. But then it all changed, and the change came from Wu-Xia, our trusted leader, himself.

"History tells us that Wu-Xia withdrew from his responsibilities and his people. No one knew why. All that's known is that he abandoned us, and when he did return, he did so with a strange weapon—the Rokura, he called it—and a demand that Monaskis change its ways.

"Not only did our proud forefathers and foremothers refuse, but they swore they'd bring war to the doorstep of every planet or moon that supported Wu-Xia. They threatened to deny him his peace through war—war the likes of which the galaxy had never seen, and when they were done, they'd have Wu-Xia's head driven onto a spike as punishment for his treason. Wu-Xia was not amused.

"He brought a reckoning to this planet that was incomprehensible. He used his power to break not only our home but also our legacy and our way of life in one single display of his might. And if that wasn't enough, he leveraged our tragedy as an example to bring all his other enemies to heel. Seeing the ruins of Monaskis, nearly every system that defied Wu-Xia's demands for peace relinquished their opposition. The wars over resources, the wars of conquest, the skirmishes over land and religion, they all ended. Wu-Xia had his peace, but it came through the death of everything Monaskis was and would ever be."

Cade listened intently, and he started to understand why Monaskis would hold a grudge against the Paragon. But the justification for it lasting this long seemed a little uncalled for.

"Look, I get your beef with Wu-Xia. I'd be pissed, too," Cade said. "But I'm not him, and what he did has nothing to do with me. You can't kill me because we happen to both be Paragons."

Ersia corkscrewed her head, expressing her confusion. "But if you are indeed the Paragon, then you have nothing to worry about. We'd never be able to so much as lay a finger on you," Ersia said. "But if you are not—if, say, you're merely imitating the legacy of the man who set a radical new course for the Monaskin people for your own benefit, then you will die."

Cade wrapped his hand around the hilt of the Rokura and tore it from the ground. He knew there was no point in explaining to Ersia his complicated relationship with the Rokura. Someone who let a person's fate be decided in the heart of a fighting pit wasn't one for finer details, Cade decided, so he only had one choice: He had to survive whatever waited for him in this pit, and he had to convince Ersia that he was the Paragon in the process.

"Nothing left to say?" Ersia mocked. "This is usually where people like you beg for mercy."

Cade groaned. "Let's just get on with it already," he said.

Ersia laughed condescendingly. "So be it."

At Ersia's raised arm, the entire arena quaked; Cade felt seismic movement beneath his feet, the shock waves tingling up his spine.

"That can't be good," Cade murmured. He'd expected a duel against one of Ersia's best guards. Maybe even a brawl where he took on a few chosen warriors.

Whatever was coming was clearly not *that*.

More tremors shook the arena, and Cade's attention was drawn to a set of massive, reinforced double doors on the other side of the pit. He dug his heels into the earth beneath his feet and gripped the Rokura tightly. The tremors grew closer, more intense, and Cade looked up to Percival, desperately seeking a clue as to what was coming his way.

"Don't hesitate, Cade! Kill it! Kill it immediately!" Percival yelled, and his outburst was met by Xeric delivering a swift punch to his guts.

Cade shifted his focus back on the double doors, which were sliding open. He was doing his best to overcome his terrified stupor when the doors burst off their tracks and flew across the stadium. And into the pit charged a gorgan beast, its immense paws chewing away at the ground as it charged toward Cade.

"What in the—" a wide-eyed Cade started to say, but he had to get busy preventing his grisly death before he could finish.

Cade sprinted to his left and dove out of the charging gorgan's

path, narrowly escaping its thunderous stampede. He somersaulted head over heels and came up looking at the luxury suite.

"I told you we shouldn't have come here!" he screamed to Percival, but he didn't have time to wait for a response. The gorgan
had stopped its wild charging with remarkable deftness, and it
was already turned and staring down its prey. Cade eyed it in return, and one thing was abundantly clear: This was no normal
gorgan.

Gorgans were enormous, terrifying beasts. Measuring about
fifteen feet from the tips of their noses to their tails, gorgans had
the capacity to be one of the galaxy's deadliest predators. Could
they use the double row of teeth—and really sharp, pointy teeth
at that—that ran the length of their narrow snouts to chew
squishy humans into an edible paste? Absolutely. Could they use
their massive paws to stomp said squishy humans into an edible
powder? Without question. They could gouge with their claws,
slice with their whip-sharp tails, or just smash with their heft.
But gorgans did none of these things. They were vegetarians.
They were pacifists. What shared the pit with Cade was not a
typical gorgan. Something was definitely wrong with it; Cade
just couldn't tell what.

The gorgan's thick hide was scarred and marked with abrasions; its teeth, while still intimidating, had taken on a green
hue, and many were missing. And the mane around its neck,
usually a quality the gorgans flaunted with pride, had been
reduced to a sickly-looking ring of wispy hair. If Cade had to
guess, this animal had been badly abused and reprogrammed
to be a vicious, dangerous killer. Its innate nature had been
snuffed out like a candle's light and had been replaced with a
murderous rage learned through whatever mistreatment it'd
suffered. Cade was suddenly filled with a righteous anger for
whoever had done this.

But while Cade was assessing the gorgan's plight, it was positioning itself for its second attack. It charged Cade once more, its legs gracefully bounding through the air as it shortened the distance to its prey with remarkable speed.

Cade thought fast. Though he was tempted to use the Rokura to slice the gorgan in half, he didn't have the heart to kill it; his pity for what the gnarly beast had endured was somehow surpassing his desire to not be eaten alive, so he had to find a compromise between the two sides. Instead of using his all-powerful weapon to both save his life and solve his problem with Ersia, Cade decided on a different course of action. As the gorgan closed in on him, Cade charged directly at it, screaming a battle cry as he went.

Just as the gorgan snapped its teeth at Cade, he spun away from its attack and slid feetfirst beneath the beast. As he skidded across the ground, Cade used his Rokura to slice at the inside of the gorgan's legs as they passed over his head. The goal was to cripple the beast and end the fight without either of them dying. While Cade was proud of his noble design, he was less enthusiastic with its result. The gorgan repositioned itself on the opposite end of the arena, and as it did, it let out a shrill, piercing scream. The damage Cade had inflicted seemed to have only made the gorgan angry. *Really* angry.

"Terrific," Cade grumbled.

Cade expected the gorgan to charge at him again, but it didn't. Instead, the gorgan started racing around the perimeter of the oval-shaped pit. Cade backed into the center of the pit so he could stay as far away from the beast as possible. But by the time the beast started its second lap, Cade realized what was happening: The gorgan had halved the distance between itself and Cade. When Cade was on one side of the pit and the gorgan on the other, he had time to dodge, even counterstrike. But with Cade in the middle, he had half the time to react and half the time to move out of the way. Which meant the next attempt the beast made for him, Cade was dead meat.

Energy began crackling at the Rokura's head. Whether he'd realized it or not, Cade had made his decision. Conflicted as he was about obliterating the gorgan, it was the only choice he had. He held the Rokura out as its energy danced a circuitous, circular orbit at its tip. He followed the beast intently with his eyes, and drowning out the arena's hollering crowd and the occasional screech from the gorgan, Cade fell back on his Rai training and slipped into a meditative state. He let every distraction that looked to cloud his own thoughts come into his mind. He didn't wrestle with them; he just let them come and then go. There were the expectations Cade had placed upon himself for meeting the standards set by his brother, Tristan, as the rightful Rokura-bearer; there were the expectations placed upon him by Percival, demanding that Cade learn to control himself and, therefore, control the Rokura; there were even the strange expectations as explained by Ga Halle, about certainty and binary absolutes. Cade let all of these things fade from his mind. He cleared his thoughts, and he considered what he wanted to become—what he needed to become—as he wielded a weapon that could change the course of history. In the quiet of his meditation, Percival's voice crept into his ear. Don't believe in me, Percival had said. Don't believe in Tristan or the weapon. Believe in *yourself.*

From the center of the pit, directly below Ersia's luxury suite, the gorgan charged. Cade was ready.

He focused his will into the Rokura, and he captured the massive beast in a surge of energy. The gorgan was halted in its tracks just short of striking distance from Cade; it snarled and hissed as Cade held it steady, though he wasn't certain how long his hold would last.

The Rokura fought Cade. Cade had seen the weapon use this

power before, back in the Quarrian spire. It held the Fatebreaker in a stasis field right before it peeled off his skin, then his muscle, and obliterated his bone until where there was once a man there was nothingness.

But Cade didn't want to kill the gorgan. He wanted something else.

As the gorgan remained trapped, time slowed to a crawl; in that drawn-out span, Cade considered the mercy he felt for the beast. None of this was the gorgan's fault. It'd been made this way, transformed into something it was not. And that was where Cade's sympathies were found, in transformations. Like the Monaskins had changed the gorgan, like the dark seeds had changed Ga Halle, so, too, was the Rokura working to change Cade. He thought back on the horror he'd felt at his friends seeing him warped by the Rokura's will when he was just moments away from atomizing Ortzo. That was not who Cade was, and Cade had no intention of altering his identity in order to claim mastery over the Rokura. Especially not under the conditions the Rokura offered, promising all the ends Cade desired—peace through the destruction of the Praxis kingdom—but through means that were unforgiving, gruesome, and frightening. Should Cade fully open that door, he couldn't even guess what would come out.

Cade wasn't going to succumb to the Rokura's nihilistic appetites, and he knew he would never transform into his brother or learn to dominate the weapon through the power of his will like Percival had wanted him to. The only chance Cade had was to tap into the part of himself that was right and true. The part that would fight for the galaxy, the part that would die for his friends if it meant keeping them safe. He used that to appeal to the goodness he felt deep in the Rokura. It was in there, somewhere. Cade felt it in the times when the Rokura saved his life; he felt it, dimly, when he meditated on the demands, dangers, and pressures the weapon had brought into his life. The pull of the Rokura's harsher and unforgiving tendencies were louder, and stronger, too. And while Cade knew he was far from being a saint, he was even further from being a power-hungry monster like Ga Halle. Cade wanted to do right with the power he'd inherited, and if he couldn't use the Rokura in that fashion, he'd sooner see it dismantled than have it become another tool to bring misery to the galaxy. There were plenty of those already.

With that in mind, Cade focused his energy into the gorgan—the beast that'd been so anguished by its physical and mental scars that it'd become something it was not. The light from the Rokura turned an iridescent white as Cade continued to concentrate despite the strain it caused. He wouldn't kill the gorgan; he wouldn't serve up its body to Ersia as proof that he was the Paragon.

Cade felt himself reaching out through the Rokura and into the gorgan; he drew from his simple desire to end the beast's suffering. There was a blinding flash that sent out a wave of light throughout the arena, and then it was over. Cade opened his eyes, fearing that what he'd attempted had been totally ignored and the Rokura had ended up splattering the gorgan's guts all over the audience just to prove a point. But as he peeked through one eye, Cade saw that the gorgan was still there and still in one piece. More than that, it was healed. Gone were its scars and abrasions. Gone was the feral, menacing look in its eyes. The gorgan lumbered toward Cade and bumped its gigantic snout against his hip. With some apprehension—the gorgan still had those teeth, and it had been trying to flay him two minutes earlier—Cade reached out his hand and petted the beast. The gorgan exhaled contentedly, and Cade heard a purr rumble from its belly.

"This is an unexpected turn of events," Ersia called out, her voice big and imposing over the arena's din. Cade shifted his attention up to her suite and found her standing at the edge once again, her hands raised to silence the murmuring crowd. "You are an unconventional Paragon and certainly a strange one, but a Paragon nonetheless. As such, I grant you your release and an offer of my help, should you still need it."

"I appreciate it, Your Majesty, but you've got it wrong," Cade said, catching his breath. "I'm not the Paragon."

The crowd gasped and started chirping like birds to one another. Ersia waved them down, silencing them once more.

"Explain," she said, eyeing Cade curiously.

"My brother was the Paragon, and this weapon belonged to him. He pulled it out of its stasis in the Quarrian spire, but he was murdered soon after. I claimed the weapon because, well . . . I was there when it all happened, and I've held it since because I guess I'm the only alternative to Ga Halle, a maniacal warlord who wants—"

Ersia raised a hand, silencing Cade. "I know all about this *Ga Halle*," she said, her words dripping with disdain. "I don't need to hear of her deeds."

Cade threw up his arms, not knowing what to say. "Look, I'm just . . . I'm trying to do my best, and I don't feel right lying to you about myself or the weapon."

"But you cured the gorgan," Ersia said. "We all witnessed it. What kind of sorcerer are you, then?"

Cade laughed. "I'm not a sorcerer, though it would be awesome if I were. I can control the Rokura . . . sort of. I control it, and sometimes it controls me. But that's why I'm here; I need your help."

"Help?" Ersia scoffed. "After you just admitted you're a fraud?"

"You know Ga Halle. That means you know what she's doing to people—to families, to children, to anyone—throughout the galaxy. She can't be allowed to continue to rule this way. I have to stop her, but I need the Rokura to do so."

Ersia was silent for a moment as she studied Cade. As she did, the gorgan stumbled next to Cade and heeled at his side.

"You really healed the gorgan with the Rokura?" Ersia asked. "That wasn't a trick?"

"I've never done anything like that," Cade replied. "But what I did was real. I know it."

"And what is it that you need from us?"

"I need to learn anything I can about Wu-Xia—how he created the Rokura, what it is, anything. If I can learn how this all works, maybe I can learn to control it better. And if I can do that, I can stop Ga Halle."

There was a pregnant pause as Cade stood, the gorgan panting at his side, waiting for Ersia's judgment. She eyed him up and down until finally she spoke.

"There's a passion in your voice, an authenticity in your words," she said. "I believe what you say is true, and because of that, I will help you."

Cade felt every muscle in his body release unbearable tension. "Okay, then. Okay," he said as he let out a deep breath. "So, how does this work? Is there an archive or something that we could access and get Wu-Xia's memoirs, journals, whatever?"

"Archives? No, we have no such thing. We have no need."

"Oh," Cade said, confused. "Then . . . where?"

"There's only one place that can give you what you seek," Ersia answered. "The Chamber of Memories."

Cade followed Ersia through a narrow tunnel where thick, green roots grew over the ceiling and walls. They clung tightly to the smooth stone surface and were so abundant Cade could barely see anything other than what looked like a sea of emerald-colored fingers gripping the world around him. Cade had asked where the roots came from, but Ersia had dodged his question.

"Did you not think we cultivated plant life on our planet?" she'd asked. "We wouldn't have lasted very long if we didn't."

Cade hadn't pressed the matter further, deciding instead to follow Percival's advice and remain cautious around Ersia. Percival didn't trust the Monaskin queen, and neither did Cade. And the deeper she led him down this tunnel, the more his distrust grew. She'd been leading them forward for some time, guiding them by lamplight, and despite agreeing to take Cade to this sacred place, she was very tight-lipped on details. Either she wasn't much of a talker or she was hiding something. Cade assumed the latter.

"Can I tell you something?" Ersia asked. "Between just the two of us?"

Cade paused. He was wary of Ersia; something about her being so young and holding so much power put him on edge. She'd also made him fight a deranged gorgan. Still, he couldn't really say no, given the circumstances. "Go for it," he said.

"I'm glad you healed the gorgan," Ersia said. "I didn't make him that way, you know. That was my brother, which is partly why he's currently held in a prison cell and will be forever."

"Why else is he locked in a cell?"

"He's a sadistic lunatic."

Cade nodded. He knew all about sadistic lunatics; they chased him around the galaxy every single day. "Is that how you came to be queen?"

"Our parents died, and he became king. He sucked at it. So Xeric and I led a revolution and won. We overthrew my brother before he could kill us all, and Monaskis has been a much better place since."

For a moment, Cade found himself liking this teenage queen. "You know, you're not nearly as awful as I'd initially thought you were," he said.

Ersia tsked at Cade. "I didn't ask."

"Look," he said, stepping in front of Ersia and blocking her path, "this banter we're developing is a ton of fun, but you have to clue me in, at least a little bit, as to what we're doing here. What is this place, and what is supposed to happen while we're here? 'Chamber of Memories' is a cool name and all, but I have no idea what the thing actually is."

"You mean you don't have a Chamber of Memories where you're from?"

"Uh, no. I'm pretty sure it's not a very common thing."

"I know," Ersia said flatly, stepping around Cade. "I was kidding."

Cade grinned and followed Ersia.

"I know you've only been on Monaskis for a short time, but have you wondered why we haven't abandoned this planet?" Ersia asked. "Let's be honest: It's literally a bombed-out ruin of what it once was. I'm told it was great at one point, but right now, it kinda sucks. I mean, just the work required to make this place sustainable . . . it's not easy."

"I didn't want to be rude," Cade said, "but yeah, I did find it weird that you all haven't left this place. I mean, I come from Kyysring, which is basically the armpit of the galaxy, and I couldn't wait to get off it. But at least it was in one piece."

"We would leave, but there's one problem," Ersia said as she led them left when they reached a fork in the tunnel. "We're connected to this planet. All Monaskins share a special bond with this place."

Cade followed Ersia, ducking low-hanging roots and maneuvering around others that bulged off the wall. This path, for whatever reason, wasn't treated to the same grooming as the previous passage; the deep scent of wild, musty moss filled the space and rushed Cade's olfactory system like a stimulant. There was something different about this tunnel, and it wasn't just the overgrowth. An indelible aura saturated it, like an otherworldly presence. In another life, Cade would chalk the feeling up to being a little creeped out by the dark, dank tunnel in the middle of a planet that wasn't supposed to exist. But he knew better now. There was something unique about this place, and Cade's sense of it only grew stronger the deeper they went.

"What do you mean you have a special bond?" Cade asked. "In what way?"

"How do I say this?" Ersia said, stroking her chin. "Monaskis possesses certain . . . properties. I wish I could explain it, but I really can't. No one can. It's something that just is. We share a bond, and the bond lasts forever."

Cade continued a step behind Ersia, pushing a root out of his way to keep pace. The root, to his surprise, was wet. Cade examined his hand and wondered where the root could possibly be drawing water from. "Forever?" Cade questioned. "In what way?"

"Well," Ersia started, trying to make what she was about to say sound as natural as possible, "when we die, we stay on Monaskis. Our bodies are buried in the ground, and our spirits become one with, you know, everything. And we can find the spirits of those who are no longer with us in the Chamber of Memories."

Cade squeezed his eyes tightly, just for a moment, and shook his head. Though he didn't think what Ersia said was a lie, he had a hard time believing that it could possibly be true—that you could just go to this chamber and visit any of the people you'd lost.

"And that's why you stay?" Cade quietly asked. "So when you die, you can join the Chamber of Memories?"

"That and so we don't leave our loved ones, and all those who've died over so many generations, behind."

Cade went to speak, but no words came out. Thoughts of Tristan and of his parents flashed across his mind. Memories, snippets of lives he'd once lived—first with his entire family, then with just Tristan—that seemed so very far away. The remembrances were accompanied by profound sorrow, and Cade knew that he'd give anything—anything in the entire galaxy—for just five minutes with his family. If fulfilling his desire meant remaining in the shell of his ancestral planet, he'd never so much as leave its atmosphere.

"You don't believe me," Ersia said after a drawn-out moment of silence.

"No, no, it's not that," Cade said. "It's just—I wish there were a Chamber of Memories everywhere. I wish . . ." He had to pause and fight back the sadness he felt growing within him. "There are some people I wish I could see again."

A sad smile flashed on Ersia's face. "I know. Anyone would feel the same, and that's why we stay hidden. We have to protect this gift at all costs. Which means when you leave, I expect you not to go blabbing about what you see. Got it?"

Cade nodded. He understood.

"Come on," Ersia said, leading them forward again. "We're not far."

Cade took a deep breath and bottled up the longing he'd begun to feel, longing for things that could never be returned to him.

"So, what's going to happen in the chamber?" Cade asked. "What have people learned from Wu-Xia? What's he like?"

Ersia stopped. She turned and looked at Cade, pity flooding her eyes. "Ummm . . . this is where things get awkward. I didn't want to tell you this before, but . . . no one's ever spoken to Wu-Xia in the Chamber of Memories. Ever."

Stifling a stream of obscenities, Cade had to grab hold of a vine to keep himself upright as vertigo began to overwhelm him.

"Are you telling me he's not in there?" Cade asked, unable to conceal how crestfallen he felt.

Ersia shrugged uncomfortably. "Maybe. We really don't know. It could be that his connection to the chamber was severed after what he did to the planet. Or maybe he is in there and he's just not talking to any of us. Maybe only the Paragon can interact with him now. We just don't know."

Cade sighed. "If only there were a Paragon around."

"Oh, have heart. After all, you got me to come around," Ersia said, slapping Cade's bicep in a way that was meant to be encouraging. "Now come, we're here."

Ersia turned and held her lantern high, revealing a tall, narrow door covered in green and yellow lichens. Cade swore it looked like the door itself was pulsing, like it had a heartbeat of its own.

"The Chamber of Memories," Ersia said, pushing open the door. Stone scraped against stone, causing a rumble that echoed down the tunnel. As the door opened, soft light escaped from the sliver that was created. "Only one person can enter at a time."

Cade stepped forward and looked at Ersia; not knowing what to say, he remained silent as he walked toward the chamber.

"I hope you find what you're looking for, Cade," Ersia said as Cade passed by. He turned and saw something in her that he couldn't pinpoint. Like pity, but not. Sadness, he thought. Like a kind of remorse.

She didn't believe he was going to find Wu-Xia, either.

But Cade couldn't turn back; he had no choice but to follow this path wherever it led. The chamber, warmer than the tunnel that led him there, seemed to beckon him inside. Cade had slipped past the threshold without even realizing it, and he felt the power of this place all around him. His nerve, for a moment, flinched, and he thought to turn back. It was too late. Cade turned around just in time to see the door closing.

He was trapped.

CHAPTER NINE

Though Kira still bore the scar of her father's attempt to kill her when she was just fifteen years old, she'd always contended that the emotional damage of what he'd done to her had healed long ago. From early adolescence on, Ebik was hardly in Kira's life, electing to instead dedicate himself to Praxis's military service. From what Kira's mother had told her, Ebik served his planet with distinction, and it was his valor, in part, that won Akima's heart. But it was power that did Ebik in. In one of her uncharacteristically candid moments—Kira's mother had shielded her daughter from the tragedy of her marriage—Akima reasoned that Ebik hadn't always been bad. She believed with unwavering devotion that he hadn't married her for her position as a Baron; he'd married her out of love. But then he changed. He craved Akima's power; it made him sick. Akima, in turn, internalized a great sense of guilt for what her power—given to her by birth, not choice—was turning her husband into. Those feelings worked in concert to wither the tree of their love down to its roots.

Lost in this dynamic was Kira. Too occupied with the political machinations and maneuvers that earned him relevance within Praxis's government, Ebik cast his daughter aside. Having received a dose of power, Ebik lusted after more. And nothing—not even his family—would stand in his way.

When her own father sliced Kira up, the physical pain was deep and profound; the emotional toll, though, was superficial. A decade removed, what bothered Kira most wasn't her father's attempt on her life; it was everything he'd done leading up to that point—his blackhearted mission to usurp his own wife's birthright—that'd taken so much from Kira.

Kira was supposed to be a Baron once she became an adult and her mother decided it was her time to step down. Unlike her father, Kira was never infatuated with the position itself; she didn't look forward to becoming a Baron for the sake of becoming a Baron. Still, Kira grieved all the things she'd hoped to do for her planet once the duty was passed down to her. She imagined her tenure as Baron as being an extension of her mother's and the legacy she'd been working so tirelessly to foster: a legacy of charity, benevolence, and justice. Even when the dark times came—when Ga Halle began her rise to power and started changing the face of Praxis—and Akima's work became more difficult, Kira understood that it also was more vital. The onus was on Akima, Kira, and people like them to push back against the darkness before it consumed too much of their world. Little did Kira or Akima know that their own father and husband was helping to manufacture the black clouds that blotted out the light in their sky.

Though Kira survived Ebik's assault, she'd been stripped of her future and her identity, and in her darkest moments, she was nearly broken by all the good she'd hoped to achieve that would forever be left undone. That's what made Kira's heart twist in her chest. Ebik had robbed her, Akima, and all of Praxis of something that he'd had no right taking, and Kira wouldn't rest until that crime was rectified.

But Kira couldn't explain all of that to Kay. She had no desire to bare her soul to someone she hardly knew, let alone someone she hadn't decided if she could trust or not. When he asked what she was doing back on Praxis, she kept it simple:

"I'm here to free my mother and put that last living Baron back in power so she can save this planet. And then I'm going to make sure Ebik stays out of her path the only way I know how."

"And how's that?" Kay asked, smiling because he knew the answer.

"By showing him the mistake he made ten years ago bringing a triblade to a blaster fight."

They were seated in what passed as the strategy room in the underground bunker Kay and his soldiers had claimed on the outskirts of the capital. Kay was lucky to know this refuge existed. A leftover from Praxis's preindustrial age, these bunkers once housed the labor force that'd been conscripted into building the planet's urban center some three hundred years prior. Praxis had enslaved its own lower class and forced them into brutal labor under miserable conditions, and everyone assumed that any vestige that remained of that dark time had long been destroyed. They were wrong. Kira shuddered when she thought about the workers who'd been forced to live below ground, cramped into this space and only allowed outside when they were called on to perform backbreaking work. She also wondered how many times the soul of her planet had to be saved from itself. Twice too many, at the very least, she ruefully thought.

Kira stood from her dusty metal chair, her nerves too tangled in a ball to let her rest for long. She was still coming down from the heat of their battle and escape, still unsure if she could trust Kay and his rebels, and, most of all, anxious to get to her mother. The room was drab with hazy light casting over the flat auburn surfaces and walls; maps of the city and Praxis's local strategic positions were tacked up behind Kay's head, but they didn't lend much in the way of pleasantness to the space. It was a dark, dank, underground pit. But Kira wasn't there for pleasantries anyway.

"What about you?" Kira asked. "Why are you here? Why are you, of all people, taking up arms against the Praxian power structure?"

"Oh, you want to listen to me now?" Kay teased.

"I'm generally more willing to listen to what someone has to say when I'm not holding a gun on them," Kira said. "So, yeah, I'm all ears."

Kay leaned over the table, taking a deep drink of the root whiskey he'd poured for himself. His eyebrows perked up, and he winced as the burn raced down his throat.

"Give me a drink of that," she said, pulling the bottle away from Kay's hand.

"Nothing settles having people trying to kill you like pouring that rocket fuel down your gullet," Kay said, raising his glass to Kira's for a toast.

She apprehensively clinked her glass against his, then took a drink. It was just as terrible as ever, and she loved it.

"So, you going to talk or keep me in suspense?" Kira asked.

Kay chuckled as he poured himself another drink. "Look, let me just be clear about something, okay? And I don't mean any offense, but I really don't care what you think of me, my soldiers, or what we're doing here. I'm not going to fall over myself trying to convince you of what's in my heart. I'm not. You and your friends have been welcomed here out of respect for your mother. Otherwise, we'd have left you in the streets where we found you. This isn't a game, and we don't take risks."

"You're welcome for that time I saved your life, by the way," Kira said with a cynical laugh.

Kay sucked in a deep breath and sneered as he forced his

gratitude out of his mouth. "You're a good soldier, there's no doubt. But that doesn't change the fact that everyone here has put their lives in my hands, and bringing you and your friends here might be putting them at risk. You don't trust me? Well, I don't know if I can trust you."

Kira smirked. "How'd you get here, Kay?"

Kay smiled in return, though his expression was laced with bitterness. "Same way you got here: the maniac you call a father."

Kira filled her drink again, then she filled Kay's. "May he die horribly," she said, lifting her glass.

"And may at least one of us be the cause," Kay said, tapping Kira's glass.

They swallowed their whiskey down, and Kay continued, "You know most of my story. Ebik took me under his wing when I was a kid. Taught me strategy, combat, weapons—then he fast-tracked me through the military ranks, getting me all the way up to the rank of Warden. Which is exactly where he wanted me to be.

"If you know Ebik, you know he doesn't do anything unless there's something in it for him. He played me with so much ease and so little remorse, I still can't believe it. The years we spent together—he'd become like a father to me—were a lie. I meant nothing to him. He was just putting me in position to help him get what he wanted."

Kay paused and ran through the process of pouring himself, and kicking back, another drink. He offered Kira another, and she shook her head.

"As the Barons' Warden, my job was to be chief of their personal security. I set up patrols at their homes, I arranged guards to accompany them on trips, you name it. My team was with the Barons at all times. But we were more than that, because the Barons had a lot of problems between them. A lot of grudges, a lot of bad blood going back years and years and years. So not only did we protect them from any outside threats, but I was in charge of internally policing each and every one of them. That's how I came to be of value to your father."

Kay moved to pour himself another drink, but Kira grabbed his hand. "Don't let him make you weak," she said.

For a moment, daggers shot out of Kay's eyes as he sneered at Kira's audacity. But his anger was just a flash, and his expression quickly softened. Kay put down the bottle and continued.

"Ebik trumped up a bunch of charges against your mother," he said. "Treason and conspiracy against the crown, in particular. The proof he had . . . there was no proof. Nothing that showed how Akima was doing a single thing that qualified as unlawful. But I trusted Ebik, and if he said that someone was a threat to Praxis and the other Barons, it *had* to be true. And with that in mind, I was obligated to act.

"The Warden is the only person with the power to arrest a Baron, and only the other Barons could convict one of their own of a crime. As Ebik played me, so he played every other Baron. Your mother was in custody and convicted of the crimes Ebik had concocted within a week. And with her out of the way and you missing, he had a clear path to take your mother's role and become a Baron, just like he always wanted."

Kira's rage settled behind her eyes and applied so much pressure that it felt like something would erupt from her forehead. She looked down at her hands and realized they were trembling.

"What about me? How did dear old Dad explain what had happened to his teenage daughter?" Kira said, fighting the urge to grit her teeth until they snapped.

"He said you were destroying evidence, trying to help your mother. And when he threatened to toss you in jail with Akima, you ran. You escaped the planet to avoid punishment."

"And you believed him?"

Kay sighed heavily. "I don't know. I look back at it all now, and

I think there was no way I could have bought into what your father was orchestrating. But at the time . . . I was so loyal to Ebik, so trusting. It was like I was under a spell.

"Eventually, though, I did sober up. Little cracks started to show in the walls Ebik was building. Then the cracks got bigger; they ran straight into the foundation, and before I knew it, everything came tumbling down. You can only fool people so much until they reach a crossroads where they either willingly decide to live the lie or they make a change. I chose the latter. And it was a good thing, because Ebik was on to me. He suspected I was starting to come out from under his thumb, and had he known it with absolute certainty, he would have had me discarded in a heartbeat."

"You went AWOL?" Kira asked.

"A little over two years ago. Went totally off the grid. Luckily, because of my position as Warden, I had comprehensive knowledge of Ebik and Ga Halle's list of 'agitators'—people who, in one way or another, resisted what they were turning our planet into. It took some doing for them to trust me and for all of us to join as a unified thing, but it happened. When Ga Halle massacred the Barons, we knew it was time for us to come out of the shadows and strike back. We've been gaining a lot of support ever since. Because what Ga Halle and Ebik have turned Praxis into—this isn't us. This isn't who we are. Not as a planet, not as a people. And I will not let these power-hungry monsters trash everything we are and commit one atrocity after another in our names."

Kira stared Kay in his eyes; there was tenacity in his gaze, a steadfastness that she had no doubt was a great asset in unifying and leading people. There wasn't a person alive who wanted to rally around someone who wasn't certain. But in those eyes— brown speckled with black—there was also hurt. In the basement of the financial center, Kira had wondered what that hurt meant to Kay, and now she knew. And more importantly, she had little doubt that it was genuine.

"You sure know how to ratchet up the intensity," Kira said as she grabbed the whiskey bottle and poured them both one more drink. "Remind me not to invite you to any parties."

Kay stroked his beard as he swirled his drink. "What? Parties are a great way to meet new people and recruit them with the power of your message."

Kira shot Kay an exasperated look.

"Come on, it's a joke," he said.

"*Is* it?"

Kay shrugged. "I don't know, maybe," he said, and he threw back his drink.

As he did, Gunk hurried into the room, a look of anxiety on his face.

"Sir, I need to speak with you," he said. "It's of the urgent-matter variety."

"You can go ahead," Kay said, motioning his hand toward Kira. "She's with us."

Gunk's eyes darted to Kira for a moment, and she could see his uncertainty. If he hadn't corrected himself, she would have walked herself across the room and backhanded him across his face. After everything she'd done for him, he owed her a life debt, not to mention a modicum of trust.

"Seriously, Gunk?" she questioned.

Gunk's head recoiled into his shoulders, and every muscle in his face went taut—which probably caused quite a strain, Kira imagined, seeing that he was made of rock. He was the portrait of discomfort. "One can never be too careful in a revolution. That's what my mother always says."

"Gunk. The message," Kay said.

After clearing his throat, the Poqlin continued. "Right. We received an urgent transmission," Gunk said. "From Akima."

Kay sprang up from his seat and gasped. Worry—very deep, Kira could plainly see, very real—was written all over his face. "What kind of transmission?" Kay asked, almost frantic. "What did it say?"

"I think you ought to see it for yourself, sir," Gunk said.

Kira's and Kay's eyes met, and Kira knew exactly what was growing within each of them: dread. They didn't waste a second dwelling on it, though. They followed Gunk out of the room, wordlessly, their paces hurried.

"We have to break her out," Kira said. She'd stood up among Kay's gathered audience of soldiers, instigators and outlaws alike, and could feel their skeptical, even scornful, eyes on her. There was nothing but silence hanging in the air, and an uncomfortable one at that. Kira looked over at Kay, who was cupping his mouth in his hand. He bore the expression of a man who'd heard something that he wished he hadn't.

"Am I the only one who was paying attention?" Kira asked, her voice conveying no shortage of disgust at the impassive audience surrounding her. "The people holding her captive are closing in; she doesn't have much time."

"We heard the message," said a squat soldier with a flat nose and eyebrows that formed a thick black slash across his forehead. He stretched his body up as far as it could reach so Kira could see him among the crowd. "And we heard Akima give clear orders: We need to get to our man on the inside and snatch whatever information Akima has to offer, and we have to do it tonight. 'No matter what it takes,' she said. I don't know about you, but that sounds pretty clear to me."

"Are you going to completely skip over the part where she suspects she's been discovered?" Kira snarled, trying her best to shove aside the image of her mother, whom she hadn't seen in over ten years, shaking as she implored her loyalists to follow orders while casually informing them she was about to be killed. She was right there in front of Kira not five minutes earlier, a blurry holographic image that was realer than anything Kira had been able to project in her head over the past decade. Real enough for her to see with her own two eyes; almost real enough for her to touch. Kira had to stifle the avalanche of emotion that threatened to overwhelm her, threatened to paralyze her. She hadn't come all this way, hadn't fought so hard so some grunt with a little bit of nerve could diminish her mother's urgency. She wouldn't let the cowardice that hid behind the call of duty have its day. "That is your commander," Kira continued, "and where I'm from—"

"You're from *here*; we know who you are, Kira Sen," the soldier groaned. "Awfully strange that you come back home and immediately our mission is strangely sabotaged. And now, you want to draw out our troops and defy your mom's orders. Seems like an unlikely coincidence, these things happening all at once."

"That's enough, Private Straker," Kay ordered from the head of the briefing room. He was standing right where Kira's mother—or at least the projection of her mother—had been standing just moments before.

"Just speaking my mind, sir," Straker said with a condescending smile. "But since I have your attention, can you remind me what the chain of command is? Do we take orders from you, or from this—"

Kira was so focused on the raw fury that was burning a hole inside of her as she listened to this Straker run his mouth that she didn't see 4-Qel stride soundlessly behind him. 4-Qel didn't say a single word; he just snapped his left hand, chopping it against the back of Straker's head. The man was knocked out instantly; his head slumped into his chest, then the forward momentum pulled him onto the ground. He landed with a thud.

"Oh no, it's happened again," 4-Qel said. "It's a reflex malfunction that I suffer from; you never know when it's going to strike."

The rest of the soldiers craned their necks to look at 4-Qel, silenced in awe.

"I'm sorry to interrupt," 4-Qel said. "Would anyone else like to follow up on Private Straker's line of conversation?"

One private, a woman who stared without blinking at 4-Qel, raised a shaky hand. 4-Qel called on her.

"Are you . . . are you a *Qel*?" she asked.

"Indeed I am. And everything you've heard about us is true."

The woman slowly lowered her hand. "I think we're good with questions."

4-Qel motioned to Kira, giving her control of the room. Kira nodded, then looked over at Kay, who arched an eyebrow and took a step back. There was a good-natured playfulness in his expression, like he was challenging Kira to win his soldiers over.

"Listen, I'm not into giving long, drawn-out speeches, and we don't have time anyway," Kira said as she paced the head of the room, connecting with as many eyes as possible as she spoke. "I know what Straker was getting at, that I'm too close to all this because Akima is my mother. My response to that is simple:

"Shut your face."

That caught a couple of smiles, which Kira wanted. She knew her best strength as a leader was in being one of them, the grunts. Not one of *them*, the commanders.

"I'm serious," Kira said. "And I know my mother gave clear orders to go after this critical information that she has to share and to not concern ourselves with her. That's a prudent call; it's noble and brave. Any leader worth her salt, myself included, should do exactly the same thing. But my squad has one simple rule, and we don't bend, break, or compromise it: No one gets left behind. *Ever.* And with or without a single person in this room, I will stand by that rule until the day I die. Which is my way of saying that I will not leave my mother—your leader—to die. All I need to know is who's with me."

"What if it's a trap?" Gunk asked. He was standing off to the side, beside Kay, his hands held together at his waist. "I'm not saying she was coerced into making that message to set us up—she would never do that—but the message didn't come over the usual secure channels, probably because she was in a rush. But that being the case, there's no telling who picked it up."

"Then the mission to get her information would be suicide either way," Kira responded.

"Not necessarily," Kay interjected. "Most of the contact with Akima is through a third party, someone on the inside. See, your mother isn't kept in prison; she's captive in the Baron's Overwatch. We have a man on the inside there; she gives messages to him, he gets them to us. That's how this exchange would go down. The kingdom doesn't know who this person is, so they wouldn't be able to intercept the exchange."

"So you think," Kira argued. "You know more than anyone that Ebik knows more than he lets on and doesn't play his hand until he has to."

"True, but if the kingdom did intercept that message, odds are they'll expect us to do something to save Akima."

"Not to mention," Gunk added, "that it's impossible to break into the Overwatch. You'd have to be a master escape artist. Or . . . or a *magician.*"

From the opposite side of the room, Mig fanned his lips. "Nope. Uh-uh. That's what they all say, but no place is impenetrable. Trust me, I know."

"It's true," 4-Qel added. "Mig is exceptional at breaking into places he doesn't belong. I wouldn't be here otherwise."

Kay sighed, but his exasperation was paired with a smile. "Well, what, then?"

Kira looked to Mig, who gave her an affirming nod. It was all she needed to cement her decision.

"We double down," Kira said without a hint of doubt in her words. "Kay, you lead a small strike team in to meet your contact, expecting the worst. I lead a stealth team in to save my mother, expecting the same."

"It's bold and risky," Kay sighed. "But I like it."

Kay turned to face his squad, speaking to them more than Kira. "We do it under one condition: volunteers only. This will be very dangerous. We're talking about going across enemy lines and with no time to prep or strategize. I'll only take people who come along willingly, and there is no shame—none—in turning down this mission."

"Fair enough," Kira agreed, then she turned to the men and women before her and asked, "No one left behind. Who's with us?"

Every hand in the room shot up.

Kira nodded, and her mouth upturned into a determined smile. "All right, then," she said. "Let's show the kingdom exactly what they're up against."

Pink and green neon flashed with nauseating brightness in Kira's eyes, and she wanted to smash every little pixel on the incomprehensibly massive screen to bits. It would do her no good but there was something to be said about striking back against the dizzying display that was scorching her eyesight. She couldn't help but curse kids—every last one of them—and their inability to have their attention drawn by anything short of a seizure-inducing billboard of light and sound. But Kira had more important things to focus on, particularly rappelling down the side of the Baron's Overwatch without being detected.

Standing ninety stories high and guarded tighter than any building in all of Praxis, the Overwatch was less a building and more a military-controlled compound. The ways in which someone trying to break in could get detected, caught, and likely killed were innumerable. Mig had hacked his way deep enough into the Overwatch mainframe to thieve just a glimpse of the security protocols in place: Sentry and alpha drones were pretty much stationed in every nook, cranny, and hallway inside the building; outside, gunners in flying mech suits, accompanied by buzzing raptors, patrolled the building's exterior and ensured no one tried to do the unthinkable.

Which is exactly what Kira, Mig, 4-Qel, and Kobe were doing.

Mig had sold Kira on the idea that scaling the side of the building with the advertisement for Yocando—the video game juggernaut—was their best bet; unlike the Overwatch's other three sides, which were all glass and sparkled with light reflected from the adjacent buildings, the side displaying the hyper Yocando ad at least offered some visual cover. They wouldn't be spotted from the drones on the inside, Mig reasoned, and the display's deep hues at least provided a chance for them to camouflage with the building. It was the only weakness Mig could find on such short notice, and even he admitted it probably wasn't the best or safest way to get inside. When Kay cemented their plan by cashing in a favor with a razor pilot who could get them to the top of the Overwatch unnoticed, the decision was made. But that didn't change the fact that busting into the Overwatch this way required people to be dumb enough to shimmy their way down from ninety stories up and do it with hardly any preparation.

Kira and her friends, apparently, were just the right kind of dumb.

"How much farther?" Kira asked, shouting into the comms headset that connected to the rest of her team. She had to shout over the buzzing din that poured off the Yocando display.

"Just a little bit more," Mig answered, his voice taut and strained. Though the plan was his, that didn't mean he liked it. Blasting off into space in grav suits or any of his similar stunts was one thing; Mig had time to prep, practice, and perfect everything he was going to do. But dropping down the side of a heavily fortified building without any planning or any proper tools—he didn't consider rope, harnesses, and grappling claws to be proper—was something totally different.

Kira, who was just above Mig with 4-Qel and Kobe above her, tightened her grip on the rope, squeezing it so she could feel the harness tighten around her waist. A gunner in a mech suit rumbled by not twenty feet behind her, and she could only hope he didn't detect the four small shapes pressed like lichens against the sea of background color; if he did, they'd be target practice.

"Here," Mig called into the comms. "Right here."

Kira lowered herself to Mig. Every muscle in her body started to feel tense and sore, and when she looked up, just a quick glance, she was surprised to see that they'd only traveled around twenty stories. The physical demands of the journey, compounded with her personal investment, threatened to deplete Kira's energy before they even got inside. She took a moment to breathe and let her body slacken; she knew better than to allow her emotions to intrude on a mission. She preached that lesson to her Omega Squadron constantly. *Keep your focus, keep your perspective.* She reminded herself that the task directly in front of her was all that mattered. First, she had to get inside the building, then she'd knock down whatever obstacle came after that and after that and so on, until there was nothing else in her way. Until she was standing face-to-face with her mother.

"This is where the gap between floors should be," Mig said,

tracing an invisible, not-so-big square against the building with his finger.

"Should be?" Kira questioned.

Mig shrugged. "Hey, you can study the schematics and do all the calculating in the world, but there's no accounting for the times numbers and reality don't align."

"And what if there are alarms between the outside of the building and the inside?"

Again, Mig shrugged. "We didn't scale the side of a building—which was terrifying, by the way—to start second-guessing, did we?"

"No," Kira said, her resolve unflagging. She started to lower herself below Mig and called into her comms as she did. "Four-Qel, get us in there."

With carefully applied strength and the precise calculations given to him by Mig, 4-Qel would be able to punch an opening in the building's exterior big enough for them all to crawl inside. And creating an opening between floors would allow them to avoid detection from the drones waiting within, at least for a little while. It was a good enough plan—and then it was completely shredded when the billboard display went completely white.

Kira looked up, stunned. Against the seamless white glow, they stood out like birds soaring in a cloudless blue sky. A sky that was patrolled by predators hungry for dinner.

"I thought the display didn't change for another hour?" Kobe yelled into the comms.

"Estimates!" Mig yelled back. "I told you it was the best I could do!"

"Both of you shut up," Kira said as she pulled herself back up toward Mig and 4-Qel. "Four-Qel, new plan—screw delicacy. Punch us in there before we're killed."

"My kind of plan," 4-Qel said right before he pounded his fist into the side of the building.

Sparks rained down on Kira from the screen's erupted display, then tiny bits of steel. 4-Qel tore away a chunk of the building's exterior, but it wasn't quite big enough for any of them to pass through.

"Four-Qel, hurry!" Kobe commanded. "Raptor incoming!"

Kira looked to her side and immediately caught an eyeful of a raptor's spotlight scanning the building up and down, left to right, as it approached from the west. It was still a good distance away, but it was coming on fast. They had a minute, maybe less, before the raptor was in range to see the four intruders hanging helplessly off the side of the building it was programmed to protect.

"Four-Qel," Kira admonished, but just as she did, a hulking chunk of shredded steel flew past her face.

"Everyone suck in your breath and move," the drone ordered. He was boosting Mig inside; his slender body just squeezing through the jagged hole 4-Qel had created.

Once inside, Mig kicked away some debris, widening the hole just a little bit. Kobe was the next to go, aided, like Mig, by the powerful drone. Kira looked past them both and saw that the raptor had narrowed the distance between them. They had seconds to get inside.

Before Kira could issue the command for 4-Qel to go next, the drone was lifting her up by her jacket and tossing her toward the opening, where Kobe and Mig were waiting to catch her.

"Hey, no!" Kira yelled, and she was about to protest on the grounds that the commander should always be the last to go, but she didn't get a chance. She was inside the building before she could say another word. And once inside, she realized something that made her heart skip a beat: The opening wasn't nearly big enough for 4-Qel to squeeze into.

"Four-Qel, don't you dare do anything stupid!" she said as

images of the drone sacrificing himself to save his friends overran her mind.

"Stupid is what we do," 4-Qel replied. "Now, please, all of you, get back."

Kira, Mig, and Kobe did as they were told; Kira was turning to crawl through the narrow space they'd been allotted when she saw 4-Qel use his powerful legs to push himself against the building. He swung away from the side and swooped back in, leading with his feet. Whatever building materials stood in his way were pulverized as 4-Qel pushed through them like a drill shredding through drywall. And once he was safely inside, he tugged on the rope that'd been mounted to support all their weight. Kira saw the grappling claw, a chunk of concrete caught in its grasp, drop past the opening.

"The raptor will see the lights are out, but at least it won't see a rope hanging off the building," 4-Qel said. "That would probably give us away."

"I don't know what we'd do without you," Kira said, smiling.

"Die," 4-Qel responded flatly. "You'd all be dead."

Kira nodded, accepting that unfiltered assessments were simply part of the package when living with a Qel.

"Okay, then," she said. "Let's get moving."

Even though they hadn't traveled that far, Kira felt like she'd trudged through miles and miles on her elbows and knees. She was sweaty and exhausted by the time the narrow ventilation space that'd been allotted between floors finally brought them to the elevator shaft. And then it was a grueling climb up six stories before they reached the floor Kay had known Kira's mother to be located on. As she pulled herself up to the ventilation shaft just above the floor they'd been slogging silently to get to, Kira couldn't help but think about how much more she enjoyed the old-fashioned method of blasting her way to where she wanted to go instead of all this sneaking-around business.

As she pulled her body into an even narrower shaft than the one before, her body heavier than she'd ever felt it, she was overwhelmed by a different kind of weight. It was like a metal cuff had been clamped around her throat, and the mass of it was nearly more than she could bear. Kira grasped at her neck, but there was nothing here. Just the weight of what waited on the other end of the shaft.

Her mother, the woman who'd risked everything to save Kira. The woman she'd missed every single day since they'd been torn apart. The woman who'd had the courage to stand up to Praxis before it became a tyrannical kingdom and was redoubling her efforts now that it was. She was the most important person in the galaxy, and Kira was holding her life in the palm of her hand. And Kira was afraid. Not nervous, not worried—this was fear. And fear, Kira knew, could swallow you from the inside out. Sweat dripped off Kira's brow, the salty droplets sliding down the contours of her face.

But all Kira had to do was think of her mother. That crystal-clear memory she held on to, for better or worse, of her father slicing Kira with his triblade. How she fell, stunned by the blood—so much blood—that soaked her shirt and poured out of the slash in the fabric. Then there was the look in his eyes—not crazy, not hysterical, but calm, totally calm as he raised the blade to finish what he'd started. And there was her mother, spearing her father with every ounce of her strength. Her frame was so slight, especially when pitted against her father's chiseled mass. Still, she overpowered him just long enough for Kira to follow her orders: She was to take the small transport ship her mother had arranged for, fly it away from Praxis, and never, ever turn back. Kira, in her panic, in her utter fear, did what she was told. But now she was back. Back to reclaim what'd been lost, what'd been taken from both of them, in whatever small measure that she could.

Fear, in all its power to overwhelm and overpower, had no chance of standing in Kira's way.

Moving slowly and silently, Kira led Mig, Kobe, and 4-Qel to the space just outside of Akima's quarters. Her prison. Through a slatted vent that looked onto the center of the room, Kira spotted at least four sentry drones and one alpha. Easy to defeat, Kira assessed, but that was considering typical means: dropping down from overhead, catching the drones off-guard, and decommissioning them the funnest way possible: with a blaster. But that method would attract a whole lot of attention, and they hadn't circumvented the countless enemies stacked from the first floor all the way up to have the alarm sounded on them now. Caution was in order.

Kira turned to Mig and signaled with her hands a sequence only he understood. He smiled and rolled a small metallic orb her way. She examined it carefully, then held the orb up to Mig. He nodded his assurance, and Kira hit him with a skeptical look. After what had happened with the magnetizer, she couldn't bring herself to feel totally at ease. Mig knew what she was thinking, and he rolled his eyes at her like a sullen teenager. Kira winked at him; Mig was so sensitive about his inventions, and that's why she gave him a hard time. If he wasn't bothered by comments about his work, then teasing him wouldn't be any fun.

Ever so carefully, Kira wrapped her fingers through the slats in the vent and pushed it open. It creaked on its dry hinges, and while the noise sounded so loud it made her cringe, the drones didn't notice. She rolled the orb over in her free hand and found the small activation button on its side. Kira closed her eyes, took a deep breath, and flipped the switch. She then dropped the orb to the ground, where it landed with a hollow *clink*. That, the drones noticed. But if they had any mind to react, they never got the chance. The orb splintered open, and from it fired a hot-pink electric bolt that spun around the room in the blink of an eye, hitting each drone in its chest as it passed. Kira didn't know what shot out of the orb, but it caused the drones to erupt into a fit of convulsions. They spasmed for just a few seconds before each of them crashed to the ground. Kira ducked her head cautiously out of the vent and surveyed the room. Every drone, all seven of them, lay facedown on the porcelain surface, smoldering like they'd just been pulled out of a fire pit.

"Just a temporary loss of power," Mig said as they all dropped to the ground. "They surge and override. Their backup systems should have them back online soon enough, so we don't have too much time."

"Let's just cut the cords on them and put them down for good," Kobe offered, standing over the nearest sentry drone.

"No," Mig ordered. "They're likely wired to the building's mainframe; complete loss of power would trigger the alarm."

As Kobe backed away from the drone, Kira examined the lock on the door. Mig followed at her side. He bit down on his finger as he studied it, making noises that didn't fill Kira with confidence.

"Can you pick it?" she asked.

"My instinct is to let Four-Qel tear it off," Mig said. "But there's no telling if it's connected to an alert system that'll sound if it's tampered with. Soooo . . ."

"So . . . what?"

Mig smiled nervously. "So, we'll just have to see if I'm as good at getting into places as I brag about."

Mig's eyes flashed to the lock, and he went to work with his set of lock-picking tools.

Kira sidestepped over to Kobe, who was standing in a fighting position, his quarter staffs at the ready.

"You expecting someone?"

"Always," Kobe responded, his voice flat. He bore a grim expression that unnerved Kira.

"Something you want to tell me?" she asked, almost suspiciously.

Kobe shook his head almost imperceptibly. "Bad feeling is all. A really bad feeling."

Kira eyed him, about to probe deeper into what Kobe meant when Mig called her.

"I've got it," he said, winded. He, too, seemed to feel the stress of the moment. "You can go in; you can go see your mom."

With a stuttered breath, Kira placed her hand on the doorknob, but then she hesitated. For as many times as she'd dreamed about this very moment, for all the times she'd envisioned reuniting with her mother after so very, very long, she never actually imagined it down to the details. Never down to what she'd say, not exactly, if she ever did see her mother again. Now, that long-pined-for moment was here, just on the other side of a door, and she felt a profound hesitancy. Something, maybe brought on by Kobe, made her intuition tingle—intuition that gave her the feeling that something wasn't quite right.

That feeling passed or was at least put off when 4-Qel placed a delicate hand on her shoulder. She looked at him, and he gave a reassuring nod. It was a reminder of his presence, telling her at the perfect moment that her friends were by her side. And whatever awaited on the other side of the door, they'd be there to face it together.

Gently, Kira eased the door open. It was heavier than she'd expected, and the hinges gave the slightest creak as the doorway slowly revealed more and more of what was previously hidden.

The room defied Kira's expectations. She'd expected her mother's captivity to be harsh and cruel. But the room was . . . peaceful. That was the word that popped to mind as Kira's eyes moved from the deep-magenta couch to the mahogany table to the many, many books that lined the far wall. And there, at the far end of the room, was a slim, proud figure with her back to the door. Her hair was gray, and her posture was assured; she sat at a writing desk, handwriting a note as Kira, Mig, 4-Qel, and Kobe stood in the doorway. She had to have known someone was there, but she didn't bother to acknowledge the presence. Not until she'd finished what she was writing. Memories of her mother's impeccable cursive came to mind as Akima delicately swooped her hand across the page; finished, she placed the cap on her pen, set it down gently, and said without turning around, "Get on with it, then."

Kira looked at Mig, who was just as speechless as she was. Here Kira was, defying the odds and all obstacles to save her mother, and she mistook her for an executioner.

"Mom?" Kira said softly as she took a step deeper into the room. "Mom, it's me."

The moment Kira spoke, Akima's posture broke. Her violent death she could handle with grace and dignity. But this—this was something different. Kira could see her mother's hands spread across the desk, her shoulders narrow, as slowly she began to pivot in her chair. Kira thought to say something but didn't; instead, she waited as, little by little, her mother's face was revealed to her. Akima stood, and for the first time in over ten years, they were looking eye to eye.

Akima placed her palm against her chest and stumbled a quarter step back. She braced herself on the back of the chair, and Kira noticed that the hand gripping the upholstery was trembling.

"Kira?" she called breathlessly.

For a moment, Kira was taken back to long afternoons in their garden, tending to their vegetables, drenched in sunshine; back to games of hide-and-seek, her mother singing her name as she searched all around for her only child, even though she knew where she was hiding; back to being tucked in at night, feeling safe in her mother's care.

Kira took a step forward, hesitant, as if at any moment the floor could disintegrate beneath her feet. "I'm here to get you, Mom," Kira said, breathing back tears. "I'm here to get you out."

Akima raced to her daughter and threw her arms around her; Kira melted into her embrace.

"Is it really you?" Akima asked as she gently held Kira's face in her hands. "How did you get here?"

Kira laughed awkwardly, and the levity was like opening the hatch to all the pent-up emotions that were ready to erupt within Kira. She felt a good measure of relief. "That's a long story. I'll tell you all about it when we're far away from here."

Kira turned back to her squad, and the moment she did, she felt queasy all over. Mig was pressing his comms unit tightly to his ear, a look of consternation on his face as he tried to hear whoever was radioing him more clearly. Kira's and Mig's eyes met, and she immediately read exactly what he was feeling: dread. Dread and panic.

"Oh no," Mig gasped.

Kira switched her comms on—she'd turned it off before stepping into her mother's chambers—and was hit by the sound of carnage. Someone—it sounded like Kay—yelled something she couldn't understand, and then the transmission cut out.

"It was a trap," Mig said. His hand slid slowly off the comms unit in his ear and over his mouth, covering it. "They had no chance."

"Are they—" Kira said, then paused to steel herself. "What's their status?"

"Full retreat. Kay said only a few of them are left, and they're fighting their way to the emergency evac."

Kira's hand had been clenched within her mother's; they were holding each other like their idea of forever had just been reduced to mere minutes. Kira felt Akima's fingers slacken, her grip loosen. And though she tried to hold on, she felt her mother slipping away from her.

"This is all my fault," Akima said as she moved away from Kira. Her steps were weak, and Kira feared she would have collapsed had she not supported herself on the back of the couch. "I should have never sent that message; it was desperate and foolish. And now . . . and now . . . all those people . . ."

Kira rushed to her mother's side, propping her up. "No," she said, her voice stern with conviction. "This is not on you. This is Praxis. This is Ebik and Ga Halle and whoever else. Not you."

Akima caressed Kira's arm and smiled the way parents do when telling their children things will be all right despite overwhelming evidence to the contrary. "I have to fix this."

"And you will; trust me, you will. We all will."

Kira shifted back to her squad and returned to command mode. It helped her force down the terrible feeling festering inside of her. "Let's get back on target. Mig, call for the roof evac. If we get moving, we should be able to make it up there in—"

"Take this," Akima said, interrupting Kira and placing a data disk in her hand. "It's everything you need to know, everything I tried to get to Kay but . . . but didn't."

Kira laughed mirthlessly. "You can tell him yourself when you see him."

Akima wiped an errant dreadlock away from Kira's face and smiled. The smile was forced, Kira could see, just as clearly as she could see the tears her mother was holding back.

"My brave little girl. I've asked *so much* of you. And now, I have to ask for even more."

"What are you talking about? Everything is going to be fine. We're going to be fine."

Kira knew this wasn't true, but she hoped just this once that her mother would be able to wave a magical wand over all her troubles the way parents do and make everything better.

"I'm so sorry," Akima said, maintaining her smile. "But you have to leave me here."

Kira wanted to collapse. She wanted to drop to her knees and let her body go limp. Yet somehow, she stayed on her feet. A small part of her tried to convince herself that Akima was making the right call, that this was best for the mission. The mission. Always the mission. Kira was sick of the very word, sick of Praxis, sick of everything. All she wanted was her mother, and it was the cruelest joke to be given this glimpse of the life she'd lost only to have it torn away.

"You must have picked the lock to get in," Akima continued, not wasting any time. "If you'd destroyed it, this room would already be overrun by drones. The same for the drones outside—I'm assuming they're only disabled? That means you can leave, and they'll never know you were here. They'll never know that the message I was trying to get out did, in fact, get out."

"No, no," Kira protested, and at once, she felt like a child again, stomping her feet, pushing back against whatever she was being told to do. But she knew then, just as she knew now, that it was futile to resist. Still, she couldn't stop herself. She couldn't let go. "You're coming with us. We have to leave, all of us."

"My daughter, my life. I wish, more than anything in the galaxy, that there were another way. But they can't know that I passed along this information. The only chance you have to stop your father is if he doesn't know you're coming."

"I don't care about Ebik. I don't care about any of this," Kira said, losing the battle to keep the tears from flowing down her face. "We lost each other once; I'm not going to lose you again. I can't."

Akima's shoulders sank into herself, and she closed her eyes. She had to reestablish her own resolve, which was weakened by her daughter's plea. When she opened her eyes again, her conviction had returned.

In that painfully brief yet infinite moment, Kira knew that she had lost her mother forever.

"He's going to destroy Praxis," Akima said. "The entire planet. They've kept the energy Ga Halle has taken from extinguishing stars all these years. Amassed it. And now they've harnessed it into a weapon that has the capacity to kill every man, woman, and child who calls this place home."

Kira gasped and staggered backward. "No . . . no, he can't."

"He can and he will," Akima said. "Ebik is capable of doing it, and worse, he's willing. His insecurity and fear dominate everything he does, and this rebellion has threatened to take away the thing he cherishes most—his power. He'd rather see Praxis destroyed with everyone on it than lose what he thinks is his. I know how he thinks, Kira. He doesn't need this planet, and neither does Ga Halle. They have the entire galaxy."

"But, Mom, I—"

"You have to stop him, Kira. Everything you need to know is on that disk. Get to the Crucible, disarm the weapon. It's the only way to stop your father."

Behind her, though distantly, Kira heard the elevator faintly ding. Someone was coming.

Mig rushed out of the room. "I can short-circuit the car, but the backup generator will kick on quickly."

"Leave," Akima said, pushing Kira toward the door.

There was no time for sentiment, no time for anything other

than fighting and surviving. Sometimes, Kira felt like those were the only two things she knew.

"I can buy you time, but you have to hurry," Akima urged.

Kira shook her head, protesting the inevitable. She was torn apart by two sides of a conflict. One side compelled her to stay, to remain at her mother's side and let someone else defeat evil this time. The other side compelled her to go, to be the obedient daughter and make the sensible, moral choice; to dig deep and rally her spirit in order to save millions of lives. Kira couldn't decide which path to choose. "I *can't*," she whispered. "Mom, I can't do this without you."

Akima wiped away her tears and kissed her daughter's forehead softly. She looked into her daughter's eyes and smiled. "All these years, I've been right by your side, Kira. I've marveled at your bravery, I've felt your wonderful heart, and I've seen all of your tremendous accomplishments. I'm so very, very proud of you, and I know you can do this without me. You already have. Now go."

Kira felt a strong yet gentle hand grasp her bicep. Out of the corner of her eye, she saw Kobe; she felt him pulling her back. "They're coming," he said, and she knew she had to go. But her feet wouldn't take her away—not until Kobe spun her around, tearing her gaze off Akima.

"Remember my sister," he said firmly. "Remember the promise I made to her, the promise we share to never let Praxis commit genocide again. Remember, Kira."

Kira looked into Kobe's eyes. She saw the pain and the resolve that coursed deep within him, and she knew it was what the fight she'd involved herself in demanded: loss and hardship. They were part of war, and Kira had to accept them regardless of the pain they caused her. Her only choice was to keep moving forward, to keep fighting until the war was won. Until the pain that Praxis brought to innumerable lives was over.

She followed Kobe out of her mother's room, allowing herself one last look at her mother. Akima waved and mouthed the words "I love you."

And as 4-Qel raised her into the ventilation shaft and Mig reset the lock on the door, Kira knew she'd just seen her mother for the final time.

CHAPTER TEN

G o back," the voice whispered. "Go back."
    It was a small voice, but a convincing one. It called from
the back of Cade's mind, making his every step all the more hesitant. Soft, green light penetrated through cracks in the walls and the ceiling, though Cade could hardly venture to guess its source. Not natural, it couldn't have been. But Cade had to rely on that light to guide him through the chamber's darkness and past the thick union of roots that hung down to his waist, one cautious step at a time. The voice called within him again, urging him to retrace his steps all the way back to the chamber's entrance. Cade knew, even with Ersia's blessing, that he didn't belong in this place, but that didn't make him feel afraid. It made him feel reverent.

His path began to slope just slightly, and it continued to steadily descend until Cade arrived at a circular trench dug about three feet below the ground's level. The trench had to be fifty feet in diameter, and tearing through its center was an enormous gnarled tree. Slowly, Cade stepped into the trench, his focus fixed

206 | MICHAEL MORECI

on the tree the entire time. As he walked toward it, his eyes followed its twisting and turning body upward. Dried, blackened bark clung like scabs to its weathered exterior; branches sprouted and curved upward, stretching as if trying to grow toward the light of a star that would never come. All the tree managed to reach was darkness, and eventually, it was swallowed by the chamber's swirling mists.

Cade circled the tree, eyeing it warily. He reached out but stopped short of running his fingers along its abrasive exterior; the dry and jagged bark looked sharp to the touch, and Cade had learned that in these kinds of situations, it was best to leave well enough alone. Whatever the tree was—a monument, maybe a grave marker—it felt sacred, like something that held great significance to someone. And that someone wasn't Cade. In fact, like the tree that improbably stood before Cade's eyes, the entire chamber was imbued with a similar sense of profundity. Cade didn't have to think hard to remember where he'd experienced this type of feeling before.

The Quarrian spire, right before Tristan removed the Rokura from its stasis and was then murdered.

Whatever this mystical and mysterious presence was, it was as palpable to Cade as the fog that rolled over the gates on Tannhauser. The sense of awe that shrouded Cade like a well-worn cloak also made him feel distant from everything around him. Maybe it was his way of dealing with the enormity of what he knew he was there to do, or maybe it was just a feeling that naturally came to people when presented with the unknown. After all, the Chamber of Memories was a place where the people of Monaskis went to commune with loved ones whose deaths should have made their absence irrevocable. Yet if the power of this place held true, then death held no authority here. Cade only wished he could somehow draw on this gift; if he could, then his brother would only be a magical call away. Cade yearned for Tristan's guidance, if only for one last time. For a single moment, Cade closed his eyes and thought of Tristan, and he sorely missed how much more the world made sense when his brother was in it. It wasn't just because of what Cade's life had become because of the Rokura, nor was it about the relentless pursuit levied on him by Ga Halle in her quest to take from Cade something that neither one of them should rightfully possess. It was simply about Cade having to adjust to a galaxy that was absent his brother; it was about how his entire grip on reality was shattered the moment his brother was killed. He rarely slept peacefully since acquiring the Rokura, but on those rare occasions when sleep came easily, he'd dream of his brother, alive and well—but like all dreams, these visions came to an end, and the sutures that stitched together his grief were torn apart by his waking life. Sometimes, Cade wondered if he'd ever acclimate to a life that was so far removed from Tristan.

His eyes still closed, Cade's mind wandered. To life, to death. It felt like the first time he'd had any real quiet since falling unconscious in the spire on Quarry, and the silence was so absolute that he could hear Tristan's voice as if it were calling out to him from the dark.

"It's remarkable, isn't it?" The words came softly to Cade, almost like they were whispered on the wind. But they weren't, Cade realized, and he popped his eyes open.

He spun around, leading with the Rokura.

No one was there.

As he searched the darkness, looking for a shadow to crawl across a patch of light, his mind remained fixed on the last time he was in a dark, mystical chamber and how an ambush led to a shido being thrust through his brother's heart. Cade wasn't about to let the same thing happen to him.

"You can sense how special it is. How . . . unique. There's a certain energy that moves throughout—even through both of us as we stand here."

The voice was behind Cade again, inexplicably. Cade turned, and this time, light caught the corner of his eyes. He stopped short of a full rotation, and just off to his right, Cade saw a man standing among the roots that hung outside the trench. The man was bathed in the same green light that illuminated the bleary space. He began to walk toward Cade, passing through the vines. Not around them—the man passed through them like they weren't even there. Or like he wasn't there.

"You—" Cade began, dismayed, even though he was looking right at—or through, depending on the angle—who he'd come to the chamber to find. "You're Wu-Xia."

"And you," Wu-Xia said, bringing his eyes to Cade's, "are Cade Sura."

Wu-Xia walked toward Cade, though his footfalls didn't make a sound. He was dressed in a simple gray cloak that clasped tightly from his neck to his waist and billowed out down his legs. Though his chest was wide and strong, his body was otherwise lithe and nimble. In the light that drizzled down into the trench, Wu-Xia moved with so much grace it seemed as if he could bob and weave around the dust motes that fluttered through the air.

"How do you know who I am?"

Wu-Xia's thin lips smiled at Cade, and almost imperceptibly, he nodded. He was just a hair taller than Cade, though Cade still felt dwarfed by his presence. Wu-Xia studied Cade with deep gray eyes that were both soulful and kind, but there was a harder edge to his glance, a steeliness behind his pupils that was as sharp as a dagger.

"If we spend our time discussing how I know what I know, we'll have time for little else," Wu-Xia said. "You have work to do."

Cade took a deep breath. He had plenty of questions about how the chamber worked, how Wu-Xia could possibly be standing in front of him, and why he'd chosen to reveal himself to Cade and no one else, but he didn't have the luxury to pursue any of that. Time was running out; the galaxy was waiting.

"Then you know why I'm here," Cade said.

Wu-Xia nodded and turned away from Cade. He approached the tree and inspected it just as Cade had moments before.

"This isn't the only one," Wu-Xia said. "There are other places in the galaxy—other beings, even—that feel the way this chamber does. That are . . . different. Some are good; some are not."

Wu-Xia continued to study the tree, and Cade studied Wu-Xia. There was mournfulness in his eyes, and Cade feared he was to blame. Wu-Xia looked like a doctor mustering the willpower to deliver a tragic diagnosis. He remained silent, and Cade considered what Wu-Xia had said, about other places in the galaxy being special. Cade knew what Wu-Xia was getting at.

"The spire on Quarry—that's another one of these places, right?"

"And now you're here, and you want me to tell you what happened in that spire. You want to know how I made the Rokura so long ago."

"If it'll help me, yeah. That's exactly what I came here for."

"You wish me to train you?" Wu-Xia said absently as he looked up the tree.

Cade shrugged. "I don't know. Is that what it takes?"

Wu-Xia looked at Cade with his mournful eyes and beckoned him to his side. "What do you think this is?" he asked once Cade was standing next to him.

Cade cocked an eyebrow. "I'm pretty sure it's a tree."

"It's more than a tree, Cade Sura. Its existence is impossible;

it shouldn't be able to grow without water and starlight, and yet here it stands. This tree is *life*, and sometimes life doesn't need a reason. Sometimes life simply is."

"I . . . I'm sorry," Cade said, bowing his head. He felt like he should know what Wu-Xia was trying to tell him—that a Paragon would be able to decode his wisdom. "I don't understand what you mean."

Wu-Xia turned away from the tree and focused his attention on Cade instead. "First, it was your parents. Then your brother. Then Jorken. Percival. And now me," Wu-Xia said. "You, Cade Sura, are always looking for someone to tell you what to do. You never allow yourself the opportunity to *be*."

"It's not like that," Cade said. His words came out low and hard.

"No? Then tell me again why you're here."

Typically, Cade would have been more than happy to offer a sardonic response in order to evade conversations that made him uncomfortable. Humor, even self-deprecation, was his shield. But as he stood feeling oppressed by the utter silence of the chamber, Cade couldn't think of anything to say. His life had veered into a direction it should have never gone the moment he'd left Kyysring for the Well. Jorken himself confirmed this deep-seated truth that festered within Cade for years, an itch he couldn't scratch. He didn't belong at the Well; he was only there because of his brother, which meant he wasn't even a real Rai. He was just *there*, and he'd never achieved enough comfort in his own life, in his own skin, to seek out a path that suited him. So, he'd followed. He'd followed Tristan to Ticus, he'd followed Jorken through training, and with both gone, he'd moved right to following Percival in the hopes he could make sense of another role he wasn't suited for. Content to pursue paths trod by others, Cade never so much as took a single step on a trail of his own making. And now, he found himself at the end of a path, in a place he didn't belong, and there was no one there to tell him where to go.

Cade stared at Wu-Xia. He tried to mine a compelling response to Wu-Xia cutting to the heart of his true identity, but there was nothing for Cade to say. Wu-Xia was right. Cade was, and always had been, a follower.

All he could do was look away.

"I shouldn't be here," Cade said. His head was angled down, and his words tumbled to the ground. "I shouldn't be doing any of this. I'm not the Paragon; I'm not the Chosen One."

"What if I told you," Wu-Xia said, "that there was no Paragon. No Chosen One."

"I'd say you're full of sh—" Cade stopped himself and cleared his throat. "I'd say that's not what I've heard. And seen. And experienced."

"Think of this place. People can come here and visit ancestors, long dead, like they were still among us. Think of the spire where I made a weapon more powerful than the galaxy has ever known. In my bones, my heart, my soul, I feel the power of these places. And you do, too. Something exists in this galaxy that is outside ourselves. Unseeable, unknowable. But it's there. The Chamber of Memories is proof of this."

Cade had been nodding along to Wu-Xia's words, but his agreeable nods transitioned into confused shakes by the time Wu-Xia was finished. "Wait . . . I don't know what you're talking about. I thought I did, but . . . no. You lost me."

Wu-Xia smiled. "The galaxy guides us, Cade. And in times of great peril or danger, times of great change, it finds someone to correct its course. It chose Percival to try to stop what was soon to happen with Praxis, and it chose your brother to, in a sense, correct its own mistake."

"And it chose you," Cade added.

"But I wasn't the first; there've been others," Wu-Xia said, then he turned to Cade with a renewed sense of mournfulness in his eyes. "I was just the first to make a terrible mistake."

Cade studied Wu-Xia, expecting to see some kind of levity to break his mien; he expected Wu-Xia to somehow betray the notion that the Paragon could make a mistake. But the break never occurred, and Cade realized Wu-Xia was telling the truth. Something terrible had happened.

Wu-Xia shifted his eyes away, and with a swipe of his hand, he brushed the space above his and Cade's heads. The arc of his movement left a black smear behind it, and in that swath of obsidian, an image began to take shape.

It was Ga Halle. She looked down at Cade, her eyes burning red, the horns twisting off her head. She said nothing, only stared at Cade, burrowing a hole into his soul. A chill ran up his spine. He'd always been frightened of Ga Halle, but in a more practical way. She was a cruel tyrant, and that was something to be fearful of, particularly when you're the one who must stop her. But now, his fear was more primal; he feared Ga Halle the way he'd feared the monster under his bed when he was just a kid. It was as if she'd become something otherworldly, something without reason. She was simply a manifestation of evil. And as Cade trembled before her, he tried to convince himself it was only an image he was seeing and nothing more. But he wasn't certain.

The black smear faded and Ga Halle with it. Cade exhaled.

"I've tried," Cade admitted. "I've tried to make myself the Paragon. I've trained. I've focused. I almost sacrificed my life for this, but I don't know that I can defeat her."

"What do you feel when you hold the Rokura?" Wu-Xia asked.

Cade looked down and studied the weapon in his hand. Right now, he felt nothing. But when he did feel something—that loud, poignant call that refused to leave him be—he knew exactly what it was.

"What do you mean?" Cade stalled.

"Don't look to me for your answer. Just tell me: What do you feel?"

"Look, it's your weapon. Or the galaxy's or . . . whatever. What I feel in it probably isn't all that important since—"

Wu-Xia stepped in front of Cade. His jaw clenched, the muscles in his face tightened, and his eyes narrowed. Cade could see the shadow of the man who'd once led the Monaskin army to conquer half the galaxy. It was more than a little scary.

"What. Do. You. *Feel?*" Wu-Xia asked.

Cade closed his eyes and drew a deep breath. He didn't need the Rokura to call to him; he could feel the shadow of its pull even when it was dormant. It was powerful and clear.

"Evil," Cade said as he opened his eyes. "I feel pure evil. It wants me to do terrible things; it compels me to do terrible things. And sometimes, I come close to giving in. I mean, there's goodness in there, too. A lot of it, and it's powerful. But I don't think it can overcome whatever this evil is."

"And that, Cade Sura, is my legacy."

Once more, Wu-Xia brushed his hand over his head, again manifesting a black smear. This one remained dark, and Cade thought maybe he was missing something. But then, an image began to brighten as blue orbs cast their illumination over the scene.

"Chrysthums," Cade pointed out. "From Quarry."

The orbs' glow grew, and Cade could see the mist-shrouded walls of the spire take shape. The chrysthums floated through the space, leading Cade's eyes to a certain point the way they had led him and Tristan to the Rokura when this whole thing started.

The orbs converged. And in their unified light, they revealed the outline of a man sitting cross-legged on the ground. Cade took a step closer to the portal Wu-Xia had created as the orbs descended, but he already knew who they'd reveal: Wu-Xia, his body projecting a blue aura as he meditated in the chrysthums' glow.

"I made the weapon in my own reflection," Wu-Xia said as he stood next to Cade. As Wu-Xia spoke, Cade watched in awe as shards of metal—or whatever the Rokura was made of—materialized and swirled above Wu-Xia's head. He remained meditative, eyes closed, as it happened.

"You must understand," Wu-Xia continued, "my life was one defined by war and conquest. I was given a weapon when I was a child, and I had one in my hands until the day I returned the Rokura to the spire where it was made."

The spire trembled all around Wu-Xia. Not as violently as when Tristan took hold of the weapon, but the walls and ceiling shook with an intensity that was impossible not to notice. As the chamber quaked, the swirling shards began to join, bonding piece by piece. Wu-Xia's body trembled—perhaps from the unstable ground he was resting on, but likely more from the strain of his focus. His lip upturned, and he seemed to be experiencing intense pain, though Cade found it hard to read his expression. Regardless of whatever Wu-Xia was enduring, his concentration didn't waver, and the Rokura continued to assemble above his head.

"Over time, I came to experience things that changed my heart and mind, but the change came too late for me. Because when I made the Rokura, I still knew evil; I *embraced* evil. There was goodness in me, too. But all too often, I used evil as a means to achieve righteous ends. All too often, I took that easy path, and I was wrong."

Cade saw the Rokura's blades forge; he saw the hilt and the staff take shape until, finally, all the pieces of the Rokura became one. The most powerful weapon the galaxy had ever known was created.

"There were two sides of my life that were entangled as deeply as the roots of this tree," Wu-Xia said. "Good. Evil. And I was convinced that, even to bring peace, you needed both; you needed, at times, what was wrong to get to what was right. And in my hubris, I thought I could control both sides in equal measure."

The spire stopped quaking, and the Rokura's light extinguished. All that remained was Wu-Xia, the chrysthums, and the weapon. Slowly, it floated down into Wu-Xia's open hands; his fingers wrapped around its hilt the moment it touched his flesh, and his eyes finally opened. In his mind, Cade was taken back to the moment Tristan united with the Rokura; Cade could see the look on his brother's face as clear as if it happened yesterday. There was peace and calm, relief and happiness. He looked how the bringer of galactic peace and justice should look, and it comforted Cade. Wu-Xia's expression brought Cade no comfort. Ferocity replaced tranquility, determination replaced calm. Wu-Xia looked like a man out to prove something deeply personal, and whatever it was, it was more important than allaying the galaxy's unrest. Suddenly, Cade thought of Monaskis—particularly how it had been destroyed by Wu-Xia's hand.

"I infused both good and evil into the Rokura, and it was the greatest mistake I've ever made."

The image of Wu-Xia in the spire faded away, and when Cade looked to Wu-Xia, he saw how heavily regret weighed on his life—and even his afterlife.

"I know in my heart that I was a good person, and I wanted to do good things, remarkable things. But I made the same mistake all good people make when trying to fight back against evil. When confronted with the galaxy's darkness, we think good will naturally overcome as if that is the natural way of things. We think evil will see the error of its ways and come around to our side. But we're wrong, and we never realize the truth until it's too late."

Cade winced. The Rokura felt heavier than ever in his grasp. "What is the truth?"

"Evil will not be negotiated with," Wu-Xia said, his face as implacable as stone. "You cannot bargain with it, you can't compromise with it, and you certainly cannot use it for your own means lest you become evil yourself. That's why I brought the Rokura back to Quarry. I used my power as the Paragon to freeze it there until someone like me—someone chosen by the galaxy, but better than I was—came along.

"Your brother was incorruptible. Percival was, too, although it only took moments of being exposed to the Rokura's true nature to take his innocence from him."

"So what do I do, then?"

"Vanquish it. It's the only way to truly stop evil. You must burn it at its roots and then burn its ashes."

"Okay . . . okay," Cade said. He nodded agreeably, but he had no idea why. "I really hope this is the part where you share some specifics and say something like, 'But there's hope . . .'"

Wu-Xia smiled and clasped Cade's shoulder. The gesture was symbolic, though; Wu-Xia was incapable of clasping anything. "Ego was my downfall. True power never comes from within your own self; it comes by learning from others, by surrendering yourself to the world around you. You need to be strong, Cade Sura, there's no question, but you must use that strength for the betterment of the whole. But you already know this."

Cade laughed defensively. "I wish you were right. Most times, when it comes to the Rokura, I don't feel like I know much of anything."

"Oh, but you do. Twice, you've done something remarkable, and you don't even realize it," Wu-Xia said, and he looked at Cade with an expression of pleasant awe. "You were prepared to surrender your life on the *War Hammer*—not to secure the Rokura's power for its own sake but to protect others. You did it to save your friends and countless other people you'll never even meet. Ga Halle would never even consider such a sacrifice; the very idea undermines the only thing she cares about, which is acquiring the weapon for no reason other than her belief that she's owed it."

"Okay, but being better than Ga Halle—morally, at least—is a goal everyone should strive for, Paragon or not."

Wu-Xia scoffed. "If that were true, then she'd have far fewer followers," he said. "There was a second instance as well—when you tamed the gorgan in the arena. You drew upon the Rokura's goodness to heal the gorgan. I've never even dreamed of something like that being possible. You laid down your ego and took a chance that could have gotten you killed. And you did it thinking only of the gorgan and its suffering. You, and you alone, brought forth the Rokura's goodness through the dark."

Cade admitted, if only to himself, that the moment with the gorgan was meaningful. If only because it felt so different from any other experience he'd had with the Rokura. It was the first time he'd used it the way *he'd* wanted to use it. He wasn't trying to mimic what he assumed Tristan would do, nor was he trying to decipher what the Rokura wanted and compromising with it just to survive. The Rokura had finally become an extension of his own self, and Cade was actually happy with what he'd been able to accomplish using the weapon's power. Cade would be comfortable—proud, even—to let Kira, Mig, and 4-Qel witness him using the Rokura in such a way, which was a stark contrast to how he'd felt about them watching him take Ortzo's head off with a concentrated blast. He'd never thought that'd be possible, but seeing the gorgan relieved of its misery gave Cade a glimmer of hope that maybe things could work out with the weapon after all.

Maybe. Because Cade still harbored many doubts.

"That's great, Wu-Xia, really. But it still doesn't change the fact that I'm not the Paragon. I'm not the person chosen by the galaxy or whatever to stabilize its course."

"No, you're not the Paragon—you're something *else*," Wu-Xia said as he looked at Cade with eyes that were both sympathetic and hopeful. "And maybe that's a good thing. You don't carry the burden of having been chosen. You're free of the rigid constraints that bound everyone who came before you, and that means you can do things that even I could not.

"I see things, Cade Sura. Being unstuck from time and space has given me more wisdom than I could have ever obtained while I was still alive. And I know you've spent so much of your life searching for your identity, for your place in the galaxy. But you've always sought the answers for these questions in anyplace other than where your real truth can be found—within your own self."

Wu-Xia stepped back to the tree and flashed his hand in its direction. "Think of this tree. Think of it and remember that life just needs to *be*—and so do you. I saw you do it in the *War Hammer* and again in the arena; you followed your own instincts, which tell you to protect others. To do for others before you do for yourself. And in those instances, you were never more powerful.

"Cade Sura, you separated the light from the darkness within the Rokura, darkness that should not, and need not, be there. What you seek lies within your own heart—you just need to be brave enough to follow it."

The aura around Wu-Xia began to fade as he slowly stepped away from Cade. Wu-Xia was leaving, and Cade suddenly felt a rush of panic throughout his body. He still had so many questions, so many things to learn and to understand. And if everything Wu-Xia knew was lost now, Cade feared it would be gone from the galaxy forever. That would leave him solely responsible for the Paragon's legacy.

"Wait!" Cade pleaded, but Wu-Xia continued to fade. "What I did with the gorgan, I don't know if I could do that again. I'm not even sure how I did it in the first place."

"Just be, Cade Sura," Wu-Xia said as the light of his existence was snuffed out. "Just *be*."

Cade bowed his head and ran his fingers through his hair. His shoulders slumped as he exhaled sharply. When he looked up again, he realized how much darker the chamber was, absent of Wu-Xia's light. It made him feel small and very much alone. Cade turned toward the exit, and the stone door rumbled itself open right on cue.

The open door let in a sound that stopped Cade in his tracks. His blood ran cold, and he had to turn his ear toward the door to confirm what he was hearing, because he couldn't believe it.

Traveling all the way though the tunnels that led to the Chamber of Memories, past the overgrown roots that threatened to bury the entire path, was the sound of blaster fire as distinct as anything Cade had ever heard. Then an explosion.

Monaskis was under attack.

Cade raced through the tunnels, his heart thumping in his ears. He needed more time to put what Wu-Xia had taught him into practice; to learn how to control the Rokura the way he had on the *War Hammer* and in the arena. But neither would happen, not now. Praxis was coming for him—they'd always be coming for him.

Unless he finally did something about it.

CHAPTER ELEVEN

Rivulets of water ran down the side of the diminutive bunker's abrasive concrete wall and pooled in accordance to the room's sloping grade. Rain had been steadily drumming the surface for hours, and Kira felt the dampness that it brought deep in her bones. Kira welcomed the steady downpour; its consistent rhythm was like white noise that sheathed her in solitude and helped detach her from the rest of the world. Secluded in her tiny space—she could simultaneously touch the walls on either end of the room—Kira worked hard to keep her mind focused, forbidding it to wander toward anything other than the mission at hand. She stood above the single twin-size bunk that was just able to squeeze inside the room and not block the door, studying the weapons cache she had laid out on the bare, musty mattress: two sidewinders, fully charged, with a half dozen extra charge packs; a whipblaster and an extra charge; a tri-blaster, because you never knew; and a half dozen proton-charged explosives, all Mig's making.

"That should do it," Kira said, and she went through the

process of checking that each blaster was fully loaded and that the explosives were free of the detonation glitches that often plagued similar models. As the serpentine streams of water passed beneath her feet, Kira felt a sense of quietude within herself. She was grateful for it. It was just her and her weapons locked inside this tiny room, and they could have been floating in the vacuum of space for all she cared. She only needed one thing: a plan. But she could always stitch one of those together along the way. What was important was that she amassed a Praxian body count on the journey from Kay's underground bunker to Praxis's nearest moon, which was where the Crucible was located.

Kira breathed deeply as she worked, considering the silence around her. She liked the idea of being surrounded by nothingness, particularly as it captured how she'd felt ever since being dragged away from her mother's quarters. She was numb from heartbreak, numb from disbelief. All she knew was that the only thing she had left of her mother was an image of her face, looking steadfast and brave, as Kira abandoned her to die. The woman who'd saved Kira from the very same evil that now threatened her own life was a picture of tranquility as she steeled herself for her eventual trip to the gallows. And all Kira could do was turn and run. To save the lives of millions—to save Praxis from total annihilation—Kira had to sacrifice the life she cherished most. Suddenly, Kira was fifteen again and overwhelmed by the enormity of the circumstances engineered by her ruthless father. But this time, it wasn't fear that threatened to paralyze her; it was rage. She thought of the series of events that led her to having to make such a damnable choice—abandoning her mother in order to save the entire planet or staying by her side as her heart compelled—and she knew that every link along that chain was poisoned by Ebik's touch.

But there was no time for distraction or for dwelling on the past, so Kira took all the love for her mother and all the fury for her father, worked them into tiny balls, and shoved them down deep within herself. They were her fuel; they were her greatest weapons against the impossible odds she was soon to face. And there was only one way to beat those odds: She had to keep fighting. That's all her life had been ever since she'd escaped Ebik— fighting to survive, fighting to find her place, fighting to protect the galaxy from the pain she knew all too well. She didn't want to think about her mother's fate; she didn't want to think about losing Cade to the Rokura's power or how cold she'd been to him before he left; she didn't want to think about the father Ebik once was, the loving, happy man she could still see in the furthest recesses of her memory. All she wanted was to take a supply of weapons that would make a small militia blanch and use them to storm the Crucible, thwart Ebik's plans, and, hopefully, end him in a hail of blaster fire at the same time.

Kira wanted to *brawl*.

The galaxy, though, had different plans. Because just as Kira was putting the final touches on calibrating her whipblaster, there was a knock at her door. She had told everyone she wanted time alone; given what she'd just gone through, she figured her wishes would be respected. But no. Whoever was there kept knocking, and Kira continued ignoring the rapping until finally it stopped. Kira breathed a sigh of relief but immediately wished she hadn't. Because seconds after the knocking on her door ended, it was replaced by someone picking the lock.

Kira knew it was Mig before he'd even finished the breaking part of his breaking and entering. He sauntered in like he was dropping by a friend's place for dinner.

"Hey, you've been in here for a few hours, so I wanted to check and see—" Mig stopped at the sight of Kira's arsenal. "WHOA. Now that . . . that's a lot of weapons."

"The door was locked, Mig," Kira said as she continued the calibration of the whipblaster.

"Yeah, I knocked, and you didn't answer. So, where are you going with all these blasters and bombs and stuff?"

"I'm going. That's all you need to know."

"You don't have to act tough and mysterious with me," Mig said as he shut the door to Kira's room. "I know you think you're going to the Crucible."

"There's no thinking about it," Kira said, still not turning to face her friend. "This is what I'm doing."

Mig sighed, and Kira could hear him sucking at his lips—a habit of his, she'd noticed, when he was stuck on what to say. "Look, I get it. What you've gone through with your dad, and now having to . . . everything with your mom. I know it's not easy, but you can't—"

"Having to leave my mom to die," Kira interrupted. "Those are the words you were looking for."

"I'm just trying to say that I get what you're—"

"No. You. Don't!" Kira turned and hurled the whipblaster against the wall; it busted into pieces. By the time the blaster parts were scattering all over the floor and bed, Kira had taken long, determined strides that brought her right in Mig's face. "Did you know, Mig? Did you know that my mom could have saved herself instead of me back when I was a kid? She knew everything Ebik was up to, and she had a tiny window to do something about it. The only option available to her was to run. But she didn't. She put everything she had into getting fake papers for *me*, drawing all the coin she could get her hands on so *I* could get away. Not her—*me*. And now, I finally had the chance to be the one to save *her*, and I blew it. She's going to die because of me."

Kira was close enough to see Mig's eyes as they subtly flickered, flashing with sudden pity. It was the last thing she wanted to see from anyone.

"Kira, you cannot think that way," Mig said, steadfast in his opposition. "Whatever happens to your mom, it's not on you. It never will be. This is the work of your dad, of Ga Halle, of every single complicit Praxian who's allowed this reign of terror to go on. Mothers have died. Brothers, sisters, children—so many people have died, and it's all because of Praxis. No one else."

"You can't tell me not to feel guilty, Mig."

"You're right," Mig replied. "But I can tell you not to feel responsible."

Kira drew a deep breath that helped to take the edge off her temper. "Fine, I'll give you that. But that doesn't change what I have to do."

Kira tried to turn back toward her weapons, but Mig was quicker. He stepped around her, blocking her path. "So, what, then? Your mom sacrificed herself so you can go on a suicide run?"

As quickly as it had fallen, Kira felt her temper rising again. Of course she understood what Akima's sacrifice was for, but she found it difficult to embrace what was supposed to happen after. Because while selflessness born out of love—not just for Kira but love for the people she represented as a Baron—was her way, it was Ebik who didn't share Akima's compassion or her patience. Akima resisted; Ebik fought. It didn't matter what obstacles were in front of him or who got hurt along the way. Ebik pushed ahead no matter the consequences, and Kira's darkest fear was the day she resembled her father in any way. And how far would her apple have fallen from the tree if she enlisted other people—friends—into her quest for revenge? She choked on trying to discern where her mother began, where her father ended, and whether there was room for her in the narrow space between.

"You're not the only one," Mig continued, filling the silence created by Kira's intense contemplation. "I may not have had a dad who tried to kill me, but neither of my parents did much to keep me alive, either. I had a zep addict for a mother and degenerate gambler for a father, and neither one ever cared where I went or if I ever came back."

Kira scoffed. "Fine, Mig. You had terrible parents. Congratulations. Is that supposed to make me feel better?"

"No, actually, it's not," Mig snapped, and Kira was taken aback by the indignation in his voice. She'd never heard such annoyance, or assertiveness, from him before. "It won't make you feel better. Nothing will make you feel better. But even at the lowest points with my crappy parents, I was never alone, and neither are you. I had Cade, Tristan, and their parents, and you have me. You have Four-Qel and Cade. Even super-weird Kobe. And none of us are going to let you die so you can avoid what you're feeling right now."

"Mig," Kira said, her eyes closed and her voice nearly down to a whisper, "do you even know what the Crucible is?"

Mig shrugged. "Not really. I know it's not on Praxis; it's on your nearest moon. And Kay is trying to find a way for us to get in before the moon reaches its farthest point from the planet. That's when, he assumes, the explosives are going to be detonated and tear Praxis apart from the inside out. As for the Crucible itself, I imagine it's some kind of military compound or something?"

"The Crucible is our prison. The previous generation of Barons built an impenetrable, inescapable jail on the moon to house the very worst prisoners—and not only from Praxis; the Barons sublet cells for prisoners from other nearby systems," Kira said. "When Ga Halle took power, she gave inmates a choice: Serve in her army or rot forever. It was a quick, efficient way to bolster her forces.

"Now, the Crucible houses anyone Praxian police deems to be a dissenter or instigator, and it's also my father's operations hub; it's Praxis's only land base, and it's guarded by the worst scum Praxis has to offer. So, trying to break *in*? No one would even dream of it."

"Then good," Mig said with a smile. "They'll never see us coming."

"Mig, you don't understand," Kira said, pinching the bridge of her nose. "Assuming we can even get in, and assuming we can get to the detonator and deactivate it before we're all killed, there's no way we get back out. This trip to the Crucible . . . it's a one-way mission."

Mig took a step away from Kira and let out an exasperated sigh. "Do you not understand what I've been saying to you? Do you not understand what we've all been through together means? I'll just spell it out: We're family. And we don't let each other go through this kind of stuff alone."

"I know we're family, Mig," Kira said as her lips curled into a bittersweet smile. "And that's exactly why I can't take any of you with me."

Kira tried to walk past Mig—going where, she didn't know, but she couldn't drag this conversation out any longer—but as she did, he grabbed hold of her elbow. Not hard, but enough to keep her attention. "You won't succeed, Kira. Alone, you won't—"

Mig's words were cut off by a sudden, intrusive sound. Kira's head whipped toward the door; she and Mig stood silently, listening for the noise to repeat. As they did, Kira gripped the sidewinder holstered at her side.

"What was that?" Mig said, his voice low.

Kira shushed him and took quiet, cautious half steps toward the door. Before she reached it, the sound echoed overhead, filling the tiny room. It was an explosion. Muffled and somewhat distant, but an explosion nonetheless.

"We have to get out of here," Kira told Mig. Any other time, Kira would have hidden her fear from everyone, especially those under her command. While Mig technically wasn't her soldier, she knew he looked to her for leadership, especially when things went bad. But this time, she couldn't hide the stricken expression on her face. They were trapped underground with nowhere to hide, and the enemy would be coming for them any minute.

They rushed to the bed, where Mig grabbed the tri-blaster. Kira took a second sidewinder while regretting how she'd busted the whipblaster even though it wasn't the most ideal weapon for close-quarters combat.

Kira went to put her hand on the door but stopped. She turned to Mig and told him, "Stay behind me, stay small, stay alert."

Mig nodded, tri-blaster at the ready. Slowly, Kira opened the metal door, using it for cover as she pushed it out. Its creaky hinges sent out an alarm so shrill it seemed like it could carry for miles. The narrow hallway leading from Kira's quarters was empty; though Kay's numbers had been thinned because of the ambush they'd suffered trying to retrieve Akima's data, Kira was alarmed to find it completely desolate.

"Where's Four-Qel?" Mig whispered. "Where's Kobe?"

Kira turned to Mig and pressed her pointer finger against her lips. She could see the panic rising within him, and as much as she wanted to remind him to keep a level head, she knew the words wouldn't matter. Even she was afraid. Something had gone terribly wrong, and odds were that something was coming for them.

Overhead, the single row of nude quirzine bulbs began to flicker; all the way down to the two overhead doors that swung out to the topside world, the line of bulbs was the only thing separating this arm of the bunker from total darkness. Kira knew what was going to happen next. It was inevitable.

"Mig, grab on to me!" Kira ordered.

Just as she felt Mig grab on to the waistband of her pants, every bulb surged, pouring white-hot light from their fragile cores.

Then they burst. There was a succinct popping noise, then the entire space went dark. More than dark. It was like Kira and Mig had suddenly been plunged into the blackest night. Kira couldn't see her hand, her weapon, or Mig. It was nothingness—real, total nothingness.

And she knew they had no time.

"Run and don't let go," she said, the words escaping her lips in gasps.

Kira charged ahead, aware of Mig's hold on her all the way. They plowed straight down the hallway toward the double doors; they were the only way in and, more importantly, the only way out. Thirty yards was all Kira needed; thirty yards to get to those doors and get out before somebody came in after them. Their footfalls slapped against the grated steel, but Kira couldn't help but feel like they were going nowhere. Her heartbeat pounded in her head, hard and fast, muffling the sound of her own ragged breathing.

She led them forward with her left arm outstretched, desperately waving it to feel for the cold metal of the stairway railing. Finally, just as another explosion thundered above their heads, Kira made contact. She gasped relief and then ran her clammy hand over the smooth surface. As she was about to take hold of it, a single beam of hazy light shone in her eyes. Kira looked up and stared at the small sliver of white that pierced through a slender crack between the double doors. The sky was ashen with rain clouds and darkening with the sun's recession below the horizon line. It was a rainy late evening on Praxis, and Kira was certain this smudge of sky was the last one she'd ever see.

"Go, go!" Kira commanded Mig as she stumbled back. "Get away from the door!"

Kira and Mig had barely pushed themselves back three steps when the double doors were flung wide open. The light, even as dull as it was, momentarily blinded them both. Kira rallied her tenacity and gripped both sidewinders tightly. She was ready to give whoever came down those stairs the fight of their life. If she was going to go, she'd be certain to take a few of her enemies with her.

Before her pupils could totally adjust to the sudden rush of light coming into the bunker, Kira's attention was captured by the sound of feet marching down the stairs. The stomping footfalls were far too heavy to be human, which meant only one thing: drones, and a lot of them.

Kira fired at will.

The indistinct shapes gained more and more clarity with every passing second, taking on the definable outline of sentry drones rushing toward her and Mig. One by one, they were blasted off their feet. Mig joined the offensive spree, cutting down every Praxian drone that tried to invade their space. Kira put a hole through one's chest and sent more than one bulbous drone head flying off its shoulders. Again and again and again they fired, shredding drone after drone. So many that they were forming a pile of scrap metal at the bottom of the stairs. But still, they kept coming.

"I'm running low on ammo!" Mig yelled, and Kira cursed the tri-blaster's low charge capacity. She kept firing with one sidewinder as she took a break with her left hand to see if she had any spare charges on her. Right as she did, she saw the lifeless corpse of one of the downed sentries rise off the ground, its body limp like a puppet on strings. Suddenly, the body was propelled forward and flew toward both Kira and Mig.

"Move!" Kira yelled. She grabbed Mig as she dove for the ground, narrowly avoiding the incoming drone. Kira collected herself as quickly as she could, firing her sidewinder erratically as she pulled herself up. She knew, though, that they were done for.

A horde of sentry drones charged down the stairs, using the break in Kira and Mig's onslaught to crush them with numbers. Mig, fresh out of ammo, was the first to fall.

"AAAH!" he screamed in agony. Kira turned, and she could only watch as he dropped to his knees, his fingers curled in on themselves, his jaw clenched tightly and teeth bared as his body convulsed uncontrollably. He dropped face-first to the floor, smoke wafting off his body.

"NO!" Kira howled, and she yanked back each of her triggers so hard that it hurt her fingers. "No!" she screamed as one sentry went down, "No!" for another, then "No!" for one more. Thoughts of her mother alone in her prison, of Ebik's smug, callous grin, of Cade losing to the Rokura burst across her mind with each pull of the trigger. Kira continued to scream her fury as she fought back, but there were too many of them and not enough of her.

She felt the blaster bolt hit her square in the chest, delivering more of an impact than the hardest punch from the strongest person. Then came the electric shocks that surged throughout her body; her muscles tensed, her bones weakened, and the rush of energy kept her awake and alert for the most painful moment she'd ever experienced. Like Mig, Kira dropped to her knees, incapable of staying upright. The electric storm within her kept rolling and rolling, and just as Kira thought she couldn't withstand any more and her heart was soon to burst, the torturous pain ended. She gasped as her body twitched uncontrollably, but the moment of respite was short-lived. Kira's eyes rolled back in her head, and every muscle and joint surrendered. Her mind immediately followed, and though Kira's instincts told her to raise her sidewinder and fight back, she couldn't lift a finger.

Kira was out cold before her head hit the ground.

When she awoke, it was to screaming.

The sound was muffled and far away; the entire world around her seemed vague and distant. Even her vision, as it slowly returned, was as murky as the stormy sky overhead. It only took a moment for Kira to realize the cause of her impaired sight. Whoever had taken her unconscious body from the bunker had dropped her in a pool of mud, and that's where she lay, half her face dug into brown sludge. Instinctually, she went to wipe the mud from her eyes but found that her hands were bound—by ionic cuffs, judging by the circuitous pulsing Kira felt at her wrists—behind her back. The best she could do was push herself up until she was positioned, unsteadily, onto her knees. Her body ached; everywhere felt battered and raw. Kira shook her head, angling it up so the rain could wash away some of the mud that obscured her vision. She regained enough focus to assess her surroundings. The earth that covered Kay's underground bunker was nothing more than a sparsely wooded field. Sickly trees grew all around, thin and bare, while even sicklier grass grew in discolored patches along the barren ground. It all took on a completely different feel, though, with dozens of sentry drones patrolling the area. Kira spotted the top of a drop ship that poked out from a gorge just ahead, but parked about thirty yards away was a smaller vessel, a Polaris-class assault shuttle. And in every space in between, drones. So many damn drones.

As Kira became more lucid, the screaming that had woken her just a moment earlier was getting closer and closer until, finally, it snapped into focus. It was Mig she heard; he was on his knees right next to her, though he was being restrained by a sentry drone that had its mechanical arm locked around Mig's neck. Mig was fighting with reckless abandon to get himself free. His muscles were taut from the strain he was putting into his resistance, and there was a frenzy in his eyes that Kira would have never guessed he was capable of. Even in the face of the life-threatening stunts they'd pulled together, Mig remained relatively even-keeled. Now, though, he was out of his head, and the sight of it alarmed Kira as she continued to regain full consciousness.

"Let him go!" Mig howled. "Wake up, Four-Qel! Wake. *UP!*"

Kira looked ahead and saw, through the rain that came down in sheets, the source of Mig's frenzied protestations. She gasped. 4-Qel's lifeless body hung in suspended animation, trapped in a shimmering blue containment field. Kira never imagined a scenario where 4-Qel could be captured—or worse. Seeing him hanging there reinforced just how desperate of a situation they were in. 4-Qel's arms hung limply at his sides, and the green light that had shone in his eyes—the light that had conveyed more life from a drone that Kira ever thought possible—was absent. All Kira could see were dark shadows covering his eyes. She trembled at the thought that 4-Qel was gone forever. Despite her body's burning soreness, she moved to get up and rush to 4-Qel's side. She knew there was nothing she could do for him, at least not yet, but she couldn't bear the thought of him trapped there all alone. As foolishly sentimental as it was, Kira was certain that, if nothing else, someone should be with him. And that someone should be Mig.

Kira got up off her knees just enough to dig her feet into the treacherous ground; though slippery, she still gained enough purchase to lunge at the sentry that was restraining Mig. She threw all her weight into the drone, knocking it over and freeing Mig in the process.

Unfortunately, Mig didn't get far.

By the time Kira looked up, Mig was on his feet but halted in place, staring down the blades of a shido.

Kira knew that black armor just as well as she knew the sadistic face of the man who wore it: Ortzo, the Fatebreaker who was responsible for untold misery across the galaxy, including the death of Cade's parents.

"Ah, ah, ah," Ortzo warned. "Your friend is going to fetch a fine bounty from the Eris royal family. They may even be so grateful for the return of their property that they'll join our kingdom at last."

"He's not property," Mig sneered.

"Look at the expression on your face," Ortzo said, mocking Mig. "So angry, so hostile. You want to kill me, don't you? And here I thought you would have missed me."

"Let him go," Mig snarled. "Or I will kill you."

Ortzo laughed sinisterly. "Oh, you will, will you? Even if you weren't bound, even if you weren't weaponless, you truly think you can do what your Qel could not? What your Paragon, or whatever you want to call him, could not? No," Ortzo sneered, "you cannot kill me. *None* of you can."

"I beg to differ," a voice called from the distance, breaking through the cacophonous rain as it pummeled the ground. The sentry beneath Kira started to push against her body weight, and Kira delivered a sharp elbow to its neck, disabling it. She then swung her head around and saw, through the haze caused by the incessant rain, Kobe.

Kira had no idea how he'd escaped whatever had happened on the surface, but he had. And now he was standing just twenty yards away, quarter staffs gripped tightly in his hands. The rain streamed down his face, but he didn't seem to even notice it; his vicious, unblinking gaze was focused on Ortzo, and Kira got the impression that it would take a lightning bolt to the head to break his concentration.

Ortzo didn't assess Kobe with the same gravity. Kira knew that was a mistake.

"Well, well, well," Ortzo said, turning his attention to Kobe. With a single gloved hand, he grabbed Mig by his right shoulder and shoved him down to the ground. "The terrorist has come to join us. How delightful."

"You've destroyed worlds," Kobe countered. "Made orphans of children, widows of spouses. Your legacy in this galaxy is one of suffering and bloodshed, yet you call me the terrorist. Ironic, wouldn't you say?"

Ortzo shrugged. "I don't care. When you're all gone and we control everything, we'll be able to call you whatever we want. Your place in history will be what we decide it is, *terrorist*."

Kobe twirled his quarter staffs and took a step forward. Ortzo drew back a little.

"I challenge you to a duel!" Kobe yelled, loud and clear. "If you're so honorable, so righteous, then you'll call off your allies. Just you and your shido against me and my staffs. Nothing else."

Ortzo paused, studying his shido as if he'd find the answer to Kobe's proposal in its blades. Kira knew he didn't have to accept the challenge, but she had a strong feeling that Ortzo's arrogance wouldn't allow him to resist. She just wondered what the plan could possibly be if Kobe did successfully defeat Ortzo. After all, they'd still be surrounded by a dozen sentries, and the drones wouldn't surrender just because a Fatebreaker—ostensibly their leader—was taken off the battlefield. Still, even if Kobe's victory achieved nothing more than the death of one of the galaxy's most dangerous, ruthless souls, Kira would be happy to call that a win.

"My shido is the weapon of only the greatest warriors. I hold it because I've earned the privilege," Ortzo said. "If you want to challenge that, so be it."

"You bring disgrace to the legacy of that weapon," Kobe sneered. "And I'll be glad to take it from you and give you what you deserve."

Ortzo dug his feet into the soft ground. "You will try."

At that, Kobe rushed toward Ortzo, quickly closing the distance between them with his remarkable speed. He went in swinging, going for a high strike with both of his staffs. Ortzo blocked the attack, but he wasn't quick enough to get his weapon in position to stop Kobe from swinging his staffs down and furiously pounding the Fatebreaker's chest. Though Ortzo was armored, Kira could tell that he felt the force of Kobe's blows ringing across his midsection.

Ortzo stumbled back but recovered quickly. He went on the offensive, lancing his shido forward, but Kobe was able to easily deflect Ortzo's attempt. As Kobe knocked Ortzo's weapon to the side, he flipped his legs upward and nailed the Fatebreaker in the face with a somersault kick; the blow knocked Ortzo's helmet clean off. It landed not far from Kira, its sharp edges digging into the muddy ground.

Blood trickled out of Ortzo's mouth, which he wiped away with the back of his hand. A mirthless smile appeared on his face as he watched Kobe stand at the ready. He was a portrait of utter calm while Ortzo—his aged, tired eyes revealed with the loss of his helmet—seemed to be coming undone.

"Percival has taught you well," Ortzo said. "You have tremendous skill, and you're no doubt fueled by emotions I can see you fighting to keep down. Anger, perhaps? But that would be too easy. No," Ortzo said with a grin. "You're grieving."

As Ortzo spoke, Kira nudged Mig.

"Hey," she whispered to him. "Can you walk? Actually, can you run?"

Mig turned and regarded her with eyes that spoke of his heartbreak. So lost in his sadness, he didn't seem to even recognize who Kira was.

"I, um . . . yeah," he said, tearing away from whatever thoughts were occupying his mind. "I can run."

"Good," Kira said, trying to sound encouraging. "See the ship over there? When Kobe puts Ortzo down, we have to grab him and run for it. It's the only chance we have."

Mig blinked hard. "But—Four-Qel."

Kira looked hard in Mig's eyes, making sure he kept his attention on her and not his captured friend. "Listen to me. We'll find a way to get him free. We will. But if we stay, we're all dead. All of us."

Mig looked over at 4-Qel, still hanging lifelessly in the containment field. He looked back at Kira, bitter resignation painted on his face, which in a way was good; he'd need that fire to get through this alive.

"Okay," Mig said, nodding. "Okay."

Kira turned back to Kobe and Ortzo, waiting for their opportunity to escape.

"You've destroyed entire worlds," Kobe said, his words laced with acid. "My world is gone because of your wretched kingdom. My family, my friends—Praxis murdered every last one of them."

"And yet you've learned nothing," Ortzo said, his words drawn out as if they were a blade twisting in Kobe's side. "They're dead because they fought back. And now you will die for the very same reason."

Both Kobe and Ortzo must have known not another word needed to be said. They rushed at each other, their weapons meeting directly between them. Ortzo altered his grip on his shido; he held it at its center, allowing him the speed needed to adjust to Kobe's rapid, rage-fueled pace. The two parried in equal measure, exchanging a series of strikes and counterstrikes. For a moment, they almost seemed equally matched, but Kobe soon put Ortzo in an uncomfortable defensive position. Some fighters, Kira knew, worked better when fighting defensively; it allowed them the chance to study their opponent and exploit their weakness. Ortzo wasn't this kind of fighter. He was used to being the aggressor, and his success lay with his ability to over-power opponents with his strength and skill. Kobe, though, never allowed Ortzo to gain enough footing to express his dominance. As the Fatebreaker again stumbled back, Kobe slammed his quarter staffs against Ortzo's chest. Ortzo tried to defend himself by drawing his leg up for a kick, but Kobe knocked the strike away with a defensive kick of his own. With remarkable fluidity, Kobe followed his defense with a roundhouse kick that connected against Ortzo's jaw. The blow sent Ortzo spinning away, but it didn't knock him down. Not yet.

Panting with both rage and exhaustion, Ortzo went back with an awkward plunge of his shido directed at Kobe's belly. Kobe sidestepped the weak attack, grabbing hold of the Fatebreaker's weapon at the same time. Drawn together, Kobe slammed his forehead twice against Ortzo's nose. Kira could hear the cracking through the rain.

"AAAH!" Ortzo screamed as he fell to his knees, expressing both his pain and his impotent fury. There was nothing he could do to defend himself against Kobe; he was beaten.

Kobe, large and imposing, stood calmly over the fallen Fate-breaker. He'd sheathed his staffs and was now in possession of Ortzo's shido, which he was examining with revulsion.

"I wonder how many souls this weapon has claimed," Kobe said.

"More than you could ever even guess, boy," Ortzo said, then he spat a wad of blood on the ground at Kobe's feet.

Kobe raised the shido above his head, ready to strike Ortzo down for good. As he did, the implacable expression on his face finally broke. Kira could see the anguish in his face, and she could only imagine the thoughts running through his head. Of his world going dark. Of holding his sister as she died in his arms. "In that case," he snarled, "what's one more?"

As he said the words, Kira bounded to her feet. "Now!" she

told Mig, and they both began to trudge as fast they could through the mud.

Kira looked to Kobe, and she saw something: Ortzo's hand, digging into his boot as the shido was about to come down on him. He pulled out something that glinted softly in the waning light.

"Kobe, look out!" she screamed, stopping dead in her tracks.

Just as Kobe was bringing the shido down, fully prepared to slice it across Ortzo's throat, the Fatebreaker pulled a blade from his boot and lunged upward with it. Had Kira not alerted Kobe, and had Kobe not been so fast, he would have been dead. The blade would have driven directly into his rib cage, leaving Kobe to suffer a slow death in the rain on Praxis. Instead, Kobe responded quickly enough to twist his body so the blade only punctured his side. He groaned once when the blade went in, then groaned again when Ortzo yanked it out.

"Never learn," Ortzo grunted as he stood over Kobe, who'd fallen to the ground. He was going to thrust his blade into Kobe again, but Kira was already charging for him.

"NO!" she screamed, driving her shoulder into Ortzo's spine. The blow knocked him away from Kobe, but he managed to stay on his feet. He turned to see who'd hit him.

"Come on, you bastard," Kira snarled. Hands bound behind her back, feet covered in mud to her ankles, she was still ready to fight. "Let's do this."

"Oh no, no," Ortzo said with a devious smile. "I have orders to bring you back alive."

Ortzo whistled loudly enough for the entire area to hear, drawing everyone's attention. "Bring the girl and her friends aboard my shuttle. Restrain them. Bring the Qel, too. I'll attend to him later," he commanded, then started to walk away but turned back. "Oh, and summon the commander as well. We're leaving, all of us."

Kira felt the presence of a dozen sentry drones closing a circle around her and Mig. The nearest drone grabbed Kobe, yanked him to his feet, and slapped a pair of ionic cuffs over his wrists. The clumsy drone wasn't at all gentle about it, and Kobe couldn't do anything but grimace in pain as he was pushed forward.

"Hey!" Kira yelled as a pair of powerful mechanical hands pulled her back by her shoulders. Before she knew it, both she and Mig were being marched alongside Kobe toward the assault shuttle, surrounded by sentry drones. As they shuffled along, Kira wondered what Ortzo had meant when he'd instructed the drones to "summon the commander," but she didn't have to consider the mystery for long. Kira looked ahead and couldn't believe her eyes. Coming out from around Ortzo's shuttle, led at blaster point by a pair of drones, was Kay.

And he wasn't wearing any cuffs.

"Son of a—" she hissed, and she tried to go after him, but she was again stopped by a sentry's inescapable grip. "You sold us out! You told Praxis where we were. You told them how to ambush us!"

"You did this!" Kay yelled as he stood just outside the circle of sentries that protected Kira and Mig. "You and Akima."

"Don't you dare say her name," Kira fired back. "Don't you—"

"I lost good men and women in a bloodbath orchestrated by your mother. She set us up, and for *nothing*. I don't know what game you two are playing, but I won't let you get away with it."

Kira breathed heavily through a snarl. As furious as she was with Kay, she was just as furious at herself for trusting him.

"Enough," Ortzo said, charging between the drones that led Kira and her friends forward. "Put this one in cuffs, too."

"What?!" Kay bellowed. "We had a deal!"

"And our arrangement will be followed to the letter once the deal is complete," Ortzo said, brushing by Kay as he was placed in cuffs.

"What deal?" Kira demanded of Ortzo. "And where are you taking us?"

Ortzo turned slowly, pointing at Kira. "I forget, Kira Sen, that you're from Praxis. Chalk it up to wanting to push filthy traitors as far out of my mind as possible. But since you're from here, you'll be able to appreciate the special treat we have in store for you. You want to know where we're going? The last place you'd ever want to go, which is also the last place you'll see:

"The Crucible."

As Ortzo walked away and boarded the shuttle, all the pieces clicked into place in Kira's mind. She looked at Kay, the anger emptying out of her. He looked back at her and delivered a subtle, conspiratorial nod.

Mig was right; Kay had been working on getting them into the Crucible.

Now all they had to do was take it over.

CHAPTER TWELVE

C ade snaked his way through the palace's winding hallways, following the thunderous eruptions toward their source. He had nearly reached what he assumed was the palace's throne room—which would have been situated just beyond the palace's front doors—when he felt the ground beneath him start to shake. The force of the quake was strong enough to nearly knock Cade off his feet; he stumbled against the powder-blue-and-white-tinted wall that looked like a sky streaked with clouds. The rumbling continued unabated, and Cade shoved himself off the wall just as bits and pieces of the ceiling began to crumble down on his head.

Then, just as Cade was about to continue his mission to find whatever trouble was battering the Monaskin palace, trouble found him.

A trio of Monaskin citizens bounded down the hallway, heading right for Cade. The de facto leader was holding one of the enormous blasters Cade had spotted the guards armed with when he'd first descended into the Monaskin core. The other two were armed with a tri-blaster and a compression pike, respectively, but Cade knew that no amount of firepower could compensate for the perseverance that came with being battle-hardened. And battle-hardened these three were not, which was probably why they were running. Cade could only hope that the Monaskin guards had a little more tenacity; sure, they looked the part of being formidable soldiers, but being isolated all these years, Cade had to figure, probably hadn't done them any favors when push came to shove—or, more specifically, when defending your turf against the galaxy's ruling power. Cade didn't know how Praxis had found him, but he had no doubt that when he found the cause of the ruckus, he'd find the bloodred banner of Praxis waving not far behind.

As the leader closed the distance between herself and Cade, she waved for him to go. "Run! Get out of here!" she screamed, and while Cade took cautious steps backward, he wasn't inclined to flee, especially since he'd come from the direction these people were heading and knew there wasn't anywhere to go. With the intention of being helpful—inspiring, even, seeing that these people had probably seen the cool stuff he was able to do with the Rokura—Cade held up his hands, urging the fleeing trio to stop. But then a weapon of some sort—Cade had no idea what it was—came spinning down the hallway and sliced clean through the leader's skull. And it kept coming. Without a moment to spare, Cade ducked just in time to watch as a gleaming, circular blade with razor-sharp teeth zipped overhead. It lodged itself in the wall behind him, thankfully without his scalp attached to it.

The two people who'd been on the run didn't waste any time getting back to their flight; they scampered around their decapitated friend, leaving her and her novelty blaster behind.

"Well, then," Cade said with a devious smile. "Looks like you're all mine."

The blaster, unsurprising, was heavier than a sack of bricks. Cade groaned as he wrapped his right hand on a handle that rose off the top of the gun; his other hand gripped what he assumed was the trigger, but it was a guess at best.

"You're not going to win any awards for being user-friendly," Cade whispered to the blaster. "But let's see what you can do."

Cade centered himself in the hallway, feeling the floor rumble beneath his feet and debris from the ceiling fluttering on his head. He was waiting for the pursuers to arrive, and thankfully, he didn't have to wait long.

A sentry drone charged from around the corner, wielding a tri-blaster in one hand and the blade-shooting weapon in the other. It abruptly stopped when it saw Cade, like it was stunned by the sight of him.

"That's the one we are looking fo—" the sentry was saying through its tinny, monotone voice modulator when Cade squeezed what he figured was the trigger. And when he did, the bulky, unwieldy, ridiculous weapon gave Cade one of the most satisfying experiences of his life.

Multicolored blaster bolts larger than any Cade had ever seen sprayed all over the passageway and shredded anything in their path. After the first sentry stumbled into the hall, it was followed by so many others, and none of them knew what was waiting for them.

Cade kept a steady hand on the trigger, mowing down drone after drone. More than mowing down, though, Cade's blaster blew the sentries to bits, the force of its strikes exploding their bodies into pieces that careened up and down the gleaming hallway. It was a pleasant sight, but not as pleasant as the blaster bolts' brilliance transforming the passageway into a kaleidoscope of light. Cade found himself grinning ear to ear as the sentry bits and pieces lined the hall, making it look like a derelict catacomb. After the journey he'd taken into the depths of his soul,

Cade was relieved to blow off some steam, and this was just the ticket. Cade would have liked to have copped to not knowing how much fun it would be to wield a hand cannon and decimate a legion of drones, but that would have been a lie. This moment was everything he'd dreamed it would be and more.

But even the best of times had to come to an end.

Without warning, the blaster's carousel of ammunition went dry. Disbelief struck Cade; he pulled on the trigger again and again just to be sure, but every squeeze was met with nothing more than a dry *click*. For a moment, Cade was more disappointed by the end of this good time than he was concerned with the enemies that were still coming for him. Reality sank back in hard for Cade, especially when he spotted a line of five sentries armed with compression pikes spread across the width of the hall, kicking aside what remained of their fallen brethren.

"Fine," Cade said, dropping the blaster and pulling out the Rokura. "We'll do this the hard way."

Cade considered testing his newfound comfort with the Rokura but figured it was best not to push his luck. Drones he could deal with, and he didn't want to get in the habit of calling on the Rokura every time he needed his back scratched. So instead, he charged the drones, thinking he'd make use of his training as a Rai. But as Cade got within striking distance, the sentries didn't move. They remained completely static, which he found odd. Undeterred, Cade was about to drive the Rokura through the centermost sentry's chest plate when, suddenly, the drone dropped face-first onto the floor. Behind it was another sentry—and this one had a blaster.

Realization slapped Cade in the face with a cold, wet hand.

He'd been tricked by drones.

"Crap," Cade said, trying to slow his momentum in time to change direction, but it was no use. The sentry fired, and before Cade knew it, he was covered in ionic netting. He tried desperately to pull the netting off him, but the anchors activated before he could get a chance; they worked in unison, pulling Cade to the ground and locking on to the floor. Cade could hardly move.

"Package acquired," a sentry intoned as it stood above him. It pulled out a small blaster and aimed it down at Cade. "Preparing for transpozzzzzrrkkk."

A blaster bolt tore through the sentry's head, creating a blackened hole the size of Cade's fist. Cade tried to jostle his head around to see who had done him a very nice favor, but he still couldn't move. From his vantage on the floor, all he could see was the line of remaining sentries; they all dropped their pikes and were reaching for their blasters when, one by one, they were nailed by blaster bolts. Every single bolt was a head shot.

"You look like you could use a hand," a voice said. Cade could move his eyes just enough to his side to see Ersia standing above him, her golden gamma blaster held up to her face.

"I think I've got it, actually," Cade said. "I was, uh, just about to—"

"Oh, shut up," Ersia said, stomping her heel on something just above Cade's head. Whatever it was, it deactivated the net's hold, and Cade was free. He got to his feet and admired his handiwork; there were drone parts everywhere, most of them showing the scorch marks from where they'd exploded. Cade still didn't know what the gun he'd wielded was, he'd have to get his hands on one. 4-Qel would love it.

"You almost finished?" she asked, standing with one hand on her blaster and the other resting on her hip.

Cade flinched, then refocused. "Where are all these drones from? What's happening?"

Ersia cocked an eyebrow. "Do I really need to explain that we're under attack? I know you're not the Paragon, but at least try to keep up with the basics."

"That can't be possible. No one even knows I'm he—" Cade's words died in his mouth as a memory flashed in his mind. A memory of what he'd thought was just a vision: Ga Halle's presence in his thoughts was far more real than he had imagined. She'd been able to see him like she was standing right there, on Monaskis, next to him. Which meant she was here, Cade was certain, and unless the ruined planet had a rear exit, he was going to have to deal with her.

"Listen," Cade said, turning toward Ersia, "you have to get off this planet and take as many of your people as you can. There's nothing Ga Halle won't do to get the Rokura. She'll kill you all."

"Wow, thanks for the advice, Cade, but I think I'll handle the war strategizing for my planet."

"So, you're not going to retreat?"

A shadow passed across Ersia's face, and Cade knew the answer before she even said it. "Never."

Cade pinched the bridge of his nose. He couldn't have the blood of the Monaskins on his hands, and he knew there'd be nothing but blood soaking the palace walls if he didn't do something about it. Ersia couldn't order her people to run; that wasn't their way, and it never would be. She'd be deemed unfit to lead if she even tried. But Praxis would make a slaughterhouse of the entire planet if that's what Ga Halle felt was necessary to get what she'd come here for, and there was no way Ersia and her forces could prevent that from happening. That left Cade with one choice—after all, Ga Halle had come here for him and him alone.

To save Monaskis, he'd have to face Ga Halle. It was a challenge he knew, deep down, he wasn't prepared for. But maybe Wu-Xia was right, and whatever he needed to control the Rokura was already within himself. Which sounded really inspiring at the time. It was less so now.

"Where is she?" Cade grimly asked as he picked up one of the sentries' B-18s. "Ga Halle. Where do I find her?"

Ersia paused and then drew in a breath; Cade could tell she was harboring something that either she didn't want to say or she didn't want him to know.

"Ersia," Cade snapped, bringing the queen back into focus. "Where?"

"On the landing pad, right where you came in," Ersia said after a moment. "But you have to pass through the throne room to get there, and that's where most of the fighting is taking place. There's no other way."

Cade eyed Ersia skeptically, and he could tell—in her darting eyes, in her dampened mood—that there was more. She was still hiding something.

"And what else?" Cade prodded. "What aren't you saying?"

Ersia turned her gaze directly to Cade; she was biting the inside of her cheek. "Well, it's your friend. Percival. He went after her. I was forced away from the platform when we fell back to inside the palace, but what I saw didn't look good."

Cade tried to maintain a steady calm, at least for the sake of outward appearances, but he knew it was no use. He was sweaty, his hands were trembling, and he felt like a vein was going to pop beneath his eyes at any moment.

"I have to get to him. I have to get to *her.*"

"Like I said, through the throne room," Ersia said, jamming a fresh charge into her gamma blaster. "We're holding those Praxian beasts there."

"Well, okay then. I'll take it from here," Cade said, turning to leave. "Thanks for leading me to your sacred chamber. It was useful. I hope."

"Uh—what?" Ersia said, sidling up to Cade. "Did you just ruffle my hair and tell me to stay put?"

"I didn't touch your hair, but you are definitely staying put."

Ersia huffed and threw up her hands. "Why, because I'm a kid?"

"No, not at all. But—"

"Oh, I see. Because I'm a woman."

"What? No!" Cade protested. "It's because you're the queen. And given your planet's history with the Paragon, it's probably best that you don't get killed on my watch."

Ersia looked at Cade flatly, then she started to laugh. "A drone? Kill *me*? Okay."

Cade knew this argument wasn't going anywhere. "For crying out loud—fine, you can come."

"Gee, thanks, Grandpa."

"Grandpa?" Cade questioned, unable to hide the umbrage he took at such an insult. "What's that supposed to mean?"

"'For crying out loud,'" Ersia said, mimicking Cade's voice. "My grandpa always used to say that."

Cade blew out an exasperated breath. "Just . . . enough. Keep your head down, and follow my lead."

Ersia smiled playfully at Cade, and together, the two strode down the hallway toward the throne room doors. The smell of blaster fire hung in the air, commingling with the ineffable scent of blood and fear. Warfare raged on the other side of a set of tall and wide double doors—chrome painted blue with the outline of a ligre's head traced in gold on each door, likely Ersia's family crest—and the sights and smells of its toll were never pleasant. Cade and Ersia stood side by side, their backs pressed against the doors, mentally preparing themselves to enter the fray.

"I hope you learned something down there with Wu-Xia," Ersia said.

Cade scoffed. "As well as I learn anything."

Without warning or even a countdown, Ersia lifted her foot— she was wearing mech boots, something Cade hadn't noticed until now—and drilled her heel squarely into the middle of the double doors. The doors flew open, splintering under the force of her kick.

Cade was stunned by what he saw. While he hadn't seen the throne room yet—he was unconscious the first time through—he felt confident in assuming it was, at this moment in time, definitely worse for wear. Monaskins seemed to have a passion for overblown décor and architecture—you had to do *something* during all those years in isolation—and there was no way that throne room, of all places, would have been any different. But now, hardly even the shadow of the Monaskins' fine taste remained.

For starters, the ceiling had been utterly ruined. A Praxis Elite Thunder Cruiser must have pounded it with its battery of heavy artillery until the fortified stonework buckled under its compromised integrity. All that remained were a few scant bricks that jutted from the ceiling's remains like fingers pried away from a hand that wouldn't open. Cade could see the Thunder Cruiser hovering right above the hole; it'd stopped its assault on the palace—Praxis wouldn't want the entire structure to come down with its own forces still inside—but drones and gunners still rappelled from the ship's impossibly large passenger hold all the way to the ground. And on their way down, they all kept a steady stream of blaster fire directed at whatever they thought they could hit. Most kept their sights on the Monaskin ground forces, but a few of the gunners directed their fire at the distinct character of not only the room but the heart and soul of Monaskis itself. Cade spotted the remnants of wall paintings that'd been shredded, reliefs that'd been obliterated; at the moment, two gunners were targeting a banner that was embroidered with primitive symbols—a historical artifact, no doubt—that hung from the ceiling to the floor. The tattered remains of two similar banners hung nearby, their lonesome ribbons gently swaying amid the chaos. This is what Praxis did. The evil kingdom wasn't satisfied killing people or even killing people en masse. They also had to kill entire cultures, wiping out as much history as possible. Praxian invasions only ended in two ways: complete abdication to the kingdom or a scorched and salted planet. After all, you couldn't create an obedient galactic hegemony without torching the character of the galaxy as is, and that's what Praxis fully intended to do.

A younger, less responsible Cade would have thrown himself right into the fray, driven by his righteous anger. But Cade knew better. He knew what was at stake. His objective wasn't to win the battle; it was to navigate it. He had to find Ga Halle and face her. And once he did, one way or another, the assault on Monaskis would be over. She'd either kill him and claim the Rokura, or he'd do the same to her and put an end to the Praxian scourge right there and then. He was really hoping for the latter.

Ersia, who was crouched behind a golden pillar adjacent to Cade, yelled something he couldn't make out. A series of blaster bolts chipped away at the pillar he was positioned behind, and the penetrating sound, combined with the crumbling marble, seemed to be as much as Cade's ears could take.

"WHAT?" Cade yelled over the ruckus.

Ersia grimaced hard at Cade, then she twisted her body around her pillar and fired off two shots. The deafening noise that'd been thrumming in Cade's ear stopped; he turned to see the gunner who'd been relentlessly firing in his direction on his back. He wasn't moving.

"Nice work," Cade told Ersia.

"Shots to the face usually do the trick, especially when they're not looking; their armor can't respond quickly enough to cover up. Plus, head shots are a lot of fun."

"Uh-huh," Cade said. "Good to know."

"Look, I was saying—"

"Down!" Cade yelled, and Ersia dropped. Right as she did, Cade fired off two bolts, scoring almost two identical head shots on a pair of creeping sentry drones.

Ersia looked behind her and spotted the downed drones. She then huffed in an agitated breath and continued. "I was *saying* that the Praxian forces are trying to bottleneck my troops to the center of the hall. That's good. They haven't plugged the area yet, and that gives us an opening. We need to join one of my squads; they can create a shield around you, punch their way to the front doors, and get you out."

Cade's eyes wandered to the heart of the battle being waged at the center of the room. Drones, gunners, and Monaskin soldiers all fell, one after another after another. Cade envisioned the human shield surrounding him, guiding him to the palace's doors, which was not a short distance. The Monaskins had to love their pomp and circumstance, because the runway leading from the entrance to the throne itself was about a thousand miles long. That was a lot of time for Cade's shield to rack up casualties—soldiers dying because of him. He couldn't stand the thought of that.

"I have a bull's-eye on my back," he said as the gears in his mind assembled an idea.

"Yeah," Ersia replied, "that's the problem. Can't you just use the Rokura to completely wipe out Praxis? That would really be helpful."

Cade grimaced. "It's . . . complicated. And if I tried, I'd probably kill just as many Monaskin soldiers as I did Praxian."

"So the weapon is good for slapping a target on you but not helping you fight back. Great."

"Well, a bull's-eye—or a benefit."

Ersia huffed in another agitated breath, and Cade took it as his cue to get to the point.

"I'm a distraction. But we can use that. See, if I break for it along this far wall, all those Praxian morons will see me. Once they do, they'll turn the attention over here, giving your troops the chance to pick them off and cover my exit."

Ersia looked sternly at Cade. "That's actually not a bad idea," she admitted.

Cade surveyed the scene. It was as good a time as any to get moving.

"Ready?" he asked.

"Always," Ersia replied with a smile.

Cade nodded, absolutely believing that Ersia was ready to blast whatever opposition standing in her way at any given moment, and took off.

Praxis had been waiting for them to do just that.

The moment Cade sprang out from behind the pillar, he was met with a barrage of countless blaster bolts screaming all around him. Thankfully, the distance to the next pillar was short, and while Praxis had been waiting for him, they hadn't accounted for Ersia. With their attention drawn to Cade, the queen picked off no fewer than six targets. While it was an impressive display of marksmanship, Cade knew those were the only clean shots Ersia was going to get; now Praxis would be targeting her as well. Not only that, but there was no telling how many more drones and gunners would join the effort to kill Cade; there were already more involved than he'd anticipated. A lot more.

"We've got a long way to go!" Cade yelled to Ersia as he took count of the eight columns that separated himself from the front doors. Behind him, the Monaskin infantry was making the most of the attention drawn toward Cade and was launching an offensive to push back against the Praxian forces. The sizzling of blaster bolts streaking back and forth intensified, and Cade knew it would only get worse.

Ersia took stock of the distance as well, then a shimmer sparked in her eye. A sly look appeared on her face. Cade didn't like it.

"Why are you making that face?" he asked. "What are you thinking?"

"You feeling lucky?" Ersia asked.

Cade drew in his lips and shook his head. He exhaled. "Not particularly."

Ersia shrugged at Cade in a way that told him "too bad" and got on her comms. "Xeric! Xeric, do you read?" she yelled into her wrist unit.

Xeric answered quickly, but Cade couldn't make out what he was saying.

"We need coverage—a lot of coverage. Order an unmanned pod car to ground in the throne room and then pull back. Get everyone away immediately. Do you copy?"

A crackling came through the comms, and then Ersia turned to Cade.

"Get ready to run."

For a moment, it was quiet. Relatively. The battle still waged, but the enemies gunning specifically for Cade and Ersia took a break from their assault. Cade figured they were waiting on him to poke his head out. But then, the Monaskin troops began to fall back. They laid down suppressive fire, and Cade had to assume that it looked to Praxis like they were retreating. It certainly looked like it to him until there was a screaming across the sky, and then Cade knew the soldiers weren't retreating; they were just getting out of the way.

Offensive fire erupted out of the Thunder Cruiser, directed at the pod that was coming in hot. The pod spun and weaved, deftly dodging the attacks as it accelerated toward the palace—right at the hole in the ceiling.

"Let's go!" Ersia said as she took hold of Cade's hand and dragged him forward. Blaster bolts came at them fast and furious, but blaster bolts were the least of Cade's problems. A transport vessel was about to crash-land on his head.

"Are you sure this is a good idea?!" Cade hollered as he kept pace with Ersia.

"No!" Ersia yelled back. "But it's all we've got!"

The screaming in the sky grew louder and louder until it was interrupted by what sounded like an explosion. Though he really didn't want to look up, Cade's eyes instinctively shot to the ceiling. The pod's rear engine was pouring out black smoke from where it'd been hit. But the Thunder Cruiser's strike didn't matter; the pod was barreling toward its objective, so enormous in the sky that Cade thought he could pick out even the tiniest detail of its protective shell as it rocketed through the hole in the palace's ceiling.

The impact was tremendous. Sure, Cade had crashed a ship before. But it was a profoundly different thing to be inside a ship during a crash, safely strapped in, rather than outside. Upon the ship hitting land, a shock wave erupted in every direction; the power of it blasted Cade clean off his feet and propelled him back with unbelievable force. He smashed against a wall, crushing both his back and the plaster in the process. Though Cade's body hurt so much he couldn't even bring himself to breathe, he raised his head just enough to see the pod gliding across the floor, leaving a trail of rubble and obliterated drones in its wake. Its momentum began to waver as it reached the stairs that led to the throne's platform, which is where the Monaskin forces had congregated. As the pod came to a halt, screeching and howling like a dying wild animal all the way, Cade acknowledged how fortunate it was that one of the engines had been knocked out before the ship hit the ground. That little bit of lost power probably saved every Monaskin life.

Beside him, Ersia lifted herself off the ground and spat blood.

"What are you waiting for?" she asked, wincing through the pain.

Cade blinked hard. He couldn't tell if his ears were ringing or if the ringing was coming straight from his brain. Regardless, it was hard for him to think clearly enough to understand what Ersia was saying.

"What?" he groggily asked.

"They're not going to stay down forever," Ersia said. "You have to go get her. Get Ga Halle."

"Sure," Cade said, barely able to stand. "Right."

Cade picked himself up and swallowed the pain that riddled his body. He stretched out his hand and helped Ersia to her feet, too.

"Thank you," Cade said. "I owe you more than I can ever repay."

Ersia nodded—dignified, royal. "Just do what that weapon was meant to do, and we'll call it even," she said.

Cade pulled the Rokura off his back and set off, half limping, toward the door. What was left of the Praxian sentries and gunners were still gathering themselves, and their numbers had thinned considerably. Unless the Thunder Cruiser had another reserve of troops, the Monaskins would be able to finish them off. Still, the damage had been done. Cade looked back one last time to see the throne room's chaos. All of this death and destruction to satiate one person's lust to obtain unlimited power. It was all so pointless, so tragic. Cade became furious as he conceptualized the scope of the misery Ga Halle had caused. Never had he been so determined to face her.

Never had he been so determined to see her fall.

"Cade Sura, the one who would be Paragon," Ga Halle mocked. "I thought you'd never make it."

Cade stood at the start of the landing platform, eyeing Ga Halle at the other end. She was exactly as she'd been when she'd appeared to Cade in his visions: the crown of daggers, the obsidian shawl that conformed to her body, the darkness in her eyes. Her containment suit had also conformed to whatever transformation she had undergone; the once-blue waves of antimatter now pulsed with inky blackness. Cade couldn't even theorize what had happened to her, and he wasn't sure that he wanted to know. Besides, his focus was elsewhere. Because just in case the unhinged ruler of the galaxy's tyrannical kingdom wasn't enough to deal with, there was more.

Ga Halle wasn't alone.

Hovering behind her were the three specters that somehow were responsible for upgrading Ga Halle from an evil despot to a magical evil despot—the dark seeds of Mankarta. Though they mainly retained their ghastly forms, their faces were more articulated than they'd been in Cade's previous encounter. Each had sculpted for itself a woman's head, pewter-toned and completely hairless. Cade couldn't decide if their lifeless faces made them more or less horrifying. As much as Cade thought it was in his best interests to keep an eye on the dark seeds—he had no idea what they were capable of—he couldn't help but dedicate his attention to Percival.

Beaten, bruised, and bloodied Percival.

He was on his knees in front of Ga Halle, and she was stroking his hair with one hand like he was her pet. With her other hand, she kept her shido pressed firmly to his throat—one swipe and Percival would be dead.

"Let him go," Cade called out. "Let him go, or I'll obliterate every inch of you down to the shriveled thing you call a soul."

"We both know you can't do that, so let me offer you a deal," Ga Halle said. "It's very simple—give me the Rokura, and I'll let Percival live. I'll let both of you live."

"I'll never let that happen," Percival snarled. "I'd sooner throw myself off this platform than let you touch that weapon."

Percival had been staring at Cade through despondent eyes, so Cade was glad when he showed that he hadn't lost his fire. Still, Cade knew the complicated history between Percival and

Ga Halle, and he knew getting beaten by her had to have broken more than his body. The loss must have been profoundly demoralizing; Percival had dedicated so much of his life to waging war against his former friend, driven by his feelings of shame and anger for having been at Ga Halle's side the moment her power-craving mania began. Shame because he'd abandoned his duty as the Paragon; anger for not being able to stop Ga Halle—to kill her—when he'd had the chance. Cade had been worried about Percival from the moment Ersia told him that he'd gone after Ga Halle. It was such a brazen and terrible idea, but Cade understood why Percival had done it. Knowing firsthand the Rokura's terrible power, Cade never faulted Percival's decision to reject the mantle of the Paragon and leave unfinished the job the weapon had started when it had tried to kill Ga Halle. But those decisions weighed heavily on Percival, because even if he'd done one of those two things differently—if he'd remained the Paragon or finished off Ga Halle—the galaxy would have been a much different place. Percival spent a lifetime trying to correct what had happened in the spire on Quarry, but he couldn't. Ga Halle had gotten too powerful, and he'd gotten too old. And now, resoundingly beaten, Percival was a man with nothing left to lose.

Cade took two steps forward on the platform. "Do you even realize what you've done to the galaxy?" he asked, unable to stifle his disgust. "Do you understand the pain you've caused?"

Ga Halle was unmoved. "You silly boy, you know nothing. Do you truly believe that a galaxy absent of me would also be absent of pain? Let me ask you this: Have you ever heard of the tribal feuding on Adama? Feuding that had gone on, until just recently, for centuries?"

"I've heard of it, yeah," Cade said.

"And do you know what life on Adama was like before the

feuds finally ended? Did the Well ever send you there to try to make peace?"

"No," Cade tersely answered.

"No. No, of course they didn't. It was too complicated for them. Too messy, and the Masters didn't like to get their hands dirty. You want to know about misery? Adama was misery personified. That planet was suffocated by a war waged by extremists. The various tribes fought their battles everywhere. On city streets, in parks, spaceports—they didn't care. Collateral damage meant nothing to them; the innocent lives they took meant nothing to them. And what was it all for? Some ridiculous disputes over land and religion that'd been going on so long no one even remembered how it had all started.

"That is misery; that is suffering. And I released those people. Not the Well, not the Galactic Alliance. *I did.*"

"So what?" Cade said, scowling. "You're branding yourself a peacekeeper now?"

Ga Halle shrugged. "At least I know what it takes to get there."

"You are seriously out of your mind." Cade's voice was on the cusp of trembling, but he kept his righteous anger from boiling over. "I mean, this peace on Adama required a whole bunch of killing, right? That's how peace is won?"

Ga Halle smiled but didn't say a word.

"Peace through terror is no peace at all," Cade growled.

"That's where you're wrong," Ga Halle said, her voice thick with conviction. "There's no having one without the other. The Well had their chance to make peace. They flooded the galaxy with aid missions and diplomacy and all their other weak attempts to justify their existence. They wanted what I'm giving the galaxy; what they got was Adama. The Well's time is over. Now, it's my turn."

Ga Halle turned around and nodded to one of the dark seeds.

At her signal, the three specters wafted in front of the Praxian queen and hovered in a straight line just over her head.

"The Rokura," Ga Halle demanded.

Cade aimed the Rokura ahead. His thoughts flew to what Wu-Xia had told him about vanquishing evil, about refusing to compromise. He remembered the gorgan; he thought of what he'd done, how he'd channeled the Rokura's light somehow through the determination of his will. Cade's heart and mind were heavy with all of this, but the clarity of what he needed to do was new, and it brought him at least a modicum of solace.

"You might have convinced yourself of this whole peacemaker line, but there's no way I'm buying it," Cade said. "Everything you've done, everything you plan to do, none of it is about you trying to bring order to the galaxy. This whole thing—all the battles and the blood—is all about you still trying to get back what you think you lost in the spire. Get over it."

There was a tense moment when Cade waited for Ga Halle to attack him in a rampage, but she didn't. She simply stood with her shido pressed against Percival's throat, her dark eyes fixed on Cade.

"And now look at you," Cade continued. "You've made yourself into something with the help of . . . whatever these dark seeds are. I don't know what it is, and I don't care. Nothing will change that you're not the Paragon, and you never will be." Cade drew a deep breath and fought back angry tears. "I know what the Paragon is; I saw it in my brother. Tristan . . ." Cade trailed off, thinking of the right words to say to capture everything he knew and felt about his brother. A bittersweet smile appeared on his face as he remembered what Wu-Xia had said. "Tristan was incorruptible. *He* was made to be this, and you disgrace everything he was by acting like you're anywhere close to being his equal."

"Give. Me. The. *Rokura*." Ga Halle's voice trembled with rage.

"*Never.*"

Ga Halle nodded; she seemed to know Cade's resistance was inevitable. She probably even hoped for it. "Then die," she said.

Ga Halle didn't have to say a word or deliver a signal. The dark seeds knew. As they flew toward Cade, the masklike faces transformed into three human skulls that burned off streaks of effervescent tendrils that glowed deep red, green, and indigo. Their decaying jaws opened wide, and from them they discharged a bloodcurdling scream. Cade wanted to cover his ears; he wanted to rip his ears from his head, but he maintained his focus. The gorgan. He'd healed the scarred beast by appealing not only to the goodness of the Rokura but also the goodness in himself. Cade had to stay committed in his heart and mind to what he wanted from the weapon. He wasn't going to defeat evil on its terms and compromise his own soul in the process, nor was he going to ever be strong enough or incorruptible enough to overcome the Rokura's strength. Cade's deepest desire was simple; he wanted to make the galaxy better. And Wu-Xia was right about the path to getting there. Evil had to be vanquished. Not by dominating it, not by bringing it to heel. The only option Cade had was to do what he did with the gorgan. He had to expunge evil, totally and completely.

Cade drew on this clarity. He fed it into the Rokura and, just like in the fighting pit, a burst of white energy was thrown from the weapon's tip. The radiant light intensified with tremendous rapidity and crackled with raw power. Still, the dark seeds continued toward Cade undeterred. They were nearly within striking distance, their long, skeletal fingers reaching out, ready to claw and tear at Cade, when he pushed the light forward. A stream of the Rokura's energy surged from its tip and propelled ahead; it halted the ghouls and began to wrap them in a force field of light. Soon, the dark seeds began to writhe and convulse; they shrieked as if suffering from torturous duress. Cade could only hope he was doing to them what he'd managed to do to the gorgan; he didn't know what the dark seeds once were, but he knew they couldn't have been born this way. At least he hoped not.

The three specters fought against Cade and the Rokura, but he didn't relent. He continued to push until, finally, the weapon's power hit its apex. The dark seeds were consumed by light that shone so brightly Cade was forced to look away.

Then it was over.

The light receded from the Rokura, though Cade felt the difference in the power it had expended. Before, it was like the weapon had been working through him, like he was merely a necessary vessel for its outward displays of might. But now, just like with the gorgan, Cade felt like he had agency in the Rokura's power; he felt like it was coming from him, rather than through him. It was natural; it was, as Wu-Xia had promised, a product of him simply being.

When the energy Cade felt cycling between himself and the weapon ended, it was once again just a weapon, no different in appearance from a shido. What changed, though, were the dark seeds. Cade turned and saw them standing just an arm's length away. Gone were the flaming skulls and the terrible shrieks; gone was the menace and the wisps of tendrils. They were now just three women, identical to one another, no older than Cade, clothed in red, green, and indigo dresses that were lavish, ornate, and unlike anything Cade had ever seen before. They seemed to be from an entirely different era.

All three women—sisters, Cade presumed—ran their fingers over their cheeks and lips as if feeling their flesh for the very first time. Or maybe, Cade considered, it was the first time in many, many years. The centermost one let out a soft laugh, then she looked at Cade. She smiled at him as a tear rolled off the contour of her cheek.

"Thank you," she whispered, and then she took hold of her

sisters' hands. They formed a circle, drawing into one another; as they did, their skin began to peel off. Little by little, more and more of the bodies disintegrated, flesh and bone drying to dust and floating away, ostensibly, to join the universe. Cade watched it go and felt, for a moment, a sense of peace within himself.

But Ga Halle shattered that feeling.

"You shouldn't have done that," she said, her voice conveying not even the slightest hint of perturbation. "We'll just have to make it even."

Ga Halle's arm barely even moved. It required hardly any effort for her to jam her shido's blade into Percival's throat and then cut.

"No," Cade whispered, barely able to muster enough air to get the simple word out of his mouth. "What have you done?"

Ga Halle shoved Percival to the ground by his hair—an unnecessary display of her dominance. For a moment, Cade thought Percival was going to get up. That he was going to fight back. But he stayed facedown on the ground, unmoving, as the crimson pooled around his head.

"NO!" Cade howled.

Ga Halle charged Cade. Her shido left a trail of Percival's blood behind her. And Cade, like Ga Halle, was transported back to the place that, in a way, he'd never leave: the Quarrian spire. He was watching his brother get murdered all over again, and he screamed with the fury he couldn't control. Tristan and Percival, both murdered in front of him; both dead because he couldn't do anything to stop it. Cade watched Ga Halle approach, and his rage intensified with every step she took. Every death, from the planets she'd snuffed out to the people Cade had loved, was because of her. And now she was going to try to kill him, too. Then Kira. Then Mig, 4-Qel, Kobe, and whoever else stood in her way. As he looked at the twisted, crazed look on Ga Halle's face, the pools of darkness that were her eyes, the daggers that grew from her head, he knew there could be no redemption for her. She was dead in her core, dead in her soul, and Cade couldn't risk keeping any variation of her in the galaxy. There'd be no saving Ga Halle.

Rage and pain swelled within him, and he poured every ounce of it into the Rokura. He called on it to do what it had done to the Fatebreaker that'd killed Tristan, what it had wanted to do countless times since then. Cade willed it to unleash its darkest desires, whatever they may be, and destroy Ga Halle. In his mind's eye, he saw her being torn apart, piece by piece, from her flesh to her bones until there was nothing left of her. Cade hoped the pain it caused Ga Halle lasted an eternity.

But nothing happened.

Cade pushed and forced everything that was inside of him into the Rokura, but it didn't respond. Ga Halle was almost on him, and he needed the Rokura to act. Now more than ever.

"Come on!" he yelled, pounding his fist against its cold metal. "Kill her!"

Ga Halle leapt high into the air; she held her shido with two hands above her head, and she was bringing it down on Cade when he gave up on the Rokura's power and used it instead like a normal shido. He blocked Ga Halle's strike at the last possible moment. In the meeting of their weapons, Cade felt Ga Halle's immense strength and the dark power that fueled it. He knew he was doomed.

Ga Halle wasted no time continuing her assault. She swung the back end of her shido around and drove it into Cade's abdomen. It doubled him over, but he recovered just enough to block Ga Halle's uppercut, also with the back end of her shido, aimed at Cade's face. Rolling away from Ga Halle, Cade shoved her shido aside and tried to drill the Rokura's blades into her containment suit. He didn't know what would happen if her suit was compromised, but he assumed it wouldn't be good.

Ga Halle, though, was fast. She knocked Cade's weapon aside and followed her defense with a swipe at Cade's midsection. He leapt back, avoiding the blow, and went at Ga Halle with a series of jabs, all of which were defended easily. As they exchanged blows, pushing back and forth across the narrow strip leading to the landing platform, Cade began to hope that Ga Halle would start taunting or mocking him. Anything to get her distracted. But she didn't utter a word, and Cade was far too devoted to keeping up with his enemy to even think about drawing her into a battle of barbs.

The effort required to combat Ga Halle's strength exhausted Cade, and he lost a step quickly. Ga Halle recognized Cade's waning stamina, and she went in for the kill.

Coming out of a defended overhead strike, Ga Halle drove her heel into Cade's knee, buckling his leg; Cade stumbled, and though he tried to recover his position quickly, he was too slow. Ga Halle swiped her shido's hilt across Cade's face, battering his right eye.

"Agh!" Cade growled, and he felt the flesh over his eyelid swelling immediately. He had only a few moments, at best, before his eye was swollen shut.

He went back at Ga Halle with a downward stab, trying to catch her off guard by going after her legs. Ga Halle wasn't fooled. She grabbed the shaft of the Rokura as he plunged it toward her, then she drove her own shido into Cade's thigh. The tips of all three blades chewed into Cade's muscle; he screamed painfully, then howled louder when Ga Halle twisted her weapon out of his flesh. Cade could hardly see, he could barely move, and he knew his punishment was just beginning.

Ga Halle struck high, and Cade defended, but the purpose of her strike was to get Cade out of position. As soon as their shidos clanged together, Ga Halle spun around Cade, narrowly avoiding falling off the landing strip, and she sliced her shido across his bicep as she passed. Behind him, she brained him with the butt of her weapon, and Cade saw stars. The blow destroyed his sense of equilibrium, and he fell to his knees.

Cade's consciousness flickered, but he was aware enough to know he was about to die. His body vertiginously swayed but was righted by a hand clenching his chin. Cade looked up to see Ga Halle, triumphant, standing above him.

"You think I'm going to kill you, don't you?"

Cade could hardly focus on her words; the only thing that kept him conscious was the hope for one chance to stop Ga Halle from getting what she wanted. As she waited for his response, Cade pooled what little energy he still possessed. It wasn't much, but with all he had, he tried to raise his arm—nearly immobile from the deep cut in the muscle—and throw the Rokura into the fathomless depths that awaited over the side of the platform.

Ga Halle stomped on Cade's wrist before it got an inch off the ground.

"That should have been the first thing you did when you stepped out here," Ga Halle mocked. "But you had to be noble and try to do what we both know you're incapable of doing."

Cade wanted to cry furious tears over what he'd done. For whatever short amount of time he had to live, he would spend it lacerating himself for not following the instinct he'd first had when the Rokura was dumped into his possession: Destroy it and run. That's what he was cut out to do. And now . . . now, it was all over. Because with a forceful tug, Ga Halle yanked the most powerful weapon in the galaxy from Cade's limp hand.

Cade expected the galaxy to shake. He expected the ground to tremble beneath him. He expected Ga Halle to exhibit some sort of display of her supremacy. But nothing was torn asunder, and there was no satisfaction expressed from his nemesis. It was just the two of them, alone on a platform on a planet that had been decimated by the very weapon now held by the most dangerous person in the universe. And all Cade could do was succumb to the darkness that was crowding the periphery of his vision. To the feelings of shame that he couldn't face, knowing his failure had damned the entire galaxy. Killing him, he realized, would have been the humane thing for Ga Halle to do, and that was probably why she didn't do it.

What happened next was a blur to Cade. The last thing he remembered was being dragged down the platform toward Ga Halle's ship.

And then, the ship exploded. The blast was just beyond his and Ga Halle's range; he felt the explosion's heat on his face, and his mind cleared as two Monaskin attack ships descended on Ga Halle. The ships opened up their cannons on Ga Halle; the first shots went wide, pelting the strip just behind Cade. Those turned out to be the only strikes that would touch the ground.

As if she'd done so a hundred times before, Ga Halle raised the Rokura skyward, directing it at the approaching ships. The weapon's tip crackled with power, and the ships, paired in a tight formation, fired down once more. But this time, Ga Halle wouldn't be caught in harm's way.

The Rokura unleashed a streak of energy, catching the ships' blasts in midair. The bolts disintegrated to ash, and the Rokura's charge continued outward, capturing the ships in a field of sizzling light. Even through the haze of his lingering disorientation, Cade knew he was witnessing something different. This is what happened, Cade understood, when someone embraced what he'd worked so hard to fight against. And even in this glimpse, it was every bit as terrifying as he knew it could be.

Within moments, the ships were torn apart, their individual pieces—like the bolts—disintegrated. The pilots, too, were caught in the Rokura's fury. And they, too, were obliterated.

"I hope you don't mind," Ga Halle said as she dragged Cade forward once again. "We'll be taking your ship."

"Just kill me," Cade said, feeling sickened not only by what he'd seen but also by what he knew was still to come.

"You'll remain alive for just a while longer," Ga Halle said. "I wouldn't want there to be any mistaking how the beloved Paragon died. So, they'll watch. Your friends, your band of renegades, the entire galaxy. They'll watch you die at my hands, and they'll know at last who their savior truly is.

"They'll know that I am their *god*."

CHAPTER THIRTEEN

A thunderclap boomed across the sky, throttling the Praxian assault shuttle. For a moment, Kira thought that the storm on Praxis had followed them all the way to Olanus, the nearest of Praxis's six moons and home to the Crucible. But she realized that the turbulence was caused by sloppy reentry executed by green pilots. Bolstering your forces through intimidation, threats, and conscription was fine for the numbers but terrible in the details. While a robust army looked good on paper, if the majority of your grunts couldn't handle flying a starship, the numbers didn't mean a whole lot. The soundest tactics, Kira believed, started with skill and morale. Ga Halle, though, liked to inundate her enemies. She liked to overwhelm. But she did so with coffers crammed with incompetent soldiers who were only there because they had to be. Stockpiling your forces with as many warm bodies as possible was conventional wisdom that most leaders followed. But most leaders weren't Kira. She was convinced that she could pit ten skilled soldiers against a hundred sloppy ones and walk away with a clean victory.

At least she hoped she could. Kira could only guess how many troops were stationed at the Crucible, and even her most conservative estimations made her wish she had more on her side. A lot more on her side. Though if reinforcements were her only hope, she might as well request to be taken straight to the firing squad when the ship landed. She needed a plan, but seeing as she was heading to a place she knew nothing about, logistically, trying to predict even one second into the future was a wasted effort. There'd be no plan, no reinforcements, and that was that. But as she looked out the narrow window high on the wall opposite her, she noticed that it wasn't raining on Olanus like it was on Praxis. At least she had that.

And she had her squad. Kobe was seated on Kira's right, unconscious. He'd lost a lot of blood, but they'd sutured him well enough to survive the trip and the questioning Kira was certain awaited him. Kay sat across from her in the shuttle's narrow hold, and he was doing his best to nudge Mig without any of the Praxian guards catching his attempts. Mig was slumped in the seat next to Kay, still reeling from 4-Qel's captivity; 4-Qel was lying prone in the middle of the hold, hovering just a few inches off the ground. Mig hadn't spoken a word since they were loaded inside; in fact, Kira wasn't certain he'd even blinked. He stared at 4-Qel, his face weighed down by his grief. His eyes had darkened, accentuating the pallor of his skin. He was in his own world, and whatever Kay was trying to convey to him wasn't getting through. He needed to be more aggressive if he was going to get Mig's attention.

Which meant he needed a distraction.

Kira cleared her throat, the rasping sound rising just above the shuttle's grinding hum, and looked at Kay without looking *at* him. When she noticed she'd caught his attention, she dipped her head to her left, just slightly, indicating the guard—Crucible guards wore reinforced tactical uniforms, all black, with matching black helmets that were broken in color only by the ruby-red shielding over their eyes—sitting next to her. He'd removed his helmet right after takeoff, and Kira was delighted by Praxis's loose regulations. He didn't know it, but this guard had given Kira just the opening she needed.

Once Kay acknowledged, subtly, that he'd received her signal—or the gist, just that he knew she was about to do *something*—Kira took a moment to scan the ship one last time. There was the guard next to her and two more at the door. All were armed with N-12 enforcer rifles, blasters that tested the limits of their holder's ability to resist recoil. The hold was small, which gave them little room to maneuver when Kay put his scheme in motion. Whatever it was, Kira didn't care. Weaponless and bound meant nothing to her. It was her three against their three, and she'd take those odds no matter what the handicap.

Kira turned her head to the guard on her left and stared. He was facing straight ahead, but she knew he noticed her looking. The muscles in his face cycled between being tense and relaxed, and his right eye darted in every direction. Kira hadn't realized it before, but this guard couldn't have been more than seventeen years old—a baby who probably had been busted for theft when he was a teenager and dumped into the Crucible because that's how crime and punishment worked on Praxis. Kira almost felt bad for him, but not bad enough to prevent herself from doing what she had to do. Not even close.

Finally, the guard turned to face Kira. He tried to look tough and hard, but he looked sleepy and constipated instead. He was closer to Kira now—the slightest bit closer—but since she was restrained to her seat, she needed every centimeter she could get.

"You got a problem?" the guard sneered.

Kira didn't reply. At least, not with words. Instead, she reared her head back and threw it forward as far as her neck and her restraints allowed. Her forehead bashed the soldier's face, catching him square in his nose; Kira felt the brittle cartilage shatter upon impact, and by the time she pulled back, his nose was already gushing blood.

"Hey!" one of the guards yelled from her spot next to the door. "What do you think you're doing?!"

As she heard the boots stomping toward her, she knew what was about to happen. She knew it from the start. So when the butt of the enforcer rifle cracked against the side of her head, smashing against her temple, she was ready for it. The blow didn't ring her bell any less, but at least she wasn't caught off guard. All that mattered was that she'd accomplished her intended effect; all Praxian eyes were on Kira, and no one was paying attention to Kay and Mig.

By the time Kira's ears stopped ringing and her vision regained its clarity, the ship's comms system was announcing they were on their landing vector heading toward the Crucible landing pad. The guard seated next to her slid his helmet back on, and Kira could feel the tension growing in this diminutive space. The Crucible couldn't have been an easy place to be stationed, and Kira's arrival, mixed with Ebik's presence and the plan he was executing, must have only made the tension even tauter. Which was good. People who were wound too tightly lacked focus and patience; they made mistakes.

Kay, on the other hand, was as calm as the soothing waters of Ohan. In fact, when Kira looked at him, he smiled.

"Hang on tight," he said, even though it was a totally redundant thing to say. They were bound to their seats; if they were held down any tighter, their bones might start to snap.

Nonetheless, Kira got the point. Because a second after his caution, an explosion tore through the assault shuttle's rear engine.

Still reeling from the blow to her head, Kira felt like the ship was doing barrel rolls as it plummeted to the ground. Everything around her was spinning uncontrollably, and even when she shut her eyes, it was like she was a die tumbling across a wellington table. The ship's alarm screamed in her ears, its long, monotone bellowing sounding like the mating call of a monster that made the aquatic depths its home. Kira held tightly to the ionic restraints that wrapped around her shoulders and kept her in place, as if gripping a hunk of ionized metal would somehow protect her from the horrific crash landing they were all about to endure. And her holding on was even more of a futile gesture when the ship's power went out and the bonds lost their charge. There was a breathless moment when she was no longer squeezed against the ship's wall. But not just that.

She was free.

The guard next to her realized what the ship's power outage meant; Kira could see the shock in his eyes. He went for his blaster—as if spraying bolts from one of the galaxy's most powerful hand cannons was in any way a bright idea—but he was too slow. Despite the ship's spiraling turbulence, Kira managed to land a chop against the guard's neck, hitting him square in the sliver of space between where his uniform and helmet failed to seamlessly connect. A gargling sound crackled from inside the guard's helmet, and Kira threw all her weight into driving her elbow into his chest, delivering one sharp blow and then another. The ship hit a pocket of air that threw Kira up and off her seat; when she came down, she was facing the rear door and the two guards who were posted there. One of them had his enforcer in his grip. It was locked on Kira and ready to fire.

A half dozen enforcer bolts tore through the hold. The room glowed a searing orange with each eruption from the powerful weapon, but the blasts never touched Kira. Not a single shot went anywhere near her. The guard hadn't fired; she never even had the chance before her chest was riddled by a barrage of blaster fire. The assault shook her body like a marionette controlled by a drunken puppeteer, then she dropped face-first onto the ground. Kira turned to look over her shoulder, fully expecting to see Kay, his hands wrapped around the enforcer and a very satisfied look on his face. But Kay wasn't holding the powerful weapon; Mig was. The look on his face was no less satisfied, but there was a dark determination in his eyes as well.

"Eat it, dirtball," he said, and he was turning his newfound blaster toward the other guard when the ship began bucking wildly.

Everyone was thrown around the hold, and Kira knew it wouldn't be long before they reached the ground. And when the ship smashed against the moon's hard surface, there would be no survivors. The ship's descent was too fast, and now it was too out of control. The shuttle would hit the ground and either explode upon impact or it would bounce and tumble, crashing into whatever was in its way until, eventually, it stopped. And by then, nothing would remain but a crumpled hunk of scrap metal and a bunch of human limbs. That meant they had only one option: They had to get off that ship. Immediately.

"Kay!" Kira yelled, drawing on all her strength to grab on to a small crevice that ran below the window. "Get the door open! We're leaving!"

The guard who'd been sitting next to Kira was coming to and reaching for a sidewinder holstered at his waist. Kay pounded three hard, quick punches into his mask and then relieved him of his gun. He turned to Kira, tucked the sidewinder into the back of her pants, and smiled. "Aye, aye, Commander," he said, then punched the guard one last time, just for good measure.

"Mig! Get Kobe!"

Mig stepped toward Kobe, who had regained consciousness but not mental clarity, but stopped. His eyes shot to 4-Qel, and panic spread over his face.

"What about Four-Qel?" he yelled. "We can't leave him in the ship!"

"We're not! We're going to push him out and hope the containment field protects him."

"What?!"

"Hey!" Kira yelled, losing her patience. "You're the one always talking about science not being exact. Now move!"

Mig stomped petulantly, but he collected Kobe. And as Kay worked on opening the door, Kira took hold of the starboard wall and used it to help keep her balance as she scaled the side of the ship. There was a footlocker next to the cockpit's door, and Kira prayed it had what she was looking for. If not, she would have wasted a whole lot of effort just to die in a horrific landing anyway.

As she reached the footlocker, a sequence of blaster shots burst from the ship's rear. Kira turned and saw that Kay had subdued the final guard; he was standing with a keycard in his hand and Mig at his side.

"Got the key!" he yelled.

"Wait there!" Kira instructed, then she flung the locker open and breathed a sigh of relief. Something, finally, had worked in her favor.

"Incoming!" she yelled, and because the nose was descending, she had to hurl the three bundles she'd grabbed upward to reach Kay, Mig, and a barely lucid Kobe. They knew exactly what to do, strapping the packages to their backs. They were booster paks—personal jet packs that provided short, controlled bursts of flight.

"What now?" Kay yelled.

"Are you serious? Open the door, grab Four-Qel, and get out!" Kira ordered. "And grab whatever weapons you can, too!"

As Kira turned to the locker, she felt an onslaught of wind at her back as she grabbed another bundle; she was strapping it to her back when the cockpit door opened right in front of her. And standing in the doorway was Ortzo.

Blood ran from his hairline down the side of his face, and Kira spotted bleariness in his eyes. She assumed he'd bashed his head open at some point after Kay's explosion detonated and was just now coming to. Just when things were finally starting to look up.

Kira hurried to throw the booster pak over her shoulders, but despite having a concussed brain, Ortzo was just quick enough to stop her from getting away. With a vicious hand, he grabbed Kira by her throat and pulled her toward him.

"You will not escape," he huffed. With his other hand, he brandished a blade, the same one he'd stabbed Kobe with. It was a triblade, a detail Kira hadn't noticed back on Praxis. The same blade Ebik had used in his attempt to kill her.

Rage and resolve bloomed within Kira. If her own father couldn't kill her with this weapon, neither would this damn Fatebreaker.

"Yes, I will," Kira snarled, and she followed her words with a kick to Ortzo's abdomen, in the same spot Kobe had pounded in their duel. Ortzo winced in pain, and Kira made the most of the distraction; she landed two quick jabs into Ortzo's face, and he staggered back against the wall, disoriented from the blows. Kira planted both of her feet against his chest and pushed off as hard as she could. She tumbled out of his grip, landing hard on the floor. By the time she was up on her knees, Ortzo was stomping toward her. But Kira had everything she needed to make her escape from Ortzo and the ship.

"Good luck with the crash landing," she said, then pressed the small button that she had gripped in her left hand. The booster pak burned, and she propelled forward, flying up and out of the ship as it barreled forward in the opposite direction. She was only seconds into her flight when she heard metal scream and fire erupt from an explosion. Kira righted her trajectory and looked to the ground. There, not far from where she was hovering, she saw a blazing plume rising from the ground, the orange and black and gray intermingling in a deadly cloud before the entire thing dissipated just as quickly as it had ignited.

Somehow, they'd escaped, and for a moment—hardly longer than a blink of an eye—Kira felt like she could relax.

But then, from the ash and the smoke that wafted from the ground, Kira spotted something unbelievable: a figure getting bigger and bigger as it headed in her direction.

"You've got to be kidding me," an exasperated Kira said.

Ortzo, a booster pak strapped to his back, was racing toward her. And he wasn't slowing down.

Kira, stunned, didn't respond quickly enough. By the time she ignited more power into her booster pak, Ortzo was on her. He crashed into her and sent them both barreling through the sky.

Booster paks, though, were designed strictly for short bursts of flight, which meant they didn't last long. As luck would have it, both Kira's and Ortzo's paks began to run out of juice at the same time. Their barreling through the sky, entangled in one another, soon turned into them falling from the sky.

It was, to a degree, a controlled fall. The booster paks were programmed to reserve enough fuel to allow the wearer to land or at least get closer to landing. Kira and Ortzo were descending, but it was a slow enough fall for them to exchange blows as they neared the ground below.

Ortzo struck first, disengaging enough from Kira to deliver an elbow against the side of her head. She reared back, but she kept a tight hold on his armor with her left hand; she used her grip to pull herself forward, and she returned leading with her fist. She popped Ortzo directly in his face, and he groaned in pain. Kobe had done a number on him, and Kira was more than happy to pour salt in his wounds.

Kira punched him again, but when she tried her luck a third time, Ortzo was ready. He swallowed her fist in his much larger hand and squeezed it hard.

"You are no match!" Ortzo yelled as he head-butted Kira.

The blow sent her head spinning, and in her daze, she realized something important: The surface was coming on fast. She noticed its rapidly increasing proximity just as she saw Ortzo reach to his side, going for his shido. Kira couldn't have that, and she couldn't be tied up with this Fatebreaker if she wanted to give herself the best chance of landing safely. Hitting the ground uncontrollably and against the pillow of Ortzo's impenetrable armor wouldn't be the best way to end this flight. In fact, it would probably kill her.

As Ortzo pulled up his arm, shido in hand, Kira swung her fist in a powerful arc, down on his elbow. The blow swatted his hand back, and it gave Kira enough time to unholster her sidewinder and shove its barrel against Ortzo's armor.

"So long, *Fatebreaker*," she said and fired three shots point-blank into Ortzo's chest.

The force of the blast propelled Ortzo away from Kira; he flipped head over heels and continued to drop down to the ground, only now he had no control over his descent. Still, Kira angled her booster pak and pursued his trajectory; she wouldn't be satisfied until she was absolutely certain the bastard Fate-breaker was dead.

Her own descent to Olanus wasn't what she'd call graceful; the booster pak was nearly out of fuel, and when she hit the rolling green pasture, she landed hard. Her body somersaulted and spun through the tall grass, but she never lost sight of Ortzo. Not for one second.

Kira sprang to her feet, sidewinder in hand. She was knee-deep in a lush, idyllic field of tall, green grass that blossomed violet poppies at its tips. In the distance, waterfalls cascaded over a ridge, reflecting the star that was setting just over the horizon. Though Kira had never been on Olanus, she'd heard of its bound-less beauty. Unfortunately, that beauty was limited to the dry season, and that only lasted about six weeks out of the year. The rest of the year, Olanus was swallowed by torrential rains and rapidly descending temperatures that led to dangerous and deadly ice storms. Kira was very, very happy to have arrived on the moon during its dry season.

With cautious steps, Kira crept toward where she'd seen Ortzo crash. A swath of grass had been crushed in his wake, and Kira was able to follow the path that it made to her prey. She antici-pated Ortzo attacking her; she expected him to pounce at any moment. But he didn't, and soon enough, Kira had visual on him, his body twisted in unnatural angles as he lay motionless on the ground.

As she drew closer, Kira spotted the subtle rising and falling of his chest; he was breathing. She'd figured he'd find a way to survive. Keeping a comfortable distance, she drew a circle around Ortzo, studying every inch of him to ensure he didn't have any surprises waiting for her. He seemed unarmed, though. He seemed defenseless. In fact, when Kira stood above Ortzo's head, she saw his shido lying in the grass just a few feet away, but out of reach. The Fatebreaker didn't even have his precious weapon on him.

"Very careful," Ortzo murmured, struggling to push out his words through the pain. "You're smart."

Kira stepped next to Ortzo and pushed him over with the ball of her foot. His body rolled over without any resistance. Kira didn't know the extent of the Fatebreaker's injuries, but she figured it was safe to say they were extensive. Yet still, he somehow held on.

For now.

Kira gripped her sidewinder, keeping it close to her side.

"And what do you plan on doing with that?" he snarled.

"The galaxy a favor," she replied.

Kira fired. Three shots, and none of them missed.

"That's for Cade's parents, you rotten son of a—"

From behind, Kira heard footsteps. She swung around, sidewinder ready, and scared the crap out of Kay.

"Whoa!" he yelped. "It's just us. Just us."

And by "us," he meant himself, a limping Kobe, and Mig, walking side by side with 4-Qel. She wanted to run and hug him, but she wasn't certain how a killer drone would respond to that.

"Did you just kill a Fatebreaker?" 4-Qel asked, the question assuring Kira that whatever had happened to him hadn't resulted in any permanent damage. "The one who murdered Cade's parents?"

Kira looked down at Ortzo—or what was left of him. He was most definitely dead.

"Yes," she said. "Yes, I did."

"Impressive," 4-Qel said, nodding his approval. "Cade's going to be so delighted."

At the mention of Cade, Kira felt a weight like an increase in gravity pulling her down, compressing her. She wondered where he was. She wondered if he'd found what he was looking for. But most of all, she wondered if he was okay.

Her worry, her longing, was cut short by Kay, who was all business.

"So, what's next?" he asked.

"I'm glad you asked," Mig interjected. "I've made some calculations and . . . well, I'm actually not glad you asked. Because according to my calculations, our forecast isn't good."

"But it's not bad, right?" Kay asked, trying to sound hopeful.

"Uh, well . . ." Mig winced.

"Just spit it out," Kira said.

"Right," Mig agreed, then he began to pace, his mind working faster than his words could convey. "Okay, so, here's the thing: Ebik needs Olanus to be at the farthest point from Praxis in order to detonate the explosives that will destroy the planet. Right? Right. So, based on a number of factors—and I won't go into detail because I know how much you guys hate learning new things—I calculated when that window, when Olanus is farthest, is going to happen. And it's soon."

"How soon?" Kira asked, though she knew she wasn't going to like the answer.

Mig swallowed hard, and his voice went high. "About two hours. Give or take a few . . . seconds."

Nobody said a word. Kira could feel the sense of hopelessness, that they'd lost before they'd begun. She felt it herself, just as she felt the weight of all the lives on Praxis, all those people going about their day not knowing that their very existence was in the hands of a gang of misfits.

But just because things looked grim didn't mean that giving up was an option. Giving up was never an option.

"We can still do this," Kira said, taking command of her squad and its fading morale. "The Crucible is right above that ridge; we can get there in no time at all. And once we get there—" Kira paused. She took a deep breath and looked directly in the eyes of each member of her squad. "We all knew what coming to Olanus would mean for us. Ninety minutes . . . we don't need to factor in an escape. We just need to get to Ebik. We need to get to his detonator and destroy them both. We've been in tight jams before, and we've—"

"Um, Kira?" Kobe interrupted. His head was tilted up, his eyes fixed on the sky. "Is that some kind of missile?"

Kira turned and, following Kobe's line of vision, saw what he was referring to: a small streak of gray cutting through the dusk sky, heading right for them.

"I guess they know we're here," Kira huffed. She turned back to her squad, who looked as despondent as ever. They were beyond the point of being inspired, of being galvanized by words that motivated them to fight for what was right. Right now, all any of them had was simple cause and effect.

"Look, there's no running. There's nowhere for us to go. Our only option is to do whatever we can to find a way into the Crucible and save the lives of millions. It's up to us and no one else. Got it?"

Kira saw blank faces surrounding her.

"GOT IT?" she yelled, and she received uniform nods in response.

"Good, then let's move," Kira said, and she handed 4-Qel her sidewinder as they all started to trot ahead. "Four-Qel, take this and use that sharp vision of yours. Whatever that thing is that's coming at us, kill it."

4-Qel took the blaster, his attention still focused on what was streaking toward them.

"Kira, I'm not sure that's a missile. I think . . . I think . . . ," he said, and though his inflection abilities were limited, it was clear that he was marveling at whatever the strange object was. He didn't seem afraid of it.

"I think that's a *person*."

CHAPTER FOURTEEN

The pain had been excruciating.

During the journey to wherever they were heading, Cade's mind shifted between agonizing lucidity and unconsciousness filled with nightmarish visions. In his waking moments, he was visited by Ga Halle treating his wounds in the most indelicate way possible. Cade knew she wanted him alive, and he assumed she wanted him well enough to at least be able to stand on his own two feet. Her means for restoring him enough to rise for his own execution weren't a concern; she sutured him, shot him full of meds, and did whatever else was essential to ensure he wouldn't be taken for an invalid when the time for her to display her dominance came. She wasn't gentle or merciful; to her, she was treating a corpse.

And when he wasn't being made worse to eventually be made better, he dreamed. Or more appropriately, he experienced an approximation of dreaming. Visions haunted his mind—visions of Ga Halle, in all her wicked glory, using the Rokura to vanquish enemy armies in their entirety; with one mighty blast, scores of people were reduced to ash, and then that ash vanished into the galaxy's abyss. She used it to decimate entire worlds; Cade saw her plunge the weapon into the surface of a planet, and every bit of it withered and died. Ga Halle, sheathed in the weapon's protective shell, laughed and laughed as mayhem ruled. And finally, Cade was forced to witness the Praxian queen turning the weapon on Kira, Mig, 4-Qel, and Kobe. They writhed in agony, and as the weapon tore them apart, they screamed for Cade to save them. But there was nothing he could do.

That's why, when Cade returned to the waking world and saw his father sitting across from him, he assumed it was just another delusion. And it was, in a manner of speaking. But it was different, and even in his weakened state, Cade recognized that. He just didn't know if it was different with a purpose or just another vision there to torture him before death.

"Hello, Cade," Benji said. "You're not looking well, my son."

Cade was lying prone on a footlocker in the cargo hold, peering at his father through glassy eyes. It took a moment, but Cade brought himself to sit up even though he hardly had the energy to do so. His wrists were shackled in ionic cuffs, which was to be expected, and as he dragged his body off the locker's cold, hard surface, Cade realized that his vision was a fraction slower than his movements; as he sat up, the image of his father still rested at a 90-degree angle. It took a second for it to turn and click into place.

"Hey, Dad," Cade finally said, his lips cracking from dehydration as he spoke. "How've you been?"

His father smiled. "Dead."

"Mmm-hmm," Cade agreed. "That's right. Bummer."

Cade dropped his head back against the *Rubicon*'s wall, and his brain sloshed around in his skull. Then he wheezed a raspy breath and wondered when Ga Halle would finish him off. As if the universe itself were in a generous mood—though Cade would have appreciated that generosity a lot more a few hours earlier— the ship slipped into a downward trajectory. Ga Halle was taking them in for a landing, and that meant Cade was soon to outlive his purpose. And that sated his curiosity. Ga Halle would be executing him soon enough.

While Cade couldn't say that he accepted his death, he also knew he couldn't fight it. He had no intention of exiting this world kicking and screaming, either. After all, what was there to thrash against? He only had himself to blame. Cade should have never been so stupid and arrogant to believe he could wield the Rokura. Even if what Wu-Xia had said were true, even if the myth of the Paragon was one big scam, that still didn't mean someone like him—an adrift nobody who couldn't win wars like Wu-Xia, couldn't battle like Percival, and couldn't lead like Tristan—should be the one to take the mantle. He was wrong on so many counts he was convinced he was getting exactly what he deserved.

Just be, Cade recalled with grim disdain. It made little sense to him then. It made even less now.

Cade dropped his head and tried to shove those thoughts out of his mind. None of that mattered at this point anyway. He opened his eyes, and sitting across from him, still, was his father. And Benji had the expression on his face that would be etched in Cade's mind, forever and always: It was a look that conveyed his father's compassion, kindness, and patience. It'd been too long, Cade rued, since he'd seen any of those things. Which made sense that he'd be seeing them now; it was the best solace his bleary mind could conjure as he cruised to his death.

"You're a persistent hallucination, I'll give you that," Cade said. "So, you here to comfort me in my final hours?"

"You've come a long way, Cade," Benji said. "Though I wouldn't have guessed anything less from you."

"That I'd foul up the entire galaxy because of my poor judgment? Yeah, I guess we all should have seen that coming."

Benji smiled and chuckled softly. "Of course not. You've been a loyal, good friend, you've inspired people all around you—"

"Through a lie," Cade interrupted. "That's an important detail, Dad."

"And," Benji continued, without missing a beat, "you've shown the potential to be more than you think you're capable of being."

Cade gave a long, exaggerated groan. "I'm not doing it. I'm sorry, Dad, but I can't listen to another person tell me all the things I need to be and how I have to do it. Besides, you're just a hallucination anyway. You're my subconscious trying to make me feel better—though, by the way, you're doing a terrible job."

Benji nodded slowly as he listened. "Let me ask you one thing. What is the first line of the Galactic Treaty?"

"Uh . . . well, it . . . um—"

"'So be it in peace or in times of conflict, this agreement will stand,'" Benji said. "Now, if I'm just a figment of your mind, how could I know something that you don't?"

"I don't know," Cade huffed. "I have that stored in my brain somewhere, I just couldn't think of it. Anyway, so what? I mean, if you're not a hallucination, then what are you? How are you here?"

"Maybe I am just in your mind," Benji admitted. "Or maybe I'm something you unlocked in the Chamber of Memories. Does it matter?"

Cade shrugged, though his motion was limited by the bonds around his wrists. "At this point, not really."

Silence fell over the *Rubicon*'s cargo hold. Cade felt shame in having to face his father after his many failures; nevertheless, the simple occasion of seeing him again brought him joy that was so robust he was close to bursting into tears.

He sighed. He had so many things to say, so many questions to ask. About Tristan, about his mother, about what happened after . . . well, after you die. But one question pushed its way through the others, loud and persistent; it was an itch in his mind, one that Cade knew he had to scratch. He needed to know the truth.

"If you're really my dad and not just, you know . . . my imagination, then I have a question for you."

"Anything," Benji said.

"Were you and Mom part of the rebellion against Praxis? Is that why they attacked that ship when you died?"

Benji sucked in a deep breath, but he didn't take his gaze from Cade, not for one moment. There was solemnity between them; Cade felt it, and he was certain his father felt it as well.

"Your mother and I were dedicated to doing what was best to help people throughout the galaxy. In whatever form that took," Benji said. "In our lives, we believed that it was the responsibility of anyone who recognized evil to fight it. We are the ones who must expel evil from the galaxy. And now, my son, that burden falls to you."

Cade hung his head. "I tried, Dad. But everything went bad. And I know you're going to try, but look at me," Cade said, gesturing to his restraints. "You can't tell me I wasn't wrong."

"Yes, I can," Benji said, his face filled with so much pity. "Forget about all this stuff with the Rokura and what the Paragon is and isn't supposed to be and remember the one true thing that you've known all your life: You are never wrong when you stand up for what's right."

Cade shook his head. "Yeah, Dad. A lot of good that maxim did you. And Mom. And me."

"I'm an idealist, Cade, and so is your mother. The last thought

I had before I died was of you and Tristan; the knowledge that I'd never see you again was worse than any pain I could ever endure. I regret, more than you can possibly know, missing your life." Benji cut himself off by pressing his fist against his mouth. He winced, the sorrow he'd experienced all those years earlier still fresh, and it took him a moment to collect himself. "Cade, you can't run. You can't hide. The only thing you can do is what you've done your entire life; you need to do whatever you can to push evil out of this world."

Deep down, Cade didn't want to die, especially not like this. Not when he still had a chance to correct everything that'd happened. He was the only one who could stop Ga Halle, and if he was going to die, he was going to die fighting. The problem, given his captivity, was how he'd manage to do much of anything. He felt the ship jostle like it was going through the atmosphere of whatever planet they were heading toward; his opportunity to do something wasn't going to last forever.

"You're right," Cade said, feeling galvanized. "You're right. But . . . it's going to be a little tough for me to put up much of a fight if I can't get out of these bonds."

"You're sitting on everything you need," Benji said.

Cade rolled his eyes. "Yeah, yeah, yeah. The power comes from within, I got it. You, Percival, and Wu-Xia can all be satisfied that you delivered that message loud and clear. And it's great, but it's not going to get me out of this mess."

"No, Cade," Benji said with a smile. "You're *sitting* on everything you need."

Cade looked down at the footlocker, and his eyes went wide when he realized what he was resting on: the grav suits.

"Oh," Cade said, getting it. But then his spirits sank when he realized what this meant. "Aw, man, I have to use a grav suit again."

Benji's gesture said it all: Cade could either use the grav suit or stay on the *Rubicon* and accept everything that came with being Ga Halle's prisoner. All things considered, the grav suit didn't seem so bad.

Cade flipped open the locker and grabbed a suit. The problem, though, was that he couldn't get a full suit on, not with his hands bonded together in front of him. Granted, he didn't need the protection of the entire suit since he wouldn't be dropping out of the *Rubicon* in outer space. At least he thought he wouldn't be. Cade started to wonder just how certain he was that the ship was on a landing vector, but he knew it didn't matter. This was what he was doing, so screw it.

In that spirit, he jammed his feet into a pair of the grav suit's boots; he did the same with the gloves, getting them as snug as possible despite his hands' limited mobility. The propulsion control was located in his right palm, so he'd at least be able to sorta maneuver his fall to the ground. It'd be hard with his hands bound, and he could have sworn he remembered Mig saying something about the suit itself being built to help distribute the propulsion thrust. But Mig spouted a lot of scientific junk; Cade didn't have the brainpower to remember it all. And it wasn't like the potential for the propulsion to send him careening out of control was going to deter him anyway.

Cade slapped a helmet on, just in case, and was ready to go. But he couldn't leave, not yet. The vision of his father standing directly over his shoulder was just that: a vision. Cade pegged it as a manifestation of his subconscious mind working overtime to compensate for his addled conscious mind and give him the information he needed in order to survive. Cade heard of people lifting dasher bikes off themselves to save their own lives, so his own brain saying, "Here's a way you don't have to die," wasn't all that ridiculous. Still, figment of his imagination or not, it was the closest Cade had come to his father since he was a kid, and his heart couldn't take that for granted. He turned around, and Benji was there, watching him with what looked to be pride.

"Dad," Cade began, and all at once, the memories of his misjudgments and mistakes came back to him. But looking at his father, Cade didn't see disappointment. He didn't see a shred of regret or the desire for Cade to be anyone else but himself. And in that instant, for the first time since the Rokura came into his possession, he felt okay. "I know I've made some, well . . . mistakes as I've tried to figure a lot of stuff out. And I'm probably harder on myself than anyone else could ever be, but still . . ." Cade paused, drew a deep breath, and stood a little taller. "I always did my best. I always did what I thought was right."

Benji beamed. "I told you you'd find your way."

Cade smiled in return, a bittersweet grin as he watched the image of his father fade away. Wu-Xia's two simple words came at him through the ether—"Just be"—and Cade growled.

"All right already," he said as he walked to the switch that controlled the cargo door's hydraulic release. "I've got it."

The moment he hit the door's release, Cade knew that an alert would route directly to the control panel informing the pilot that—oh, crap—the ship was opening up. It wouldn't take Ga Halle much to figure out what was happening, and Cade knew she'd be none too happy about him trying to escape. The thought made Cade smile. She could stomp and huff all she wanted; he was leaving.

Cade punched the little orange button that got the hydraulic system going. As if in tiny increments, the door started to open. Bit by bit by bit. Cade didn't remember it being so slow.

"Comeoncomeoncomeon," he murmured, expecting Ga Halle to storm into the bay and use the Rokura to tear his flesh from his skeleton.

Cade stepped onto the door as it was lowering, slid off one of his grav suit boots, and started to hop on one foot, hoping it would help the door open faster. The hopping wasn't proving to be all that effective, though Cade was just finding his groove when the door connecting the cargo bay to the *Rubicon*'s cockpit slid open. Ga Halle stood in the open space, Rokura in hand and an incredulous look on her face.

"What are you doing?" she shouted.

Cade stopped his bouncing and thought to answer, but all he did was suck in a lot of air. When he actually thought about it, he wasn't sure what he was doing. He was down to one grav suit boot, his hopping wasn't at all effective, and he was suddenly aware of how painfully ridiculous he looked.

"What are you *doing*?!" Ga Halle repeated. This time, she asked the question with the Rokura. It was pointed straight at Cade, and he saw the familiar lights of its power sparkling at its tip.

Cade looked over his shoulder; it seemed like the door was open just enough for him to slide out of it. And what was even better was that they weren't in space anymore, so at least death wasn't a certainty once he plunged out of the ship. The odds were still pretty good that he wouldn't land in one piece, but at least his demise wasn't a guarantee.

When Cade turned back to face Ga Halle, he did so with an expression of defiance. He didn't feel bold. In fact, he was terrified of the Rokura and its growing energy, but he refused to give Ga Halle the satisfaction of seeing him scared.

"I'm leaving!" Cade yelled. "I'd rather kill myself than be your pawn."

"You'll die," Ga Halle snarled, "when I tell you to die."

"I don't think so," Cade said, then he dropped against the hard surface, rolled to the narrow space the still-opening door had provided, and slipped out of the ship.

For a moment, Cade smiled. He would've paid to see the look on Ga Halle's face as he slipped right between her fingers. She must have thought he was so stupid.

But then Cade realized something: He *was* stupid. This was a horrible idea. Because now, he was free-falling to the ground, which wasn't all that far, and he couldn't even kick on his grav suit. Not yet, at least. His fall had to be convincing; Ga Halle couldn't know that he survived. Cade needed all the time he could get to escape, and being dead was the best way to keep Ga Halle and her forces off his back.

So, he had to just fall.

The planet below him raced into view, and Cade was surprised by how pleasant it seemed. Fields of lush, vivid green pastures rolled as far as he could see, interrupted only by the lakes and waterfalls dotted across the landscape. And, save for a towering stone edifice in the south that blighted the idyllic forest surrounding it, that planet was abandoned. There was no sign of human life anywhere, and that perplexed Cade, not only because he wondered why such a beautiful place was uninhabited but because he had no clue where he was.

Feeling like he'd reached a safe-enough distance from the *Rubicon*—Cade had looked back a few times to check if Ga Halle had decided to change course and crash the ship directly through him; she hadn't—Cade kicked the grav suit to life. Energy pulsed through his hands and on his one foot, and before Cade knew it, he was uncontrollably spinning and twirling. The distribution of thrust was completely out of whack, far too powerful for Cade's body to balance. Every time he gave power to the grav suit, he was sent careening.

The trick, Cade learned, was in short bursts. He'd stopped the thrust altogether in order to straighten out, and once he had his head above his feet once again, Cade fed the grav suit the smallest bit of juice. Then a little more, then a little more. In each increment, he felt the grav suit's power pushing against his fall, which meant he was slowing down, but the power wasn't strong enough to pinball him around the sky.

Of course, he wasn't slowing down enough, and Cade didn't need Mig's brainpower to know that the rate in which he was approaching the ground and the rate of his deceleration weren't going to make for a nice, smooth landing.

Cade was going to crash. Again.

The ground was fast approaching; Cade could see the finer details of the swaying grass and the poppies it bore. Collision was imminent, and just before Cade nailed the ground, he pushed maximum burn into the pieces of the grav suit. While it did send him tumbling, it also created the most resistance possible and softened the blow of his landing.

Still, Cade smashed into the ground. He tore through grass and poppies; he sent dirt erupting with his impact. His body rolled and bounced for a good fifteen yards until, finally, he came to a stop, facedown.

That's where he stayed for a good five minutes, afraid to move any of his limbs out of fear that they'd fall off if he tried. But once he realized he was fine, that he was in no worse shape than he'd been before he'd jumped out of the *Rubicon*, he got to his knees and spit a clump of dirt out of his mouth. He opened his eyes, and the first thing he saw were blasters. A bunch of them, and they were all trained on him.

"Oh," he said. "Hey . . ."

CHAPTER FIFTEEN

H ey, guys."
Kira couldn't believe her eyes. She froze, sidewinder limp in her hand, and she felt her heart skip a beat. The galaxy had taken a lot from her—the father she once knew, her mother, and it'd almost taken an essential piece of who she was when she'd nearly surrendered her will to fight. As devastating as those losses were, and as much as Kira cursed the unfair hand she'd been dealt, she knew there was more to the galaxy than the pain it inflicted. The stars, the planets, and all the spaces between contained more mysteries than anyone could ever hope to fathom. In her boundless love and generosity, Akima bestowed many gifts upon her daughter, but the greatest gift she ever shared was her sense of awe for the unknowable galaxy; Kira knew wonder, and no matter how dark her life's journey became at times, she always found solace in looking out to the stars, just as she'd done so many times with her mother, and imagining what could possibly be out there. Akima maintained that the galaxy was far richer and more complex than even the best

scientists gave it credit for. There were unique, special places that defied fundamental laws of nature; there were occurrences that should not have been possible but transpired nonetheless.

And now, ostensibly when Kira needed it the most, one such unlikely occurrence happened right before her eyes:

Cade had fallen out of the sky and back into her life.

Kira didn't hesitate. She shrugged off how dumbfounded she felt—Mig, Kobe, 4-Qel, and even Kay shared her agape expression—and as Cade rose to his feet, Kira ran to him; she threw her arms around his shoulders and pressed herself close to him, needing to feel as much of him as possible. Kira could tell by the way he was grunting that she was hurting him, but she didn't care. She couldn't let go.

"I'm sorry," Kira whispered into Cade's ear. "I'm sorry for how I was before you left. If those had been the last words I said to you, I . . . I . . ."

"It's okay," Cade said, and he tried to clasp his arms around her but remembered they were still restrained. 4-Qel, though, fixed that problem by breaking his hands free.

"I shouldn't have left like that," Cade continued. "I should have found a way to keep us together, to keep us all together."

They stood like that for a few moments more, wrapped in each other's embrace. Cade broke the silence.

"I wish we could stay like this for so much longer," Cade said, "but you're hurting me."

Kira pulled back and straightened out Cade's shirt, which had gotten twisted around his body during his landing. "Sorry about that," Kira said as she tried not to wince at all of Cade's visible injuries.

"Your grip is really strong," Cade said, "and my body is really sore."

"So, this is pretty weird," Mig said, stepping close to Cade and examining him as if to make sure it was really him. "You just happened to drop out of the sky, *right* where we are, without even knowing we were here?"

"Oh, I'm fine. Nice to see you, too, Mig," Cade chirped in his most condescending tone.

Mig shrugged. "Hey, I'm just asking ques— Wait, are you wearing pieces of my customized grav equipment?" Mig asked, his tone shifting from cautiously inquisitive to accusatory. "Where's the other boot? Don't tell me you lost a boot, Cade."

Cade brushed Mig off. "Relax, okay? It's on the *Rubicon*."

"And who's flying the *Rubicon*?" Kira asked, adding to Mig's cross-examination.

Cade nodded and sucked in his lips. He'd been so caught up in losing the Rokura that it didn't occur to him that he'd also lost Kira's prized starcruiser. "That . . . you know, it's all a long story. Let's just focus on the fact that I'm here and . . . we have this nice reunion. With that strange guy over there," Cade said, gesturing to Kay.

"Name's Kay," Kay said, extending his hand to Cade. "Good to meet the actual Paragon. It's an honor."

"Yeah, about that," Cade said as he shook Kay's hand. "We've got a lot of gaps to fill in. A lot. But, first of all, where are we? And why are you all here?"

"Why are you here?" Mig asked, still sounding like an accusation.

"Mig, you're one stupid question away from getting punched in the face," Cade said as his response.

"Look, we don't have time for this," Kira said as she stepped in the center of the group, taking charge. "A lot happened since you went your way and we went ours. I'm going to tell you really quickly what you need to know, and then we have to move."

And Kira did. She summarized the revolution on Praxis, the solar bombs embedded near the planet's core, and how they had less than two hours to infiltrate the Crucible and stop Ebik from killing millions of people. She stopped short of relaying what'd transpired with her mother; that was a wound she'd share with Cade another time.

Cade, for his part, listened intently to Kira's summary. There was something about him, though; something had changed. While Cade would always be Cade—he'd always act cavalierly to mask his insecurities; he'd always use humor as a shield against his own self-reproach—whatever had happened to him on his journey returned him with a little more depth. Kira would never say this to him aloud, but Cade seemed like he'd matured. He might even be able to fool people into thinking he'd cultivated a bit of wisdom within himself.

"So . . . this Crucible," Cade began. "That doesn't happen to be a giant stone tower about a mile away and over the ridge, does it? I saw it, well, on my way down. It looks . . . how do I say this nicely? It looks totally impenetrable. And I thought that *before* I knew it used to be a super-max prison."

"But things just got all the easier," Kay said, clapping Cade's shoulder. "You're the Paragon; you have the most powerful weapon in the galaxy, and you can use it to blast us wherever we need to go. Nobody and nothing will stand in our way now."

Cade recoiled out of Kay's grasp; he got especially squirmy at the mention of the Rokura, and Kira began to wonder, with no small amount of panic, where the weapon was. It definitely wasn't in Cade's hands. Or on his body.

"Cade," Kira said, trying to sound patient, "is there something you want to tell us?"

Cade pursed his lips and gingerly shook his head. In short time, though, the rebuking that was waging within him subsided, and he began to answer Kira's question. "You see, my journey, like yours, was also full of many surprises. In fact—"

"You lost the Rokura, didn't you?" Kira asked, cutting to the chase. It was the merciful thing to do.

"Lose it? No. No, I know exactly where it is."

"Where?" Kira asked, already dubious of where this was heading.

"Ga Halle has it. On the *Rubicon*. Which she also took from me."

Nobody said a word. There was a time when Kira would have scorned Cade for such an epic failure, but she couldn't bring herself to react that way now. Whatever caused Cade to suffer this loss wasn't just a case of him messing things up; this was deeper and more profound than that. Kira could see him bearing grief and regret, she could see him shouldering the burden of whatever had happened.

"The important thing," 4-Qel said, patting Cade's back, "is that you're okay."

"Wow, thanks, Four-Qel," Cade said. "That means a lot."

"Oh, no, I was being sarcastic," 4-Qel said, his hand spread over his chest plate, signaling his embarrassment. "You allowed the galaxy's most powerful, destructive weapon to fall into the hands of a maniacal tyrant. This is a catastrophe."

Cade shoved 4-Qel away and stood next to Kira in the center of the group. The look on his face spoke to Kira's observation that Cade had, in some way, changed.

"Listen, Ga Halle isn't the same person she used to be. She's changed in ways that . . . it's too hard for me to even explain. But that doesn't even matter, because she only got the Rokura because of me. I misused the weapon, and it's my fault. I can fix it, though. I think—no, I *know* how to beat her. I know what to do with the Rokura. I just need a—" Cade's eyes searched around, and as luck would have it, they fixed on Ortzo's shido sticking out of the ground just a few feet ahead. "Here we go, a weapon. But—"

Cade stopped in his tracks, just a short distance from Ortzo's dead body. He turned and looked at Kira, a stunned expression on his face. "Did you kill Ortzo?" he asked.

"Damn right I did," Kira said, flexing just a little with the pride she felt at taking down one of the galaxy's premier badasses. She let her desire to boast of her conquest subside, prioritizing their need to stay on task above all else.

"Look, it's great that you've had this epiphany with the Rokura," Kira said, "but we still have our mission. Millions of lives are at stake, right here, right now, and we have to stop Praxis from being torn apart."

"I know, the Crucible," Cade said, a touch of solemnity in his voice. "That has to be where Ga Halle was heading, and it's where we're heading, too."

"All the paths are converging," Kay added. "I think it's time we faced our enemies."

Kira's and Cade's eyes met, and they seemed to share an understanding: Their paths did more than converge; they intertwined. And neither would let their paths break apart again.

Feeling her team growing antsy, Kira knew it was time to put their nervous energy to work. But one question lingered in her mind, one she didn't want to ask for fear of the answer.

"Where's Percival?" Kira asked, drawing closer to Cade.

"He . . ." Cade began. He stopped, then he closed his eyes and let out a deep, mournful breath. "Ga Halle. She killed him."

Kira gently grabbed Cade by his bicep and turned him toward her. "I know you two didn't always see eye to eye . . . but he meant a lot to you. To all of us. I'm sorry."

"I'm sorry, too," Cade said as he turned and shuffled forward. "But not as sorry as Ga Halle is gonna be."

With Kira taking the lead, Cade, Mig, 4-Qel, Kobe, and Kay began their journey toward the Crucible. They walked at a brisk pace, as time was at a premium. Ahead, the nearest star was setting just over the ridge, its waning light shimmering off the rolling surface of the waterfall. There was beauty in the juxtaposition of the water's raging current and the light's ability to play off its chaos.

It gave Kira an idea.

"Kay, you know the schematics of the Crucible, right?" she asked.

"Yes and no. I have a bird's-eye grasp, but I couldn't tell you, say, how to access the garbage chute."

"That's fine, I just need to know one thing: Does the Crucible have any ancillary buildings? Any satellite structures, anything connected to it in any way?"

Kay thought for a moment. "Yes," he said eagerly. "There's a powering station nearby, tucked in the forest. Why?"

"Because Ebik needs a signal to set off the detonations, right?" Kira questioned, the ideas in her mind starting to gain momentum. "Mig, if we got inside this powering station, could we cut off the signal between here and the planet?"

Mig rocked his head back and forth and weighed the possibility with his hands. "Maybe," he said, though not with the conviction Kira would have liked. "The signal could be relayed independently of the Crucible. But," Mig continued, and Kira could almost hear the cogs turning in that big, beautiful brain of his, "even if we can't kill the signal, if we get inside the station, we could at least mess some stuff up."

"Like what?" Kira said, a devilish smile forming.

"I dunno." Mig shrugged. "There's no telling what that station is used for, what's routed in and out of it. Get me in there, and I'm sure I'll be able to wreck something."

That was good enough for Kira. If they couldn't stop Ebik's plans at the powering station, they'd at least strike a blow at the Crucible.

And that's how they'd do this: blow after blow after blow until the whole thing crumbled down.

They stalked through the forest on soft feet, crouching tactically with their weapons hot. By the time they closed in on the power station, the darkening sky provided them with just enough cover to move stealthily forward, staying low and close to trees. It'd been some time since Kira had been part of a ground assault mission, since before she'd formed Omega Squadron at the Well. Like muscle memory, the experience of embarking on a raid all came back to her, and she at once felt exhilarated and scared, pining for the moment when it would be all over. She didn't like how fast and messy they were; even with the best planning, storming an enemy on their turf was never a predictable endeavor. But soldiers, Kira knew better than anyone, weren't made in training, nor were they made in the war room. Soldiers were made in combat, on the ground or between the stars. Strategizing was great, and simulations were fine, but nothing kept a soldier alive to fight another day more than his or her instincts, reflexes, and plain old common sense.

Kira could only hope that her combat instincts were as sharp as they once were. And, as the commanding officer driving this mission, that her squad's instincts were even better.

A break in the forest's otherwise tightly packed trees signified the start of a clearing, which was exactly what Kira had been looking for. Kay's memory of the Crucible's powering station led them in this direction, and given how vast the forest seemed to be, they were lucky to be on the right path. Kira held up her fist, signaling for her squad to stop. She turned and pointed to 4-Qel and called him to the front. She needed his eyes to see deeper and with more clarity, thanks to his nighttime vision, into the area ahead.

"There's a structure ahead, a little more than fifty yards out," 4-Qel relayed to Kira in his quietest tone. "Guards. I see four patrolling, all very near the structure."

Taking down four unsuspecting grunts wasn't a problem; taking them down quickly and silently was where things got tricky. Even if they were on a regimented patrol pattern, she didn't have time to figure out the rotation, not with the clock ticking. They had roughly eighty-five precious minutes until Praxis was turned into an asteroid belt, and allocating time to four patr—

"I can neutralize the guards."

Kira startled at Kobe's hushed voice. He'd snuck up behind her without making a sound, as if to prove his point. Kira didn't doubt Kobe's abilities; he was skilled in ways she didn't even understand. But he was injured, and the stakes were a little too high to find out what he was—and, more importantly, wasn't— capable of by throwing him into a situation that had absolutely no margin for error. She explained to him as much, but Kobe wouldn't accept it.

"I know my limits," Kobe said, and he held up a pair of tree branches the size and shape of his quarter staffs. Kira hadn't even noticed him picking them up along the way. "There won't be a sound."

It didn't take long for Kira to run through her options and realize she had none. Even hobbled by injury, Kobe was the best stealth option they had. While Kira had learned plenty of lifesaving tactics from her commanding officers, she'd taught herself one or two as well. Particularly, she'd learned the value of flexibility. Of improvising. You use what you have, and don't give a second thought to what you don't. Getting caught thinking— or worse, overthinking—was just another way to end up dead.

"All right, you've got this," Kira whispered, then she brandished her sidewinder for Kobe to see. "But I'm your backup. I'll set off a thousand alarms before we lose anyone else."

Kobe nodded, and after 4-Qel relayed the guards' positions— three on the north side of the station, one more on the south— Kira was off, following the silent warrior through the dark forest.

First up was the lone guard on the station's south end. Kira huddled into the shadow of a tree a few yards out and watched as Kobe stalked his prey. Lithely, he darted between the trees leading up to the guard like they were put their specifically for him to traverse between; he spun and pressed his back against a trunk just large enough to conceal his frame and waited. The guard was walking past the tree that concealed Kobe, and the moment he moved completely past it, Kobe went around the other side, behind the guard, and battered him into unconsciousness.

One down.

Kira moved in an arc through the trees, following Kobe's movement as he hugged the station's outer wall, cloaked in the darkness it cast. The station itself wasn't the imposing structure Kira envisioned it being. It was a squat, gray concrete bunker with a corrugated metal roof. A satellite was perched atop, and Kira hoped that destroying it would cripple Ebik's ability to commit genocide from thousands of miles away. It wasn't a lot to ask.

Kobe reached the northeast corner the exact moment a guard was turning toward his position. Had Kobe so much as taken a step around to the other side, he and the guard would have collided. Kobe, as if drawing from a sixth sense, instead pushed himself into the corner, concealing himself completely in shadow. The guard passed by without noticing him, but he didn't get far. Kobe reached out and pulled him back into the darkness. Moments later, Kobe emerged; the guard did not.

Two down.

The two remaining guards would be a problem. They were engaged in conversation and had been since Kira made eyes on them. Worse, they were centrally positioned on the building's side, and there was no way to sneak up on them from either side. Kobe and Kira exchanged a look; they both knew they didn't have this kind of time to waste. Kira reached down, grabbed a stick, and held it between her hands; breaking it, she figured, would be subtle enough to draw the guards' attention and too inconspicuous to warrant an alarm. She held the stick up for Kobe to see; he nodded and crouched into his position, make-shift staffs gripped tightly. Kira snapped the stick, and it sounded like a firecracker thrown into a monastery. The guards heard it pop, and after a moment of conferring, they headed toward its source. Kira was already belly-down on the ground, but she could still see the guards approaching, and Kobe waiting, through the thin grass that obscured her line of sight. Tension made knots of Kira's stomach as the guards stepped past Kobe's position. They didn't even flinch toward his direction.

In a flash, Kobe pounced. He leapt from behind the soldiers, greeting the first with a staff against the back of his head. The guard immediately dropped to the ground with a thud; he didn't move again. The second turned, faster than Kira would have expected, and nearly had her blaster raised on Kobe by the time she was facing him. Smartly, Kobe crashed his left-handed staff against the guard's fingers, preventing her from getting a shot off. Before the guard could react, Kobe drilled her with an uppercut blow with his right-handed staff, then followed it with a roundhouse kick that sent the guard spinning off her feet. She smashed to the ground and, like her mates, was out cold.

Kira thought the coast was clear. She pulled herself off the ground, but just as she was about to step toward Kobe, she sensed something at her side. The moment she turned, she identified what had triggered her internal radar: a previously unseen fifth guard, deeper in the forest, not ten yards away. Their eyes met at the exact same time, and Kira could only watch as the guard's blaster sprang up in his hands. He had her dead to rights, but he didn't fire. The guard didn't do anything but alter his expression in the subtlest way. In an instant, his face went from cold indifference to confusion. Then he collapsed to the ground.

Standing behind him was Cade, bloody shido in hand.

The squad regrouped at the station's front entrance. A reinforced blast door shielded the only way in or out, and that would have presented a problem had Mig not swiped a security keycard off one of the fallen guards.

"The minute those doors open and whoever's inside sees us and not their squad mates, there's going to be trouble," Kira assessed. "We need to be faster than fast; we cannot let any of them trigger an alarm."

"It's risky, firing blindly into a space you can't visualize against an unknown number of enemies," 4-Qel said contemplatively as he studied the door.

Kira shrugged. "Yeah, it's a risk, but—"

"Leave it to me," 4-Qel interrupted, sounding chipper. "I'll kill them."

Kira's glance met Cade's, and she saw on his face a skeptical expression that matched her own. 4-Qel possessed physicality—strength, speed, and agility—that no living person could even dream of matching. But there was a lot at stake here. And if 4-Qel missed just one guard, they'd be screwed.

"Imagine you're in that station right now and the doors open," 4-Qel said, picking up on Kira's doubt, "but it's not the people you know standing in the entrance. No, it's an angry Qel. Do you respond as a good soldier would, hit the alarm, and fight for your position, or do you mess your pants?"

"The latter, most definitely," Kay chimed in.

"That moment of hesitation is all I'll need."

Kira nodded her acquiescence. She lived and died by trusting her squad, and she knew she could certainly do worse than trusting a determined Qel.

Keycard in hand, 4-Qel was as ready as he'd ever be. He was just about to open the doors when he looked back at Kira.

"If you're still concerned over this, just know that while I don't show it, I'm upset over being shut down and placed in a containment field," 4-Qel said. "*Very* upset."

"Okeydoke," Kira responded. 4-Qel's words sank in, and knowing that the drone was not only determined but also angry made her feel a lot better.

4-Qel swiped the card, and the door hissed and belched steam at its corners as it slid open. From her position a few paces back from the station and off to the side—there was likely to be errant blaster shots coming from within—she could just barely see inside. From what she could tell, there were five guards for 4-Qel to deal with. Four were seated at a table—playing tatow, it looked like—and one was at the door. He was dressed down to his skivvies with a look in his eyes that said he was either drunk or shaking off a heavy slumber.

"It ain't break time yet, get back—" he said, but stopped himself. His gruff demeanor flushed out of him in the blink of an eye. Being utterly dumbfounded took its place. A stupefied "What?" was his final word.

4-Qel grabbed the guard by his head and, without exerting a shred of effort, lifted him off the ground, snapping his neck in the process and then whipping his lifeless body at his four mates.

What followed was a blur of death.

Needing only three bounding strides, 4-Qel rushed the remaining guards who were all in various stages of confusion and

disarray, having had a corpse flung at them. They tried to collect themselves, they tried to fight back, but it was no use. 4-Qel
was too fast, too strong, and too skilled.

The lethal drone attacked with the meticulous precision of a
surgeon. One guard was quicker than the rest, and she managed
to get her hand on the butt of her sidewinder, holstered at her
side; 4-Qel grabbed that hand, snapped it, and launched the
guard headfirst into a wall. Kira wasn't sure how many verte-
brae broke upon impact, but it was enough to crumple the guard
like an accordion. In the process, 4-Qel somehow managed to
come up with her blaster, a modified outpost pistol, and he fired
two shots apiece at the nearest guards, getting them both right
in their chests. The final guard was a moment away from meeting the same fate, but he'd managed to arm himself with a chair
before 4-Qel could get the pistol aimed. The guard swung the
chair at 4-Qel with all his might; the chair splintered in a dozen
pieces, shattering upon impact. 4-Qel was undisturbed. Kira
assumed that, if anything, getting smacked with the chair only
made 4-Qel madder.

4-Qel lifted the last remaining guard off his feet and pulled
him close. The guard resisted, kicking and punching because,
well, he had to do *something*. But there was no gain in his efforts.
4-Qel held him in his grasp and studied him as if he were trying
to peer into the man's soul.

"You're on the wrong side of this war," 4-Qel said, then he
crushed his head against the guard's face—once, twice, three
times, mashing it to bloody pancake batter.

His job done, 4-Qel tossed the guard aside and turned to the
front door.

"All clear!" he called, signaling his friends with a goofy wave.

They all entered the station, doing their best to ignore the
grim scene all around. Mig bolted right to the computer terminal at the far end and got to work. Kira couldn't even pretend

to know or understand the finer details of his capabilities. 4-Qel stood over him, protective of his friend as always—more so now, it seemed, since his brief encounter with being decommissioned.

Meanwhile, Kira, Cade, and Kay gathered at the mouth of the station. They seemed to share the same sentiment: This was a nice start, but there was still a long way to go and not a lot of time to get there.

"So," Cade began, getting the question that was on the tip of all of their tongues out there, "if Mig can't shut down the signal from here and we have to infiltrate the giant, heavily fortified, heavily guarded prison turned fortress . . . how do we do that?"

Kira snickered. "Very carefully."

"Yeah, but seriously," Cade said, his face flashing real concern. "How arc we going to pull this thing off?"

"We're going to watch each other's backs, and we're going to make the most of what we have," Kira said, pushing as much conviction into her voice as possible. Leaders were confident; leaders were inspiring. She had been taught that ad nauseam. But there was one thing she'd taught herself about being the person responsible for the lives of others: Leaders were honest. And so she added, "Also, we're going to remember that we don't have a choice."

Cade and Kay both nodded, satisfied. Their concerns weren't completely allayed, but they'd never be. Leaders were there to keep you alive and moving to the next objective.

"I've got bad news," Mig said, and the entire squad gathered around him at the computer terminal. "Ebik's signal exists independently of what transmits on and off Olanus. I can't shut it down from here."

Before anyone could so much as slump their shoulders, Kira cast aside the one door that wouldn't open and directed their focus into finding one that would.

"What *can* you do from here?" she asked. "This station has to be operational and guarded for a reason."

Mig smiled. "I was just about to get to that," he said, then he spun around in his seat so he faced the terminal again.

Mig punched some keys, and suddenly, a three-dimensional projection of the Crucible flashed above their heads. A bunch of red dots blinked from the bottom of the projection all the way to the top.

"The security protocol," Mig said with pride. "Not everyone would have figured out how to do this, but luckily for you, you have one of the galaxy's best hackers on your side."

"Do . . . what?" Cade asked.

"I push a button, and boom," Mig said, snapping his fingers. "Every locked door, every locked gate, including the one that blocks the entrance, is open."

"So not only will we be able to get in," Kira said, her smile growing wider and wider as she pictured what Mig's meddling would accomplish, "but all the inmates will be able to get out."

"Chaos." Mig beamed, hardly able to contain himself.

Kira liked what she was hearing. She nodded, mentally projecting an image of the Crucible as it would soon be—overrun by its own inmates, mayhem and carnage reigning. Between the security outage and Ortzo's missing shuttle, Ebik would definitely know something was wrong. It wouldn't matter, though. He wouldn't risk detonating the planet until he was at a safe enough distance, and Kira was going to hit him with all she had before that time came. Let him see his walls crumbling in the meantime. Let him know that his end was nigh.

"As a bonus," Mig continued, "I can also kill the lights. They'd be totally blind and wouldn't see us coming until we were rushing the front gate."

Kira's smile turned into a determined sneer. "How soon can you do both?"

Mig gestured his ease at doing what he wanted, when he wanted. "At your word," he answered.

Kira looked at her team and saw in them the same unwavering clarity of purpose she felt within herself. They knew as well as she did that once Mig did his thing, there'd be no stopping, no slowing down. The siege of the Crucible would begin.

She was ready.

They were ready.

"Do it," she commanded.

It was the blackest night any of them had ever seen.

Under Olanus's moonless sky, Kira charged through the dark forest, following 4-Qel, who barreled through any obstacles that stood in the way. Her squad trailed behind dutifully, none of them knowing how long they'd have to capitalize on the mayhem they'd manufactured. They ran with all they had, weapons hot and wits sharp, ready for anything. Kira could see the Crucible through the trees, that oppressive, obsidian obelisk, and she wondered where Ebik would be hiding within it. The lights of his command chamber were out; all of the lights on the Crucible were out.

When Kira burst through the tree line, just two steps behind 4-Qel, she immediately identified what was happening: the Crucible had erupted into a riot. A long, narrow strip of unleveled stone led from a faraway landing pad all the way to the fortress's outer wall, but the space where an impassable gate should have been was empty. The Crucible was wide open.

With 4-Qel at her side and her squad at her back, Kira kept running toward their destination. With every step she took, the space just past where the gate normally separated Olanus from the incongruent world that existed within the Crucible's walls became clearer and clearer. They were heading toward a court-yard; massive stone pillars and bronze monuments of larger-than-life figures—heroes of the Praxian war machine, Kira guessed—were scattered from the entrance all the way to the Crucible's front door. The courtyard had to span about fifty yards, and at the moment, the space was raging with a furious battle. Former prisoners—political prisoners, enemies of the Praxis kingdom—went toe to toe with guards with the ferocity one would expect from someone given the opportunity to strike back against their tormentors.

But still, they were losing.

The guards had the numbers—if Kira had to guess, she'd say the guards were around one hundred strong, while the prison-ers would be lucky to number sixty. The guards had compres-sion pikes and E-9 tri-blasters, and though the prisoners had managed to get their hands on some weapons of their own, they were still overmatched. It wouldn't be long before the prisoners were back in their cells, or worse.

Kira ordered 4-Qel to take cover ahead; there was a concrete pedestal at the mouth of the courtyard—holding up a statue of some undoubtedly cruel Praxian warlord; it had to be if the den-izens of the Crucible paid it worship—that was large enough for them all to regroup behind before they entered the fray. They slid to the designated spot, unseen by any of the combatants within.

"Those inmates," Kay said, gasping for air, "they're going to all get slaughtered. We have to do something."

Kira snuck a quick glance over the pedestal, hoping that, some-how in the past minute, the prisoners had found a way to rally and take command of their fight for freedom. They hadn't.

"We caused this battle," Kay continued. "We can't just use these people as a distraction for our own ends."

"I know, I know," Kira agreed, tortured over the idea of having to weigh cost against benefit. She could command her squad to join the fray, and together they'd crush the guards. But then what? The prisoners had no way off the planet, and there was absolutely nowhere on Olanus to go. And this didn't even take into account how committing the time to save them would undermine their efforts to prevent genocide. There was that small detail to account for as well.

"Mig, how much time before Ebik can detonate his weapon?" Kira asked, her anxiety growing more and more as she entertained the idea of taking any detour from their mission.

"About thirty-seven minutes," Mig replied, looking queasy.

Kira gritted her teeth. They still had to make it all the way up the tower. They still had to infiltrate her father's command chamber, take out whatever guards he was sure to be hiding behind, and disable his detonator. Still. They couldn't just leave the prisoners they'd freed to be slaughtered. That was something Ebik would do.

"All right, listen up," Kira said, cutting right to the chase. There was no time to expend on anything other than essentials. "We have no choice but to punch our way through this courtyard. Our time is short, and our mission couldn't be more vital. But—"

"Kira, these prisoners need—" Kay interrupted pleadingly.

"*But*," Kira continued, "that doesn't mean that we can't help along the way. Those guards are nothing but grunts and thugs, and we're—"

"The Black Star Renegades," Mig proudly pronounced.

Kira rolled her eyes. "Not what I was going to say. Not even close."

"You're welcome," Mig said.

After an exasperated breath, Kira continued. "Just remember we don't have all day. We *have* to keep moving forward. We do what we can along the way, but forward motion is nonnegotiable. Got it?"

Everyone nodded.

"All right, then," Kira said, steeling herself for what was about to happen. "Follow my lead."

Leading with a sidewinder in each hand—she'd relieved one of the powering station guards of hers after Cade called dibs on the outpost pistol—Kira charged into battle. The guards, caught completely unaware, were target practice. Kira fired four shots, and four guards went down. She saw another seven fall in the space just ahead of her, all of them taking bolts from someone on her squad. It wasn't enough to appreciably thin their numbers, but it was a start.

The task of mowing down Crucible guards became much more difficult, though, once the guards realized they were being ambushed. They weren't so easy to hit anymore; in fact, some of them even started to fight back.

Nonetheless, Kira stayed true to her directive. She fired, she dodged, she took cover. And no matter what, she continued to push forward.

Coming around a pillar, she blasted two bolts into a guard who'd been popping shots in her vicinity from his tri-blaster. Kira was thankful for the weapon's terrible aim; a more precise weapon might have done more than chew chunks off the pillar's mortar. Each of her bolts hit the guard square in the chest, propelling him off his feet. But while Kira was focused on the guard with the tri-blaster, she didn't notice one of his mates coming at her with a compression pike. The guard rushed in from Kira's blind side, swinging the pike down in an arc that would have crushed Kira's skull had she not arched her body back at the absolute last moment. The pike smashed against the ground, its weight and momentum pulling the guard with it—and right into Kira's swinging elbow. Bouncing back from narrowly missing her head being split like a maga fruit, Kira delivered her weight into her hip and twisted it around; she threw her right elbow out, her timing perfect to catch the guard just as she was passing by Kira's face. She tumbled backward, far enough for Kira to down her with one shot.

Kira took a moment to assess. Her squad was close by, as they should be; Mig and 4-Qel worked in tandem, staying tethered to one another as they cleared a path for them to push through and others to follow; Kay's battle training helped him predict his enemy's moves and stay at least one step ahead; though injured, Kobe still moved faster and with more fluidity than anyone around him; and Cade was Cade, blasting and attacking guards with his outpost pistol in one hand and his shido in the other like he was allergic to battle strategies. And he was. Cade relied on intuition, which both amazed and terrified Kira. Still, Cade and everyone else brought their own character to her squad, and that was exactly the way Kira liked it.

They'd pushed their way halfway up the courtyard without much resistance; as Kira predicted, like much of Praxis's armed forces, the guards weren't what anyone would consider elite. They were fodder feeding the kingdom's war machine, as expendable as the uniforms on their backs. With Kira's squad's help, the tide was turning; the prisoners—maybe no better trained than the guards, but certainly with more to fight for— took control of the battle, and it wouldn't be long before the courtyard, and their freedom, was theirs.

Through the last remaining wave of guards, Kira spotted the open doorway that led into the Crucible. It wasn't far. Just a little more fighting, a little more adversity, and they'd be inside. It was one more obstacle down on the path to reaching, and stopping, Ebik.

But then, just as Kira was whipping her sidewinder across a guard's face, a light splashed in her eyes. Kira had to shield her face and step out of the light's beam; her vision regained, Kira surveyed the scene and realized that the battle had come to a halt. Every single combatant on both sides had stopped, and they were all looking up. Kira followed their gaze and found, clamped against the outer wall, a trio of spotlights burning brightly, illuminating the darkness. She tried to convince herself that the lights must have been running on a backup generator and were running in conjunction with an emergency protocol. But she knew that was just wishful thinking. Something else was happening.

It only took a moment for her to find out what.

"Kira Sen, you and your rabble have made what I suppose will be considered a noble attempt to fight for your cause," a voice said, crackling through an unseen intercom. "Unfortunately, you're not nearly as clever or resourceful as you think you are."

Her eyes fixed on the sky—less on the light's burning beams and more on the darkness around them—Kira hadn't noticed Cade sidestepping next to her.

"Is that—" he began, but Kira cut him off.

"Ebik," she said, feelings of anger, dread, suspense, and betrayal pushing down within her like a coil.

"I've been a step ahead of you the entire time, and I always will be," Ebik continued. "Your attempted rebellion is over. It was over before it ever began. Good-bye, Kira."

The intercom popped and then cut out. The entire courtyard waited in suspended animation, knowing something was going to happen. Kira thought to start firing again, to blast and scream and battle until every last charge was spent, until every shred of her will to fight was exhausted. But she knew she was trapped; she just didn't know to what extent.

As abruptly as they'd turned on, the spotlights cut off. A shadow pressed down on the entire courtyard once again, and everyone took a startled half step back. Mig, 4-Qel, Kobe, and Kay had all managed to gravitate toward Cade and Kira. They formed a circle, tight and close.

"This is bad," Mig said. "What's going to happen? Kira, what is he going to do?"

Kira couldn't answer. She surveyed the scene, her eyes examining every visible inch of the courtyard, trying to figure out what trap Ebik could have laid for them. Disbelief overwhelmed her, disbelief and a creeping, growing sense of shame. The contradiction of those feelings—Kira couldn't believe Ebik had managed to pull the rug out from under her, yet she was ashamed that she hadn't been able to prevent it—didn't matter. All that mattered was that they were losing. That everything was slipping through her fingers. Never in her life did she consider retreat a viable option. She'd retreated the day Ebik nearly killed her and took her mother prisoner, and she vowed never to do it again. But now, it was the only option. She wouldn't see her friends die fighting for a mission that she knew they could no longer complete. Ebik had won; the only thing Kira could do was minimize her losses.

But almost like Ebik was reading her mind, like he had somehow implanted himself inside her head, he took that option away, too. She was about to call for their retreat; she was about to lead them back into the forest and figure out what to do from there when she heard a subtle sound coming from within the Crucible, soft and distant but growing. It distracted her and the rest of them for just long enough.

"What is *that*?" Kay asked. They'd all turned their attention toward the open double doors that led into the fortress. Kira squinted, trying to get a better look inside, but it was no help. The entrance was a seamless onyx wall, and she couldn't see an inch past it.

"Is that screaming?" Cade asked as the sound became louder and closer.

Blood rushed to Kira's head. The screaming only got louder, but it was drowned out by her heart pumping in her ears.

"GO! RUN!" Kira screamed, but it was too late. The moment she turned, her squad right with her, the outer gate rolled on its track and slammed shut.

They were trapped inside.

"Oh no," Mig murmured.

Kira whipped around and faced her squad; they looked how she felt—terrified. They were huddled behind one of the courtyard's monuments, soon to be swallowed by their enemy. In that moment, Kira recalled an obscure lesson she'd learned about leadership, one she'd never understood until now: Squads needed leaders to win, but they needed leaders even more to lose. Ebik could get the upper hand on them, he could throw whatever he had in their path, and maybe this would be their last stand. But if it were, she wouldn't let them go down like this. Not on her watch.

"Listen to me, all of you, right now," Kira said, having to project her voice over the incoming yelling. "We've faced impossible odds, and we've come out on the other side. My mother once told me that the only time you lose is when you give up, and we are *not* giving up."

Kira could see the resolve of her squad returning. Cade, Kobe, and Kay were ready. 4-Qel was made ready. But Mig wasn't there. He wasn't a warrior; he wasn't even a soldier. Kira knew he needed more.

"And do you know why?" she asked, slamming a fresh charge into her sidewinder and catching Mig's eyes. "Because we're the Black Star Renegades, and we'll show everyone who stands in our path what that means."

Kira twisted her head around the monument toward the Crucible's door; the onslaught had arrived. Soldiers upon soldiers rushed through the door, screaming a vicious battle cry all the way through. Kira couldn't even estimate how many. *A lot* was the best she could do.

The Praxian forces rushed toward them, and Kira and her squad used their coverage to thin their ranks. Kira fired blast after blast, targeting enemies indiscriminately. But even after she'd depleted a charge and had to reload, she realized the opposition hadn't thinned one bit.

As the horde closed in on their position, Kira committed to keeping one eye on each of her squad mates as she fought. Slowly, her unit was breaking; everyone was being pulled in different directions, farther and farther away from her, and they, like her, were being overwhelmed. Kira turned and fired two blasts into the chest of a guard taking aim at her, then she fired another shot into the guts of one who'd just missed her face with a blast of his own. Another guard charged at her, leading with a compression pike, and Kira fired again and again, but whatever armor he was wearing protected him from her strikes. She fired a blast that deflected off his helmet, then another that merely scratched his chest plating. He was nearly on her, and just as she was about to dive to the ground, she saw a shido's blade smash against his face. The guard went down, and Cade, standing over him, gave Kira a wink.

"That's two you owe me," he said.

Kira fired in his direction, and Cade nearly leapt out of his skin. He might have even squealed, but the battle was too loud for Kira to tell. Cade looked at Kira, stunned, and Kira gestured to the ground behind him; there, a soldier who was about to slice Cade with her triblade lay facedown.

"Okay, one," Cade said, swallowing hard.

The fighting continued with Kira and her squad staying alive but not making a dent in the opposition. Not only that, but fatigue was setting in. Kobe had a wound on his bicep from where, best as Kira could guess, a pike had gotten him; the circle of enemies around Kay was drawing closer; and Mig undoubtedly would have been done for were it not for 4-Qel—and even 4-Qel seemed to be struggling to keep up. They were losing, and Kira knew it wouldn't be long before, one by one, they all fell.

Kira mowed down another two soldiers, then she searched the battlefield for Cade. Left, right—he was nowhere to be seen. Kira pushed forward against the horde, blasting and blasting until her trigger fingers got sore, but there was no Cade. She kicked out a nearby soldier's knee and fired down on him; she dodged a pike and shot out her attacker's legs, and her eyes continued to scan. But she couldn't find Cade.

"Kira!" she heard a voice scream to her side. She looked, and Mig was frantically pointing to an area across from Kira. "Four-Qel sees Cade! He's in trouble!"

After removing three guards from her path by way of incessant blaster fire, Kira got a clearer look at Cade's position. It wasn't good. He was practically swarmed by Praxian soldiers and guards, and he was losing ground fast. It made sense that they'd dedicate so much manpower to capturing him, or worse; even with Ga Halle's theft of the Rokura, Cade was a loose end that needed to be tied. Kira regretted not having taken that into account.

Blasting, dodging, punching, and kicking, she was closing in on him. And Cade was putting up nothing short of a heroic fight against impossible odds. He *had* changed. He was using his outpost pistol only as a backup, and Kira found herself marveling at his focus and skill. The latter was always there—he'd trained with the Masters the same as everyone else at the Well; he'd spent years of his life being molded into a Rai. But he had never become one. Not until now.

Cade ducked around a pike's swipe, slicing out the legs of his would-be attacker; he grabbed a guard as he went back up, spinning him to deflect incoming blaster fire, then he pushed that guard into the firing soldier, turned, and thrust his shido's blade across the chest of a soldier who was trying to get him from behind. He was fast and attentive; his attacks were economical, not wasting a single movement.

But there were too many enemies for Cade—or anyone—to fight forever. And when a soldier on Cade's blind side trained her A-10 on him, all Kira could do was scream. There were too many other soldiers and guards in her path, and Cade had no idea he was a trigger pull away from dying.

"CADE!" Kira yelled, but her voice was inaudible, completely drowned out.

Drowned out by an explosion coming from overhead.

CHAPTER SIXTEEN

S moldering detritus descended from above, furious bits and chunks of erupted masonry that tore through the air on their way to the ground. The once impenetrable Crucible stood well above all of Olanus, and in its time it had withstood the moon's harsh elements. It had withstood prisoners' riots and their out-right attempts to tear the fortress to the ground. But never had it been wounded until now.

Reflexively, Cade covered his head and backpedaled away at the roar of the eruption in the sky. As debris rained down, Cade looked up and saw that a chunk of the Crucible's south-facing wall had been chewed from its side; while the damage wasn't nearly enough to bring the fortress down—it was more cosmetic than anything—it stood as proof of its vulnerability. Whoever had the moxie to lead this attack—Cade was dying to know as he searched the dark, cloudy night sky but saw nothing—had shattered the myth of the Crucible's indestructibility, and Cade hoped they'd be back for more.

In the relative hush that'd descended over the battle since the moment the Crucible had what amounted to a diamond-shaped chasm scored out of its exterior, Cade heard his name, faint and muffled. He turned to his right and saw Kira charging at him as she screamed, "Look out!" Kira pointed to Cade's three o'clock; he turned back around quickly and saw a soldier aiming her attention—and her A-10—back on him. Cade didn't think, nor did he hesitate; he reacted. With a quick sidearm motion, he flung his shido. The weapon whistled through the air, and in a moment's time, it found its home; its three blades buried into the soldier's chest, hitting her just as she pulled the trigger. The shot went wide, screaming past Cade's head.

"We're even," Kira said as she reached his side, nearly out of breath. She shoved a fresh charge into each of her sidewinders. The soldiers and guards were turning their attention away from the Crucible's wound and shifting it back to Cade and his friends. The impossible battle was about to start all over again. Cade was thrilled. He blasted the two nearest soldiers directly in their chests, the force of the outpost pistol knocking them clear off their feet. The soldiers continued to swarm, more and more standing between Cade and his shido was closing. Cade needed that weapon if he wanted to live; things were looking grim for him and his friends, and they were sure to only get worse.

"I'll be right back," Cade told Kira, and he felt she wanted to say something in return but he couldn't wait. Cade took off, racing toward his shido as his enemies absorbed it into their ranks. The first guard that stood in his way, a middle-aged man with a mangled face, turned his A-10 on Cade, but Cade was too fast. One shot from his outpost pistol, and the guard was down. Cade blasted one soldier in his knee, then sent another one spinning with a perfectly placed shot to his arm. As he continued to run, Cade spotted a towering, muscular man with a scar running over his eye, and a crazed smile spread across his face as he waited for Cade. He was a beast of a man who squeezed a power pike in his hands and looked eager to take Cade's head off. The shido sticking out of the downed guard was right behind him, and that left Cade no choice but to keep running.

Cade dug his feet into the hard ground, one after another, and just as he was within striking range of the beast, Cade broke into a slide. Perfectly timed, Cade skidded directly beneath the massive swing of the beast's pike and arrived right in front of his shido. He gripped the weapon and yanked it out of the soldier's chest; he turned to swipe it at the beast but was stopped by a roaring sound bursting from the sky. Cade looked up, and through the black clouds he saw what might have been the sweetest thing he'd ever laid his eyes on: Kira's Omega Squadron charging toward the Crucible. And they weren't alone, either. Trailing the rear was a trio of armored transport vessels. He didn't know their specific model, but Cade knew a troop jumper when he saw one.

The cavalry had arrived.

The Omega Squadron, eight in total, spread out into attack formation. Six of the Echoes unleashed a barrage of offensive strikes on the Crucible, their streaks of orange proton blasts looking like fire against the night sky. Strike after strike pounded into the Crucible, obliterating more and more of its surface. Repulsion cannons were stationed up and down its walls, but either Ebik hadn't gotten them back online after Mig cut out the power, or he didn't have anyone left to man the bulbous stations. Stone and brick crumbled to the ground, showering the courtyard with the Crucible's wreckage. The offensive pass would be the only clean one the Echoes would get, though; just as they finished their strike, a squad of Praxian Intruders, launching from the Crucible's interior, took to the sky and went after the Echoes.

Meanwhile, the two remaining Echoes swooped low to the ground and screamed right at the battlefield. Cade knew they wouldn't open fire. Everyone he was with knew that. But the

Praxian guards and soldiers didn't share that knowledge, and as the starfighters zeroed in on their position, the Praxian troops either ran for cover behind the courtyard's monuments or dropped to the ground, terrified for their lives. They wouldn't stay down forever, but the flyby served its purpose; following on the Echoes' tails were the transport vessels, and with the Praxian forces running for cover, the transports had a pristine window to hit the ground and unload their troops. At least three dozen soldiers, all armed, stormed the battlefield.

Just like that, they had a fair fight on their hands.

As if magnetically drawn together, Cade realized that he had been reunited with Kira, Mig, 4-Qel, Kobe, and Kay. They were once again joined in a tight circle, protected by a monument's base. All around them, Praxis's forces were on the run. They tried to regroup, tried to assert defensive barriers to keep the incoming forces back, but they had no chance. Soon enough, Cade wagered, they'd be retreating back inside the Crucible.

"How'd your squad know to come here?" Kira asked Kay, her voice unable to disguise her delighted incredulity. "And how did you get Omega here?"

"Give me some credit, Sen," Kay replied. "You didn't think I'd send us into the galaxy's darkest corner without a backup plan, did you?"

"So, what do we do now?" Mig anxiously asked. "We've got about sixteen minutes to go, and a whole lot of Crucible to make our way throu—"

Across the battlefield, Cade heard a voice calling out; when he looked over, he saw a clumsy Poqlin heading toward them. "Guys! Hey, guys!" the Poqlin yelled, waving toward Cade and his friends.

"Who is *this* guy?" Cade asked.

"Your replacement," 4-Qel dryly responded. "The swap was hardly noticeable."

"Hilarious, Qel," Cade groused. "Really glad you're developing a sense of humor."

"Hey, everybody!" the Poqlin said as he joined the group. Winded, he put his hands on his knees and drew a deep breath before continuing. "Who's the new guy? Oh, is this Cade? Are you Cade, the all-powerful ninja sorcerer?"

"Um . . . yes?" Cade replied.

"Well, it's a pleasure to mee—"

"Gunk, enough," Kay commanded. "Go lead the troops."

"Oh," Gunk said with a chuckle as he assessed the battle around him, "right."

"We need to get to that chamber, but damn it," Kira said as she surveyed the battle still waging just ahead. "We'd still have to fight our way through all of *that*," she said, gesturing. "We don't have time."

Cade surveyed the scene, desperate to find something that Kira wasn't seeing. They needed an idea, and they needed it five minutes ago. Kira, he knew, thought linearly; Cade, on the other hand, thought in loops and circles and dead ends. It's why they made a good team. But Cade understood that if he was going to seek out a solution that Kira hadn't already seen, it would have to be something unconventional.

Then it hit him, and he went running.

"Wait!" Cade yelled at the top of his lungs. He was sprinting as fast as his legs would take him, flashing his arms above his head as he tried to stop the last remaining transport vehicle from leaving. "Don't go! We need you! STOP!"

Just as the pilot was taking off, just as the ship was raising off the ground, the pilot turned in Cade's direction and saw the madman waving him down. He shot Cade a look that said, "Yeah, right," and he was about to hightail it off Olanus. And he would have, had he not spotted Kay trailing behind Cade.

Cade reached the ship and jumped into it through its exposed side.

"Listen, we need you," Cade huffed. "I mean, we need your ship. Get out."

"What? No," the pilot said. "I take orders from—"

"You heard him," Kay said, entering the cockpit. "Get off the ship."

The pilot grumbled and did what he was told. The second he was gone, Cade hopped into the pilot's seat and took the stick.

"What are we doing?" Kira asked, a touch of impatience in her voice.

"Getting us to the chamber," Cade replied. "We don't have time to push our way through the battle and into that fortress. Who knows what we'll even find in there? This is our shortcut, so strap yourself in, all of you, and hold on tight."

"Wait a second. Are you going to crash us into the chamber?" Mig asked from the rear of the ship. "Why do your plans always involve crashing things?!"

"Hey, this time it's justified!" Cade snapped. "Now strap in and be quiet. This is gonna be bumpy."

Cade lifted the transport ship off the ground. It was heavy and slow, and its maneuverability stank. "This should be interesting," he said to himself.

As it chugged skyward, Cade messed with switches and buttons, trying to find a weapons array. It would be nice if they could defend themselves.

"Hey, Kay," Cade called. "Where are the weapons on this thing?"

"Doesn't have one," Kay called. "This thing's slow enough without cannons strapped to it."

Cade looked up and saw the dogfight raging in the exact space he was heading. Echoes and Intruders vied for domination, igniting the sky with one blast after another as they twirled and spun, avoiding enemy fire. Cade's ship, in comparison, couldn't blast, spin, or twirl, so how he was going to make it through the melee, even for the brief window of time he had to be in it, was anyone's guess. But this was the only option they had, and if anyone was going to be reckless enough to try, Cade knew it had to be him.

Cade rose the transport ship to the necessary altitude; he needed to be just above the chamber on top of the Crucible, but not by much, for what he was going to do. Once in position, he jammed the stick as hard as he could and sent the ship rocketing—sort of—toward the chamber. And that's when an Intruder caught the ship in its sights.

The first volley buzzed directly past the ship's narrow viewport; Cade knew they were in trouble even before the second blast caught the ship's closed starboard side—the side opposite the one troops disembarked from—and rocked it so hard that it was nearly sent spinning out of control. A klaxon screeched in the cockpit, its shrill alarm pretty much capturing how Cade felt on the inside. The shields were already toast, so one more strike like that would make crashing seem like shore leave on a luxury cruise.

Cade was closing in on the chamber, but the Intruder was coming around for another pass. At its velocity, there was no way he'd reach the chamber before that Intruder had them in its sights again.

Which gave Cade an idea.

"Four-Qel, the side door," Cade yelled, "throw it off!"

Everyone was silent.

"You want me to destroy our own ship?" 4-Qel finally said.

"Time's a factor here. Now do it!" Cade commanded.

Cade heard 4-Qel lumber to the starboard side; he heard the door slide open, fast, and the sound of it rolling on its wheels was followed by the sound of shredding metal as 4-Qel tore it from the ship.

"Happy?" 4-Qel asked.

Cade glanced to his left; the Intruder was nearly on them.

"Not yet," he said. "Now strap back in and, everyone, hug the wall!"

"*Cade*," Kira warned, "you are *not* going to do what I think you're going to do, are you?"

"I can't read minds, so I'm just going to act like I have no idea what you mean," Cade said, keeping his eyes on the Intruder the entire time. It was angling behind the ship, trying to catch it from behind for a clear shot. "Now, wait for it, everyone . . . wait for it . . .

"HOLD ON!"

Just as the Intruder came into range, Cade threw the stick to the side and spun the ship at a forty-five-degree angle so the hole 4-Qel had created was facing their enemy. Right at that moment, the Intruder fired, and its powerful blast passed right through the transport ship and into Ebik's chamber. The glass there was reinforced, and it was durable, but not enough to withstand a direct hit from an Intruder. The panel shattered, utterly ruined.

Cade grabbed the stick and angled the ship back toward the hole in the chamber created by the Intruder. He locked its trajectory and stood up from his seat.

"Come on, let's move," Cade said. "If you don't want to crash into the chamber, then we need to jump."

The group hesitated, but then Kira stepped in. She got up from her seat and clapped her hands. When she spoke, she had the voice of total authority.

"You heard him! Move!" she ordered, and everyone obeyed.

The hole was fast approaching, and while Cade knew jumping from a moving ship wasn't ideal, it was better than crashing it into the chamber and hoping he could bring it to a stop.

With Kira at his side, Cade stood on the lip of the transport ship as it zeroed in on its flyby pattern, which would take them right where they needed to be. Mere seconds separated them from their destination, and Cade was compelled to use them the best he could. He knew what they were about to encounter, and he knew what it meant.

"You okay?" he turned to Kira and asked.

"Ready for this to be over," she said, taking his hand in hers. "Ready for all of this to be over."

Cade looked at Kira and smiled; he knew exactly what she meant. She smiled in return.

And then they jumped.

Cade came down hard on the chamber's floor, and his hand separated from Kira's in the process. He rolled with the fall, and while he didn't expect to get a break when he landed, he also didn't anticipate looking up and being greeted with a shido.

Cade rolled just as the shido came down, and he barely avoided having its blade buried in his skull. As the Fatebreaker that'd attacked him pulled the weapon from the floor, Cade swept out her leg, then rolled back; he joined his team, pulled out his shido, and assessed the situation.

The chamber was like a maze. Command stations, standing about waist height, were staggered throughout the room, positioned in a circular formation. The effect was a circuitous path from the chamber's core to its outer walls. And the winding path, however it was traversed, led to two Fatebreakers who stood at the opposite end of the chamber, fully armored, ready to fight. Behind them, a squad of sentry drones, armed with a mixture of pikes and blasters. Cade almost expected there to be more, but Ebik had played a heavy hand trying to get rid of Cade and his friends, and his numbers were either dead or retreating.

And speaking of Ebik, he was nowhere to be found.

"We were hoping we'd have the opportunity to face you," the

Fatebreaker who'd attacked Cade said. "It would be such a shame to see someone of your stature bested by someone . . . less worthy. But we," the Fatebreaker said, gesturing to her companion, "are perfectly worthy of ending you at last."

Cade rolled his eyes. "My goodness, are you *all* so theatrical?"

The Fatebreaker didn't respond, and Cade used the opportunity to get everyone on task.

"Listen, this is what we do," Cade said, turning to face his friends. "Four-Qel and I will take care of the Fatebreakers. Kay, Mig, Kobe, you take care of the sentries and whoever else wanders up here.

"Kira," Cade said, trying to grab her eyes, which were searching the room. A look of deep concern—caused by her father's absence, no doubt—rested on her face. "*Kira.*"

Kira finally fixed her gaze on Cade.

"You have to find Ebik," he said.

A smile appeared on Kira's face, the kind of smile that pushed out all her former worry.

"Don't worry," she said. "I know exactly where he is."

CHAPTER SEVENTEEN

Metal bashed together, the sound of its impact spreading throughout the entire chamber. Cade's shido pounded against the Fatebreaker's shido just as the other Fatebreaker's weapon had his strike blocked by 4-Qel's arm. The clash signaled the start of the skirmish; as the duels began, the drones pressed their attack, firing blasters or coming at Kira, Mig, Kobe, and Kay with their pikes. Kobe moved fast and efficiently, even with his injury seemingly aggravated by his fall into the chamber, and he disabled the nearest drone as it fired in his direction. Kay worked in his own way, spraying blaster fire to keep the drones at bay. And just as Mig was about to lay down some return fire of his own, Kira grabbed his arm and pulled him back. They crouched behind one of the stations, covered from the battle taking place just over their heads.

"Mig, forget what Cade told you to do," Kira said. "You need to find the detonator. Right here, right now, and you need to—"

A blaster bolt sizzled above them, then another pounded the station's outer shell. Kira growled and leapt up. She fired a shot from her sidewinder that nailed the drone right between its eyes, splitting its head.

"*Anyway*," she continued, "find the detonator. Disable it. You hear me?"

Mig looked at Kira, confused. "But Ebik has the detonator."

Kira smiled. "No," she said, certainty giving strength to her words. "He absolutely does not.

"Now find the right console; it's in this room. I'll cover you on my way out."

Mig shook his head; his body shivered. "Wait, wait. You're not staying with me?"

Kira looked to the floor; she closed her eyes and took a deep breath, steeling her resolve. She knew she should stay at Mig's side and keep him safe while he did his work. But that's what her squad was there for; they kept one another safe, and she had to trust that. And that trust freed her to do what she had to do, not as a leader or a commander but for herself, personally.

She had to confront her father. She had to end this.

"But there are only eleven minutes left," Mig said, a sad desperation in his eyes.

"Then move fast, Mig," Kira said. She clasped his shoulders and drew his gaze to meet hers. "You can do this. I know you can."

Mig drew in his lips and vigorously nodded. "Okay," he said. "Okay."

Kira smiled. "Okay," she said, then scouted the scene beyond the cover of their command station. The number of drones had already been pared down to six. She saw a few more stagger into the room, but it wasn't much of a reinforcement. Praxis's Olanus forces—Ebik's forces—were nearly depleted. This was almost over.

"Follow my lead," Kira said, "and keep your head down."

Mig held his sidewinder up to his face, holding it steady. Kira did the same and spun out from behind the station. She fired three shots, hitting a drone that was charging at Kobe with its pike. One shot in its knee and two in its torso were enough to send it to the floor. That drone out of the way, Kira blasted a series of shots across the chamber, sending a trio of drones ducking for cover.

"Now, Mig!" she ordered, and Mig scrambled to the nearest station and got to work.

Kira darted through the chamber; 4-Qel and Cade seemed to be holding their own against the Fatebreakers. It even seemed that Cade had his opponent on the defensive and could finish her off soon enough. United with 4-Qel, they'd be too much for the remaining Fatebreaker to handle. Kobe and Kay, meanwhile, continued to thin the drones, mindful of the reinforcements coming in. As she reached a thin metallic door just off the side of the entrance, Kira assured herself that her squad had this under control. They could do this. She drew in a deep breath and looked down at the keypad adjacent to the door. She knew what the password would be; it was the password Ebik had used since she'd entered this world.

Kira punched in the five digits for her birthday, and the door slid open. She took one step into the room, and all was darkness. The door slid shut behind her, leaving Kira no choice but to move forward. She took hesitant steps, each one taking her closer to the room's single light source: a projection of Praxis, centered among the surrounding stars, covering the far wall. The planet's deep auburn glow was faint from this distance, but it still radiated light. It was alive. But the figure who stood in front of the projection wanted that all to end. Ebik remained motionless, his back to Kira, as she drew closer and closer. The room's silence was heavy and profound.

"I don't have many memories from my childhood," Kira said, her voice sounding small, as if she and Ebik were floating in the space that was projected on the screen. That, after all, was the intended effect. "Some of them I've lost; most of them I've pushed away. But I remember the room you built—total darkness except for a view of the sky. It was for the headaches you'd get. You practically lived there."

Ebik remained motionless, his crimson uniform as crisp as ever. He was a statue like the ones he'd had erected in the courtyard. Doubtless, he'd envisioned the day when one such memorial would be built in his honor.

"Why?" Kira asked. It was the question she'd been wanting to unburden her soul of for years. "Why did you do this to me? To Mom? We were a family, we . . . we were so much more than anything you have now. *Why?*"

Ebik didn't answer. He didn't even move, his focus instead fixed on Praxis spinning in the vacuum of space. Kira knew no answer he could give would satisfy her; nothing he could say would heal her wounds. But he wouldn't dismiss her. Not after all these years, not after everything.

"Answer me, Dad," Kira said as tears formed in the corners of her eyes. Tears she let flow. "I need you to tell me."

Ebik shook his head and laughed derisively. "Your vision is still so . . . small. When you were a child, there was a time I thought you'd get it. But no. You're like your mother, always wanting to fix what is broken rather than build something new over the ashes of what's meant to burn."

A sad smile spread on Kira's face. Part of her felt unburdened by his words. For as long as she could remember, everything she knew painted Ebik as a monster; he was a dark force in her life, the source of all her anger and fear, the reason she was incapable of trusting anyone enough to experience love again. He was doubtless still that monster, but he was also a small, pathetic man. A man who knew nothing but satisfying desires that could never be sated, all while he lost anything with value, anything with meaning, that once existed in his life. Kira hated her father, and that would never change. But she pitied him as well.

"Was it worth it?" she asked. "Look at you. You're reviled by half the galaxy, if not more. You're a murderer."

Ebik shrugged. "I told you we were building on the ashes of the old world. Those fires don't start themselves."

"And after everything, can you say that you have what you want?"

"I'm about to," Ebik said, and he finally turned to face his daughter. Kira saw the emptiness in his eyes, the absolute lack of heart or soul. There was nothing there, and there never would be. "I know why you're here, daughter. You think you can stop me. You think you can prevent the destruction of Praxis, which is mere moments away. I hate to break it to you, but you've failed once again. I knew you'd put all your focus in coming for me, though I'm impressed you made it this far. Nonetheless, I still took proper precautions. That's why the detonator isn't on me. I don't have it."

"I know," Kira said, and a triumphant smile made her face glow.

Ebik flinched. He tried not to show it; he tried to maintain his stoic, untouchable presence, but Kira saw a little tremor twitch the muscles in his cheeks. As he turned back to the projection of their home world, Kira had no doubt that her task had been completed. She'd trusted Mig and her squad to do their job, and they wouldn't let her down. That's what family did.

Ebik's fist rolled into a ball at his side. Praxis was supposed to have erupted into countless bits of debris; the rebellion should have been over, and the ripple effect would have surely sent the Black Star Renegades scrambling in fear. Then the galaxy at large, seeing the Praxis kingdom's power and its willingness to punish anyone for their defiance, would cower indefinitely. The war would be over; the galaxy would be won.

But that's not what happened.

"What have you done?" Ebik snarled.

"I outsmarted you," Kira responded.

"No," Ebik growled, his head shaking as if he could reject what had happened. "No, no, *no*. This was the end. I was supposed to *rule*."

Now, it was Kira's turn to remain silent.

"You think I'm going to let you enjoy this victory? You think I'm going to let you walk out of here?" Ebik asked as he slowly reached for the blaster at his side.

"Don't do it," Kira warned.

Ebik spun, his officer blaster in hand. Kira had a sidewinder in each hand. She was faster than Ebik and probably a better shot. Ebik knew all of this. But he wasn't betting on skill. Ebik was betting that Kira couldn't shoot her own father.

He was wrong.

"I'll kill y—" Ebik exclaimed as he came around, but Kira was waiting. She brought her sidewinder up before Ebik could even fully turn, and she fired a pair of bolts directly into his chest. Ebik doubled over, and he gasped. His face bore an expression of anguish. Ebik didn't know what it meant to lose, and Kira imagined that caused him more pain than the two holes she'd drilled in his body.

Slowly, Ebik's hand reached to cover his wounds, but it didn't make it. He collapsed onto his back.

Kira stood over her father as he faded away. Ebik didn't look at her, though. His eyes were fixed on Praxis, his greatest triumph turned into his greatest failure.

"I could have had . . . everything . . . ," he said, forcing the words out.

Kira kicked his blaster away from his hand. "You did have everything, you fool," she said, then she turned and left her father to die.

Kira opened the door leading back into the chamber and was met by 4-Qel's raised fist.

"Aaaaah!" he yelled.

Kira fell back into the doorframe. "What are you screaming about?" she asked.

"You startled me," 4-Qel said. "I was going to punch the door down and come save you."

Kira was about to question how she could possibly scare 4-Qel, but she stopped herself. Instead, she smiled at the big killer drone and patted his arm. "Thanks for trying to come after me."

Kira took a quick survey of the room. The Fatebreakers were down; all the drones had been defeated, and no more were entering the room. It was, at last, over. And more importantly, her friends were all fine and, once again, they were together. She looked them over, all of them—herself included—dirty, weary, and battle-damaged. Except for Mig. He was nonchalantly whistling, waiting for recognition.

"Did you have something to say, Mig?" Kira teased.

"Me? Oh no. No, no. Just taking it all in."

Kira playfully rolled her eyes. "You did a great job. Thank you."

Mig gestured cavalierly. "All in a day's work for the Black Star Renegades and their leader, Mig, the savior of planets."

Kira's eyes narrowed. "Don't push it."

"Gunk and the rest of my forces are mopping up what's left of Praxis's ground forces," Kay said. He sounded proud, and he had every right to be. "The stupid ones are still putting up a fight, but most have surrendered."

"You trained them well, Warden," Kira said.

Kay smiled, but his smile quickly faded. He cleared his throat and stretched his neck uncomfortably. "I'm sorry to ask, but I have to know. Is Ebik—"

"Dead," Kira said flatly. "He's dead."

"Understood," Kay said, then asked nothing further.

Cade stepped closer to Kira; she could see how utterly exhausted he was. Physically and emotionally. She shared the same depletion; there was nothing left within her. Kira felt like she was going to need to sleep for weeks once they got off this moon.

"You okay?" Cade asked softly.

Kira thought about it. There was a lot to process still, and even with this victory, the war wasn't over. But that wasn't what Cade was talking about; he meant the here and now, and at the moment, that was the only place Kira wanted to be. "Yeah," she said. "I am. And I think I will be."

"Good," Cade said, and Kira could see his eyes light up as he looked into hers. "Good. Now, come on, let's get out of here."

They moved to leave, all of them, but the moment Kira's back was turned, she heard something. Something humming in the distance, but coming closer. The sound was familiar.

Kira stopped dead in her tracks.

"Do you hear that?" she asked.

Cade shook off Kira's concern. "Just a ship," he said. "The Poqlins are still patrolling over us."

"No," Kira said, her heart sinking down in her chest. "That's *my* ship."

No one had time to respond. The glass lining the chamber behind them erupted, blasting tiny shards in their direction. Kira covered herself, protecting her face out of instinct. And by the time she lowered her arm, the *Rubicon* was in sight, hovering in front of the space that'd just been opened. Her ship was positioned with its rear, which was open, facing them.

Ga Halle strode down the *Rubicon*'s ramp, Rokura in hand, and into the chamber.

"Go!" Cade yelled. "Get out of here, all of you!"

But it was too late. Before Kira could move, before Mig, 4-Qel, Kobe, or Kay could move, they were wrapped up in a blast of energy. It enveloped all five of them and lifted them off the ground. Everything from that point was pure nothingness. Kira couldn't carry a single thought in her head. All she knew was pain. Pain like burning, like electrocution, like suffocation consuming her body all at once.

Her body was being torn apart, and there was nothing she could do to stop it.

CHAPTER EIGHTEEN

"C ade," Ga Halle said as her face slowly twisted toward him. "I've been looking for you."

The Rokura blasted a stream of unimaginable energy from its tip; Cade knew this moment well, but never from this side of things. He'd always been the one controlling—or perhaps merely delegating—the Rokura's raw power. It was unlike anything in the known galaxy, and its purpose wasn't just to destroy and kill; it was to obliterate. It wiped whatever it levied its might on clean out of existence, and Cade could hardly even grasp what that meant. Whatever it was, it was happening to his friends. He looked over and couldn't stand the sight of them so riddled with pain and torture. So utterly consumed by the Rokura's debilitating impact, they didn't even look to him for help. They weren't capable of even that.

Cade fixed his gaze on Ga Halle. She was cast against the dark, cloudy sky, the light of the Rokura giving her face an ethereal glow. She looked utterly deranged.

"I suppose, in a way, I have you to thank for my recent

epiphany," Ga Halle continued. "I once thought I could change hearts and minds; I wanted to give people a chance to see how valuable what I offered them was. If they could see how my domination was *necessary*, they'd submit. But system after system, rebellion after rebellion, some people never learn. Just like your friends.

"But now I know what must be done. I know that mercy is a fruitless endeavor, and there's no reason for me to even act like there's an option for this galaxy to do anything but bow to my will."

There was no reasoning Cade could offer. No argument, no plea that would penetrate Ga Halle's twisted consciousness. She was evil, through and through; the Rokura's darkness and the evil Wu-Xia had placed into it had found its home.

But that didn't mean the light was extinguished. It didn't mean this fight was over.

"You're going to watch your friends die, Cade Sura," Ga Halle said. "Then you will join them."

Cade looked back at his friends. It wouldn't be long before their flesh began to disintegrate. Before they were ground to dust and scrubbed from the galaxy. They were writhing in the pain the Rokura caused them; seeing them like that, seeing them suffer, filled Cade with determination like he'd never felt before. The idea of them and the light they all possessed being snuffed out of this world gave him a sense of purpose he never knew.

His father promised he'd find his way. He was right, and this was it.

Cade's thoughts stayed with his father, and in a flash, it all made sense. It was his responsibility to fight evil. To expel it from this world. And that's exactly what he was going to do.

He stepped toward his friends, the light that poured over them shining brightly in his eyes. He could feel the heat and the power radiating off it.

Behind him, Ga Halle cackled loudly and maniacally. "Eager to join your friends?" she asked.

Cade turned back to Ga Halle, his eyes narrowed on her, his lip upturned to a snarl.

"You're not going to show any mercy, Ga Halle?" he yelled, throwing his voice over the Rokura's crackling pulse. Cade looked one last time at his tortured friends, then he turned back to Ga Halle. "Then neither will I."

His heart pounding, his breath shallow, his body trembling, Cade stuck out his hand and took hold of Kira's. In an instant, he was swallowed by the Rokura's destructive, frenzied power.

All Cade could think of was how he was going to die. His flesh itched and burned like every molecule was engulfed in flames. His bones rattled and pulsed, feeling as if they were going to swell and erupt. Soon, all too soon, the Rokura was going to consume him, mind, body, and soul. And then, Cade would be done for. And the galaxy would be lost.

In the precious moments he had, while he could still maintain a train of thought, Cade had to act. Through the agony, Cade fought with all his strength to lift the shido in his right hand; he wanted to scream as he resisted the furious weight that pushed against his arm, but he didn't want to misallocate one bit of his energy. Everything he had, everything he was, went into raising that shido. And once he had it level with his chest and directed outward, Cade pushed back against the Rokura.

He recalled what he'd done for the gorgan back on Monaskis. In that moment, Cade had followed his own desire and willed the Rokura to act as he'd wanted it to act, not the way he'd thought Tristan or Percival would have willed it. It was all Cade. And his impulse was simple: He wanted to cure the gorgan of the torment it'd suffered. He wanted to drive the evil that'd been instilled into the beast out and let it be free once more. And that changed everything. Cade felt power roaring through the

Rokura, but it was different. Up until that moment, the weapon acted on Cade's behalf only to subtly—or, at times, not so subtly—draw Cade to its side; it wanted to seduce Cade with the magnitude of its power. The darkness was in control, and even when it saved Cade's life, it only did so to keep him alive until the time it could coax him into submitting to its terrible will. Its lighter half had been there the entire time as well, and Cade felt it, but his action in the Monaskis fighting pit brought it out of dormancy.

And now, as Cade was enveloped in the Rokura's destructive force, he was also connected to it. He could feel its might circulating through him, but he was also able to reach out, knowing what he was looking for, and link to its source. And there, buried deep below its darkness and the strength it had been given by Ga Halle's insidious hand, Cade detected the Rokura's light still burning within it.

Cade called on the light to come to his aid; he screamed for it to help him in his fight to eradicate the darkness.

And the Rokura's light answered.

Suddenly, the suffering Cade was enduring began to diminish. He began to regain control of his mind and body, and as the light rose within the Rokura, Cade was able to add his own will to the fight. Together, they pushed back against their enemies.

Ga Halle realized what was happening. Cade knew she must have felt the resistance within her, and her reaction to being contested drove her mad. "You will not take this from me!" she screamed as the look on her face turned manic.

Cade felt a surge of energy rush through the Rokura, into his shido, and then riddle his body. It pushed him back, and he felt the pain he'd endured at the apex of the Rokura's hold on him start to return.

Drawing deep within himself, Cade resisted. He pushed so

hard that it increased the pain he was enduring. It was all he could do to hold on. But it wasn't enough.

Little by little, the Rokura's darkness began to resume control. Cade felt his entire body radiate pain as his enemy worked to annihilate his very being. He looked down at his arm, the one outstretched as it held forth the shido; the skin of his exposed forearm was beginning to flake away. In moments, he'd be erased from existence, and he wanted to scream out his despair. He'd failed. He'd failed the galaxy, his father, and himself, and in the face of such shame, he almost welcomed the oblivion that was soon to come. He certainly couldn't live in a world where he shouldered the weight of such disappointment.

But then, just as the pain was about to overwhelm him so thoroughly that he'd no longer be able to hold a thought in his head, he felt a gentle squeeze on his hand. He looked down, and he saw Kira's fingers interlaced in his own. Fighting against the force trying to keep him down, Cade lifted his gaze so he met Kira's. To his disbelief, Kira looked at him with love. She looked at him with what might have even been pride. And behind her, Mig, 4-Qel, Kobe, and Kay all shared that look, like they were grateful to Cade for fighting for them. For trying.

That's when it hit him.

Learning, as Wu-Xia has said, "to be" had opened the Rokura's light to him. Understanding his responsibility to fight against evil had given him purpose. But power? That came from his friends. If there was one true thing that Cade could rely on in this entire galaxy, it was that he was better when Kira, Mig, 4-Qel, Kobe, and now even Kay were by his side. All of them were better together.

In a flash, Cade felt his power—*their* power—surge.

A blast fired against Ga Halle, so strong that it caused her to stumble backward. Cade felt her trying to push back, but she was overwhelmed. She howled and fought with more than she had to give, but it was no use. Together, Cade and his friends were too strong for her.

"*How?*" Ga Halle screamed. "How is this even possible?!"

Feeling the Rokura's light circulating through him, warm and bright, Cade squeezed Kira's hand, and he unleashed a surge of energy that burst throughout the entire chamber. The remaining glass was shattered, the command stations were torn from the floor, and Ga Halle, howling her futile resistance, was blasted out of the chamber.

In the blink of an eye, the power that'd been thundering throughout the entire space was extinguished. The Rokura, lying on the ground where it'd been torn from Ga Halle's grip, was at rest once more.

But it was different.

Cade picked the weapon off the ground; at once, it felt lighter in his grip. But not only that, the Rokura was no longer gray. It had taken on a dull white sheen from its hilt to its head. Cade closed his eyes and reached out into the weapon. He felt the light bounding throughout, buoyant. It was free of the darkness that'd encumbered it since its inception, and Cade felt harmony between himself and the weapon.

"Well," he heard Kobe say over his shoulder, "that was intense."

Cade turned around. His friends were all there, alive and well. He might have never seen a better sight in all his life.

"Whoa, man," Mig said, pointing at Cade, "your hair's all white!"

"Are you serious?!" Cade groaned.

Mig couldn't contain his smile. "Nah, I'm messing with you. Just your weapon."

Cade rolled his eyes, though he was glad that some things would never change.

"All right, all right," Kira said, waving everyone ahead, "party's over. For real this time, let's get off this rock. I don't ever want to see this moon again."

Everyone was more than happy to follow Kira's order, and they shuffled their weary bodies toward the *Rubicon*, which was still hovering just outside the chamber.

"This turn of events begs a particular question," 4-Qel said as he approached Cade. "Whatever you just did, does this mean you're now the Chosen One? Are you, Cade Sura, the true Paragon?"

Cade could only smile as he looked up at his drone friend. "There is no Chosen One," he said. "I'm just someone who's guided by the galaxy, and I'm lucky to have good people around me to help me along the way."

"Hmmph," 4-Qel said as he continued on his way. "'Guided by the galaxy.' That's a nice thought. Ridiculous, but nice."

Everyone filed onto the *Rubicon*. Cade was the last to board, and he found Kira waiting for him at the top of the ramp.

"I got your ship back," he said as he strode next to Kira.

She didn't say a word. She simply grabbed him by his shirt, pulled him close, and kissed him, long and deep.

When it was over, Cade was numb. He blinked fast and hard, and his brain refused to let him say a word, knowing he'd say the absolute wrong thing. Kira wasn't sticking around for it anyway.

"Not so bad, Cade Sura," she said, leaving him to stare out into space as the ship closed. "Not so bad."

The *Rubicon* rocketed through the atmosphere, and Cade was still standing exactly where Kira had left him.

CHAPTER NINETEEN

They remained in the *Rubicon* for days. Licking their wounds, attending to their grief, recovering from everything they'd endured on Praxis, Monaskis, and Olanus. Each of them had been pushed to their limits in so many ways, yet they'd managed to accomplish more than they had dreamed possible. And they'd done it together.

Cade had passed the time sleeping; the Rokura's drain on him was profound, and he felt like he hadn't rested in years. Kay couldn't put his work on hold for a moment; he stayed in communication with Gunk and the other Praxian forces as they overran the scattered strongholds that refused to surrender. Kira mainly kept to herself, dealing with her grief in her own way. Mig and 4-Qel pretty much played tatow the entire time. They'd even coaxed Kobe into joining their game, and Cade had been watching them for a few hands now, silently so as not to be noticed, from the ramp overlooking the cargo hold. He enjoyed seeing them let loose; he liked listening to them laugh and horse around.

He was about to turn back to the cockpit when he spotted Mig being, well, Mig. Even in a game among friends, Mig couldn't help but cheat.

"Are you supposed to deal from the bottom of the deck?" Cade asked.

Mig jumped, startled, and the deck of cards he'd been dealing flew out of his hands.

"What? Who, me?" he asked, trying to sound innocent.

"Cheater," 4-Qel reprimanded.

Mig chuckled uncomfortably and began to back away. "Look, wait, I can explain."

"You owe us coin," Kobe said, closing in on Mig with 4-Qel at his side.

"Well, yes and no. I mean, some of those hands I won fair and square. And I might have already spent some when we stopped for supplies, so—"

"What will the punishment be?" 4-Qel asked Kobe.

Kobe shrugged. "I'm sure we can get creative."

Mig backed into a stack of boxes, knocking them over. There was nowhere else for him to go. "Hey, Cade! Cade, help me out here! Tell these guys to be reasonable; it's just a game. It's just—"

Cade shot Mig a salute, then turned and walked away. "I'm sure you can handle it, Mig. You wouldn't have made it this far in life if you couldn't."

As he approached the cockpit, Cade heard Kira's and Kay's voices ahead; they reminded him that Kay had made plans to leave the *Rubicon*. Gunk was sending a transport vessel to retrieve him and take him back to Praxis. Though Cade didn't know Kay all that well, he was sad to see him go. He was a dedicated soldier, and a tenacious one at that; both reminded him of Percival, and Cade wished the former Paragon were there to see everything that'd happened. He wished Percival had known that his belief in Cade had been warranted.

"Are you sure this is a good idea?" Kay was saying as Cade entered the cockpit.

"Come on," Kira said, "look at me. I'm not exactly Baron material. I mean, if it makes you feel better, just think of this position as temporary. I'm appointing you just until I come back to claim my title."

"Are you going to come back?" Kay asked uneasily.

"Absolutely not."

Kay laughed and stuck out his hand for Kira to take. "I'm damn glad to have known you, Kira Sen. And I want you to know one thing before I leave, and you'd better never forget it. Your mother was proud of you. I spent my share of time with her, and I can't remember one time she didn't mention you. She was the best I've ever known, though let me tell you—the apple hasn't fallen far from the tree."

Kira looked at Kay's hand, then looked back at him. She pushed Kay's gesture away and wrapped him in a hug.

"Thank you," Kira whispered.

When Kay pulled out of the embrace, his eyes were getting moist. "Now look what you made me do," he said, wiping away a tear that threatened to roll down his cheek. "I can't lead a planetary coup like this."

Kira smiled. "You'll do just fine."

Kay nodded to Kira, shook Cade's hand, then he was off.

"So, he's going to lead Praxis?" Cade asked.

"Better him than me," Kira replied, her voice conveying how much of a blaster bolt she was dodging by squirming out of the possibility of having to get involved in politics.

Cade turned toward the viewport. A dwarf star shone in the distance, and numerous points of light swirled around it. Planets and dust reflected its glow, filling the spaces between with shimmering light. Together, hand in hand, Cade and Kira walked closer to the viewport for a better look.

"Look at us," Cade said after a moment of comfortable silence. "We sacked the tyrannical kingdom's home planet and bested the galaxy's most powerful weapon. Who would've thought?"

"Me," Kira said flatly. "I never had a doubt in my mind."

"No," Cade said, turning toward her. "I bet you never did."

He leaned over and they kissed; Cade reached out and felt the smoothness of Kira's cheek. He felt her hand on his arm, soft but strong. There was no more Rokura pushing inside his head, no more agony over trying to be something he wasn't and failing. Cade's world was quiet; it was peaceful. It was a moment he wanted to stay in forever.

And then the comms crackled. Captain Temple's gruff voice came through, cagey as ever. There was no better person to utterly shatter the harmony of the moment. Kira and Cade pulled away from each other, both of them smiling.

"I'd better—" Kira began.

Cade groaned. "Yeah, yeah."

Kira cleared her throat and picked up the comms. "This is Kira. Good to hear from you, Captain."

"Well, it's about time!" Temple scolded. "You think overtaking Praxis gives you license to take a holiday?"

"Yes," Kira said.

"Well, erm . . . ," Temple faltered. "You're right. Just let me know next time."

"What's the latest?" Kira asked, getting to it. As she did, the cockpit door slid open; Mig, 4-Qel, and Kobe strolled inside.

"We're hearing chatter from one end of the galaxy to the next. People are talking, Kira," Temple said, his voice sounding as upbeat as it got. "If a Praxian rebellion can take the planet back from right under the kingdom's noses, then there's real hope for us all. We're gaining support. We're gaining numbers. In short, we might just win this thing."

Kira turned and looked toward her squad—her friends, her

family. They'd joined Cade at the viewport, and they were all looking to her. She knew exactly what their expressions meant.

"We're on our way back, Captain," she said. "We'll see you at the rendezvous point."

Kira joined her friends at the viewport, and together they took a moment to stare out to the galaxy, vast, wide, and bright. It was something worth fighting for, and it always would be.

"So, what do we do now?" Mig asked.

"Now comes the fun part," Kira said. "Now we go free the galaxy."

ACKNOWLEDGMENTS

As I sit down to write these acknowledgments, I can't help but be a bit overwhelmed by all the amazing people I'm so lucky to have in my life and can thank.

Writing these books—and I say this without an ounce of hyperbole—has been the time of my life. Creatively and personally, being able to sit down for the past two years and craft stories about a group of misfits fighting a war in space has been more fun, and more fulfilling, than anything I could possibly hope for. And for that, I thank everyone who has joined me on this adventure. If you've read the first book, if you're holding this one in your hands, please know that I am grateful—so very grateful—that you picked my story among so many stories. It means the world to me.

Yet not a word would have been written without my family. My wife, Alissa, is so patient with the many demands that writing a book requires, and she reminds me to step outside myself. She makes life fun, and I know she always will. My two boys and their imaginations, hearts, and joy inspire me to tell stories more than anything in the world.

I'm also fortunate to have an agent who I can call a friend. Jason Yarn works so hard on my behalf; he's honest when I know it's not easy to be honest, and his always-sharp insight continues to make me a better writer.

And, of course, there's my editor, Marc Resnick. None of this would exist without him. He is the alpha of the Black Star Renegades universe and one of the best guys I know. Marc, I will always, always be thankful for the once-in-a-lifetime chance you've given me.

To everyone at St. Martin's Press, from the designers to marketing to publicity and everyone in between, thank you for your talents and dedication.

I owe a great deal of thanks to Tim Daniel, my good friend who has helped me in more ways than I can count. And my aunt, Tracy, who is a better beta reader than I deserve. She, Chad McGavok, and Dirk Vanover were a tremendous help in shaping this book when I needed it most.

And my parents, who have supported me for so long and gave me the strength to follow my dreams.

To my friends—thank you all.

I hope everyone has had as much fun reading these books as I've had writing them.

I sign off, now, as any true *Star Wars* fan would:

May the Force be with you, always.

GLOSSARY

PEOPLE

Cade Sura—He's the Paragon . . . but not really. While he does wield the Rokura—a mythical, all-powerful weapon—his self-doubt and lack of confidence prevent him from truly mastering the weapon. Still, he fights alongside his friends to free the galaxy from the evil Praxis kingdom.

Ebik—Ga Halle's top commander and Kira's father. He's a vicious strategist who craves power—first, he connived his way into the Baron's Quorum, then he betrayed them in his quest to rise in Praxis's ranks. Nothing will stand in his way, not even his own daughter.

4-Qel—Hailing from Eris, 4-Qel is a drone built specifically to protect the royal family. But every line of Qel is decommissioned (i.e., murdered) upon the creation of the subsequent model. Since the Qels are up to model 6-Qel, 4-Qel should have been disposed of, but somehow, he escaped.

Ga Halle—The self-appointed queen of the Praxis kingdom. With the Barons out of her way—removed by Ga Halle herself—she rules her kingdom and the galaxy with an iron fist. But no power is enough for her, not until she claims what she thinks is rightfully hers: the Rokura.

Gunk—One of Kay's commanders, a Poqlin who arrived in Praxis as a refugee. Like all Poqlins, Gunk has a rock-hard exterior and a very, very dry sense of humor.

Kira Sen—The leader of the Black Star Renegades. Kira is a fearless pilot and loyal friend; she plays by her own rules and demands a lot from the people she leads, but no more than she gives. Kira's a fearless, audacious fighter in the battle for galactic freedom.

Kobe—Percival's lead soldier, once a prized candidate to remove the Rokura from its stasis. A survivor of a great tragedy—he lost his entire family to Praxis's planet-killing *War Hammer*—Kobe is a skilled warrior and master of hand-to-hand combat.

Lux Ersia—The teenage queen of Monaskis. Despite her age, she's not to be trifled with; she's smart, sharp, and handy with a blaster.

Mig—Cade and Tristan's best friend; an engineering genius, con artist, and scoundrel, Mig travels the galaxy running various schemes, gambling, and causing mischief wherever he and his pal 4-Qel go.

Percival—Before there was Tristan, there was Percival. Percival removed the Rokura long before Tristan ever had his hands on it. Terrified by the weapon's power, he returned the weapon and went into hiding, determined never to have anything to do with the Rokura again. He has since joined forces with Cade and Kira.

Ortzo—Ga Halle's lead Fatebreaker—highly trained warriors who serve Ga Halle's every command, whether it be political assassination, squashing a resistance, or other similar deeds.

Tristan Sura—Cade's older brother and the one who pulled the Rokura from its stasis. He was murdered by a hidden assassin immediately after claiming his birthright.

Warden Kay—Ebik's former right-hand man. He betrayed Kira and her family when she was young, though he claims now to be leading the uprising on Praxis.

Wu-Xia—Fabled warrior who forged the Rokura and used it to bring peace to the galaxy.

PLACES

Kyysring—Known for its criminal delights, Kyysring is the place people go to get what they can't have and do what they're not supposed to. Though most of it is covered by an uninhabitable desert, its small city and spaceport pack in enough character to rival the most bustling core worlds. It's also where Cade, Tristan, and Mig grew up.

Monaskis—Wu-Xia's birthplace. The planet, though, was supposedly decimated; it exists only in legend, known as the Ruined Empire of Monaskis.

Olanus—One of Praxis's six moons and home to the Crucible, a prison compound housing the galaxy's worst criminals that also serves as Ebik's fortress.

Praxis—An urban planet just beyond the Inner Cluster, Praxis has grown to annex other worlds, spreading its flag across the stars as it looks to rule the entire galaxy.

Quarry—A forlorn planet that once cultivated a rare spice that was traded throughout the entire galaxy. But that was before Praxis unleashed its star-killing wrath on Quarry, blanketing it in eternal darkness and ensuring no one would be able to remove the legendary Rokura from its stasis.

Raja Prime—The home base of the Black Star Renegades. It is an agricultural moon in the Vossalos system chosen by Percival for its secluded location and mountainous topography, giving them plenty of aerial coverage in the planet's valleys.

Ticus—A mountainous, idyllic world isolated outside the Inner Cluster. For centuries, it served as a destination for religious pilgrimages. After the death of Wu-Xia, it evolved into the Well, a place for spiritual warriors to train as they defended peace and justice throughout the galaxy.

COOL STUFF

The Chamber of Memories—A mysterious, mystical cavern deep in the heart of Monaskis.

Fatebreakers—Agents of Ga Halle, these highly trained, brutal warriors do her dirty work.

Nucletoid bomb—Though small in size, nucletoid bombs contain a concentrated amount of nucleoi, enough to decimate large areas of land with a single charge.

Outpost pistol—Poorly made and, thus, inexpensive blasters that are common to street gangs and other low-level criminals. They're known for backfire malfunctions more than anything else.

Paragon—According to legend, the Paragon is the one person who can release the Rokura from its stasis and bring peace to the galaxy.

Power pike—A mysterious weapon wielded by the Darklanders. Unlike similar electricity-charged weapons, the power pike is charged not just at its head but throughout the entire staff.

Quarter staffs—Short, compact staffs used specifically for hand-to-hand combat. Wielded by Kobe.

Quanta staff—Long, heavy metallic staffs that are charged with electricity that pours off the massive blade that tips this weapon.

Rai—Warriors trained, physically and spiritually, to fight for peace and justice throughout the galaxy. They follow the example set by Wu-Xia, the man who forged the Rokura.

Rokura—A mystical weapon, forged by Wu-Xia in the Quarrian spire, that is said to have the power, when wielded by the Paragon, to bring peace to the galaxy.

Sidewinder—A powerful sidearm that's standard issue to the Well's forces and commonly carried by many others throughout the galaxy. Its slender size makes it easy to holster, and its adjustable barrels allow for different discharge settings, ammunition, and range.

Shido—Designed after the Rokura, shidos are bo staffs studded by three blades at their tops. A powerful electric cell embedded in the staff pours electricity from the tips of its blades when activated.

The Well—Located on the planet Ticus, the Well is the nexus for warriors from around the galaxy to train to become Rai. It's grown to also house a peacekeeping infantry of ground soldiers and starfighter pilots.

31901064462411